THE LEAGUE OF LONELY WAR WOMEN

ANDIE NEWTON

One More Chapter
a division of HarperCollins*Publishers*
1 London Bridge Street
London SE1 9GF
www.harpercollins.co.uk
HarperCollins*Publishers*
Macken House, 39/40 Mayor Street Upper,
Dublin 1, D01 C9W8, Ireland

This paperback edition 2026

1

First published in Great Britain in ebook format by
HarperCollins*Publishers* 2026
Copyright © Andie Newton 2026
Andie Newton asserts the moral right to
be identified as the author of this work

A catalogue record of this book is available from the British Library

ISBN: 978-0-00-879975-5

This novel is entirely a work of fiction. The names, characters and incidents portrayed in it are the work of the author's imagination. Any resemblance to actual persons, living or dead, events or localities is fictionalised or coincidental.

Printed and bound in the UK using 100% Renewable Electricity
by CPI Group (UK) Ltd

All rights reserved. No part of this publication may be reproduced, stored in a retrieval system, or transmitted, in any form or by any means, electronic, mechanical, photocopying, recording or otherwise, without the prior permission of the publishers.

Without limiting the exclusive rights of any author, contributor or the publisher of this publication, any unauthorised use of this publication to train generative artificial intelligence (AI) technologies is expressly prohibited. HarperCollins also exercise their rights under Article 4(3) of the Digital Single Market Directive 2019/790 and expressly reserve this publication from the text and data mining exception.

Also by Andie Newton

A Child for the Reich
The Secret Pianist
The Ghost House
The Last Flight from Moscow
The Housewives of Atomic Lane

Andie Newton is a *USA Today* bestselling author of historical fiction. Her work has been published in multiple languages and has topped ebook bestseller charts all over the world. She holds a bachelor's degree in history from Washington State University and a master's in teaching. When she's not writing gritty war stories about women, you can usually find her trail running in the desert and stopping to pet every dog that crosses her path. She lives in the beautiful Pacific Northwest with her family.

- instagram.com/andienewtonauthor
- facebook.com/NewtonAuthor
- x.com/AndieNewton
- bookbub.com/authors/andie-newton

For Matt, Zane, and Drew

Prologue

September 1, 1944
Third Army Command Tent
France

The rain had been especially vicious that night on the Western Front, soaking the boys of the Third Army and the command staff, even the ones poring over maps in the tent, when a lone German hobbled up to their checkpoint, hands in the air.

The soldier on guard drew his weapon as soon as he saw the *feldgrau* uniform.

"Don't shoot!" The German lifted his hands higher. "Please, I surrender."

The soldier roughly searched the German for weapons but found a crinkly piece of paper instead.

"What's this? A letter from your lover?" The soldier waved it in his face for an answer, but the German remained silent.

"Get inside." He nudged him with his gun to walk into the tent and answer to his sergeant.

"Another Kraut, Sarge. Had this in his pocket."

Standing near a flickering lantern, the sergeant unraveled the paper—a flyer, it turned out—and noticed a small heart printed in one corner, something meant to be worn on a lapel. The text was flowery and written in German.

The rain drummed against the tent.

"Well, I'll be damned," the sergeant said, a lit cigarette bobbing on his lips. He'd seen a lot of unbelievable things on the battlefield, but he'd never come across something like this before.

Others were intrigued and tried to catch a glimpse over his shoulder. "What does it say, Sarge?"

"Looks like all a German soldier needs to do for a little companionship is wear a paper heart."

He passed the flyer to his translator to read aloud for all to hear.

"'We German women realize it is our duty to our fighting men to help however we can. Your wife, sweetheart, or mother is one of us, doing her duty for the Fatherland. The dreams you had at the front and the longings of your lonely nights will be fulfilled… The League of Lonely War Women is here for you.'"

They all had a laugh, some more loudly than others, calling the German women adulterers and red-light Rosies, but the prisoner showed no emotion, nor said one word.

"Get him out of here," the sergeant said.

They hauled him away to sit with the others who'd surrendered that night. As the command staff got back to their maps and the war, the sergeant shook his head.

"The League of Lonely War Women," he said to himself. "The brass aren't going to believe this one."

Chapter One

One Week Later
Office of Strategic Services
Grosvenor Square, London

I stood in front of the wall map, eyes shifting, following the strings I'd used to connect the pieces of intelligence together like silken spider webs. I had a feeling about a small tire factory just outside Bonn, and after sifting through agent reports and translating German documents about supplies, I was sure the Nazis had split their tire production. Though I knew my partner, Junie, and I needed more than some statistics and a solid hunch to take down the hall to the boys in the Enemy Objectives Unit. We needed another source if we were going to recommend a target, and the only other source was two hours late.

I tugged on my uniform tie, feeling choked, then itchy from the wool skirt suit we had to wear in the Women's Army Corps. Our civilian friends from the Office of Strategic

Services, who bunked, ate, and worked with us, were lucky because they could wear lovely dresses and high heels of their choosing.

"I can't breathe in this thing," I said, finally pulling the tie from my neck and flinging it onto my desk. I turned to Junie. "Where are they? We ordered that list ages ago."

"You know the boys in Military Intelligence, Viv. They take their own sweet time, like sun tea left out on the stoop, especially when it's one of us girls requesting information."

Barbara Bennington looked up from her desk. She'd been listening and watching us for the last three hours. "You two WACs find something?"

I crossed my arms, glancing back at the map. I'd already determined the number of boxcars between Cologne and Bonn had increased based on the reports, but I looked again because Barbara had a way of distracting me. We could also use a visual confirmation, such as an aerial photo, or…

I thumbed through the reports on my desk like a dog trying to find a bone.

Barbara tapped her desk. "Viv?"

Junie stood from her chair. "Pipe down, Babs. Besides, don't you have your own targets to worry about?"

Barbara indeed had her own targets to worry about, and by the look of the file folders on her desk and the orderly way she kept her stacks of paper, I knew she was getting close to writing up a recommendation of her own.

It was no secret that the OSS girls were in direct competition with the WACs over enemy target recommendations. We had an unofficial tally by the door, for God's sake. However, it was considered bad luck to discuss it during working hours, especially after what happened to

Penny, an analyst from Connecticut, who mistranslated one of her German sources. We heard there were more than five hundred civilian casualties after she recommended the wrong target. She never recovered and went back home, some say to an asylum.

Nobody wanted to be Penny.

A messenger from Military Intelligence finally arrived with the list we'd been waiting for. Junie sprinted back after signing for it, flapping the paper in the air as she maneuvered around desks, causing more than a few to look. My heart raced as I ran my finger down the paper, checking off a hundred serial numbers in ascending order, numbers lifted from German tires confiscated in France and sent to the scrap yard in East London for repurposing.

I looked up when I realized what we had.

"Junie," I breathed. "You know what this means?"

The Germans didn't think we were smart enough to compare serial numbers—they couldn't have. Each number was unique to its factory. That little tire factory in Bonn had not only increased production, it was also supplying Hitler's Germany with military-grade aero tires.

Barbara stood, hands on her hips. "You have a recommendation or what?" she barked.

Every eye turned toward us, fingers frozen on typewriter keys and cigarettes paused mid-air, waiting for my reply.

I slowly crossed my arms. "Maybe."

A mad rush of flying papers and analysts comparing notes followed. I squeezed Junie's arm when I saw that Barbara had photographs.

"We need a visual."

"Of what? Tires?" She put both hands on her head, but then

slapped her thighs when Barbara started rolling a piece of paper into her typewriter. We had to be first down the hall, but more so, the intelligence in our report had to be plumb and plenty. If Barbara had more sources, her team's recommendation would bypass ours. That's when I remembered something from a field agent's report a while back—something about a big contract, a man, and the strange way he smoked his pipe.

I pulled Junie in close next to my filing cabinet for privacy. "Do you remember that report…" I thumbed through the files, starting at the front. "About a man with a handlebar mustache and glasses, boasting about a big contract near Bonn a month before production increased? I thought he was with munitions, but now…"

Junie gasped. "You think he was talking about tires?"

I found the file and read through the report. "Listen to this. It says he smokes a pipe from the front of his mouth like a baby with a bottle." I looked up. "If we can somehow connect him to the tire factory using this information…"

"My God, Viv. You translated that weeks ago. How the heck did you remember that?"

I had an excellent memory when it came to appearances. It was even better if I'd seen the person face to face, but in this case, it was a report—someone in the field who was following the Reich's chief production czar to a meeting and overheard a conversation in a café. If he was who I thought he was, then the description could serve as my visual.

"Never mind how." I grabbed Junie by the shoulders. "Start typing. Explain the significance of serial numbers first, then list them in order, with their location."

Junie nodded, loading her typewriter with paper.

Barbara had heard every word and was swiftly ordering her partner, Kitty, to pull more files. "We're on the same team, Viv," she said.

Aside from the general competition between the WACs and the OSS girls, there was a promotion on the line: a position in the field was the rumor, one where only the best would be considered, and we were definitely the best teams from each agency.

"Of course we are, Babs. But you know how it is." I blew her a kiss as I scooted past her desk, then bolted from the room, first breaking into a fast walk, then running into the stairwell and down to the bottom floor to talk to Jim, the records keeper.

The OSS had files on every manufacturing company in Germany as well as some in France. Jim was supposed to service OSS requests first, but it was known that he did favors for the ones he liked and for those who made time to have a conversation, rather than taking their papers and leaving right away. He also didn't like being rushed.

"Another request?" he asked.

I shrugged one shoulder before filling out the request card, thinking carefully about what questions I wanted to ask and which file I wanted him to pull.

"Ask stupid questions, get stupid answers," he said.

"Boy, do I know it." I'd been downstairs three times in the last three days. "But I know exactly what to ask this time."

"Mmm." He examined the card while I tried playing it cool, as if I had plenty of time, even though I was slowly running out of it. At the top of the hour, the boys at the end of the hall would be at lunch, and nobody—not even Barbara

Bennington—would bother the EOU boys while they were eating.

"Take your time," I said, looking at my nails, then to the ceiling where the OSS girls' heels clicked wildly across the floor, possibly from a burst of excitement. I couldn't help but think it was because Barbara was about to take her recommendation down the hall. My heart sped up. I had to do something. "Did you like the cookies I brought in last week?"

He looked confused. "That was you?"

I smiled.

"I did like them. Thank you. But how'd you get Quaker Oats? Reminded me of back home."

"You could tell I used Quaker Oats?" I smirked, but I had no idea about the brand because Marla Smith in the OSS had made them with ingredients her mother had shipped her from Kansas, no less.

"I'm practically a spy, Jim. I can get lots of things. But right now, I need the answer to these questions." I gestured to the note card in his hand.

"Give me a second."

I breathed a sigh of relief—he was looking—but I was still eyeing the clock. After a brief search, he pulled a thick file folder from the shelf behind him. "Bonn Tire Factory." He glanced up after flipping through some of the loose papers inside. "Small output, mostly novelty tires. Founded in thirty-one by a…"

I nodded. "Never mind that. What does he look like? The owner—investor. The man in charge?" I twirled my fingers, imitating a handlebar mustache and repeating what I'd already written on the card. "Has a mustache? Smokes a pipe?"

I held my breath, waiting for what seemed like an eternity when, in reality, it was only a few seconds.

"Yeah."

I reached for my chest. "You don't say…"

"Says here he smokes a pipe from the front of his mouth like a cigarette, rather than the side." Jim puckered his lips, then looked rather confused by that image, or maybe it was horror. "Now, that's a hell of a detail to include."

I jotted down the particular wording, the file and report numbers, and the date. "Thanks, Jim!" I said before dashing off. He threw his hands up, disappointed I was leaving, and I told him I'd bring him more cookies the following afternoon.

I quietly slipped back onto my floor, finding Barbara still at her desk. I had time, but wasn't sure how much. I was still breathing heavily from the sprint up the stairs as I made my way to my desk. I gave Junie a get-out-of-my-chair look, trying not to cause too much attention, but my big secret wasn't much of a secret after Barbara looked up from her typewriter.

I slid into my chair, fingers at the ready, taking a scan of what she'd typed out already.

"Go, Viv!" Junie said.

Kitty cheered Barbara on, and we were in a dead heat. *Clack, clack, clack.* A curl fell into my eyes. *Ding!* I hit the return bar back, biting down on the pencil between my teeth. *Clack, clack, clack…*

Barbara typed just as fast, and soon the other teams were watching, half the floor cheering for Barbara and the other half—the WACs—cheering for Junie and me.

"Don't be a Penny, Viv. It's not worth it," Barbara said as she typed.

Ding! I pulled the pencil from my teeth. "Funny, I was

going to say the same thing to you." I ripped the paper from the typewriter and gave it to Junie, who checked all my work. "Well?"

She gave me a nod, and we bundled our evidence, facts, and figures, then wound a rubber band around all of it before walking calmly away with our precious recommendation. We were professionals, after all, but once out of sight, we bolted down the hall before the boys left for lunch.

I got ready to knock, hand poised, when Barbara burst into the hallway behind us with her report in hand. I gasped, and Junie opened the door, skipping the customary knock for a well-rounded hello to the gatekeeper, Robert, the lead in the Enemy Objectives Unit.

He was the one we had to impress first. Junie stood next to me, shoulder to shoulder, when I realized I didn't have my tie on. I hoped he wouldn't notice because part of our professionalism was our uniform, even if I loathed it.

Junie stiffened. "Enemy target recommendation from the WACs, sir. Privates Junie Beatrice Knight and Vivien Allen."

His gaze swept over both of us before diverting to the wire basket. "Leave it there," he said.

Barbara stepped in behind us.

"One more, sir." She smiled. "Only this one is from the women in the Office of Strategic Services—Special Analyst division. Barbara Bennington and Kitty Meyer."

"Basket," he said to Barbara, who swiped her hands together after placing her heavy recommendation on top of ours, swallowing it whole. Seconds later, he shooed us all into the hallway so he could close the door for lunch. We had barely made it.

"Our status is secure, Viv."

"Same. How ironic," I said. "Don't bother wondering whose it's going to be because it isn't a competition now. You're second."

"Oh, yeah?" She looked at my neck. "You forgot your tie, Viv."

I reached for my collar. "I meant to do that."

"Still feeling secure?"

We watched her walk away to meet up with the OSS girls at the end of the hall, who were heading to the mess in the basement. "Don't pay attention to her, Junes."

"I need that promotion, Viv," Junie whispered. "It's the only hope my daughter and I have of getting out of Gillespie County. A college education doesn't grow on trees where I come from, you know that."

"You'll get there, Junie. I promise." We hooked our fingers for a shake. "You'll be a regular Annie Rice in no time, a college graduate. A real modern woman—someone who has it all."

Junie's daughter wasn't even three yet, but she was already planning her future by bettering her own with a college education at Georgetown University. Annie Rice, one of the first women to be admitted, was her hero, and had been her whole life. She'd even named her daughter Annie.

She scoffed playfully.

"Junes, trust me, we have this in the bag! Remember, we both speak German. Hell, you're one inch from being a Hun." I elbowed her, and a laugh peeped from the side of her mouth.

"Yeah, you might be right about that."

Junie was a bitty thing with blue eyes and brassy hair, but

that wasn't why I teased her. It was known that between the two of us, she spoke German the best, having lived there as a child, whereas I'd just visited my grandparents during the summer, up until my grandfather was arrested and sent to a political prison for charges unknown.

I also needed the promotion, but for other reasons. My parents didn't support my decision to join the Women's Army Corps and become a WAC. *Leave the war to the men*, they had told me after my brother, George, became a decorated hero in the Pacific Theater. *Join Volunteer Services and serve donuts at the VFW instead.*

"I'm going to be decorated too, Mom and Dad," I murmured. "And it won't involve donuts."

"What?" Junie looked up.

"Nothing," I said. "Come on, let's get to the mess before all the seats are taken." I put my arm around her, and we walked down the winding staircase for lunch in the basement.

We'd missed the first wave of diners, but they'd left us plenty to remember them by. The tabletops were a minefield of crumbs and glops of spaghetti sauce with a few curly noodles that had missed someone's mouth. The second wave mainly consisted of the OSS girls from our floor and, of course, Barbara and her partner, Kitty.

They looked smug, sitting close together in their light and airy dresses with their trays of spaghetti. I shifted in my uniform jacket. "The OSS are trained to be irritating, didn't you know that? Question one on their exit exam was to list all the ways to look righteous."

Junie gave me a look—downcast eyes and a slight smirk—before we burst out laughing, which got them sitting up a little straighter.

A few WACs from our floor finally made it downstairs, so we didn't feel as outnumbered among the others. We ate our spaghetti, which was steaming hot today, as opposed to the usual lukewarm sauce and soggy noodles.

"Did you see how thick her recommendation was?" Junie whispered over her tray. "Too thick."

It was, and I'd noted it, but Barbara was known to be long-winded. It was the quality of the recommendation that mattered. Ours was quality. I twisted a forkful of spaghetti.

"Yeah, I saw it," I said, but I said it a little too loudly, and Barbara took that as an opportunity to make small talk.

She scooted closer. "So, who do you think won?"

"Pipe down, Babs," Junie said. "If the major gets wind that we have a competition going, we'll all be dismissed. You want that?"

"Of course, I don't want that." She made a motion of zipping her lips. "No more words from me on that matter. I do wonder, though, whose report is the strongest. Did you remember to include a visual?"

"Is the Pope Catholic?" Junie asked, shoveling a heaping forkful of spaghetti into her mouth. "Of course we did. We're not new at this. Did you?"

She laughed. "We had three photographs!"

Junie swallowed her spaghetti in one gulp. "Three?" she mouthed to me.

"She's fibbing," I mouthed back.

I could tell Junie was nervous by how fast she was eating,

but no amount of talking or reassuring would convince her—she'd stop worrying once our target was chosen.

"What was your recommendation?" I asked Barbara.

"A lady never tells."

Her voice gave me a noticeable shiver. "It's their training," I whispered over my tray to Junie, who almost laughed but managed to hold it in.

"You heard about the promotion, didn't you?" Barbara asked.

The Office of Strategic Services hadn't talked about the promotion in public spaces, despite my best efforts to eavesdrop.

Junie stiffened, her fork in her fist. "What do you know about it?"

"Well, truth be known, I did hear a few things despite the particulars being *hush-hush*," Barbara said.

Hush-hush was code for a secret mission, and the only way that word of a secret mission would have passed down from the top floor to ours was if it had been passed over pillows in the melty candlelight.

I whispered to Junie from the side of my mouth. "So, some tart in the OSS slept with her boss?"

"Shh!" Junie pressed her lips together to keep from laughing. "What if it was her?"

Barbara leaned toward us, trying to listen.

"Babs isn't the tart. She'd ask questions through the whole thing, and you know those OSS guys don't like questions. Especially during you-know-what." I rolled my eyes.

With that, Junie exploded with laughter.

"All right." Barbara carefully set her fork down. "What are you talking about? Me?"

"Don't be silly." I cleared my throat. I didn't want her to know I was cracking jokes at her expense, because in all honesty, Barbara was a fine analyst. I just thought we were better, and I'd say anything to make Junie feel better. "I'm just wondering what you know exactly," I said. "So, what do you know? How secret of a secret mission is it?"

Barbara scooted her chair completely over, followed by Kitty. "It's in the field. Must know German," she said, which was moot. All secret missions required agents to be fluent in German. "But the best part..." She was whispering now. "It pays three times as much as we're getting here as analysts."

I whistled. "Three times as much. Are you sure you got that right? I never heard of such a thing, and trust me, I've tried."

"That's true," Junie said. "Viv here has had her ear stuck to the registers for days."

I kicked Junie under the table, which got a surprised look from Barbara.

"Did you hear anything else about the mission?" I wondered where it was headquartered. All of us dreamed of an undercover job in Vienna, surveilling munitions and train depots.

"Rome," she said. "That's the rumor anyway."

Rome? That didn't sound much different from London. I supposed it didn't matter where the headquarters was, as long as it involved a promotion.

"Hey, you girls wanna go out with us tonight?" Kitty asked. "Lots of servicemen meet up at The Crown pub down the street."

Junie sneered. "You know we can't."

"Why not?" Barbara asked. "It'll be fun, and don't you deserve to let off a little steam?"

"Yeah," Kitty said. "Everyone leaves."

I scoffed. "Not the WACs. Haven't you noticed?" We weren't allowed out of our townhouse at night. In fact, our corporal strictly forbade us from going anywhere other than the OSS office.

"Now that you mention it, I guess I have noticed." Barbara checked her teeth in the reflection on a clean knife. "Pity. Sometimes there's dancing. The barmaid has a jukebox she likes to bring out for some extra coin. You like dancing, don't you?"

Officers from the top floor pounded down the winding staircase into the mess kitchen, some in standard uniforms, but a few in uniforms I didn't recognize. They resembled the army's official olive drab fatigues, but in the right light, they appeared black. One caught my eye as he reached the bottom rung. Not terribly tall, but with thick, dark hair and cool blue eyes. A real cutie pie.

Barbara tapped the table when she realized my attention had strayed. "Viv, are you listening?"

I closed my eyes briefly to refocus. "Of course, I'm listening. You mentioned dancing."

Boy, did I want to go dancing. The clubs back home were fined for playing their jukeboxes, even when it was to help pay for the war. Most places couldn't afford the extra expense, which left sparse dance floors and not a lot of partners to choose from, especially since the ones my age were enlisted and those who weren't were at home with their wives.

"As I was saying, lots of servicemen will be there. The pubs stay open late for them. But not the OSS officers. I guess they get enough of us in the office, because I haven't seen them there."

Barbara took Kitty by the hand to leave.

"Count us in," I said, and they froze just after they stood.

Junie's jaw dropped. "Viv—"

"You'll come?" Barbara looked pleased, but I thought it was because she saw it as an opportunity to press us about our recommendation.

"Yeah. What time?"

"Eight o'clock," Kitty said. "Meet you on the street outside the townhouse."

Junie waited for them to leave the mess. "We can't go," she rasped over her tray. "We'll get in trouble. And we're on the verge of getting promoted, remember?"

"Socializing sounds like a luxury—a reward—for all our hard work. Think about it, will you? Please."

"Humph!" Junie finished her spaghetti without another word. The cutie pie I'd been looking at chose our table to sit with his friend. He was close enough to listen in on what we'd say, yet far enough away to have a private conversation. I shifted in my seat, and when I saw him look over, I pressed my napkin to my lips, leaving a perfectly formed red lipstick print.

"So, tonight," I said, setting the napkin next to my tray. "Eight o'clock. The Crown pub."

I felt his eyes on me.

"Yeah, I know." Junie shoved the last forkful of spaghetti into her mouth. "But I'm still thinking about it, Viv."

"Crown pub tonight," I said again, but this time with a nod.

Junie swallowed, eyes lifting from her plate to take in the other occupants of our table, then turning her sights on me as she realized I'd repeated our plans so they would hear.

She wadded her napkin up and tossed it on her tray of half-eaten spaghetti. "Anyone tell you that you talk too much?"

I smirked. "Does that matter if it works?"

"Come on, let's go." She turned to the man seated next to me as we got up to leave. "We're not going to a pub."

He looked confused.

Chapter Two

After work, we walked down to our townhouse as usual and got ready for inspection with the rest of the WACs. Junie restated her case on all the reasons why we shouldn't go to The Crown pub with Barbara and Kitty. "We need to stay focused, and you know how you get. One drink, and you'll be in the clouds."

"You're reaching." After tucking in my bed sheets, I started on the top cover, pulling tightly; Corporal Baker would notice if it wasn't stiff as a board. "When was the last time I was in the clouds? We deserve a night out."

I counted up how many hours we'd worked on the recommendation, how many days. I didn't see what the harm was, especially since we weren't going somewhere questionable.

"I'm apprehensive because it's against WAC rules." She leaned in with a rasp. "I'm trying to get us promoted, in case you forgot."

"You're going to give yourself a stomachache from

worrying all the time. Trust me, will you? This promotion is ours. I typed most of the report, for God's sake. I remember what's in it. Besides, I feel it in my bones."

She laughed, but I was serious.

"Feel it in your bones? It's bad luck to talk as if you already have it. Kind of like spending money you've been promised but haven't received. And by the way, Viv, your bones aren't always right."

I pretended to be offended, placing a hand on my chest. "They are too!"

"You only want to see if that officer shows up after that stunt you pulled in the mess. Don't think I didn't see that lip print you left him on your napkin."

"You're being silly now," I said, but she was partially correct. The other part of me just wanted to see him again.

"Am I? Babs told you the OSS guys never show up at The Crown, so you wanted to prove her wrong. It's always a competition to you, isn't it?"

Corporal Baker was on the bottom floor, making her rounds. Girls ran to their cots for a few last-minute nips and tucks, but we were mainly squared away. After inspection, we'd eat or read or sleep, but I hadn't accepted our fate.

I smoothed my tie flat while standing at the foot of my bed. "I'm going to ask her for permission."

Junie turned. "Who?"

"Corporal Baker, of course." I looked straight ahead, chin up.

She laughed once—a pop of noise. "Sure. Ask her."

"If she says yes, will you go?" The last thing I wanted to do was go to the pub without Junie.

"You're crazy. You know that?"

A WAC peeped into our room on the way to hers. "Corporal's coming!"

"Will you go?" I asked again.

She took a moment to think. I knew that if I pressed her enough, she'd at least meet me halfway. "I'll go if she says it's all right." The scamper of standard-issue WAC heels dissipated from the halls into each room. "But she'll say no!" Junie frowned when she saw me smile. "I feel it in my bones," she ended in a mumble.

"We'll see whose bones are right," I said.

Corporal Baker was agreeable if you knew how to approach her. If I blurted something about dancing and seemed too eager, she'd definitely say no. I had to ease into it.

She knocked on the doorframe first, which I always appreciated, before taking one giant step into our room with her hands behind her back. "Hello, darlings!"

She inspected our bureaus and seemed pleased with mine. "Very nice," she said, giving the top a long swipe with her finger. She paused at Junie's bureau.

"Junie..."

We both looked over. Junie had left her playing jacks out. We weren't allowed to have anything on top of our bureaus, but they were a reminder to Junie of what she'd left behind, and who she was really fighting for—her daughter—and Corporal Baker knew this. "We've talked about leaving these out." She handed the jacks to Junie, who shoved them into her pocket.

"Yes, ma'am."

After a check of our beds and closet, Corporal Baker said we were clear before being interrupted by mail call—a letter from my mother. She always sent a letter after George received another medal. I wondered what heroic act he'd executed this time.

Corporal Baker turned on her heel to leave, and I stopped her with a reach of my hand.

She gave me a curious look. I really shouldn't have touched her. "Yes, Private Allen?"

My mouth hung open for a moment. I looked to Junie, then back to Corporal Baker.

"Ma'am…" I stuffed the letter under my pillow. "As you know, Junie and I turned in a recommendation today."

"I do know. It's all the talk from the brass right now."

"It is?" Junie asked.

"We worked several days on it," I said. "In fact, yesterday we stayed late." I nodded, hoping she'd nod along, but she grimaced instead, probably wondering where I was going with my explanation. "To put it bluntly, ma'am. We've been invited to the pub at the end of the—"

She shook her head before I could even finish.

"The servicemen will catcall you in the street. I've heard them call you sweet cheeks as it is. What do you think they'll call you this time?"

I refrained from telling her that they catcalled us because she called us darlings out in the open while we were in uniform—she even snapped her fingers at us for added measure. "The OSS girls invited us. Their major gave them permission."

I let that information hang in the air.

"I see." She sighed with a rub of her forehead, and that's when I knew I had a chance, combined with the longer pause than usual. "Well, you have been working hard," she said, and I clapped once, but she was quick to settle me down.

"But ultimately, it is Major Richardson's decision. He's worried his WACs will get caught outside in the middle of a raid. It's his way of keeping you all safe."

Major Richardson was a veteran from the first war, a dedicated man and a stickler for rules, but also more grandfatherly and old-fashioned than most. I believed he wanted to protect us, yet it was also a way for him to maintain the respect of his unit.

Barbara and Kitty clipped down the hallway just then, talking as they passed our door about the pub and doing their hair. Corporal Baker's gaze lingered in their direction well after Barbara and Kitty had trotted off. I was still waiting for her decision.

"But I'll ask him. It's the least I can do for you two after that recommendation." She smiled on her way out.

I turned to Junie. "She's asking."

"I heard, Viv," Junie said, playing with the jacks on her nightstand.

As soon as Corporal Baker placed a call to Major Richardson from the downstairs phone, Pepper Coddington and Nancy Lewis rushed to our room, clinging to the doorframe and poking their heads inside. "You girls get in trouble?"

"No way, not us," Junie said.

"Hey, you want to go to a pub tonight?" I asked.

Pepper's mouth hung open. "You mean it?"

"We can't go," Nancy said.

Junie swiped up the jacks with one hand and the little ball with the other. "Viv here asked for permission, and you know how she is."

"Pushy?" Pepper asked, bright-eyed like she'd just won a

prize, but when she saw my eyes narrow, she shrank a bit. "Persistent, I mean."

"Yeah," I said, arms folded. "Persistent. We deserve a night out, girls. Don't you think so?"

Pepper clapped. "I'll go tell Marsha and Karen—"

"Not so fast, Pep," I said. "Corporal Baker hasn't said we can go, yet."

Barbara and Kitty passed by again, but this time they were whispering.

"What about the air raids?" Nancy asked. "Aren't you scared about being caught outside?"

Junie and I hadn't experienced a German air raid, not like some of the other WACs who arrived before D-Day in the spring. We'd heard that the flying bombs were something to fear, though, mostly because you couldn't hear them before they landed—only a slight flicker of the lights before the explosion in most cases. With a blitz, at least you knew they were coming and could get a running start.

"Scared? I've never said that word. Besides, it's just for a couple of hours, and the OSS's major isn't worried."

"Hmm." Nancy folded her arms.

The private who was dishing out the mail was back, popping her head inside. "This one's for you, Nance, and one for Pepper." She handed them letters. "That's all."

I turned to Junie. "Maybe a letter for you tomorrow."

"Yeah."

Junie's mother was taking care of her daughter while she was in Europe and had been sending regular updates, mostly reminding her how proud her daughter would be of Junie once the war was over and not to worry. But those posts had become more and more infrequent.

"The corporal's coming," Piper whispered, and we froze, listening to Corporal Baker walking up the stairs.

I held my breath.

"Darlings?" Corporal Baker called, knocking a second before stepping into our room. I straightened. "Don't be out past ten o'clock."

I exhaled, smiling. "You have my word! Thank you—"

She looked us up and down. "I don't care about your word. It's an order. And also, you'll be representing the Women's Army Corps. No civvies."

"Ten o'clock. Absolutely. Thank you, Corporal Baker." I turned to Junie, who looked surprised. Pepper and Nancy scooted off to tell the rest of the WACs. Squeals of delight rippled down the hall.

"How do you do that?" Junie shook her head.

"Do what?"

"Charm the pants off people."

I blew on my fingernails. "It's another one of my gifts. So, you're going?" I was beaming and trying not to say, "I told you so," but I sort of was. "You're making good on the bet?"

"Of course, I'm making good on it. I'm not a cheat. But I want you to know I think this idea of yours stinks to high heaven."

"Noted." I fixed my hair in the mirror, brushing my chestnut strands into curls near my shoulders. "But trust me, you'll thank me later."

"No way. Not a chance."

I twirled around with the brush in my hand. "Oh, come on, Junie. I'm doing you a favor. We'll be promoted soon and leaving this place. You'll see. This very well could be our last night in London, and who knows when we'll be back. We're going to a pub."

"There you go again, spending money you don't have."

"Oh, I have it. You have it, too."

She pointed her finger at me. "And you promise? Ten o'clock, not a second after?"

"I promise."

Barbara and Kitty met us outside near the street, along with Pepper, Nancy, and a few other WACs who trailed behind.

"I didn't know you all were coming," Barbara said.

"Well, you invite one WAC, you get ten of them." I shrugged. "What can I say?"

"You can say thank you."

I patted her shoulder. "Thanks, Babs!" I smiled.

Barbara rolled her eyes. "Try to keep up."

We followed her down the street. The trees hung over the pavement, green and lush; it was hard to tell there was a war going on from Grosvenor Square, save for all the American service members. We got a few whistles about our legs and comments about our uniforms. "Hey, shortcake," one said to Junie. "You look good enough to eat."

"Airmail has arrived, boys," another said, referring to me. "Hey, sweet cheeks!"

Barbara looked a little jealous. "All that because of a uniform?"

"No," Junie said. "We're gorgeous, don't you know?" She fluffed a brassy wave of hair above her shoulder, which was more of a frizz after walking. We waited on the corner while the policeman directed traffic. "So, Babs," Junie said, "tell us your recommendation."

He blew his whistle and told us to walk.

Barbara laughed deeply from her chest. "And why should I?"

I sped up a step. "You tell us yours, and we'll tell you ours." Junie glared at me. I assume she expected Barbara to tell us her secrets without anything in return, but I knew better. "I'll spill everything."

After a brief discussion with Kitty, Barbara informed us that they had intelligence about a secret oil refinery. They'd confirmed it with agents on the ground and those three photographs she'd mentioned earlier.

Junie jabbed me once with her elbow. It was a good find. But so was our tire factory.

"You know there are a lot of dummy refineries out there," Junie piped.

"It's not a dummy," Barbara said, then she turned to me, and I suppose it was because she didn't expect Junie to tell her the truth. "And yours?"

"A clandestine tire factory. I have facts, figures, and serial numbers to prove it."

She looked surprised. "That is good." She raised her eyebrows after a few thoughtful seconds had passed. "And you gals came up with that on your own? Well, who knows. Maybe the promotion isn't what it seems. Maybe it's not respectable."

"What do you mean, not respectable?" I asked.

"The things those Germans spew into the ears of their lovers…" Barbara stopped in front of a little pub painted green and gold. "Look, we all want to make a difference. But not all of us can go all the way. Are you willing to lose a friend over it or die trying?" She looked up at the marquee. "We're here! The Crown pub."

Junie edged in between us. "Are you saying the OSS is going to promote their best to be German prostitutes in the field?"

"I didn't say that," she said. "But if I were promoted, I wouldn't care what the job was. I'm here to serve."

Junie scoffed, then turned to me, slightly scolding. "Don't listen to her."

"Now," Barbara said, smoothing back her dark hair where she'd set it with lotion. "You WACs try not to embarrass us, all right?" She pulled a tube of military-issue red lipstick from her pocketbook and rudely smoothed it over her lips without a compact mirror, and I wondered just who would be embarrassing whom.

Pepper, Nancy, and the others huddled around us after Babs and Kitty walked inside.

"Remember what Corporal Baker said—ten o'clock. That's an order." I looked at my watch. "That gives us almost two hours." There was a brief discussion about whether we should all walk back together, but some of the girls didn't want to stay the entire time. It was agreed that we would leave with our partners at a suitable time, as long as we were all back safe and sound by curfew.

The smell of tobacco and beer filtered out the door when it opened, along with the building commotion of people having a good time. "Junie." I offered her my arm, and together, we stepped into The Crown pub. The barmaid's daughters ran between the barstools and tables, collecting sweets from the

American GIs as they smoked and drank pints with suds an inch thick.

"Well, what do you think?" I asked.

"It's smaller and smokier than I thought."

We took a seat at a raised table near the bar and ordered two pints. She held her beer up to the single lightbulb above our heads. "I don't like drinking beer I can't see through." She wiped her mouth with the back of her hand after taking a bitter sip. "Is it time to go yet?"

"We just got here."

I sat back in my chair and listened to others talk about the war like a disease they'd just received the remedy for. There was hope and some excitement and the occasional warning of a flying bomb, which always, without fail, got everyone to take a drink with shouts of one going up Hitler's bum.

I kept checking my watch; an hour passed, and my dark-haired OSS officer still hadn't shown up. I swore he had been listening. And what man wouldn't follow two beautiful women to a pub when it was clear I was inviting him? Defeat was a bitter pill, even if I'd only come up with the plan haphazardly in the mess.

I sighed with the thought of leaving when Junie jabbed me repeatedly in the side, spilling my beer. "Viv!"

"Dang it, what?" I sopped up the suds with a napkin.

"Look who's here." She pointed with her eyes.

I covered my mouth. The OSS officer had walked in, and he was as handsome as ever with all that dark hair and those shining blue eyes that could send a flutter through a thousand WAC hearts. Even Barbara looked a little shocked to see him. I did note that he was wearing a different uniform than the one he'd worn to lunch.

"Well, well…" I said, straightening. "Take that, Babs."

Junie studied me for a moment, looking at Barbara and then at him. "So, I was right? It was a competition, wasn't it?"

I shrugged one shoulder. "Maybe."

"If he comes over and talks to you, then I'll be thoroughly impressed."

"Oh, *then* you'll be impressed?"

We watched him talk to another man and take seats at a table for four. "He brought his friend from the mess." I slipped off my chair. "Let's go talk to them."

"Wait a minute." Junie pulled me back by my uniform sleeve. "I think we should head back. What if…" She looked at her watch. "I don't…"

"It's not like we're going to marry them and stay all night. It's a few more minutes of fun, and remember, we deserve it." I took her by the hand and dragged her through the crowd.

"Wait, Viv," she rasped. "I don't want to lose track—"

We were at their table.

"Hello," I said to both of them, but I was looking at the one with the dark hair. "Do I know you?" I resisted calling him a cutie pie. "You look very familiar."

He paused before answering, giving me a slow-burning smile. "You look familiar, too."

"Must be the uniform." I smoothed my tie flat. "Name's Viv Allen." I held my hand out for a shake.

"Hal Cunningham," he said before pointing to his friend. "This is my pal, Bill Sams."

We sat down. I got comfortable.

"So, Hal," I said. "Is it a habit of yours to listen in on conversations of beautiful women?"

"Listen in?" He laughed after grinning. "Well, you

practically asked me to come, didn't you? Like a date." He pulled my lipstick-printed napkin from his pocket.

Now, it was me laughing. "Oh, that? I was wiping off my lipstick. It wasn't a request, surely." I patted my hair.

"Well, since I figure you're going to be my wife someday, I thought we should at least meet."

"Oh, that's rich," Junie piped. "Viv here doesn't fall for corny lines like that."

I wadded the napkin and tossed it over my shoulder. "She's right."

"But it's not a line," he said.

I rolled my eyes. "Oh, sure," I said, but I'd started to feel a little warm around the collar, not sure what to say or do, so I took a long sudsy drink of my beer.

"Your uniform is different than the one I saw you in earlier," I said.

"Is it? Funny you noticed." He smoothed his front pockets to his chest.

"I'm an analyst, so I notice these things. Why the change?" I asked, boldly thinking he might throw me a bone, but he was quiet. I decided to change the subject. "Been to many pubs? This is our first and last," I said. "We were promoted, leave soon for a secret assignment."

"Viv—" Junie set her beer down. "You're talking too much."

Hal and Bill looked confused, and I had to explain because my goal was to win Hal over, and that wasn't going to work if I left her comment hanging. "Truth is, we haven't been promoted *yet*. Soon to be official, though. Junie doesn't like me talking about it before it's confirmed."

"We're being promoted," Hal said. "Though it is official."

"Oh, really?" I asked. "Good thing we met tonight, then." I held my glass up for a toast. "Here's to Berlin," I said, then threw my voice to the crowd, "and shoving a flying bomb up Hitler's—"

A cheer erupted, accompanied by glasses clinking and spilling suds.

"Where are you from?" Hal asked me.

"Maryland," I said. "Where are you from?"

"Ohio," he said. "You know there's only a state between us as the crow flies."

I smiled, taking another drink from my pint. But he must be a fool to think we'd ever see one another after this night.

The barmaid rolled a jukebox past the tables and into the back. Servicemen grabbed their gals by the hand. It was then I noticed Barbara and Kitty had gotten up to leave, but we still had time, according to my watch.

I reached for Junie's hand on the table. "We're not leaving this place without a dance." I bobbed on my stool even before the music started.

"No, Viv," she said, shaking her head, but I was nodding. "You're acting crazy." She tapped her watch. "It's almost ten. Babs and Kitty already left!" She hiked her thumb at the door. "And where's Pepper and Nancy?"

"I don't know."

"That's because they left, Viv. For the townhouse," she said as if I didn't know. "I really think we should get going. This idea doesn't sit right. I don't want to do anything—"

"One dance, Junie. Five minutes, tops. Could you give me that? It took ten to walk here, and we have just over twenty minutes to get back." I placed my hands on her shoulders. "Trust me. We'll make it."

She'd folded her arms and tried to look tough and resolved, but she started to melt the longer I pleaded. "Fine." She rechecked her watch. "Five minutes. But that's all. Not a second more. Actually, you've already lost a minute while we talked. Four minutes."

"You have my word," I said.

"Phooey on your word. It's an order, remember?"

Hal took my hand, and the next several minutes were a blur while we danced in the warm and smoky back room of the pub. Couples squeezed in, knocking shoulders, smiling, laughing, and twirling. I loosened my tie while I was heating up.

"You know the jitterbug?" he asked.

"What?" I cupped my ear because it was hard to hear over the music and the roar of the crowd.

"The jitterbug!"

"Oh, yeah. I love the jitterbug!" I said, just as the music changed to Glenn Miller. There was a joyous wave over the crowd with "In the Mood" blasting from the jukebox. My cheeks hurt from smiling, and my shoes pinched my toes, but damn, I couldn't stop. This was what I needed and deserved for all my hard work. That promotion was ours. I felt it in my bones, no matter what Junie had said.

"Hey, you got a fella back home?" he asked.

"No." I kept dancing and smiling, and boy, was I getting warm. He whipped me around in a spin. "Why?" I asked, but he never got to answer because Junie butted in between us on the dance floor.

"Viv!"

"Junes!" I pushed her to the side as if it were a fun little game we were playing, but I knew she was trying to lead me away, and I was sure I had at least two minutes left. Hal gave me a twirl.

"Viv!" she said again, but this time she'd shouted.

"What?" I stopped dancing, out of breath and sweaty.

The lights flickered. "Flying bomb!" someone shouted into the air, and a cheer erupted over the dance floor. "Up Hitler's—"

The lights cut out with the music.

Boom.

Chapter Three

The dance floor cleared out like a pack of rats running for the exit. Hal was gone, and I lost Junie in the dark rush of the crowd, but she found me on the pavement, pressing my palms to my ears.

"Junie!" We hugged quickly. The blackness of the city was even more menacing than the sirens, with the occasional blasts from the flying bombs serving as a scant source of light. We had to get to safety. We had to get back to the townhouse!

We ran across the street for Grosvenor Square, just two gray figures among a hundred, scurrying through cars and throngs of chaotic people up to our front steps. We pounded on the door while twisting the locked doorknob, but to no avail. The WACs and the OSS girls had already taken cover in the shelter.

"What do we do?" I pounded some more, though I knew it was a lost cause.

We cowered below the door, shaking, until Corporal Baker found us outside sometime after midnight, still huddled together on the front steps. She ordered us to our rooms and told us not to leave until further instructions.

The next morning, the townhouse was busy with girls getting ready for work while we lay on our beds, fully dressed in our uniforms, awaiting our fate with the ring of the sirens still ripe in my ears. Babs made sure to come see us before leaving for work, leaning in through the doorway.

"How's your status now, Viv?" She giggled.

I threw a pillow at her, missing her face and hitting the doorjamb instead. "Damn her," I muttered, then turned to Junie as she lay with her legs crossed at the ankle and her hands folded on top of her chest.

"We're the new Penny," Junie blurted. "Humiliated, tucked-tailed. Failures. She got her translations wrong, but we're about to get canned for not getting back on time?"

I sat up, unsure of what to say because I knew it was my fault, and she was upset. No, she was more than upset—she was hurt.

"We should have left earlier, Viv. Now my dreams are lost." She covered her face and whimpered.

"Junie, I—"

She ripped her hands away. "Damn it, Viv. We should have left The Crown when I first said so. Hell, we shouldn't have gone at all. I knew it was a stinker of an idea. Something was going to happen..." Her eyes shifted to mine. "Surely, you must have felt that in your bones."

"I'm sorry, Junie. I really am." I squeezed her hand, which thawed her out a bit because she wasn't glaring anymore. "I'm a real pain in your ass, aren't I?" I asked, and a laugh peeped from behind her pressed lips.

"Don't do that."

"Do what?"

"Try to make me laugh. I'm serious."

I'd been making Junie laugh since we met on day one. While she was prepared for the role even before we were issued our uniforms, wearing a gray skirt suit and a tie like the rest of the recruits, I clicked my way onto the Daytona Beach Army Airfield after a long bus ride, wearing heels, a bright yellow dress, and jingly jewelry.

I realized immediately what my parents had done when they said they'd called ahead and confirmed it was a social, a get-to-know before my actual first day. It was their way of trying to get me to quit the WACs—or be demoted to the donut wagons—before I'd even started.

I'd had to think on my feet, which was one of my strengths, even with so many eyes on me. "You mean this isn't the Goldman bar mitzvah?" I had said, snapping my fingers. "Damn, wrong invitation."

Junie had burst out laughing, and we'd been friends ever since.

"Can you forgive me?" I asked.

She moved her hand out from under mine. "Yeah. But next time you're given an order, you need to stick to it. All right?"

"I'll stick to it. I promise." Our argument was over, and I was relieved she'd forgiven me. The letter I received last night from my mother slipped out from under my pillow. I slowly picked it up off the floor, having forgotten about it.

"Are you going to open it?" Junie asked.

I stared at the postage marks, the stamps, and my mother's handwriting. The envelope felt a little padded, too—more than one sheet of paper. My brother must have really done something heroic to warrant more than one page of writing.

I slipped it back under my pillow. "Maybe later." I got up to pace the room.

Junie played with her jacks from her bedside, throwing them down on the nightstand, hand after hand after hand. "It's times like this I really miss my daughter."

I wasn't sure what to say, knowing that if we went home, Junie's dreams for her and Annie would turn to dust.

"There isn't anything on God's green earth I wouldn't do for her. You'll understand someday." The jacks fell from her palm onto the table. "I…" She looked up. "I'm sorry, Viv. I didn't mean—"

"It's all right." I sat on my bed.

Her eyes clenched. "No—"

"Junie," I said. "I mean it. It's all right."

The army doctor told me I might be sterile. I couldn't bring myself to write to my parents with that kind of news, so only Junie and the doctor knew that secret.

"Besides, that doctor doesn't know everything. He could be wrong," I said, but the truth was I trusted doctors who had medical degrees.

"Yeah!" she said with a nod. "He doesn't know everything." She scooped up her jacks and stuffed them in her pocket. "Sorry about Hal."

"What do you mean?"

"Looked like you liked him. Now he's gone. Didn't have a second to say goodbye before the bombing."

"I think I did like him for a few moments. I mean, what wasn't there to like? He was dark and handsome, and he knew how to dance. He also took the bait and went to The Crown on purpose, but can you believe that pick-up line of his?"

I scoffed, but I just wanted to know if she thought it had some truth to it.

I bit my lip, waiting for her to respond.

"It was one of the worst I'd heard, honestly," she said. "Had to come meet you because you'll be my future wife…" She laughed. "That's wishful thinking."

"Yeah." I shrugged after thinking about it. "I guess it doesn't matter now, does it? I'll never see him again."

The townhouse was quiet for some time after the women left for headquarters, so it was shocking, though not unexpected, when we heard a commotion with the arrival of Major Richardson. First, it was the thud of his footsteps in the foyer. Then it was his voice. Scratchy and commanding and angry.

We scrambled to stand at attention, listening to Corporal Baker get chewed out for trusting us and for pitching the idea to him in the first place. "These analysts are my responsibility. I don't care what the OSS thinks or how they handle their staff. I have my own problems and my own rules!" he shouted as if he were angrier at himself than with us.

"Yes, Major Richardson," she kept saying.

"And what's this I hear about one of them not wearing their tie and looking sloppy on the floor?"

"Viv, put this on," Junie whispered, handing me my tie that was still lying on my bed.

He paced the wood floors, shouting indiscriminately, and I imagined he did so with his arms behind his back, turning on his heel every time he made it to the other side of the room. Then it was quiet. Dead quiet.

I tied my tie around my neck.

"Did he leave?" she whispered.

"I don't know," I whispered back, then we heard the tap of Corporal Baker's shoes coming up the main staircase.

I hurriedly smoothed my tie flat as her steps came closer and closer to our door before she burst into our room without her customary knock. "Downstairs, you two." She paused with a brief press of her lips. "Now."

I turned to Junie after she left. "No 'darlings'?"

"Come on." Junie took me by the hand, and off we went.

Major Richardson had never been to our townhouse, as far as I knew. This was going to be bad—as bad as they come. I felt it twisting in my stomach, then throbbing in my head when I saw him waiting for us by the door with his hands behind his back, chin up, and watching us over his cheeks.

"Private Knight," he said through his teeth. "Private Allen. Nice of you to come home, finally." He paused, giving us a scrutinizing look before narrowing in on my tie. "Did you have a good time dancing while your fellow WACs were in the shelter, wondering where the hell you were?"

I opened my mouth to say something, but then snapped it closed because even I knew better.

"Ladies, you have tested my patience more than once," he said, but he was looking me dead in the eyes as he spoke, not Junie. "I know about the competition on the floor. Do you know how dangerous that can be? That's how mistakes are made—rushing toward a recommendation when real lives are at stake. This is not a competition. This is war!"

"Yes, Major," I said.

"I told you," Junie said to me under her breath.

"You're not so innocent in this, are you, Private Knight? As her partner, you share everything. The decisions, the burden, and the consequences."

"Yes, Major."

"And you, Private Allen, disobeying a direct order, no matter how frivolous it may seem to you, is egregious. And to think it was your brother, Corporal George Allen, that I read about just this morning in the *Flight Deck*, earning the Distinguished Flying Cross medal."

"George made the service newspaper?"

"Mmm. Shot down six enemy planes in a single action over the Pacific."

The letter. I knew it. *Good job, Georgie.* I loved my brother, and I was glad to hear he was doing so well, despite my parents constantly throwing his accomplishments in my face.

"Private Allen, why did you join the Army Corps?"

Proving my parents wrong was on the tip of my tongue. So was not taking no for an answer. "Because I want to do my part. Help win the war."

"Don't we all…"

He paced in front of us, and I wondered what was going to happen because he could have ordered us home long before this conversation even started. He clicked his heels once, standing even straighter. "Private Knight," he said, and we both tensed. "I understand you know German fluently."

"I lived there, Major. Came over eleven years ago."

He turned to me. "And you, Private Allen. I understand you know German fluently as well."

"Yes, Major. My parents were born in Bavaria, and I spent regular summers there visiting my grandparents until they died."

He nodded as if he already knew, which, of course, he did. "Well, you two. It is your lucky day."

"It is?" Junie and I looked at each other.

"I wanted to send you home, but the truth is, you've been promoted. You're going to Rome."

My heart thumped. "Sir, does this mean—"

"It means you're working for the Office of Strategic Services now." He turned to leave. "Good job on that tire factory. It was a direct hit."

I covered my mouth in pure disbelief, though at the same time, I knew that promotion was ours; I had felt it. "Junie Beatrice Knight, do you know what this means?"

Junie nodded incessantly.

"All right, darlings," Corporal Baker said. "You heard him. Pack your bags. Oh, and girls. Don't screw this up. You pull any of that competition baloney in Rome, and you'll be serving up donuts back home in Volunteer Services, if you're lucky."

"Yes, ma'am!" I said.

She motioned toward the stairs. "Now, go pack. You have a transport plane to catch."

We dashed upstairs, where Junie and I hooked fingers.

"I told you I felt it in my bones, Junie."

We arrived in Rome in the middle of the afternoon on what we were told was a typical Roman summer day since the Allies had seized the capital—dusty, hot, and dry. We were met by Sergeant Manzo, who was wounded during the push over the Gustav Line; he wasn't recovered enough to return to active duty but wasn't injured enough to convalesce. "They don't know what to do with me. What can I say? So, they stuck me with the OSS. First time to Italy?"

We followed him across the tarmac with our bags slung

over our shoulders. "Yes, first time. You make it sound like we're on vacation."

He turned to us, cigar tucked in the corner of his mouth. "Well, you *are* staying in a villa."

"A villa?"

"It's department headquarters. In the city."

He walked off toward a jeep, and we hurried along behind him, dressed in men's khakis and metal helmets, which were going to take some getting used to—I was just glad there was no tie. God, it was hot.

"All right, sweethearts," he said, though it didn't have the same ring to it as when Corporal Baker called us "darlings." He pointed to his jeep, and we hopped inside, me in the front and Junie in the back.

The engine rattled like a jalopy, jingling and clanking as if it had just driven out of a battlefield. "Hold on!"

We took off with a lurch down a dusty street among the military vehicles that quickly turned into a series of twisty, one-way streets with more pushcarts and small cars with squeaky horns than I'd ever seen or heard before. Warm wind blew into our faces.

"You should have heard the cheering in the street," he said as he drove. "The old timers from the first war were the first to cheer, then the women came next, and they were dressed in fancy dresses—what a sight for sore eyes. There wasn't a deprived soldier to be had in the Fifth Army." He laughed, pulling his cigar from his mouth and looking at us.

"Prostitutes?"

He swerved to avoid a woman on her bicycle who came out of nowhere. "I guess you don't want to hear about that." He tucked his cigar back into his mouth.

We pulled up to a villa on a narrow side street that was already off a different side street with hanging laundry and women standing in doorways. "Don't let the nice faces fool you. Watch out!"

I heaved my duffel bag over my shoulder in the street. I didn't expect the smell, which was a cross between sewer, fish, and roses, rising from the baking cobblestones. "What do you mean, watch out?"

He took a deliberate look down both ends of the street. A man who'd been smoking casually and watching us drive up had turned his back. "Not everyone was happy to see us push the Germans out. Some continue to support Mussolini."

"How do you know? Turned backs?"

"Let's just say I eat sauce from a can and pasta sent from home." He put the jeep in gear and drove off, leaving us in the street with our duffel bags, facing a gated double door.

"Should we knock?" Junie asked.

I thought it was odd to knock. In London, we walked right into the headquarters. This place felt like someone's home, with potted plants and a gargoyle doorknocker, which was just another indication that things were different here in Rome.

"I guess." I gave the knocker a rap.

I casually glanced over my shoulder. A woman with slick, dark hair and a low-cut dress walked into the street to get a better look at us, encouraged by the others watching from terraces and saying things in Italian I couldn't understand, motioning with pursed hands.

A greasy American man smoking a cigarette opened the door. "Ah, finally. Come in." He waved for us to walk inside, then shouted at the woman in the street with a forceful sway of his arm. "*Ciao! Bye! Get lost!*"

He closed the door with an exhausted breath. "Snooping Italians. Have to know everything," he mumbled, his cigarette bobbing on his lip.

Junie and I waited for directions in the dim entryway, which felt warmer than outside. I wasn't sure what to expect, but the thought crossed my mind that we were not in the right place.

"Is this the—"

"Shh!" He pressed a finger to his lips. "They can hear you out there. Yes, this is the place. Now, go on. The meeting is going to start in five minutes." He pointed down a long and wide hallway with his cigarette. "In the back."

I pulled at my collar. "I hope it's cooler back there."

He scoffed. "What did you expect? Olive groves and fresh breezes? It's still technically summer for a few days. Wartime summer at that. My advice is to get used to it." He pointed again to the back, this time with his finger.

I followed Junie down the hallway that opened into a terracotta courtyard with empty planters and a dry cherub fountain. I fanned my neck.

"Where do we go now?"

There were two hallways to choose from and one closed door.

"How am I supposed to know, Viv?"

A woman who looked like she was part of housekeeping, wearing an apron with a rag wrapped around her head, stood in the corner smoking and watching. "Excuse me," I said, but she started to walk away. I moved toward her. "Wait. Stop. Do you speak English?"

She blinked and blinked.

Junie edged me out of the way, pointing to her lips and talking slowly. "The meeting?"

She held both her cheeks. "Yes, yes. Of course. That way to the meeting." She pointed down one of the hallways. Her English was surprisingly good, considering the way she looked at us.

"That was strange."

"It's all strange," Junie said. "Let's go."

We walked on with our duffel bags over our shoulders when we heard the commotion of voices. There was some relief on my part because I still wasn't sure we were at the right place. Then we saw the uniforms—khakis, helmets, lipstick—and ten other women with duffel bags like us.

We entered the room, surrounded by stained glass that had been covered with heavy tapestries and three rows of empty church pews.

"Oh, good, we're all here," a woman said, standing at a podium that very well could have been a pulpit. "The meeting will start in a moment."

I plopped my duffel bag and helmet to my feet, but Junie's eyes went to the vaulted ceiling, the covered glass, and the stone floor. "Viv, this is a…"

"A chapel? That's my guess," another woman said. "It's about ten degrees cooler in here than anywhere else in the villa. Hi, I'm Pudge." She shook both our hands before pointing to the girl next to her. "This is my partner, Dot."

Dot held her hand up for a wave. "Pleasure."

Dot was strikingly petite, with dark brown hair and thick lashes to match. Her accent was astonishing, and I pegged her as being from New Jersey, but when she spoke German, she sounded exactly like what I imagined Eva Braun to sound like.

Pudge was on the plain side but with voluptuous curves and sandy-blonde hair.

"Vivien Allen," I said after Junie introduced herself.

They were from France, having dropped in a week after D-Day as part of a larger OSS team. Both were analysts who set up offices in vacated French chateaus once used by the Reich.

"So, you gals ready for this secret mission? Better be. We're genuine now. Best of the best," Pudge said.

"Nah, I came here for the food," I said, which got a peep of laughter from Junie.

"Be serious, Viv."

"Ah, a wisecracker," Pudge said, smiling. "Good to know."

I looked over the other ladies, hair frazzled from the heat and tired, but otherwise ready for work. "All women? That's interesting."

"Nothing is interesting about it," Dot piped. "The OSS has gathered its best, and it's no wonder they're all women. Pudge and I here—" she hiked her thumb "—single-handedly unmasked a double agent with our intelligence. What did you two do?"

"We took down a tire factory," Junie said, which got a whistle from both of them.

"Not bad, not bad indeed," Dot said.

"Do either of you know what the mission is?" I asked.

"We weren't told." Pudge elbowed Dot as if they'd already discussed it. "But whatever it is, I bet we'll be handling guns. Right, Dot?"

"Don't listen to her," Dot said, looking at us. "She hasn't overheard anything. Just wishful thinking."

"We'll probably be analysts here at the villa," Junie said. "Maybe listening to German radio transmissions."

I shook my head. "That's not it. We could have done that in France or even in London."

"She's right." Pudge pointed at me. "We could have done that in France."

"This mission is more comprehensive, with increased stakes," I said.

"Sure pays well," Junie said.

"Our chance to shine," Dot said under her breath.

Our chance to shine.

The lady at the podium told us to take a seat, and we slid into the pews.

"I'm Lieutenant Cora Hughes." She cleared her throat, which echoed much louder than it should have in the tiny stone chapel, because we were hanging on to every word and breath. "But it's safer if you don't address my rank in public and just call me Cora…"

Cora said she was a trained lawyer, originally from Prague, and knew six languages fluently. Seven if you count Italian, but she didn't, saying she could only speak it conversationally. She was clearly the type of person who didn't have to study, then showed up on exam day and got perfect scores. I could tell that right away, which meant this mission really was genuine, like Pudge said, because it was led by a woman of such caliber.

"Now, let's cut to the chase, shall we? Time to tell you why you're here." Girls nodded, controlling their excitement, but you could feel it pulsating in the air, especially after Cora pulled flyers from her briefcase and began to pass them out. "The details are in the print."

I reached for Junie's hand, smiling. "We deserve this," I mouthed. "We'll be heroes."

Chapter Four

Dot took a flyer from Cora and passed the rest down. My heart ticked up, watching the flyers change hands before finally reaching me. I eagerly glanced over the page. I was expecting a list of objectives or a list of target items—munitions, encampments, or names of collaborators—but instead, it was a letter written in German.

I turned to Junie for an explanation, but she shrugged.

DEAR FRONTLINE SOLDIER!

WHEN WILL YOU HAVE LEAVE AGAIN?

WHEN WILL YOU BE ABLE TO FORGET YOUR ARDUOUS SOLDIER'S DUTIES FOR A WHILE? WE AT HOME KNOW OF YOUR HEROIC STRUGGLE. WE UNDERSTAND THAT EVEN THE BRAVEST GET TIRED SOMETIMES AND NEED ... TENDERNESS, AND HEALTHY ENJOYMENT.

WE ARE WAITING FOR YOU:
For you who must spend your leave in a foreign town; for you whom the war has deprived of a home…

WE ARE WAITING FOR YOU:
Cut our symbol from this letter. In every coffee shop, in every bar and railway station, pin it to your lapel so that it can be clearly seen. A member of our association will soon contact you… There are members everywhere because we women understand our duties to the homeland and to its defenders.

We have been separated from our men for many years. Your wife, sister, or lover is one of us… We think of you and Germany's future. That which rests, rusts.

THE ASSOCIATION OF THE LEAGUE OF LONELY WAR WOMEN

One by one, each of us looked up after reading. At the bottom of the letter was a perforated drawing of a heart.

You could have heard a pin drop.

"This is a copy of a flyer that was found in the pocket of a German soldier. A few days later, an article appeared in *The Washington Post*, suggesting exactly what the note implies—all a German soldier on leave has to do to get some affection is pin a heart to their lapel and a member of the League of Lonely War Women would be there to serve." She paused, but we were still silent. "I wrote this, along with hundreds of others, which were dropped over Germany in a massive black propaganda campaign that I designed for the Morale Operations Branch of the OSS."

Morale Operations? What exactly was she asking us to do? Maybe I'd misunderstood. I read through the letter again, thinking I had missed something, because surely, she wasn't telling us we were these lonely German war women, was she?

Junie stood up. "So, ahh…" She crossed her arms. "Ma'am, are you asking us to go undercover inside Nazi Germany?"

Dot stood next. "And be German prostitutes?"

I gulped.

There was a commotion of unrest, with some taken aback at the prospect of going undercover in Nazi Germany, which was more dangerous than going behind enemy lines in France and Italy, while others were more concerned about their morality and what their future husbands would say. A blonde from Florida clutched her neck as if she were wearing her mother's pearls.

Cora stepped away from the podium. "It's companionship, a listening ear. A friendly voice. The campaign is intended to lower their morale, take advantage of their loneliness from being far from home, and sow paranoia about their own wives and girlfriends talking to other men—"

"At the expense of our purity?" Dot had raised her voice.

Cora's lips pressed. "As the best agents we have at our disposal, surely you can read the explicit meaning of the text. Being friendly and gathering intelligence doesn't risk one's purity."

Dot slowly sat back down.

"Ladies, this campaign is working, and we think there's excellent potential to do more. A lot more. You will infiltrate select German villages and look for the heart we asked German soldiers to wear while on leave." She held the flyer up, giving the perforated heart a tap. "Talk to them. Befriend them. A woman can get more information about German supply lines and rearmaments than a man with a knife to a soldier's throat."

"Be their friendly ear?" I asked. "Indulge them. Get them to drink one or two more ales?"

"Yes. There's a saying among the German troops that the enemy might be listening, but they won't expect the enemy to be a German woman."

"Why not train local women?" Junie asked. "There has to be supporters in Italy and France, just behind enemy lines. Seems less dangerous than sending us into Germany as a first response."

"We tried," Cora said. "Don't get me wrong, we had limited success, but they aren't analysts. They don't know how to dissect and connect information that, at first glance, appears inconsequential. They don't know what questions to ask."

"Ask stupid questions, and you get stupid answers," I said under my breath to Junie, but Cora heard me.

"That's exactly right. The mannerisms of a native-born German are ingrained in all of you, and with your training, well, the perfect spies for us are the women in this room right now."

"You said German soldiers on leave?" Dot questioned.

Cora nodded. "Yes, that's right."

"Field soldiers. Low-ranking soldiers? Not…"

She was asking about the SS, and if you could have heard a pin drop earlier, you could have heard a feather after that question, because Cora closed her eyes briefly, and it wasn't something that looked unconscious. It was reflective and calculated—we all saw it.

"It is impossible to know what ranks or who in the German command will be wearing a heart."

Dot turned to Pudge, and although they were whispering, they were loud enough for us all to hear.

"Cora's right," Pudge said. "There isn't anything in the flyer—"

"It's what it doesn't say that bothers me," Dot said through her teeth.

"I'll say it for the last time, this mission requires you to ask questions. Nothing more. Now, if you're staying, then I expect you to find a bedroom and get something to eat in the kitchen. Those that can't handle a little conversation and clever deception ... well, I suppose now is your chance to leave. You are the best, but also replaceable, if need be."

Nobody moved, aside from a few turning heads, wondering who, if anyone, would leave, when the blonde from Florida stood, followed by her partner, and then quietly walked out with their bags.

Cora remained stoic until we'd lost sight of them walking through the courtyard before clipping pointedly down the aisle. She paused in the doorway.

"Anyone else?" she said, turning her head toward us. She pulled one of the servicemen on her team into the chapel. "Call up the replacement team we have on stand-by to cover the women who just left. They'll be six hours behind, so I'll meet them at the airport tomorrow."

Dot stood again. "So, we can just leave if we want to? Return to our old posts and not be demoted?"

"There's a transport plane leaving Rome in forty-five

minutes." Cora's voice was stern, though she looked casually unaffected, lighting a cigarette. "Choose wisely. This is an incredible opportunity, something that separates the good from the best." She turned on her heel and left.

Girls whispered among themselves.

"Undercover *inside* Nazi Germany…" Junie said. "I never thought—"

"None of us did," Pudge said. "But I'll do anything to help win the war. My grandfather was murdered at Flossenbürg Prison, like so many others who dared to talk critically of Hitler's regime. Even if I have to have casual conversations with Nazis, I will do it."

I reached for Pudge's arm. "My grandfather was a political prisoner too, Pudge, at Flossenbürg."

"I don't know…" Dot said, scanning the flyer. "It reads as if there's information left out. Doesn't it?"

Slowly, the teams began to leave to pick out their bedrooms. One girl stopped at the end of the pew with her partner, giving Dot a glance over. "You should leave if you have cold feet." She smiled. "Like Cora said."

They laughed as they left, and Dot crossed her arms.

"Leave her alone. She's Jewish," Pudge shouted. "She has more to risk than you."

I reached for my duffel bag because I had nothing to think about, and started to follow the others out, but Junie didn't move.

"Are you having second thoughts?" I asked her. "Look, all we have to do is ask questions—"

"It's not that." She chewed her fingernails after motioning for me to talk in the corner for privacy. "I know exactly what I'm getting myself into."

Pudge and Dot returned to their conversation, with Dot pointing to the flyer again and Pudge shaking her head. "There better not be SS, Pudge, or so help me..." Dot paused after a few seconds, folded the flyer up, and slipped it into her pocket. When they hugged, I thought whatever Pudge had said must have finally convinced Dot to stay.

"Then what's the problem?" I asked. "Let's go! We're missing out on the bedroom pick."

Junie pulled me back by the sleeve. "Undercover in Nazi Germany, Viv," she whispered.

"Yes, yes, and you're practically a Hun, Junie."

When she closed her eyes, I realized it was the wrong time to make a joke in an attempt to get her to laugh.

"Viv, you're not listening to me. I've thought about it, believe me. It's a big promotion... I don't really have a choice. But you do. I need to know that you understand the risks. Have you thought about it?"

Dot and Pudge tossed their duffel bags over their shoulders. Everyone seemed to have decided or was on the verge of doing so. My heart was racing at the thought of being the last team left inside the chapel.

"Yeah, I've thought about it. You said it yourself, I talk a lot, and it sounds like that's a skill we're going to need. We can do this," I said, rushing because I just wanted to get upstairs and get a bedroom. "Come on, let's go—"

"You gals want to share a bedroom with us?" Pudge said from the doorway.

We both turned, looking at her for a split second before I grabbed Junie by the shoulders. "Look, Junie. I've thought about it, all right. Now, are we picking a bedroom or what?"

Another team stood with their bags, ready to look for a bedroom.

"As long as you're sure," she said.

"I'm sure. Let's go!"

We hooked our fingers for a shake, then heaved our bags over our shoulders and followed Pudge and Dot out.

We crossed through the courtyard where Cora's servicemen were busy bringing in supplies. They didn't seem bothered by us hauling our lumpy duffels through their work zone, or particularly interested in us at all.

"No whistling?" Junie asked over her shoulder.

I tucked my helmet under my arm. "We're losing our touch, Junes," I said, fluffing some life into my flat hair, when I stopped short. "Wait. I've seen those uniforms before."

Hal. They appeared official in the army's olive drab color, yet also dark, almost black in the right light. There was a flutter in my chest, which surprised me.

"Fat chance, Viv," Junie said as if reading my mind. "Of all the places. He's not here."

"Yeah," I said, but I had another look down the hallway anyway.

There wasn't much of a choice of rooms after all. All were simple and small. I looked out the equally small window for a view of a brick building and a peekaboo sliver of blue sky.

"Welcome to Rome," I said under my breath.

Pudge and Dot took the beds along the far wall. Junie and I got the ones near the door. All our stomachs were growling, and I couldn't remember the last time we ate—back in

London, before our transport, was my best memory. We threw our bags onto our thin mattresses, but only stayed for a moment because we had been warned that the food was running out. We tried like hell to freshen up, all four of us sharing a tiny mirror and hairbrush, before finally giving up and skedaddling back down the stairs in search of the kitchen.

"Smell that?" Junie asked. "I hope that's pasta and sauce, and I hope it's better than what they serve us in the mess."

"I don't care what it is, as long as it's good," I said, but when we stepped into the kitchen, we found crates of canned Chef Boyardee marked U.S. ARMY on the floor and a half a dozen empty cans on the counter. Sergeant Manzo, the driver who picked us up from the airport, was the cook, stirring a cauldron of canned American spaghetti over an open flame.

"Howdy." He ladled up bowls for us four. "Last of the chow until tomorrow morning." He motioned with his head to an Italian girl with the slickest black hair I'd ever seen, who handed us each a checkered napkin. A bowl of shiny red apples sat on the counter. Junie reached for one and received a slap on her hand.

"Hey!" Junie said.

"You ask first!" the girl snapped in broken English.

"Ladies, meet Francesca," Manzo said. "Don't cross her."

We took seats around a large marble slab in the middle of the room with a team from Michigan. Francesca watched us, hands on her hips.

"Someone doesn't want us here," I said.

"She'll get over it," Pudge said, taking the seat next to me. "She probably doesn't even know English beyond a few phrases."

"Shh!" Dot said. "You'll upset her more. At least do that for me since I stayed."

Junie and I shared a glance. Dot made it sound like Pudge was in debt to her, which only increased my curiosity. I twirled the spaghetti around my fork, briefly considering keeping my mouth shut, but I couldn't resist. "Pudge must have said all the right words to get you to reconsider, because I was sure you were headed to that transport plane."

Pudge looked up while Dot blotted her lips on a napkin. "She said the usual—what she always says to get me to agree, and I listened, yet again, for some reason. I still think some text was left off that flyer. Didn't you see it? Didn't you notice?"

It turned awkwardly quiet.

I shoved a forkful of spaghetti in my mouth, and so did Junie.

"What did you say to convince her, Pudge?" I asked after swallowing.

"I reminded her that we are the best, that's all." Pudge pulled her pink handkerchief from her pocket. "I also reminded her I had my lucky hanky. Nothing has gone wrong since I've had it."

Dot rolled her eyes. "I'm not staying because of your lucky hanky, and you know that."

"I'm staying for the money," Junie said. "Just want to be upfront about that. I'm as patriotic as the next agent, don't get me wrong. But money talks where I come from. Money changes lives."

"Hey, did you see those servicemen with Cora?" Pudge whistled.

"They were recruited especially for some clandestine

mission, just like us," Dot said. "Of course, they won't talk about it. Not that we asked."

"Their uniforms... Where are they from?" I asked.

"London, I think. Well, one of them is because I overheard him. Dark hair." Dot raised her hand to show height, then had to stand on her chair to get a little taller. "About this tall. A special unit is all I know," she said.

"Don't get your hopes up, Viv," Junie said.

"What hopes?" Pudge looked instantly intrigued. "You got something going on with one of the servicemen?"

I scoffed. "Hardly," I said, but my hopes were up, no matter what Junie said.

"Pudge, she's smiling after scoffing," Dot said. "Don't need to be an OSS analyst to know what that means." They both laughed.

"Fine," I said. "There was this one fella I met at a pub."

Junie almost spit out her spaghetti. "No, no. Tell the truth." All eyes were on Junie now as she pointed to me over the table. "She conned an OSS agent into following us to a pub for the sole purpose of having a dance and to prove to another girl she could do it."

The team from Michigan looked up, and even Francesca turned her ear in our direction.

"And you got the dance?" Pudge asked.

I shrugged one shoulder. "Of course I did," I said, and the women howled. "But no kiss, in case you were wondering."

Pudge looked a bit disappointed. "Why not?"

"Because a flying bomb ruined my chance. Ruined my dance, too."

"Damn the Nazis," Pudge said with a snap of her fingers. "We'll get 'em, you wait and see."

We clinked our forks together as if to toast, then laughed.

"Hey, do you ladies think the OSS will continue after this war?" Dot asked.

"Are you thinking of staying in the army?"

"I have plans. I'm not saying it wouldn't be nice to be asked. I just have plans. It's a big house with a lot of kids, kind of plan. And a husband."

"You got the husband picked out?" I asked.

"Yeah, I do." She pulled a locket out from under her uniform and showed us a photo of her sweetheart. "His name is Benjamin, but everyone calls him Ben. He doesn't know it yet, but we're getting married just as soon as this damn war is over."

"It's all she talks about," Pudge said. "Though if she stayed, she'd be the one at the top. The one with the desk and giving the orders." She pointed at Dot with her fork. "You know I'm right."

"Yeah, well, you know what Pudge wants to do?" Dot asked.

Pudge sat up with a tug on her collar. "I'm going to retire to the beach after this war."

"Retire?" I laughed. Pudge was young, as young as us, early twenties, and retirement was something you did when you were old and brittle. "A little young to be thinking about retiring, aren't you?"

"Oh, not immediately. A few years from now. Enough time for me to collect all my paychecks and find a nice beach to sit on." She kicked back with her feet on an empty stool and pretended to be sunning herself. "I think a tropical beach sounds nice. One with pineapples and—"

"Nuts?" Dot asked. "I know one nut that will be there."

"Very funny." Pudge plunked her boots to the floor and sat normally again. "I wrote a postcard, I'll have you know, dated ten years from now, so it's official. One day, I'm going to mail it."

"What does it say?" I asked.

Pudge gulped down a forkful of Chef Boyardee. "Gorgeous! Wish you were here."

"Wish you were here?" Dot asked. "Well, who are you going to mail it to?"

"You!" she said. "It's colorful, got a nice little palm tree on it." She motioned to Junie with her chin. "What about you? Do you have plans for after?"

"I'm getting an education. It's for me and my daughter's future."

"That's right, she's going to college," I said.

Pudge and Dot's gaze shifted to Junie's bare ring finger. "College, huh?" Pudge said after taking a thoughtful bite. "And for your daughter, you said?"

"Yes," Junie said carefully.

Now they knew. Junie had a daughter, and she didn't have a ring on. There was an unwritten code among us women not to ask about such things during the war. Still, if they'd asked, Junie would have told them he'd died in Pearl Harbor—a brave sailor on the USS *Arizona*, a story she thought up when the army asked her the same question during recruitment. She wouldn't have made it past the interview if she'd told the army the truth, that he'd left them both the moment he found out she was pregnant, and she hasn't seen him since.

"What about you, Viv?"

I thumbed my chest. "Me? I'm going to live next door to Junie, of course. Knocking on her door every Sunday for a cup of sugar, Tuesday for oil, and Thursday for flour. You know, the typical things annoying neighbors do."

Everyone laughed except the team from Michigan, who were now talking between themselves in raspy whispers. "You understand we're going undercover into Nazi Germany tomorrow, don't you?" one said.

All four of us gave them a look. Junie wiped her mouth, and Pudge and Dot swallowed a heap of spaghetti they'd shoved into their mouths.

"Of course, we know," I finally said.

"Doesn't sound like it. Maybe the replacement team coming in will take things more seriously than you four."

"Replacements?"

"The women who are replacing the team who walked out of the chapel," she said. "Were you not there? Maybe you had clouds in your eyes or cotton in your ears." She rolled her eyes, laughing.

I stood, my stool screeching across the tile floor. "Don't roll your eyes at me."

They both stood, which got everyone to stand. "I know who you are. You're Viv Allen from the London office, right? We heard."

"What did you hear?" I asked.

"You take risks when lives are on the line. Everyone knows about the little competition you've got going on your floor in Grosvenor Square, trying to get ahead. How irresponsible."

She looked like Snow White with her cupid's bow mouth and rosy cheeks, but had the gall of a man to bring up Grosvenor Square.

I snapped my fingers. "You're irresponsible, talking about rumors and not facts."

"Yeah? Here's a fact for you. One slip-up, and the Nazis will convict you without a trial, that is, if they don't hang you in the square first." They moved to leave. "If you don't take this mission seriously, well…" She gave the kill motion to her lily-white neck.

After they left, the kitchen turned deathly quiet.

"She's a wet blanket," Pudge said after a few moments. "We know the risks. Don't have to be reminded." She scoffed. "Necks and hanging ropes. Scared isn't my middle name."

I shoved two or three forkfuls of spaghetti into my mouth.

When Junie had asked if I'd thought about *it*, my mind was only on the pretending part—pretending to be one of the lonely German war women, not what it would be like to get caught and to be hanged in the square. I scraped my plate while Junie watched me.

"Viv?" Junie tapped the marble slab. "You all right?" she asked softly.

"Yeah." I shrugged, continuing to scrape my plate until all the red sauce was gone. "Why wouldn't I be?"

"Well, that's enough for me," Pudge said, first pushing her plate away and getting up, followed by Dot.

"Me too," Junie said.

After cleaning our dishes and turning off the lights, I followed everyone up, feeling my throat where my tie would normally be choking me.

The sun had slipped behind the buildings, and although it had cooled off a little, our room was still uncomfortable and stagnant. Nobody mentioned what was said in the kitchen, though I went to bed thinking about it and tossed and turned for a good hour before a nightmare woke me up.

"Junie—" I sat up, slicked with sweat and my heart

thumping like a rabbit's. I thought I was having a heart attack and frantically felt my chest and then my neck, where I swore I felt burns from the rope.

Junie stirred only slightly, then roused enough to talk when she saw I was sitting. "Viv?" she whispered over her pillow. "What's wrong?"

I swallowed hard. "Nothing." I was still feeling my neck and chest when I swung my feet around and felt the cool terracotta tiles underneath, which provided some comfort. "Go back to bed."

Junie rolled back over, and Pudge was snoring; I could barely make out the lump in Dot's bed.

My head pounded.

I slipped on my khakis to go back into the kitchen for some water, because that's what I was taught to do: have a glass of water, and everything would be better. I padded down the stairs into the kitchen, where I closed my eyes at the sink. Suddenly, proving to my parents that I was an American hero wasn't so important. I held my forehead.

Junie flicked the lights on, rubbing her eyes in the doorway. "Viv?" she asked, squinting.

I gulped painfully, not sure what to say. She'd tried to warn me about the risks in the chapel, and I brushed her off. I also had never said the word "scared" before—not to her.

"It's okay." She shuffled toward me, arms out, and gave me a hug. "We'll be together."

Chapter Five

We were woken up in the dead of night with orders to get dressed and to meet downstairs in the chapel.

"Boy, Cora was serious when she said our day was going to start early," I said, throwing on my pants with both feet at once.

"No kidding," Pudge said, followed by Dot.

Junie and I raced downstairs ahead of everyone else. The servicemen from the courtyard were back. On a hunch, I asked if one of them knew a guy named Hal.

"Who?" He looked a little annoyed, and in an instant, that little spark I held close from yesterday—the little bit of hope—was snuffed out like a cigarette under a shoe.

The girls had caught up to us, bumping into my shoulder and telling me to move.

"Nobody," I said, but he'd already turned away.

Junie had heard everything. "You didn't really think..." She patted my shoulder after a pause. "You did think. Sorry, Viv."

"It was a long shot. Worth a try, right?"

"You know how many Hals we have in the war?" He'd turned back around. "A thousand, at least."

"Yeah?" Junie stepped toward him. "But probably not many wearing that uniform," she said. "So, lay off."

Cora called for us from the chapel doors, tapping her watch.

"Come on." Junie led me to where the rest of the girls had already sat down in the pews.

Cora waited until we were quiet, standing in the aisle and holding a box overflowing with dresses. "In less than an hour, you'll be at the airport, preparing to parachute into Nazi Germany."

I turned to Junie. "Parachute?" I mouthed.

"How else?"

"The bags you brought with you from your last post stay in Rome," Cora said. "Everything stays in Rome. Your jewelry, your American cosmetics…"

Junie pulled her pocket inside out to show me she'd already left her jacks behind. I squeezed her hand briefly.

"After parachuting, you'll ditch your uniform in the forest for one of these dresses." Cora plopped the box down. "All good German women wear nice clothes despite the rations." She flung dresses to apprehensive hands. A striped one landed in my lap, and a floral one landed in Junie's.

We switched after comparing.

"It's not a fashion contest, ladies." Cora handed us our document booklet, followed by a piece of paper. "This is your German Kennkarte. Don't lose it. Also, a flyer with your new identities to memorize. Our team within the Morale Operations Branch is small but efficient. You remember Hector, don't you?"

The greasy guy who'd let us into the villa introduced himself as the one who designed and printed our documents.

"Good, aren't they?" Cora asked. "Almost uncannily good."

Our documents were tattered and worn-looking as if we'd had them for years, and our biographical information was detailed and specific to each agent. My name was Hannah, and Junie's was Gerta. And Cora was right. They were uncannily good. Even the date stamps looked naturally faded, matching the purported age of the document.

I read through my biographical information: I was from Munich, the only daughter of Hans and Marie Urlacher, who had long since passed away. This wasn't a stretch, as I used to visit my grandparents not far away in the country. I showed Junie the paper, pointing to Munich.

"Is that where your cousin Ina lives?" she whispered.

"Close. She's at my grandparents' old house in Starnberg." My cousin and I were best friends up until my grandfather was arrested and sent to a political prison.

Cora cleared her throat. "Something you want to say, Agent Allen?"

All eyes shifted to me.

"Ahh…" I sat up. "I have family near Munich. A cousin. What if our paths cross?"

There were a few laughs.

"Unlikely. Germany is huge," Cora said, as if I didn't know, then went on about how we all had family connections in Germany, and that was why we were chosen, after all. "Is there anything else?"

"What if we do, though … see our family." We should be prepared for the possibility, but the room had turned quiet, and I realized that it sounded as if I might seek my cousin out, which I definitely wasn't going to do. "Accidentally see them, of course."

"Do you think your family would turn you in?" Cora asked.

My cousin and I shared the same grandparents, in the end—God rest their souls. I hoped she'd support me, but I heard how family members had turned on each other in the war. Junie elbowed me to answer. Girls who were looking had twisted around in the pews even more.

"I don't know."

Cora smiled, but it was more of an annoying *can we move on?* kind of smile. "As long as you keep to the mission and do as you're told, I highly doubt any of you will bump into family members. As I said, Germany is a huge country."

We were grouped with Pudge and Dot to make a team of four. Our first objective was to reach the alpine village of Füssen undetected, a popular place for soldiers while on leave from the Italian Front. We were given basic information on what to do after landing and how to find our hotel. Our limited directions on how to behave were outlined in the League of Lonely War Women flyer—talk to soldiers, be their friend in a casual, crowded setting, and get them to answer our questions.

Junie leaned into my ear. "Have you been to Füssen?"

I shook my head no.

"It's a tourist town with a river and pebbly beaches," she whispered.

"I have one warning," Cora said. "Don't go digging up bones. We have trained ground spies for complex surveillance missions, and the last thing I need is for one of you to go on a remote scouting mission without support. You could risk our entire operation, and I've spent too much blood, sweat, and tears to make this campaign successful." She looked at her watch again.

In addition to our documents, we were given a map and a handbag full of reichsmarks to last many days. It sounded so easy. Incredibly easy, but still, we would be inside Nazi Germany, and we'd have to be friendly and interested in German soldiers. Never did I think the letter I'd write home about my heroics would involve flirting with Germans.

"Viv," Junie whispered, which snapped me from my thoughts.

"What?"

She pointed to Cora, who was looking at me. "Any more questions?"

"Yeah. How long will we be there, and how do we get out?" I asked.

"Follow me." She clapped once when we didn't move. "Now!"

We scooted out of the pews and followed her down the aisle.

"Does it feel like we're being rushed?" Dot asked Pudge. "At this rate, we'll be in Germany by sunup."

In the courtyard, we had company in the form of real German women—locals.

"Each group will have an escort." Cora pointed to three women. Ava, a sleek woman with glossy blonde hair and probably in her late twenties, was assigned to us. "They have personal connections to the area and in the Wehrmacht, which will be of some assistance to you on the ground. However, their main purpose is to help you escape after seven days. They've done it already. You'll be in good hands."

"Where did you get these broads?" Pudge asked.

Cora cleared her throat. "These women were personally plucked from POW camps in France—Nazi collaborators with a zest for a … a new life, let's say."

"Collaborators?" someone asked out loud, followed by a few gasps.

"Like I said, they have deep connections, connections that will help you," Cora said.

With the right clothes on, Ava would look like one of the prostitutes outside, only she had blue eyes, blonde hair, and the perfect German scowl. The mission didn't feel safer with her added to our team. In fact, it felt more dangerous.

"Is she joking with us?" Pudge asked me out of the corner of her mouth. "We're going in with a collaborator?"

Dot put her hands on her hips. Junie stood still.

"Ma'am," I said. "I mean, Cora, I don't—"

"They are trusted and have already proved themselves," Cora said. "Anything else?"

I think we all took a hard swallow from her tone.

"No," we all said.

"I thought so."

Ava winked. Then, in a forced way, Cora prompted us to shake her hand.

"Look for me at your hotel on the first night," Ava said. "In the lobby. Six o'clock sharp."

I pulled my hand back as soon as I could.

Parachutes were distributed, and we were instructed to form a line by the cherub fountain, where a small platform had been set up with sandbags.

"Did I ever tell you I was afraid of heights," I said to Junie.

"It's all right, Viv. I'll be there with you." Junie smiled as if parachuting was going to be a breeze, forgetting the fact that we had to jump out of a plane first.

I examined my pack and was shown where the pull string was, then shuffled forward a step, where the serviceman I had talked to earlier was directing us. "It's very easy. Jump like this and pull the string." He demonstrated, then pointed to the sandbag steps.

As girls ahead of me made their jumps, I felt sick watching, even if we were still on the ground.

"Hey," the serviceman said to me as I passed. "Turns out there is a Hal."

"There is?" I followed Junie up the sandbag steps. "Here? In the villa?" I quickly scanned the courtyard over everyone's heads now that I was a little higher.

"I don't know where he is. Not here, though."

"Is he about this tall?" I said, raising my hand for height. "Dark hair?"

He shook his head, suddenly not interested at all.

Junie had made it to the top of the sandbags where Cora was now instructing her to jump off the small platform, both feet flat and arms crisscrossed. "Maybe it's him, Viv," she said after she'd jumped.

I landed next to her. Pudge followed, then Dot. "Who? That Hal from the pub?" Pudge asked.

I shrugged and didn't give it too much thought because what were the chances, after all?

We all shushed after Cora jumped. "Now." Cora lit a cigarette and had two or three hardy puffs before stamping it out with her foot. "Transport is waiting for you out front."

Pudge's stomach growled. "What about breakfast?"

"The war waits for nobody." Cora turned on her heel to walk out. "Follow me."

She snapped, and we hurried behind her, down the corridor to the street where agents climbed into rumbling lorries in the dark. The prostitutes were up, peering down at us from the dim, candlelit spaces of their open bedroom windows.

"I wonder who the replacements are," I said. "Aren't any of you curious? If they are nearly as good as us, then some of us must know them, right?"

"I'm wondering," Pudge said. "Not gonna lie."

"I couldn't care less," Junie said.

"Me neither," Dot said.

Manzo, our wounded soldier-turned-driver-turned-cook, was also Ava's handler and was waiting outside. He pointed to our lorry and shouted for us to get in. Junie and Dot went first, but Cora ushered Pudge and me into a different one at the last second.

"Sit down," Cora said. "We need to talk."

Pudge and I exchanged a questioning look as our lorry sputtered away behind Junie and Dot's, making us shift and sway.

"I have a special side mission for you two."

I thumbed my chest. "For me and Pudge?"

"The OSS is desperate to locate SS Officer Joseph Engle. He's been spotted near Füssen, and we believe he might live somewhere nearby, but nobody can confirm it. He's elusive, sneaky, and also brutal. Slick blond hair, yellowy fingernails with ridges like valleys, crystalline eyes, and his blood type tattooed right above his elbow." She tapped her inner forearm.

"You want us to find him?" Pudge asked. "To do that, we'd have to ask questions to people other than soldiers, and you just got done telling us not to dig up bones."

"I don't want you to find him. I want you to be aware of him so that you can report back if you see him or if you hear someone mention him. Absolutely, don't go digging up bones. He's probably paid off most of Füssen for their silence and protection. If you see him, I want to know about it, but don't go anywhere near him."

I turned to Pudge. "We'll talk to Junie and Dot—"

"You can't," she said. "The orders are for you two. Nobody else can know. It's for safety. He's that brutal."

"I don't understand, ma'am," Pudge said.

"What happens if you get caught? Germans can tell if you're hiding something during an interrogation. They're masters at it. Don't put them at risk."

"Why us?" Pudge asked.

"You know why, don't you?" she asked, but Pudge and I didn't say a word. "Because you're the best in this unit. Your partners only a thin hair behind, and since you'll be working separately but together, it makes sense to tell the both of you."

"What has he done? Why all the secrecy?" I asked.

"I don't know all the details, but I can tell you he was one of the founding commandants at Flossenbürg, if you know what that means." She paused, searching our horrified faces.

"Both our grandfathers were political prisoners there," I said.

"Ah!" Cora opened the lorry doors and hopped out. "Then you know exactly what I mean when I say he's dangerous." She immediately began talking to one of her crew about the replacement team that had just flown in to take the spot of the women who had quit, leaving Pudge and me alone to sort out what she'd just said.

"Pudge, a commandant at Flossenbürg?" I asked. "God, I hate that this is what we have in common. And what do we do if we see him? Pretend that we don't? He very well could be the SS guard who took my grandfather on his death march. You've read the reports. Brutal is a compliment."

"We can't think about that." She took me by the shoulders. "This is what we're going to do. We play it cool, like we always do. If we see him, we'll write it in our report like she told us to. We concentrate on the soldiers and the paper hearts. And honestly, what's the chance we'd really see him? It's like finding a needle in a haystack."

She had a point. What were the chances? Cora said he was secretive and elusive.

"Yeah?"

"Yeah."

She motioned to hop out. "Come on. They're waiting. And we have a plane to jump out of."

"Don't remind me."

Sergeants barked for us to move along the tarmac and find our aircraft. We found Junie and Dot a vehicle away and locked arms. "There you are," I said as if we had accidentally been separated. Headlamps, torches, and landing lights lit up our faces while servicemen ran here and there to checkpoints and planes.

"Viv!" Junie said, and I stopped suddenly. She pointed her pinky finger at some servicemen. Lights flashed willy-nilly, making it hard to distinguish one from another until she said, "Isn't that Hal?"

My hands clamped over my mouth. "Junie!" My heart

thrashed against my ribs. *Boom—boom—boom*. "What—What do I do?"

Junie pushed me toward him. "You talk to him."

"Hal!" I yelled as loud as I could over the roar of the planes and vehicles, and when he turned at the sound of his name, my stomach did a little flip.

He looked as surprised as I was to see him in Rome. "Viv? Viv Allen? What are you doing here?" He took me by the arms, and I wondered if he was going to kiss me. My lips were ready if he was. He looked like he wanted to.

"I could ask you the same thing!"

All I kept thinking about was how I was about to jump out of a plane into Nazi Germany, and what if I never saw him again?

"Allen!" Manzo shouted for me from the plane where all the girls were waiting in line, and I felt the moment building where Hal would walk away, and I'd miss my chance.

He took a hard look at the plane and how we were dressed. "Be careful, will ya?"

"So, that's it?" I said, meaning, no kiss? After meeting again in such serendipitous circumstances? A propeller buzzed nearby.

"Ah, hell," I said, and I grabbed the front of his shirt with both hands and planted a smacker right on his face—a kiss of legends with the propeller wind blowing over us and fluttering my hair. Manzo broke us up.

"Come on, you. Plane's waiting!" He pulled me away with my lips still in a pucker, watching Hal disappear in the darkness, but I saw him smile, and I carried that with me because I knew I'd need it once I was in that plane over Nazi Germany. I got in line behind Junie.

"Well, well. Vivien Allen has a boyfriend," Junie said.

I was in a daze, feeling my lips with my fingertips. "Who says?"

"Me, of course. I can see it now. Little white picket fence and a blue house. All newlyweds should have a blue house. I'll live next door with little Annie, and I'll borrow sugar every day."

I scoffed. "Stop it," I said, but then reconsidered. "You think so?" I closed my eyes. Hal was gone, but the memory remained, along with the fluttering butterflies in my stomach.

"I do think so. I'm even more impressed now than I was in London. He followed you to the pub and then all the way to Italy!"

I turned to look back one last time, just on the off chance that Hal was still standing in the shadows, but he was nowhere to be found. We boarded the aircraft, a gutted cylinder with metal seats, lap belts, and dangling, netted hand rings to hold onto. Ava lumbered into the plane last after having a few words with Manzo.

"So that was him, huh? What's the chances of that?" Pudge asked. "Cute. Not as cute as Winston back home, but cute."

"Who's Winston?" I asked.

"It's the fake boyfriend she invented," Dot said, which got a jab in the side from Pudge.

"Is not." Pudge smiled, and they shared a laugh between themselves.

The engine started up. Manzo gave Junie an army shovel to bury our clothes upon landing. "Keep it away from your pack when jumping," he said, and that's when it hit me. What if my pack doesn't open?

I gripped my pack straps tightly when my heart took on a

different kind of thrashing. "Is your heart racing? I don't know if it's because I saw Hal or because we're about to jump out of a plane." I closed my eyes momentarily as we took to the sky. "I think … I think it could be both."

Junie reached for her straps. "It's both."

Manzo barked at Ava to take a seat after she insisted on standing, and there was a little back and forth, but then the journey was relatively quiet, especially after we snuck over the Gustav Line without a hint of being seen. We knew we'd crossed the Alps when we started to drop in altitude. "You guys ready?" Pudge asked.

"Yeah," I said, but I wasn't ready at all. My hands were shaking.

Manzo and Ava were at it again, but this time, things looked more tense. He frowned with his arms crossed while her fists were clenched. "What do you think they're arguing about?" Junie asked.

"God, who knows. Maybe she tried to sleep with Manzo, and he said no."

Junie gave me a look.

"He has standards too, no?"

She laughed. "Maybe, but I think it's something else." We watched them intently, but it wasn't until we dropped below the clouds that we could hear them, and it wasn't over a romp in his jeep like we thought.

"You're about to jump out of a plane!" Manzo yelled at her, while she yelled back at him in German, saying she was pregnant with a Gestapo officer's baby, and that for her efforts in Germany, she wanted the U.S. Army to pay for an abortion when she got back, or she wasn't jumping at all.

She ripped off her parachute and shoved it at him.

"You get this back on…" They fought over the parachute, each pushing it toward the other.

The pilot shouted for us to get ready to jump. "Sixty seconds!"

Manzo opened the side hatch, and we stood. The wind was merciless and cold, making it hard to breathe. We inched toward the hatch, arms crisscrossed with a hand on that pull string.

"Junie!" I wasn't sure about this, but the closer we got to the hatch, I realized I'd have to jump, sure or not. Junie let go of her pull string to guide me closer to her.

"I'm right here next to you, sis," she said.

Manzo forcibly strapped the parachute back onto Ava, but now Pudge was yelling that she didn't trust Ava, and neither did Dot. "I'm not going with her!" Dot yelled, which got Junie and me to stop.

"The sun is rising!" The pilot barked from the cockpit. A sliver of sun sliced through the sky. We had to jump, or we'd be shot at. "Jump!"

But still, none of us moved, paralyzed by what we'd heard and witnessed, and that's when Manzo must have realized that this mission was more than a little in trouble: it was about to end before it even got started. He puffed past Ava and reached for Dot, tossing her out, followed by Pudge, then Junie before going for me.

"Cross your arms!" he screamed when I flailed, and one by one, we followed each other down into Nazi Germany with the sun just beginning to break over the horizon.

Chapter Six

I landed on my back in the forest as softly as a brick, with my parachute pillowing around me, leaving my heart somewhere in the clouds. The menacing sound of barking dogs brought me back to life with a gasping breath. "Junie!"

I felt heavy and disoriented and struggled to stand. I called for her again, and when she didn't answer, I panicked more than I already had, thrashing against the tangled parachute pulling at my ankles. "Jun—"

"Viv."

I clutched my chest. "Where are you?" The rising sun barely lit up the spaces between the tall trees.

"Over here." She shuffled through the kindling behind me when I heard another noise. This one from above.

Ava. She sailed between the treetops with her breezy blonde hair to land in a bald spot several yards away. We watched her unhook her pack and change into street clothes.

"Where are the others?" I whispered.

I worried they'd flown off course, or worse, were hung up

in a tree, but moments later, Pudge and Dot rushed up behind us with their parachutes wadded in their arms.

"Well, look at that," Pudge said, eyes on Ava.

The dogs barked again, a little closer this time, giving me a jolt.

"Hurry and change." Junie dug the hole with the shovel Manzo had given her, while we shed our packs and uniforms for dresses and nice shoes.

"How far away are we?" Pudge asked.

"Not far," Junie said. "I recognize that valley from the map." She pointed with her head to a shadowy strip of trees that disappeared off a cliff.

Dot twisted into her dress. I brushed my hair back with my fingers, and Pudge shoved her feet into her shoes.

"Where do you think the other agents landed?" I asked.

"Not our business." Junie slung dirt over our things and buried the shovel. "All right. I think we're ready."

We were women out for an alpine walk, nicely dressed and with hair as presentable as we could muster, considering we'd just jumped out of an airplane.

I repeated our rendezvous plans for after we made it into Füssen. We'd take opposing routes into the village to Hotel Hirsch and meet in the lobby that evening. "Don't be late," I said. "We'll think something happened to you." I took a steady step. "All right, go!"

"Wait!" Pudge said. "What do we do about Ava?"

All of us turned. Ava was trying to find where we'd landed, subtly calling for us using our German names. Junie motioned for us to take cover behind some bushes.

"She almost ruined the entire mission. Maybe she still wants to ruin it," Dot said.

"We have to trust her," Junie said. "She's the one who's introducing us to her contacts in the Wehrmacht tonight, remember? She's also our escape out of here."

A breeze swept through the tree branches, blowing some leaves to the ground.

"You mean if she doesn't turn us in first," Dot said. "We can't forget she's a collaborator. It's gotta be bad luck to have a collaborator on your team. What if she's a—"

"Jinx?" I asked.

Ava spied us through the tree branches. "Stand," Junie whispered.

An awkward pause followed with her studying us as we studied her, only interrupted by the sharp bark of the dogs closing in somewhere above us in the hills. Ava turned and disappeared down the mountain, but I had frozen, looking for the dogs.

Junie pushed me to move, and Pudge pushed Dot. "Let's go." We left the opposite way, traversing rapidly through thickets and mountain meadows until finding the valley path we'd been looking for, where we could finally take a breath and walk normally.

"You didn't tell me you were scared of dogs," Junie said.

"I'm not."

"I'm trained to read the signs, Viv. You were trembling with each bark."

"Well, who isn't afraid of barking dogs? Especially ones that might be after you."

We kept walking.

The mountains were breathtaking in the golden morning light. But the Lech River was what caught my eye, a glistening strip of blue that cut through the valley like a satin ribbon, reminding me what I loved about Germany the most—its unspoiled nature—but had been lost to me for so long.

"We should pop out right about here." Junie pointed to a service road on the map. "Now is probably as good a time as any to start speaking German." She stuffed the map in her handbag. "And only German."

I agreed. "Between you and me, Junes. I trust Ava about as far as I can throw her." I lowered my voice in case of a mountain echo. "We don't know what was said after we jumped. Did Manzo toss her out too? Or did she jump with plans to expose us and get back at the OSS for denying her an abortion?"

"You're the best analyst I know, Viv. Read her like you read someone from the files. What do you think?"

I thought about her eyes mostly, how they weren't crystal blue but cloudy as if they'd witnessed things she wasn't proud of, and what about her palm when she shook my hand in Rome? It was soft, yet also rough with a few small calluses; she'd had servants in France and was used to living a good life. The conditions at the POW camp must have been an adjustment for her. She wouldn't want to go back there, but whose side was she really on? It depended on whether we truly believed her story about rehabilitating her reputation.

"And?" Junie asked.

"I'm undecided."

Junie looked over her shoulder to the mountains where we'd come from, then to where we were headed. "Well, one way or the other, we're going to find out her intentions. By the end of seven days, Ava will either be known as a darling for her good deeds or a villainous double-crosser who played a role in our deaths."

We followed the road just like we'd discussed and popped out of the forest and into a residential area along the Lech, which brought us to the village.

"Where is everyone?" We kept walking, and after so many quiet blocks, a man came out of his side entrance like he was headed down the street, only to turn on his heel and go back inside. "It's like they are hiding."

"Maybe they don't want to be seen," she said. "You've read the reports. Neighbors turning on neighbors."

The man had closed his door only to peek at us through his window split. I wasn't sure if he was keeping or learning secrets, which gave me a shiver.

We found the tram with the help from the map. After a brief wait, we boarded to find mostly empty seats and a tram that screeched its way toward Old Town Square in Füssen, rather than rolled. Posters had been pasted inside the car calling for all boys as young as twelve to join the fight.

"Twelve," I said just above a whisper.

Junie shook her head. "They're recruiting from Hitler Youth. Do you think… Does that mean?"

"The soldiers we meet might be children? God, I hope not. We'll have to inquire about ages, though, ask questions, and put that in our report."

Slowly, the village changed into a charming alpine town with a smattering of passersby and police directing traffic. And soldiers. Many in uniform, clad in the all-too-familiar Wehrmacht *feldgrau*, though Füssen was a place to rest. They seemed unaware of those around them and instead walked determinedly down the pavement with nowhere in particular to go, smoking and sometimes talking to themselves, before stepping into beer halls where available young women had gathered and waited.

"Stay close," I said, once we reached our stop.

In many ways, it felt as if our mission had officially started the moment my foot stepped off that tram. Every move, every gesture, accent, or innuendo would be scrutinized. We hooked arms and crossed the street, stepping over the curb and walking underneath a Nazi Party flag rippling with bold patriotism just below the hotel's marquee.

"It's different in person, isn't it?" I said after realizing I'd held my breath.

"Yes," was Junie's response.

I opened the door to the lobby and interrupted a commotion at the front desk. A couple checking in had paid for portage from the train station, but their bags hadn't arrived. I gave Junie's arm a squeeze. We didn't have bags either, and we hadn't thought up a plan to explain.

The front desk clerk snapped for me to come forward. "Fräulein, next." His eyes skirted to the floor, looking for our luggage. Junie gave me a look that said I'd better hurry up and think of something because she was blank. My heart was pounding more than my head, but that didn't bother me as much as my sweaty palms.

I smiled, stepping forward, my eyes flicking once to Hitler's portrait hanging on the wall behind him. The couple was still talking about their bags.

I turned to them, completely ignoring the clerk. "Your bags were stolen too?" I asked. "Did you make a report?" I hiked my thumb toward the train station, even though it was several blocks away. "The police are very helpful. We were not the only ones either."

The man pressed his hand to his breast pocket. "Stolen? In Füssen?" he asked. "No, no... They are just late. How can there be thieves when there are so many Wehrmacht around?"

I shrugged. "Füssen is a holiday spot, no?" My eyes flicked again to Hitler's portrait.

The man talked to his wife off to the side about contacting the police. I cleared my throat. "One room please, two beds," I said to the clerk. "Friends traveling together." I smiled for good measure, then turned to Junie. "Very glad we were able to get out of Munich for a few days."

The desk clerk opened his ledger and after checking for a room, handed me a registration card and pencil. "First time to Füssen? I suggest an excursion to the Lech and the waterfall while the weather is still nice. Single travelers like to go there for a day of sun and ... soldiers."

"That sounds wonderful, doesn't it?" I said. "Perhaps a picnic by the falls?"

Junie nodded. "Oh, yes."

He watched me fill out the card, writing down all the essential things from my documents. When I got to the part that asked for my address in Munich, the lead broke. Cora didn't give me an address, and the only one on my Kennkarte was for the issuing office. I covered the card with my hand, stalling, while he gave me a new pencil. Making up a story about our bags was nothing compared to an address. My entire identity could be foiled if I picked one that didn't exist.

I was still stalling. "Is something wrong?"

I created a fake address in the university district and hoped for the best. "Just wondering where we can buy some necessities while we are without our luggage. New dresses, that sort of thing." I handed him the card. "Is there a clothing boutique nearby?"

He studied the address. My head pounded, and I looked for a way to distract myself. Off to the side, through a set of black double French doors, I saw a quaint biergarten with a ceiling of dark wooden beams and an outdoor patio. A bartender cleaned a glass while talking to a man drinking a half-liter of beer at the bar.

"Across the street," he said.

"What?"

He looked up from the card. "Frau Schneider might have something for you. Next to the violin shop and below the apartment building. She sells women's clothes."

"Oh. Yes. Excellent." After paying for the room with some of the reichsmarks Cora had given us, I hooked Junie's arm, and we made our way across the street to Frau Schneider's clothing boutique instead of our room.

"That was quick thinking about the luggage, Viv," she said once we were standing on the curb. "You've always been good at thinking on your feet." We began to cross the street.

I didn't dare tell her I made up the address or had nearly lost my composure coming up with the luggage story. It was different thinking on my feet in Nazi Germany than in London, and boy, did I feel that more now than ever. I felt my forehead. I wasn't used to being nervous.

"Are you all right?"

I turned, giving her a little nod. "Yeah," I said, but my head was still pounding.

"You sure?"

"I promise. Trust me." I motioned to the shop to go inside.

Frau Schneider was very accommodating, though hardly sympathetic after we said our luggage had been stolen. "I see," she said, ticking her tongue. "You weren't taking care of your possessions. It is your fault." She slid her glasses up the bridge of her nose, gazing at us.

The racks were thin because of the clothing rations, but what she had was exquisite for German fashion. The finest lace from Paris and good Bavarian wool coats for the upcoming winter months. Junie and I needed dresses, and since the weather was on the cusp of changing, she'd marked down most of her summer frocks.

A violinist next door practiced on one of his instruments for sale.

"First time to Füssen? We are known for our violins. And hospitality, of course."

I held a geometric patterned dress to my shoulders. The fabric was silky with a fashionable waist tie and a high neck. It was elegant and sophisticated, but also reserved. Precisely what the German soldiers would be expecting their wives to wear.

"And you said you're from Munich? Whereabout?" She paused after I gave her a strange look. "I have family there and wondered if we knew someone in common, of course."

I didn't believe her story for a second, but I answered her just the same. "The university district."

"Ahh," she said, then paused again. "I see."

She turned on her heel and walked to her counter for us to pay, tallying up the total. "Not many people can holiday anymore with the war, and it's getting late in the season," she said, adding up the price tags. "How are you girls managing?"

So that was why she wanted to know where I lived. She didn't think we could afford to pay. I felt some relief from this and worked hard not to show it on my face. "My supervisor insisted I break away," I said so that she knew I wasn't a student. "He was very specific about Füssen, too, and told me to bring my friend. Said we'd have a good stay here."

"He sent you here specifically, with all these Wehrmacht around?" She pointed out the window as if we hadn't seen the soldiers walking around in groups. "What do you do for work?"

I hesitated. "I'm a secretary."

Junie's eyes shifted.

I smiled.

"There's only one reason single women come to Füssen…" She coughed into her fist. "Well, I'm sure you can guess by now. Wives come sometimes, but the others…"

"Only here for one thing? Oh, goodness. Our focus is to relax." I batted the air. "I'm sure he didn't know."

"Mmm." Frau Schneider opened her ledger and recorded the sale, her eyes lifting after reaching the final figure. "Now, you girls are sure you can manage?"

I had to think up another story to explain how we could afford the bill, which was expensive, even for a full-time secretary.

"I'm so glad we found your shop." I pulled the reichsmarks from my handbag and counted them while I talked. "My grandparents left me a large inheritance. Nice to know there are still some places to buy fine things during the war, and the delightful serenade from next door is lovely as well."

Her mouth was hanging open from the stack of cash still in my hands after fanning out what I owed her on the counter.

"And cologne?" She reached for a perfume bottle and gave us a misting, something that had turned yellow and hadn't sold. "Smells lovely on you. Do you like it?"

It was worse than a wet dog. I smiled. "Add it to the total and some toiletries, while you are at it. A brush, undergarments…"

"And a tie! Young women love wearing smart ties these days." She pulled one from a navy suit on display and attempted to tie it around my collar.

"No!" The violinist stopped playing next door, and the shop turned silent, which made my exclamation sound more like a yell. I cleared my throat. "I mean, no thank you."

Junie was smiling from the side of the counter.

"Very well then…" Frau Schneider reluctantly put the tie away. "Do come again. I'll have my assistant bring your bags over." She clapped. "Klara!"

Her assistant came rushing in from a side door that opened into a larger apartment building, looking flustered and out of breath. "Yes?" She smiled.

"These lovely ladies need help with their bags. Do you have time?"

"Of course," she said, still out of breath and reaching for the bags. "I have time."

"Klara is my niece," she said. "We live just a few feet away." She pointed to the side door and the ground-floor apartment. "Just over there."

Klara looked about thirteen, with bobbed brown hair and a bow.

"Shall we be off?" she asked.

We walked back into the hotel lobby to find the couple who had complained about their luggage were now talking to the police. I quickly looked away when the husband's finger lifted in my direction, making a mention of me as if I had something to add.

I guided Klara toward the lift and pretended we were continuing a deep conversation that we'd started outside. "What a lovely boutique, Klara. How long have you been working there, did you say?"

She seemed startled by the small talk and confused about how to answer.

I took the garment bag. "That's all right. I think we have it."

She took off before I'd finished talking. We waited for the lift, listening to it rumble down floor after floor. "That was strange—" Junie had started to say but was silenced by the sudden appearance of two men, one with blond hair, walking down the hallway to the lobby while drinking a whisky. The other had dark, pomade-slicked hair with his sleeves rolled up to his elbows.

"Excuse us," the blond said as a courtesy, but somehow managed to brush against my arm. He took a second look over his shoulder after passing, his gaze skirting down my backside and over to Junie's. In London, he would have called me sweet cheeks.

His friend laughed after saying something I couldn't hear, the sound low and throaty, more like a frog's croak than a laugh.

"We caught their attention," Junie said in the lift.

"Being German isn't going to be the problem. It's the stories we tell and keeping those straight." I patted my forehead where I felt a sweat forming. I didn't have a choice about the luggage, but I did have a choice about telling Frau Schneider I was a secretary, which wasn't part of the biographical information Cora had given me. "We should go over exactly what our stories are before we talk to anyone else."

Junie agreed. We were trained to ask questions, see inferences where someone else wouldn't see anything at all, and draw near certain conclusions from clues. That was an analyst's job, but still, we needed to be prepared to answer detailed questions about our home life in Germany, beyond who our parents were and where we grew up.

We tried to rest before we went out that night, but how could we rest? The beds were hard and the hallways were noisy, but also, my mind was on so many things. Pudge, Dot, Ava—if they'd made it out of the forest. I checked my watch. We had plans to meet downstairs soon.

"Who do you think Ava will introduce us to?" I asked.

"Men, like the one who eyed us in the hallway, is my guess. Does it matter? A heart is a heart, and that's all we're looking for. As long as she doesn't keep any secrets from us, we'll be fine."

"Yeah," I said. "Secrets."

We changed for an evening out, paying extra attention to our hair, but there was only so much we could do with water and a brush. We were lucky enough to have a room with a noisy toilet to mask our voices. However, it only lasted so long before the toilet filled up with water again. We had to turn the radio on for added noise, which was unbearable for other reasons.

"We had a radio when I was little." Junie tuned the station to the propaganda channel. "The music was a little different back then."

"It's not just the music, is it?" I gazed out the window to the street below, watching passersby through the rippling Nazi Party flags pitched off building eaves. "It was startling walking through the streets today, and even just being in Füssen. Germany is…"

"The same, but also like a foreign land." Junie checked her watch. "We should get those stories straight."

We huddled on the floor, just below the radio's speaker, after I closed the curtains.

"I was a secretary for a newspaper before I joined the WACs," I said. "Pushing paper around and getting my boss coffee is about all I did. I can draw on those experiences and make them uniquely German since I told Frau Schneider I was a secretary. I told her I lived in the university district because that's what I put down on the registration card. I think that's where you should live."

"I think so too."

"What's your occupation?" I asked.

She shrugged one shoulder. "One of us should be a student if we live in the university district. But how did we meet?"

"We should just say we're sisters. It would be easier."

"We look nothing like each other, and my documents are different."

Junie was right. I was slender with chestnut hair and ruby-red lips, and she was small—a whole three inches shorter than me with brassy hair. The differences in our surnames could be explained, though, if we were questioned. "Yeah, but I feel like we're sisters. That part won't be an act."

She put her arm around me. "We met at a café a year ago. Been friends ever since. Sound good?"

Sounded plausible and simple enough to remember. "Are you ready for this? Are *we* ready?"

Junie scoffed. "It's a little late to change our minds."

I closed my eyes. "That's not what I mean. Are you worried about getting close to the soldiers? We'll have to flirt a little to get them to open up. What if one tries to steal a kiss?"

Junie grimaced. "There better not be any child soldiers."

I had a sickening moan, winding a curl around my finger.

"One day, Viv, when this is all over and we're gossiping over our shared picket fence, I'll remind you about that time you pretended to be a patriotic German, flirting with soldiers, and how great you were at it. An Academy Award-worthy performance!"

A laugh peeped between my lips. "I'm supposed to be the one that makes you laugh, remember?"

"Focus on why you're here," she said. "I'm doing this for my daughter and a better life, and you're doing it for that letter you want to write. And also for our boys, of course. We want to help win the war. We'll be back in Rome very soon, and you and Hal will be smooching in the kitchen over cans of Chef Boyardee before you know it." She patted my shoulder. "Come on, let's get going. I bet Ava's in the lobby waiting, and Pudge and Dot."

Chapter Seven

We opened our door to find Ava standing in the hallway and about to knock when she was supposed to meet us downstairs. "Hallo." She looked like she'd had a hot bath, and her floral perfume smelled fresh and expensive, not the kind that had been on a shelf for years and had turned yellow like Frau Schneider's. She'd been in someone's home. Her hair had also been set with curlers, and those would be too expensive to buy.

I looked down both ends of the hallway. "You said to meet you downstairs with Pudge and Dot."

"They aren't there." She turned on her heel for the elevator.

"Not there?" I mouthed to Junie.

"Don't worry," she mouthed back.

We followed Ava into the elevator where I studied her. She had stockings on.

"Why are you looking at me like that?" she asked.

"Where did you come from?" I asked. "Not a hotel."

"I live across the street."

I raised my eyebrows. "Your lover's apartment?"

Junie nudged me for my tone.

"Does it matter?" She fluffed her shiny hair. "You know I have lived here before, so it should not be a surprise. Third-floor apartment. You are welcome to visit any time, as my guests. We are long-lost friends, no?" She hit the stop button on the lift, suspending us between two floors. "I called for you in the forest," she rasped. "Looked like you were hiding when we're supposed to be a team."

I hit the button to resume. "We are a team." The lift squealed from the restart. "And in that regard, it would be nice if you followed our agreed-upon rules."

She rolled her eyes.

"Now, remember our names are Hannah and Gerta."

Ava scoffed, shoving her clutch under her arm. "Don't patronize me."

We reached the ground floor with a shudder. I turned to Junie just before the doors opened. "Look for the heart. Listen and ask questions."

"My God, you patronize everyone, don't you?" Ava piped, just before she walked out.

Junie pulled me back by the elbow. "Don't let her get to you. I like it when you repeat plans. Focus on what our job is. That's it."

I nodded. We hooked fingers for a quick shake, then stepped into the hallway, following Ava into the lobby.

"You must tell me where you purchased your dresses," Ava said as she walked, a laugh peeping between her lips. "They are simply divine." A soldier kissing his visiting wife walked the opposite way in the hall, only taking a moment to come up for some air to see where they were going. "This way, friends," Ava said as they passed.

Calling us "friends" sounded suspicious all on its own, and it was clear she was poking fun at our dress choices. I wanted to trust her—I did—but she was making it unnecessarily complicated and difficult.

"Are you all right?" Junie asked.

I smiled. "Of course."

Still no sign of Pudge and Dot. I checked my watch, twisting it on my wrist. It was only one minute after the top of the hour. The hotel desk clerk eyed me as I passed, staring at my legs.

I cleared my throat.

We entered into the hotel's biergarten with Ava, which was more of a social space, with plenty of carved pine tables for people to gather before heading to the connecting restaurant. The musty odor of cooked pork and cold potatoes I smelled was actually coming from the houndstooth drapes that divided the room from the restaurant, I'd decided, because all that was being served at this hour was beer and spirits.

Ava lingered near the doorway with her body angled to accentuate her curves. "Oh, good, they're here," she said. "This way."

We followed her through clouds of cigar smoke and hoarse laughter, the bartender still washing a glass as before, and the day drinker tipping back his beer at the bar. Violin music played softly from somewhere in the restaurant behind the drapes.

Here we go.

She led us to a table of men drinking half-liters of beer or whisky with ice. It was impossible to know who was who with their street clothes on, but I quickly summarized the fitter ones, with the tucked-in shirts and clean-close shaves, were either sergeants or lieutenants who stayed out of harm's way. Whereas the soldiers, I imagined, would be gruffer and look like the day drinker at the bar—weathered, quiet, and exhausted from being on the front and trying to stay alive.

Ava kissed the few who knew her on the cheek, and they called her "pet," which I also filed away for later. "Oh, but call me Ava in public," she'd tell them, acting bashful and coy, which was quite the skill. She was good, and I found myself wondering if she had learned those traits in prison or before.

Nobody had hearts pinned to their lapels. Most were blond, or gray and old. I caught myself looking at their hands—get a peek at their fingernails to find Engle—but from where I stood, it was hard to tell if anyone had yellowy fingernails. Cora would remind me that it wasn't my mission to find him, only to report back if he crossed our path, and with that, I pushed him from my thoughts.

I had one job to do right now, not two, and I was going to do it expertly, damn it.

I stood a little straighter.

"Gentlemen, may I introduce Hannah and Gerta, dear friends of mine visiting from the city." She swayed her arm as if she'd brought hunks of meat to choose from, then told us to sit, directing Junie to take a chair at the far end of the table. More drinks were brought out, cigarettes and cigars were passed around, and talk about the war was like a whisper in the wind.

I took my seat.

Four of the men struck me the most. One man had a scar above his eyebrow, another had rounded pink cheeks, while the two others were older—grandfatherly-looking—with mustaches, one gray, the other brown, but both were bald.

"I bet you want to know how we met," Ava said, lighting a cigarette and making up a story about how we practiced gymnastics together in the Faith and Beauty Society when we were nineteen, even going into detail about our uniforms and instructors. "And now we are women, having a drink in this quaint little village."

Faith and Beauty Society. The Third Reich's club for young German women who were devoted to Hitler's cause. It was surprising how easily she came up with the stories.

Ava turned to me, pulling the cigarette from her mouth and leaving a smudge of pink lipstick on the filter. "Isn't that right?"

A whisky was set down in front of me. I detested whisky. "Mmm. Hmm." I took a sip. Junie laughed at the end of the table. Her voice was different when she spoke German to a German man, more mature.

"I trust these women with my life," Ava said. "The Faith and Beauty Society does that to women. It creates everlasting bonds that test time. There are no secrets between us."

The man with the scar above his eyebrow pointed at her with his glass. "But don't all women keep secrets?"

Ava's eyes narrowed in a sultry, seductive way. "Not good German women, and not true friends." She gave me a wink as we raised our glasses for a toast. "To true friends," Ava said, which they all repeated.

A man walked in. The one from the hallway who'd

undressed us with his eyes. He took a seat next to Junie, and I instinctively took a drink of my whisky only to immediately set it back down.

Felt like my insides were on fire. I reached for my stomach.

"You don't like whisky?" Ava glanced at the man at the bar.

"I'm—"

"Go get something else, then." She dismissed me with a wave of her hand, and I took that as a firm invitation to go see about the lonely day drinker, who'd never left his stool. I had to hand it to her; it was a swift move. She wasn't just good. She was great. At least in terms of the casual nuances and looking comfortable while doing it.

"Yes, Fräulein?" the bartender asked.

I nonchalantly looked into the lobby. Still, no sign of Pudge and Dot. I checked my watch; it was twenty minutes after the hour. My armpits started to sweat. "Schnapps, please," I said, then turned toward the man at the bar. "Hallo."

He nodded once. I was struck by his gaze in that brief second his eyes had flicked to mine. Not the way a woman should be struck by a man's eyes, but in a way where I knew he was swimming in unequal parts pain, hopelessness, and hurt.

The bartender pulled a clean glass out from under the bar, and while he reached for a bottle to pour, I stole a peek at the man's uniform underneath his jacket. He was a soldier, and from the gruffness of his beard and the way he exhaustedly sat hunched over on his stool, you would have thought he'd just walked off the battlefield a few moments before.

"Was the whisky too strong for you?" the bartender asked.

"A little." I patted my stomach.

"Are you waiting for your husband?" He filled my glass

with schnapps. "We have a lot of soldiers coming in from the front lately."

I twiddled my bare ringer finger. "I'm not married," I said. The soldier shifted as if he was not only listening but paying attention. I looked for a paper heart on his lapel. "I'm here with my friend." I pointed behind me.

"The one in the yellow dress?" the bartender asked.

The others had gotten up, leaving Junie sitting close to the man who'd eyed us in the hallway. He leaned into her ear to say something, and she laughed and laughed with a playful bat of his hand.

The soldier took a guarded peek over his shoulder.

"Yes, that's her." I smiled. "That's my friend."

The soldier stood, and not so steadily. "Check." He quietly downed the last of his drink but then slammed the empty glass on the bar, giving me a little jump. After paying, he left like a troubled wind, passing by the windows with a lumbered gait and a cigarette pinched between his lips.

"Was it something I said?" I asked.

The bartender counted the coins he'd left him. "Don't get too shook up over that soldier, Fräulein. He just lost his wife."

I clutched my chest. "His wife died?"

"A different kind of loss. Füssen isn't a place you want your wife waiting alone for very long."

"It isn't?" My heart sped up, thinking he was alluding to one of Cora's flyers. "What's the matter with Füssen?"

"Well, in that soldier's case—" he leaned over the bar for privacy "—by the time he arrived from the front, she'd already found herself another man to keep her company." I heard Junie laughing again, but above that, I heard Ava tell her table that it was getting late, even though we'd only been in the biergarten for twenty-five minutes.

"Poor sap. He was wounded in Italy and has been here for weeks, drowning his sorrows in beer or whatever drink he's up for that day. Did you notice his limp? Took a bullet in the leg, is what he told me."

"That's awful." I downed my drink, then stood to leave, reaching into my handbag and searching for a few coins to pay for my tab. "Was the affair with another soldier?" I asked, trying to sound interested, but I was also being nosy.

"No." He gestured to the man with Junie. "She had an affair with him."

"Oh?" I turned around to look just as Ava slunk up beside me, smoothing a blonde curl away from her cheek.

"It's been a long day. Nightcap in my apartment?" She didn't wait for me to answer. "Good. Follow me."

I thanked the bartender and followed Ava out. Junie was just a few steps behind. He'd given me more information than he knew, though I'd yet to see a heart pinned to anyone's lapel.

There was still no sign of Pudge and Dot in the lobby.

Junie locked arms with me on the curb. "They'll be here," she said, knowing I was thinking about them. "Remember, they took a longer route."

"I guess." We hurried across the street. "I don't want to go to Ava's. Why didn't we stay just a little longer?"

"I'm glad we left. That German we saw in the hallway, he asked me to dance but had very little to say about the war and preferred to comment about my arms and neck, so it would have been a waste of my time."

"The bartender said he stole another man's wife."

"I wouldn't doubt that. He's smooth, attractive, and has his mind on one thing."

We'd made it across the street. "Heart?" I asked.

"No heart."

Ava's apartment was a nice building, despite the wobbly handrail that broke free of the plaster with the tiniest bit of pressure applied to it. Frau Schneider's apartment was right next to the stairs. They must know each other.

"Watch the handrail," I said. "These stairs are narrow and dangerous. I hope that isn't a sign."

Junie gave me a look.

"You're not thinking the same thing?"

"I think you're being dramatic. You don't like her either, but it's getting to you. Don't let it get to you."

Ava had the penthouse apartment. On the outside, it was just a simple wooden door, but upon entering, it was clear Ava didn't live in just any old apartment. There were rich furnishings, gold lamps, and crystal chandeliers. I noted the scent of dust, which she explained was because she hadn't been back in a year. It was warmer than it should be, which I attributed to the windows not being open. Portraits hung on the wall, men, women—maybe a sister—and even children. If I didn't know any better, I'd say that Ava had quite the family.

"They are not my children," she said after slipping on a cream robe and putting her hair up. "None of them are my relatives."

"You buy portraits of strangers?"

"I buy paintings of value. These may or may not have value. I know enough about war to know that not all art should be displayed as an original. This painting hangs downstairs as well. It's a Duval, if you know anything about artists. Called *The Reckoning*. Only one of them is real."

I blinked. Ava was strange, and getting stranger the longer we talked.

She let out an exhausted breath and relaxed on the couch with a rub of her feet. "Nice work, ladies," she said. "We'll repeat that tomorrow. I heard the Lech is popular with the Wehrmacht and has a beach for relaxing. We should go there. I believe I know where to go."

"We heard that also," Junie said.

"There's opposition at the front among the ranks," Ava said. "Did you hear that, too?"

"Shh! Keep your voice down," I rasped. "Someone could be listening." I pointed to the floor.

She shook her head as if I was being unreasonable. "Relax."

"Viv has a point," Junie said. "And she's the best—"

"I own the apartment below, and it's empty, and there's nobody above because we are on the top floor." Ava searched her handbag for a key and after she couldn't find it, told Junie that there was a spare key hidden on the top of the doorframe. "Go and check the apartment yourself, because I know you don't trust me."

I watched Ava finish rubbing her feet on the couch, making relaxing noises in her silky robe, until Junie came back up from checking the apartment. "She's telling the truth. Nobody is there."

"Well, in that case, as the landlord, you should fix that handrail," I said. "We almost died on the way up."

Ava rolled her eyes. "You two need acting lessons. The soldiers you'll meet tomorrow will notice you don't like me.

I hope the other two aren't like you. If they made it out of the forest, that is."

"Why would you say that?" I asked. "They made it."

"They weren't downstairs, and you heard the dogs barking on the mountain, didn't you?" she asked. "You can't be sure. In fact, we might see them hanging in the square at sunup."

I gasped. "How can you—"

"They weren't caught," Junie said. "I know because those were officers downstairs. If they'd caught American spies in the forest, we would have heard some whisperings in the biergarten. Maybe even in the street."

Ava smiled sheepishly. "I guess we will know tomorrow, won't we? Speaking of, we should meet for breakfast at the hotel restaurant in the morning. If the other two are here, they will know to look for us there."

"Thank you for that thoughtful analysis, Ava." It was late, and I'd had enough of Ava's apartment and company. "Come on, Junes, let's leave."

"No." Ava looked up, one hand still rubbing the arch of her foot. "You must wait another fifteen minutes. It would be rude to leave sooner."

I checked my watch to mark the time before moving toward the window for a peek out of the curtains. I trailed car headlamps and couples walking with my gaze. Our hotel on the other side of the street was visible from her window, and it didn't escape me that she could see into our room if our curtains were open. People might ask questions as to why we weren't staying with her if we were long-lost friends. The apartment below had a large balcony. We could be staying there, especially since she owned it. I moved to open the window and catch a breeze.

"Keep it closed, and the curtains," Ava said from the couch. "I never leave them open."

I turned around against the open curtains, arms folded. "Why aren't we staying with you?"

"Please, my curtains."

"Why aren't we staying with you?" I repeated.

She got up to close the curtains herself, but I blocked her.

"Because I didn't know what condition this building would be in when plans were made for you to stay at the hotel," she said. "I've been gone for a while, and since D-Day, my accountant hasn't forwarded rent payments or made attempts at communication. The first thing I did today in Füssen was visit him and tell him the fate of my husband, implying the resistance killed him, but I couldn't be sure." She attempted to reach behind me for the curtain. "He's an insatiable gossip. Word of my story had already spread before I met you in the restaurant."

"What happened to your husband?"

"He left to check on one of our properties in the French countryside, and he never returned. Now, will you please move so I can close my curtains—"

I finally moved. "Does Cora know this?" Junie looked as concerned as I was; it could have easily been the Germans that killed him.

"She knows." Ava crossed her arms. "And I know you heard me on the plane. I had a Gestapo lover. I believe he had something to do with my husband's disappearance. The properties were in my name for tax reasons. Similar to this apartment and the flat I have in Munich. He was a small cog in the wheel of our relationship, even if our union was a marriage of convenience."

"And this lover of yours… What does he think happened to you?"

"He was shot by the resistance just as soon as the city was liberated. I was taken to a prisoner camp," she said. "Don't feel sorry for me. I didn't love him. I used him to gather information for when the Allies finally invaded. The only ones able to vouch for me are either dead, displaced, or in prison. The French didn't believe me, but the Americans did, and I'm thankful."

"Why would we feel sorry for you?" I asked. "And why would you want to go back to France when you're German?"

Her lips pursed from having to answer so many of my questions. "I built a life for myself in France, and I want it back. Once they know the truth and what lengths I've gone to for the Allies, the locals will change their minds. Just two things stand in my way of getting what I want. One is my reputation, and the other…" Her hand moved ever so slightly to her belly.

Junie pulled me to the side to talk privately. "I think you've talked enough for tonight and asked enough questions," she said. "Save it for the biergarten and the soldiers. All right?"

"Biergarten?" Suddenly, I just realized I had forgotten to pay my tab. "Oh, no! I forgot to pay for my drink at the hotel. He'll think I stole from him, skipped out on purpose."

"What?" Ava was aghast. "You forgot to pay? That is such an American thing to do. A German would never forget. What if he alerted the police? That's the last thing—"

"Pipe down, Ava," I said. "It was a mistake. I should blame you, now that I think of it, I was about to pay, and then you interrupted me, and I left the coins at the bottom of my handbag."

"We should leave," Junie said.

At the door, Ava offered us some advice. "Be careful what you say in the stairwell. You never know who is at the bottom or at the top and might be listening." She studied my face. "You don't trust me, even now, do you?"

"I trust you about as far as I can throw you," I said.

"It doesn't matter. We are associated now. Everyone knows." She motioned with her finger for us to come closer. "Here's some advice," she whispered. "If anything happens to me, run, because it'll only be a matter of time before they get you, too."

My eyes narrowed. "Is that a threat or a warning?"

Junie dragged me away by the arm. "Come on, Viv."

"Good night, friends!" Ava said loudly, her voice echoing down the stairwell.

I grabbed hold of that flimsy handrail. "Get your handrail fixed, Ava. Someone's going to break their neck if you don't watch it—"

She closed the door before I finished talking.

Once outside, we hooked each other's arms to cross the street. For a Tuesday night, the streets were lively, with Wehrmacht lumbering into beer halls only to leave with a pep in their step and a woman on their arm, lips locked.

"What was the point of bringing up the dogs?" I asked. "We obviously heard them."

"As I said before, don't let her get to you. If Pudge and Dot aren't in their room by now, then they're in a beer hall, probably talking to soldiers. Look at all of them." She motioned to the streets. "What do your bones say? I know you've already spoken to them."

"Forget my bones." She was trying to make me laugh, and

now was not the time. "I'm more worried about my unpaid tab."

We made it to the lobby. "Be genuinely apologetic, and he'll understand. You're a good German, remember? I'll see you in the room."

Junie took the elevator up to our room while I went to apologize profusely to the bartender, and to my delight, he appeared shocked that I'd worried about it. "One of Ava's friends paid for your tab," he said. "No need to fear."

"Oh, what a relief," I said, and as I put on my best surprised face, I noted that he knew Ava. And he didn't call her Fräulein, which meant he knew her casually and well. "I only realized a few moments ago and raced over." I tucked the reichsmarks back into my handbag. "I'm just a little absent-minded sometimes, especially when I'm enjoying myself."

He dried a glass with a bar towel. "I understand."

I sat down on the stool, but mainly because I wanted to survey who had moved into the restaurant and who was still socializing in the biergarten. I asked for another drink. Ava's friends from earlier appeared to be gone, and so was the man Junie had been talking with.

"Fräulein..." the bartender said, but then hesitated after pouring me a shot of schnapps.

"Yes?" I sat up.

"Pardon me, but you remind me of my daughter, and I simply couldn't live with myself if I didn't pass on a warning."

I reached for my chest. "A warning?"

He leaned over the bar, whispering, "About the man your friend was with."

"You already told me about him," I said, but I phrased it in a way that begged for more information. "No need to worry. They were just talking."

His face took on a grave appearance. "You don't understand."

"What do you mean?"

"He asked about her." The barmaid called him away to help with a check dispute between herself and two men. Voices were raised, and the barmaid looked a little frantic. "Just…" He wadded up his bar towel and rushed away. "Tell your friend to be careful."

Chapter Eight

The next morning, we waited at the hotel restaurant for Pudge and Dot, but after thirty minutes, there was still no sign of them, or Ava for that matter, and we'd already ordered. I was having a tough time coming up with plausible excuses that didn't include them getting caught.

"It's getting late," I said, checking my watch for the tenth time.

Junie took a sip of her tea. "I know."

"What if they were caught, or one of the other teams was caught?"

The waiter startled me with our food. A single potato pancake and sliced warm apple. He set the plate down in front of me, but I could only push the food around with my fork. Junie sent her toast back for more toasting until it was burnt, only to then scrape all the burnt parts off with a knife.

"It's funny how we've switched places."

I set my fork down. "What do you mean?"

"I'm usually the worried one." With a final scrape of her

knife, she spread a thin layer of jam over her toast. "Eat," she said, then whispered, "before you look suspicious."

"I would have been fine if Ava hadn't mentioned the dogs, and what about that ominous warning to run if something happened to her? I'll be better once they arrive and are safely seated at this table."

She held back a laugh. "That's not how worrying works. You think you'll feel better, but soon you'll find something else to worry about. It's inevitable."

"I won't." I ate the apple from my fork, but then I had to spit it into my napkin because of my nervous stomach. "Not me. I'll be fine once they walk through that door."

"We'll see."

A few minutes passed, maybe even five. They still hadn't shown up. "I'll be right back."

"Where are you—" she'd started to ask when the waiter appeared out of nowhere and poured her another cup of tea. She waited patiently for him to leave, smiling and looking relaxed until he left. "Where are you going?" she rasped.

"Powder room."

"Stay," she said, but I couldn't sit still any longer with a cold potato pancake in front of me. I stood, wadding up my linen napkin, and was about to leave it in a lump on the table when I carefully folded it back up and placed it next to my plate like a good German. I glanced at the waiter and the other diners; nobody had been looking, except Junie.

"Hold it together," she said under her breath. "You're worrying for nothing."

The bathroom was a single stall with a sink and a toilet. I locked the door and took a few deep breaths, reminding myself that we'd parachuted into Nazi Germany and already established ourselves as visiting guests. If Pudge and Dot had been caught, there would have been talk about it, and Füssen appeared quiet. Nobody was patrolling the streets, talking to people in the cafés, or checking in with the hotels. Only soldiers on leave with women hanging off their arms.

I was worrying for nothing, I decided. Just like Junie said.

I walked back into the breakfast room to find Pudge and Dot seated and ordering breakfast. I stumbled over my own feet, then smiled.

"Hallo." I gently placed my napkin on my lap after sitting back down. My heart was hammering, but in a good way because I was relieved.

"Hallo," both of them said.

"See?" Junie said.

We waited for the waiter to finish taking their order—eggs with milk—and then Dot leaned over the table after he'd left.

"God, are we glad to see you!" she said.

"Yeah," Pudge said. "We thought maybe the dogs got you. There was a lot of barking."

"We thought the dogs got you two," I said.

"Did they get Ava?" Dot asked, her eyebrows slightly arched. "I kind of hope so."

"No. She's here." I pointed across the street. "In fact, she owns an apartment over there."

"That sounds convenient," Pudge said.

"Yeah," Dot said. "Real convenient."

The waiter was back at our table again, but this time to say they were out of eggs. "Food shortages." He gave a slight nod. "Please forgive us at this time."

Half of what was on the menu wasn't available because of rations and food shortages. They ended up getting what we ordered—a single potato pancake from a batter that was already made. He left, and then it was me leaning over the table.

"Now, where were you last night? We were supposed to meet you in the lobby." The waiter was back, but this time, he was setting down some cutlery. We waited again. "This pancake is delightful," I said to Junie, who agreed, mouth full of tea.

He left again, and they explained that they had accidentally taken an even longer route, had to backtrack, and got too close to the dogs. After finding the hotel and buying some clothes, they'd missed the rendezvous with us in the lobby, and thought it was better to stay in their room until the morning.

"Well, I'm just glad you're both here now," Junie said. I agreed.

We told them about last night with Ava and our plans to go to the river after breakfast.

"Who's at the river?" Dot asked.

"Who else? Wehrmacht," I said. "Apparently, it's quite the spot for single women and soldiers. We'll fit right in. Might have to hold some hands."

Dot looked at Pudge, who reassured her everything would be all right.

Their pancakes arrived, and now we were just waiting on Ava. I watched the apartment across the street. Junie watched the pavement, and Pudge and Dot watched the road.

"There she is." At half past ten, Ava emerged from her apartment, dressed in a flowing white dress with a basket hooked on her arm. Instead of bursting through the dining room doors, she floated in, sitting down at our table and waving the waiter away.

I reminded her she was late.

"I had some last-minute arrangements to take care of." She looked at Pudge and Dot. "So glad to see you. I worried you might be hanging in the square."

They gave her a disgusted look, and rightfully so. Junie dismissed her comment entirely and instead asked, "What kind of arrangements?"

"I didn't want to take the tram to the river. We'd have to walk a few blocks and down an embankment to get to the riverbank, and I have new shoes on." She lifted her foot so we could see her cream pumps. "I secured a ride from a friend of a friend. What luck he was available!"

"I don't believe in luck," Pudge said, and that drew a pointed look from Ava.

"Me neither," Dot said.

A black car pulled up outside. "He's here," Ava said at the same time whisperings of a dashing gentleman in a flashy car swept through the restaurant. The waiter handed me the check. Pudge and Dot had gotten up after a quick scrape of their plates.

"See," Junie said. "You had nothing to worry about. We even have a ride to the river. That is, until you find something else to worry about."

I dug into my handbag for reichsmarks.

"Meet you outside."

Pudge and Dot left with Junie. I briefly saw them getting into the car as I settled the bill, and I did a double take. That man Junie talked with last night, the one who asked her for a dance. "Damn, there's my something else to worry about," I mumbled, but then rethought. He was only giving us a ride. That's all. Didn't matter what the bartender said because we'd all be together. And what German man in Füssen wasn't a womanizer? That was why we were here.

Ava kept chattering about luck. "Be on your best behavior," she said after the waiter walked away.

I counted the change in my palm. "I'm always on my best behavior."

She gave her hair a toss, looking toward the street and smiling. "Yes, well, the last thing I want to do is upset Joseph Engle."

I dropped the change, spilling coins on the floor like a shattered glass.

"Who?" I asked, but it was almost a shriek while one of the coins rolled round and round and round in a circle.

Ava laughed off my reaction when the diners stared, then pulled me to the floor to pick the coins up. "What has gotten into you?" she asked, reaching for the coins. "People are staring." She stood a second later, bringing me up with her.

"Ahh… Ahh…" My heart pounded, my head, light. "Joseph Engle?" Out the window, he was smiling and looking gentlemanly, helping the girls into his car—and not just any car, now that I had a better look. A sleek Mercedes 770. The kind SS officers drove.

"Yes, that's right. Why?" She leaned into my ear. "Do you know him?"

"No," I quickly replied. "I mean, only from what I saw of him last night." A smile flashed on my face, not knowing if she had done this on purpose, and until I found out, I'd have to play dumb. "Everything is fine." I did my best to straighten my skirt and appear unaffected, but my chest was still pounding, and my head was screaming. "I'll meet you outside. Just going to freshen up," I lied. "Be right there."

Ava left to get into Engle's car as I watched. *It's a ride to the river. That's all.* The situation wasn't any graver than it had been a few seconds ago before I knew his name, I told myself. She settled into the middle of the front seat with Dot by the door.

I walked outside to where Engle was holding the back door open, taking a deep breath with my head held high, but that did next to nothing to calm myself. "Thank you." I could barely get the words out, thinking of my grandfather and how he'd be turning in his grave if he knew I'd said "thank you" to Joseph Engle.

"You're welcome." He smiled, and I looked into his eyes. They were striking, just like Cora had said. Crystals in the sun. He made my skin crawl.

Junie didn't want to sit in the middle, so we switched places, and I squished in next to Pudge. I clutched my handbag on my lap after pulling a scarf out and covering my hair with a sharp yank of the fabric under my chin.

I waited for Pudge to recognize him as we drove off. He would have introduced himself to her as Joseph, I imagined, which was common enough, and blond hair wasn't an original trait, but it was only a matter of time before she saw the other signs, like his fingernails.

The wind whipped and whirled from having the top down, with the breeze rustling his silky hair. He adjusted his rearview mirror with his right hand, and there it was in the reflection: the tattoo—the faded gray letters of his blood type near his elbow—a unique position for that kind of tattoo when usually the SS had them higher up on their inner bicep for concealment.

"Is the wind bothersome?" he asked, looking into the back

seat.

"No." My scarf tails tickled my chin. "Thank you," I said yet again. My fists clenched momentarily.

Pudge seemed unaware of his tattoo, though she was looking in that direction. I checked my watch—we'd been driving for several minutes and should be there soon. Füssen bordered the river; you could walk there from the square, but the beach and park were a little further down.

Ava and Engle made small talk in the front seat. They clearly had a friend in common, but I didn't know who that was. He never mentioned the Reich, or what he did in the SS, or that he was even an officer, which went along with what Cora said: he was secretive.

"What a luxurious car, Joseph." Ava felt the smooth leather seats. "This must have cost you a fortune. So nice of you to give us a ride. What a treat!"

"You are most welcome." His voice was smooth, almost kind, and pleasant. A good German boy from the city. His accent led me to believe he was from Berlin.

"And you go to the Lech often?" Ava asked.

"No, no... It's a popular place for Wehrmacht to rest before they're brought back to the front at the end of their respite." He looked up, mentioning the clouds and how the temperatures would be changing soon with the coming fall weather. "Did I hear that you are from Munich?" he asked us in the back.

Junie piped up, pulling her eyes away from the countryside. "Close friends on a short holiday." She held her scarf in place as it rippled and flapped.

I closed my eyes, telling myself that we'd be there soon—a matter of seconds now—and that he wasn't staying with us at the river. Why would he stay? He admitted it was a place for soldiers, and an officer wouldn't mingle with soldiers. I heard his voice much clearer with my eyes closed. I wondered what his last words to my grandfather were.

He laughed, and my eyes popped open.

"You must be someone important to afford this car, Joseph," Ava said. "You can tell us." She bashfully patted his arm with a giggle, which he seemed to enjoy. "Are you important?"

I squeezed my handbag a little tighter. Engle was important. Boy, was he.

"Are you a member of the Party?" Ava asked pointedly.

I held my breath, and if it wasn't for the wind, you would have heard a pin drop with how quiet we all were, each of us looking straight ahead as if we weren't paying attention to the conversation, but we clearly were.

He gave Ava a nod. "I am a member."

Dot shifted in the front seat after he let that bomb drop.

"Then we are in good company! We were in the Faith and Beauty Society." Ava whirled her finger around, pointing to us all. "That's where we met."

His eyes flicked to us sitting in the back, but he didn't seem too interested—it was only a glance through the rearview mirror. He must have handfuls of Faith and Beauty women throwing themselves at his feet, and Ava certainly wasn't hiding her gratitude. He struck me as the type of man who chased a challenge since he was all too keen to steal that soldier's wife—a woman who had traveled and was waiting for her husband.

"Joseph," Ava said, with a little shift of the eyes to me in the back. "Do you know a good repairman? I need a handrail fixed. Apparently, some klutz almost died holding on to it."

Junie tapped my arm with that comment. Her message was clear: don't react.

"Can I turn on some music?" Ava's hand was already on the dial.

"Be my guest," he said.

She turned on the radio, and after a few seconds of trying to find a station, she found a state-run channel. Pudge looked dead ahead as Ava and Engle sang along from the front seat, all three of us in the back swaying subtly from the car's turns and movements. Engle reached behind his neck for a scratch, exposing his fingernails, yellowy as a Crayola crayon, with ridges deeper than most valleys. The hands of a killer.

Pudge cleared her throat. *"Hannah?"*

I squeezed my handbag just a little tighter. "Yes?" Engle and Ava were still singing, and while he wasn't looking, and nobody else was either, I glanced in Pudge's direction, talking through my teeth. "I know."

With that, Pudge crossed her arms, looking out the windshield like me.

"Great day for a picnic," Junie said.

I rechecked my watch. We should be there. God, why weren't we there yet?

"We're here!" Ava said, just as I heard the pop and grind of gravel under the tires. The ride was over. I felt the relief deeply.

Ava immediately hopped out and was looking for a spot to put her picnic basket, but the beach was crowded. Pudge and I were just as quick, ready to say goodbye to Engle, but he got out of the car instead of driving away, calling Junie toward him for a conversation near the fender.

Dot beelined for the river where women splashed each

other and soldiers watched lazily from the beach. "He's SS," she said in passing, not wanting to stay another second in his company.

The tram arrived, letting off a handful of young women, giggling with their picnic baskets on their way over to the river to wait for soldiers.

Pudge squeezed my arm. "Jesus, Viv. Did she do this on purpose?"

"You think she did?"

"I hope not. For her sake," she said.

Ava tiptoed through the grass, looking unaware and fanciful with her lazy day picnic basket and blanket. By now, two minutes had passed since we'd arrived, and Engle was still chatting with Junie. I let out a huff.

"They're getting to know each other," Pudge said. "He's leaning against the fender, Viv. Arms casually folded and looking flirty."

"Don't you think I see that?" I'd snapped at her when I didn't mean to. "I never thought I'd see him again."

"Again?"

I sighed. "I saw him last night."

"What? Where?"

I told her how he tried to dance with Junie, and how I'd heard he has a reputation for stealing other men's wives. "The bartender told me to warn Junie about him. I had no way of knowing his identity beforehand because I wasn't close enough to see the signs, and he wasn't wearing a uniform. I don't think he wears it when he's not on duty."

"Cora said he was secretive, remember? And brutal."

"I know."

On the surface, he looked like a nice guy. A German with

blond hair and an expensive car, giving a few young women a ride. For free, too, without expecting a return favor. He had been, for all intents and purposes, hospitable.

"Out of all the other SS officers in Germany ... the one from Flossenbürg," Pudge said. "God, I hate the sight of him."

"You think I don't? What happened to our grandfathers is just the tip of the iceberg, if the OSS want him so badly."

"Where do you think he lives?" Pudge asked.

"That's the million-dollar question, isn't it? Where does he sleep at night?" The longer they talked, the more I thought I should tell Junie the truth, come clean about our little side mission, regardless of my orders to stay quiet. "What are we going to do?" I asked.

"I can tell you what we're not going to do, and that's talk about our side mission to our partners. Dot will never speak to me again. Besides, it's our order."

My heart raced, then nearly exploded when Engle laughed at something Junie had said.

"Maybe this is the last we'll see of him."

Engle showed Junie something from his glove compartment, and just when I thought he'd never leave, he finally opened his car door and got in.

"Maybe," I said, but I had a feeling he was like a bad penny, and one thing I'd learned was that bad pennies always show back up. I placed a hand on my chest.

"I'd better go see about Dot. I'll see you after." Pudge walked away to join Dot at the beach where some soldiers were playing a game with their shirts off.

Ava called me from the blanket. "Hannah! Oh, Hannah, darling." She waved dramatically over her head. "Come over here, will you? I want you to meet … well, a hero!" She was sitting with a soldier, smoking a cigarette.

Junie was on her way back after Engle drove away, hooking my arm so that we could walk together. "You're drawing attention. Ava's calling you." The walk was a short one, made longer by taking slow and lazy steps. The sun shone between two mountain peaks, its warm rays glistening off the slow-moving Lech and onto the shore. "It's gorgeous here. If only for the war—"

"What was he talking to you about for so long?"

"The weather mostly. He said he preferred the city over the country, except on days like this."

"Oh, yeah? What did he show you?"

"His camera. He's a photographer in his free time. Why are you asking me this? I know he's SS. His car gave him away."

"Be careful, Junie," I said. "The bartender told me to warn you last night, when I went back to pay my bill. I didn't think I had to mention it because I had no idea we'd see him again. Now that we know he's SS…"

"I'm always careful," she said.

She unhooked our arms to hold my hand just as a German plane buzzed overhead. "Airmail," she said, pointing. "Your mother must have found you."

"Not now," I said.

She dropped my hand. "Hey. Everything is fine. It's all working out. Now, let's get to work." She nodded, which got me to nod. "All right?"

"All right."

We made it to the blanket where Ava and the soldier were sitting.

"Hallo, you two!" Ava smiled. "I want to introduce you to this soldier."

Only he wasn't just a soldier. He was a soldier with a paper heart pinned to his collar. He blindly felt for the pin. "Good… Good afternoon." He tried to get up, but we told him to stay seated. "I hear you are from—" he pulled Cora's flyer from his pocket along with a few twisted licorice wrappers "—from the League of Lonely War Women."

Chapter Nine

The soldier had unfolded and folded the flyer so many times it had split and ripped in the creases until the text had disappeared. "Is it true?" he asked, shoving it back into his pocket. "You are them?"

"We are." Now, my heart was racing for another reason. "And I brought some friends." I motioned toward Pudge and Dot, but there were so many couples in between, necking on blankets.

"Tell them, Hans," Ava said, patting his shoulder. "Tell them all about yourself."

He shoved a piece of licorice in his mouth, then went on to talk about how he was stationed near the Gustav Line and was waiting for a two o'clock bus to take him, and the rest of the Wehrmacht at the river, back to their posts. He was squeezing the last few moments out of his leave.

He looked young, but his eyes had a tormented glaze to them from the war, so I couldn't be sure. I hoped he wasn't one of the boys recruited directly from the Hitler Youth.

"How old are you, Hans?" I held my breath.

"Eighteen." He swept a lock of blond hair from his forehead. "But going on thirty." He laughed at his own joke.

"Drink?" I smiled, pulling a bottle of wine from the picnic basket. "Best to make these last minutes of rest count, no?" I poured him a glass and then moved to fill ours. "Where are you from, Hans?"

"Tell me about you." He chewed his licorice like a boy, taking wet, sloppy swallows with no regard for others. "Do you have a husband? Where are you from?"

These were the kind of questions we were prepared for. "I'm from Munich," I said. "And no, I don't have a husband, but some of us do."

Junie drank delicately from her glass.

"I see." He sat up slightly after looking like he was getting more comfortable. "I have a sister in Munich. Do you know Anna Muller? Is she a member?"

"Anna Muller?" I gave him my best surprised face. "From Munich? Blonde, blue eyes," I said because it wasn't that hard to guess looking at him. "Yes, I do know Anna. She's a great woman. Proud."

"Tell her to stop," he said. "I don't want her part of the league."

"Stop? Why?"

"Because she's married. Her husband will divorce her, if he hasn't already, like other soldiers I know."

"Divorce?" Junie and I looked at each other. This was the kind of intelligence we needed. "You don't say…"

Ava topped off our glasses with more wine, and time moved lazily into the afternoon with small talk about German strength and our beloved Führer. He told us about morale, which was sinking by the day, and that his unit was moving east of the Gustav Line after their respite. However, the most significant piece of information came when he complained about the lack of food, specifically naming the town from which supplies and rearmaments were being shipped. "Enough about that. The weather and company are too good to waste on such topics." He closed his eyes and lay flat on his back.

Pudge and Dot moved to a blanket near us when Ava waved a friend over, a good-looking man in a blue collared shirt and sporty, tan pants. "This is Karl, everyone," Ava said. "He's on an extended respite."

I recognized him from the biergarten. He seemed to take a liking to Dot and even tried to feed her a grape. I watched him pet her hand, then, in a bold move, he kissed her cheek. "The war will be over soon," Karl said. "The Reich is strong. Do not fear, Fräulein," he said into Dot's ear.

He leaned in further, first gently touching her hand, then kissing her neck, not once, not twice, but continuous nibbles from her ear to her collarbone. She pretended to be interested, but I could tell she felt absolutely sick about having to be his girl for the hour when she was supposed to only be a listening ear.

"Where do you serve, Karl?" I asked, trying to get him to stop, but he either didn't hear me or didn't want to answer, scooching so close to Dot that to be any closer, he'd have to climb on top of her. "Gustav Line?" I added.

He popped up for air, mid-kiss on her neck. Dot froze, then he went in for a proper kiss on her lips, which she couldn't stop without a scene. Afterward, he just laughed and laughed and laughed, like he'd stolen a cookie from the cookie jar.

"Soldiers, Gustav Line… Can't we talk about something other than the war?" Hans asked.

Karl must have decided Dot wasn't worth his time because he got up as he was still laughing and moved on.

Pudge reached for Dot's hand, but she yanked it out from under hers to fold her arms.

Hans curled up on the blanket with his knees tucked up to his chest. Junie gestured for me to pet his head. "There, there, soldier," I said, resting my hand on his head, feeling his warm locks and even warmer scalp from the sun.

We talked about what we liked best about home. The smell of bread on a cool autumn day. The cowbells in the country and the enzian growing wild in the mountains. Out of the blue, he wept silently in his hands, talking about his mother and his childhood.

"There, there, soldier," I said, again. "The war won't last forever."

Hans sat up and wiped his cheeks of tears. "I said I don't want to talk about the war!" he bellowed.

None of us moved. My heart raced, first from being yelled at, then from the look on his face, which had changed. He wasn't that eighteen-year-old who looked thirty from the war, but an angry, vengeful man with protruding blood vessels in his neck.

He reached for the wine bottle and took several gulping drinks before tossing the empty bottle in the grass. He reached for my bare leg, his calloused, searching fingers disappearing under the hem of my dress.

I scooted back, but his hand outstretched the length of my thigh, nearly reaching my underpants.

"That's enough," I said, standing, when luckily, his bus

pulled up, lurching to a stop with a poof of exhaust. "Your bus is here." I smoothed my skirt against my legs. "Better be off."

Wehrmacht, fresh from the front line, poured out of the bus with their rucksacks while the others boarded as sleepwalkers called back home.

"Do you need help?" I reached to help him up, but he pulled away, giving me a confused, angry look, as if we'd been in the middle of lovemaking and I'd suddenly had an urge to clean house.

I waited for him to leave after he adjusted his rucksack, but he just stood and stared, first at me, then at the others on the blanket before grabbing my hand and pulling me toward him.

Junie stood. "They'll leave without you!"

He wrapped his arms around my waist and dug his tongue into my mouth, grunting. I managed to give him a little shove. "You little whore," he said sourly before walking off.

Junie and I watched in a daze as he headed off toward the bus, stopping to talk to another soldier who'd just arrived, then pointing at us like a free buffet.

I spat in the grass, suddenly tasting his licorice in my mouth. "Water." I spat again, then my legs folded underneath me, and I collapsed to the ground. "Do we have water?"

"We only have wine." Ava had a silly smile on her face. She'd done her duty, and apparently, she thought I'd done mine.

Junie poured me some wine, which I heartily drank, when suddenly the other soldier Hans had talked to was at our spot and looking for a place to sit.

"No room," I said, drawing in the blankets until he moved on.

The five of us remained. Ava, buffing her fingernails, Dot

with her back still to us, and Pudge and Junie quiet on the blanket. I held my head.

"For what it's worth," Junie said, "we did our jobs and found out quite a lot about what they know regarding the League of Lonely War Women."

"Yeah," I said. "We did our jobs all right. Regular heroes. A glorious day."

Dot's eyes narrowed in on Ava. "Did you know that Joseph Engle was SS?"

Ava scoffed at first, then pulled a mirrored compact from her bag. "No, I didn't know, but Karl was SS once." She padded her nose with powder, but it was Pudge's face that turned white.

"What did you say?" Dot asked. "The man who had his lips on me..." She felt her neck where he had kissed her all over. "He was SS?"

"Yes, that's him. He has an injury and is currently off duty for a while. Oh, that's right, you weren't in the biergarten last night when he told me the story. I thought you knew."

Dot's jaw tightened. "We're supposed to chat with soldiers," she said. "Karl is not our target, yet you let him cozy up to me without a peep?"

Ava shrugged. "Didn't Cora tell you? There's no guarantee who you'll be talking to, soldiers, SS. Hell, even a civilian if it means the right information." She went back to powdering her nose.

"Well, he's not my target." Dot crossed her arms tightly. "I want to go. We've done our job for the day. Right, Junie? You said as much."

Junie nodded. "We have done our job."

Ava tapped her watch. "Well, unless you want Karl to give us a ride home, we'll have to wait for the tram."

Dot glared at Ava, then addressed us all. "Just to be clear, I'm not sitting with any more soldiers today."

Soldiers walked by aimlessly, hoping for an offer, but we ignored them by picking at our nails or closing our eyes to the sun, soaking in the warmth. I drank the last of the wine, thinking of all the things I could have done differently with Hans.

"You think we'll see someone we know?" Pudge asked. "I don't care what Cora says. Germany is a big country, but it's also small."

"If anyone has a chance, it's me," I said. "My cousin lives not that far from here, in a big yellow house near the Berg Palace."

"The only women who come to Füssen alone are looking for one thing," Junie said. "I don't think your cousin is one of those."

"What about the other agents?" I asked. "You think we'll see them? Better yet, you think they're having success?"

"I've been thinking the same thing," Pudge said. "What if one of them dug up bones, as Cora called it. Got her hands on some real intelligence."

"They better not have dug up anything," Dot said, looking appalled. "We were warned about going off on our own." She twisted around, looking at the road. "When does that tram arrive? It must be getting close." She handed me the basket to start cleaning up.

I got up, picking up Hans's licorice wrappers from the blanket and the empty wine bottles, when a laugh carried through the trees, followed by a voice. Someone familiar.

I looked toward the river with my hand shielding my eyes and saw Barbara Bennington and Kitty Meyer.

"Oh, no." The basket fell from my hands, with all the contents spilling out onto the blanket. Half-nibbled cheese, crackers, and wrappers. "It can't be…"

"What?" Junie asked.

I pointed with my pinky to the two women playfully splashing each other along the bank. Their skirts were pulled up and tied under their belts with their shoes on the shore. "Babs and Kitty."

Dot squinted to see. "Who are Babs and Kitty?"

Junie explained who they were and how there was no love lost when we left London for Rome. "They'll do anything to get ahead, and they love a competition. It was between us and them for this promotion."

I shook my head as they frolicked in the water, laughing, drenched to the bone. "I don't understand. What are they doing here?"

"They are the replacements for the team that quit in the chapel," Ava said, buffing her nails.

I shot her a look. "How do you know?"

She shrugged. "Why else would they be here? Besides…" She pointed to another woman sitting on the shore. "They have an escort. I saw her at the villa."

The escort was as striking as Ava, with glistening hair and a way with the soldiers, calling them toward her with a mere curl of her finger.

"Just look at them," Pudge said. "Talking and schmoozing those soldiers. Naturals. They look like prostitutes, don't they?"

Their wet dresses clung to their bodies, leaving little to the imagination.

"Yeah," I said through my teeth. There was another man with them. Dark, pomade-slicked hair, with his sleeves rolled up to his elbows. Looked like a dress shirt. White, clean. He smoked casually on a blanket with their escort. I pointed nonchalantly. "I've seen him before."

"In London?"

"No…" His hair wasn't what piqued my interest; it was his sleeves, but I still couldn't put my finger on it. "That's not it."

Then he laughed, and he sounded like a croaking frog even from so far away. I covered my mouth. "Oh my God," I said just as quickly as I dropped my hand. "He was with Engle last night in the hotel hallway. I'm going to talk to them."

"No, don't," Junie said.

"Why not?" I asked.

"We left the competition in London, remember? Don't bring it here. Besides, the risks are too great."

"What risks?" I asked. "It's just a chat."

"You know what I mean. We shouldn't be seen talking to them. We stay with our group. Don't go." Junie grabbed hold of my arm after I hesitated. "I mean it, Viv. This idea doesn't sit right. It's a stinker of an idea. I can smell it a mile away."

"When your best friend has a feeling, you should listen to her," Ava said from the blanket.

"You don't have any friends, so what do you know?" I snapped back.

"Viv," Junie said just above a whisper. "Please, don't go."

"Let's pack up." Dot cleaned up the mess from the basket. Junie turned away to help her, leaving me and Pudge to talk privately.

"Are you thinking what I'm thinking?" Pudge asked out of the corner of her mouth.

"That Babs and Kitty are digging up bones?" I looked back at Junie, still helping Dot with the basket. "Let's just say, it's ironic that out of all the soldiers here, they picked one of Engle's friends to cozy up to."

"There's only one way to find out."

I nodded, and without another word, we walked toward the river, leaving our partners and Ava behind.

"We will say we're sorry when it's over, and they'll forgive us," I said, to make it feel all right.

Pudge scoffed. "It will take more than a sorry with Dot. She never wanted to come here to begin with. I talked her into it."

"What did you say?" I asked.

Pudge didn't answer, and then we were at the river, slipping off our shoes, joining the giggles and laughs of the other women. Babs was the first to look over, wiping a clingy curl from her cheek with her already wet hand and slicking it behind her ear.

It took her a moment to come and talk to us, pretending to get a ball they'd been throwing and had conveniently missed.

"Hallo," she said.

"Hallo," I said back, nudging pebbles with my toes.

There was another man with them, military-like with short hair, and wearing some kind of uniform that wasn't SS or Wehrmacht, but he was just far enough away that I couldn't make out the patches or branch.

Barbara looked Pudge up and down.

"She's one of us," I said.

Barbara smirked. "As I gather." She looked toward Junie in the grass. "I see another familiar face. Oh … and she looks mad. Did you really think coming over here was a good idea? Junie probably warned you. What is that she always says? *Stinker of an idea.* You should listen to her more often."

"Clam up, Babs. Find any hearts? What's your status?"

She didn't seem to care a lick of what I asked, and instead, sized Pudge up again, probably wondering what her name was and if she'd heard of her.

"She's better than you, Babs. Top of her class. That's all you need to know."

"Is that so?" Barbara smiled.

"Yeah, that's so," Pudge said. "But this isn't a competition, is it?"

"What's your status?" I asked again.

Barbara took her time answering, looking toward the trees as if we were talking about the birds. "My status is … secure," she said, finally. "What's yours?"

"Same."

Kitty walked up seconds later, laughing and smiling, then turning dead serious once she was close enough. "Viv. It was a bad idea coming over here."

"Yeah, that's what Babs said. I see you caught yourselves some real German dreamboats over there. They don't look like soldiers. Who are they?"

Barbara looked confused. "How can you tell?"

"Yeah, well, I guess you can't tell by first glance. That's why you're always second place."

Pudge gave Kitty the ball to take back over to their beach.

"So, do you know their names, or what?" I asked.

"Why, so you can take them for yourselves?" She rolled her eyes. "I have to tell you, I'm surprised to see you here.

I thought as soon as you found out you'd have to sleep with Germans, you'd be on the first plane to the donut wagons."

"That's not part of the mission."

She scoffed. "Whoever told you that was lying. We were fully briefed about the first mission and told what the women who came before us had done. Didn't you read the flyer?"

"Of course we did."

"Then surely you remember the passage where it said the longings of your lonely nights will be fulfilled. No inhibitions."

Pudge and I looked at each other. That was not mentioned in the flyer we read, and the only information Cora provided about the women who came before us was that they had trouble asking the right questions.

"I hope coming over here was worth it. Junie is still scowling." She walked away slowly, splashing her way back over to her German boyfriend.

"Let's go." Pudge and I walked briskly away.

"You're right. They aren't soldiers," Pudge said. "They are police, or maybe Abwehr." She looked back once. "Whoever they are, they live here."

"How do you know?"

"Their blanket. It was from someone's home, like Ava's is from her home. Look around."

The girlfriends and wives who'd come to meet their soldiers from out of town had checkered blankets they purchased from a shop. The locals had crocheted blankets from home.

"What do you think about what she said?" Pudge asked. "The flyer, no inhibitions…"

"You mean, do I think Cora lied to us?" I asked. "I wouldn't trust anything that comes out of Babs's mouth. She's trying to get ahead and is probably trying to rattle us. But if we were given a different flyer to read in the chapel than what was dropped, then that means—"

"Dot was right all along." Pudge nodded to herself. "I'll say this, that Hans seemed to expect something from a member of the League of Lonely War Women, didn't he?" She looked at me. "And it wasn't just an ear."

We walked back to Junie and Dot, who hadn't moved and stared at us with ferocious intensity. "I'm sorry," I blurted before either of them could say a word.

"Me too," Pudge said. "We had to do it."

They both turned on their heels toward the tram. Ava looked like she wanted to berate us, but swiftly changed her stance when a soldier walked past. "Such a nice day." Ava gestured toward the tram that had just rolled in. "Shall we?"

We hiked up the embankment to the tram stop. Junie and Dot never said a word, even after boarding and taking seats in the back. Ava, full of conversation, sat up front with the driver, making small talk about the weather and where to get a good drink in Füssen. We were the only passengers, everyone else preferring to soak up the last bit of summer sun before the days turned cool.

I took a seat in the back next to Pudge while Junie and Dot ignored us. I figured I'd fall on the sword and admit to her it was a competition because that's what she expected and what she'd believe.

I waited until the tram had left the river and we'd been traveling for a few minutes. "I know you didn't want us to go, but it was good we did. They are up to something, conducting their own research, likely for an additional report they plan to submit. Which you know will get them pushed right to the top,

Junie." I made a buzzing noise before squishing my palms together. "Flatting us right out on the curb—"

"Will you stop it?" she said. "Making me laugh this time isn't going to work."

"But they are up to something," I said.

"Well, good for them," Junie said. "It might get them killed."

"I want to go home," Dot said, looking out the window.

"Promise me," Junie said. "Don't risk our lives again like that. Now we're connected to them. Those men they were with saw you. It's dangerous."

I scoffed, but she was right, and I knew I had to admit what we'd done wasn't smart. "All right. It was a bad idea. I know that now. I won't risk your life, or Dot's, again for something so stupid. I'm sorry."

Pudge also apologized to Dot. "I'm sorry." They hugged. "I broke your trust. It won't happen again."

Ava was still chatting with the driver, laughing and carrying on like she hadn't a care in the world.

"And what about Ava?" I asked. "Has today changed your thoughts about her?"

We stared at her from the back as the tram squealed to a stop. Dot was the first one to stand, holding on to the handrail. "No," she said, followed by Pudge, shaking her head.

Chapter Ten

Ava turned syrupy again the moment her shoes hit the curb. "I'll see you tomorrow, friends." She hooked the picnic basket on her arm while leaning in to give us kisses. "We should go shopping. It's what tourists do. See you bright and early."

I shuddered when her lips pressed against my cheek.

"See you tomorrow," Junie said. "Shopping. Looking forward to it." A few people looked. Junie added in a wave.

My tongue felt pasty. "I can still taste licorice."

Dot shivered, feeling her arms. "His touch was everywhere." She felt for her lips, then looked away in shame.

"We can get a table inside and talk. It'll be easier than whispering in our rooms."

We took a table in the biergarten near the houndstooth drapes, where it was more private. Dot immediately slumped over the table after the barmaid brought our drinks.

"How many days do we have left?" I asked.

"Several," Pudge said.

"Well, in those days we have left, we better not be seeing SS Officer Joseph Engle again," Dot said. "And when I get home, I'm not mentioning anything about what happened at that river. I'll make something up before I admit to riding in a car with an SS officer on the way to a picnic. In my report, we poisoned him, or ran him off the road, or … or…"

"Shot him? I mean, if you're going to lie, might as well tell a whopper," Junie said.

"I wanted to shoot him." Tears welled in her eyes, and I worried they'd spill over her cheeks. I handed her a napkin left on a nearby table. "I wish I could turn back time. Maybe I would." She calmed herself down enough to take a few breaths. "I know Ava denied it, but I think she set up a ride with Engle on purpose. She's probably across the street making plans to expose us right now."

"I don't believe that," Junie said. "The fact is, if Ava was going to turn us in, she would have done it already, and we'd all be hanging in the square. You know that. It's just easier not to like her."

"We didn't need to take a car to the river," Dot said. "We took the tram back, so why didn't we take it there? Because of her shoes? Those two sure were chatty in the front seat on the drive over."

Junie swatted the air; she was done entertaining such ideas about Ava.

"Chatty is a good way to describe it," I said. "And we should note that."

The barmaid was back and asked if we wanted to sit in the restaurant when it opened. None of us were hungry, but to maintain the appearance of women on holiday, Pudge said they would be back after freshening up, even though they were done for the night. Junie got up to leave with them.

"I'll be right behind you." I pointed to my half-liter of beer, which I'd barely touched.

"Don't be too long." Junie kissed my cheek and then followed them out.

I needed something more substantial than beer, and water wasn't going to do, not this time. I took a seat at the bar, having a look at the top-shelf bottles of liquor. "Whisky."

The bartender dried a glass. "But … you don't like whisky."

I was surprised he'd remembered. "I'd like to give it another try. Whisky, please."

The lonely soldier from yesterday took the seat beside me, sitting down with a laborious *umph* from having to swing his wounded leg around.

"Suit yourself, but just for the record, I don't think you'll like it today if you didn't like it yesterday." He poured me a glass after serving the soldier a half-liter of beer, then left us alone, walking off to somewhere in the back unseen.

I held my face, elbows on the bar, trying to digest the day. I tipped back my glass and immediately regretted it. "God!" I hissed, feeling the burn of the alcohol as it slid down my throat.

The soldier chuckled, watching.

"Feels like I drank fire. Does it ever stop?" I sucked in some air through my teeth, wincing.

"Yes. But only after a few more slogs." He motioned to the bottle for me to help myself, but I couldn't bring myself to.

"I should have listened to the bartender." I held out my

hand for a shake and introduced myself by my German name. "Hannah."

To my surprise, he shook it. "Gunther." His palm was weathered and cold with a thousand little cuts along his fingers.

"Come here often?" I asked because it was the only thing I thought about asking.

He turned toward me. It was the first time I saw his face and not just his profile. Sandy-colored eyebrows, hazel eyes, and in need of a shave. "You're the only one who's tried to talk to me in three days, aside from the bartender."

"Well, you're a little hard to approach," I said.

"Me?" He seemed genuinely surprised I'd think that, then relented. "I've had some bad luck. I guess it shows."

"Has sitting at the bar helped?"

"A little." He paused, taking time to drink his beer. "I'm wiser because of it. Sit around this bar long enough, and you'll be wiser, too."

"In what way?"

He looked toward the restaurant, then out into the lobby where the desk clerk and the housekeeper were talking, him leaning into her ear, brushing her hair away, which looked odd at first glance. "Well, for example, that desk clerk out there."

"I see him."

"Looks like he's having a conversation with the housekeeper, but they're having a lover's spat. They've been lovers for weeks."

"Really?" I should have suspected it with how close they were talking, too close for work acquaintances.

"You don't believe me?"

"I didn't say that."

"Go ahead, try me with something else. Take your pick. From the lobby to the restaurant."

The dinner rush was more of a trickle, and nobody looked interesting enough to ask about. "What about him?" The bartender had come out from the back and was talking to the restaurant hostess.

"He knows more than your priest, but he keeps his mouth shut unless you invite the conversation. Then he blathers on until the end of time. Talks too much for his own good, if you ask me."

"Knows as much as my priest…" I repeated because it was a tantalizing admission. "I know the type," I said, thinking of Jim in Records back at Grosvenor Square.

"He likes you, by the way. The desk clerk made a comment about your backside earlier today, and he said you were a good German and to leave you alone. This bartender doesn't say that about many people."

I blinked. "The bartender said that? About me?"

He nodded, taking another drink. "Go ahead, try me again."

"All right." I looked around the room, my back and elbows on the bar.

Two elegantly dressed women walked in and took a seat in the shadowy back, in a booth meant for three. Thick heels and crepe dresses with fur collars—too sophisticated for a place like this, even for the restaurant. One had pink rhinestone earrings, and normally, I wouldn't take a second glance, but she was making a fuss about her hat covering them.

I was still looking when Engle walked in behind them, standing in between the French doors, adjusting his cuffs.

"Know anything about him?" I grumbled, turning my back

on Engle as he followed the women. I certainly didn't expect Gunther to answer, but he leaned into my ear.

"Whispering about an SS officer behind his back is dangerous." He set his glass mug down and motioned for the bartender. "But talking about Joseph Engle is suicide."

He paid for both our tabs, then got up and left in the swiftest way he could with his wounded leg thumping against the floor on his way out.

"Gunther, wait," I said, but I wasn't sure what else I'd say. "Sorry" came to mind.

The bartender counted out his change. "You two are friends?"

"He's polite." I watched Gunther on the pavement through the windows. "A gentleman, which is hard to find in Füssen." Darkness had settled between the buildings, causing me to lose sight of him once he crossed the street. That was the second time I'd seen him leave the property in that direction. "He's not staying at the hotel?"

The bartender ticked his tongue. "And stay in the room that was meant for him and his wife?" He shook his head. "No, I suppose that was too much for him. He rented a flat nearby, keeps to himself mostly. Always here early, and then usually leaves when you-know-who arrives." His eyes flicked to Engle.

"Do you blame him?" I asked.

"Can't say I do."

The violinist started his set on the other side of the drapes, filling the room with a sweet sound, but was eclipsed by Engle's boisterous laugh and the women's obnoxious giggles.

The sound of him enjoying himself made my skin crawl.

I thought about my grandfather, who deserved to be here. The only thing worse than a tyrannical leader is a person who watches and does nothing, he told me the last time I saw him, almost preemptively explaining the reasons for his arrest, which came a year later. And here I was in the same room with the man who murdered him, and all I was doing was listening.

The clink of toasts came from Engle's table and more flirty laughs. I said goodbye to the bartender and left, unable to stand it any longer, only I ran into Pudge in the lobby. "What are you doing back?"

She showed me the hanky in her pocket, which she'd dropped and had to come back to find. "But I'm glad I found you. I have…" She glanced at the front desk clerk, who was busy with the housekeeper. "I can't stop thinking about what Dot said—going back in time and doing things differently."

"Shh—" I ushered her into the long hallway that led to the stairs behind the biergarten. The walls were thin enough to hear some light chatter from the booths and music from the violinist, masking our conversation.

"What are you saying?"

Laughter erupted on the other side of the wall, eclipsing the violinist. They sounded drunk. A man and a woman, I knew that much. It was probably Engle.

"I don't know what I'm saying," she said. "I don't know what to do. All I know is that we had an opportunity to ask questions, and we didn't."

"I'd give anything to know where he lives," I said. "Hand that information over to the OSS. I wish I'd paid attention more to what he and Ava were talking about up in the front."

"That's another thing. What if Ava really is in cahoots with Engle? Dot thinks so. Don't we have a duty to find out?"

We did have a duty to find out. There was only one problem: if Engle grew suspicious of us, then Cora Hughes would be the least of our problems, knowing his reputation. We really would be hanging in the square by week's end.

"We need to keep our eyes and ears open in regard to them. We should at least do that."

"Agreed." She turned, leaving me in the hallway.

The violinist had changed to a piano ensemble with a singer, and she was encouraging people to come dance. Then I heard Engle. I was sure it was him because his laugh echoed through the wall in a way that was both irritating and intimidating. He'd asked a woman for a dance, and when he mentioned her sparkling earrings, I pressed my ear to the wall for a listen.

"I haven't spoken to her," I heard the woman say, clearly as part of a previous conversation. "But you have? What on earth about?"

I pressed my ear even harder to the wall, only now the singer was talking to the pianist about the beat and what song to play next. I waited patiently, eyes searching the ceiling as if that would help discern between voices.

"You know I can't tell you," he said.

"I don't understand. Why so much secrecy about Ava?" she asked. "Can't you tell me that?"

I covered my mouth. *My God*. Dot might be right.

The music started up at the same time footsteps padded down the stairs. I hurriedly pretended to be looking for something in my handbag, back to the wall.

"You again?" a man asked.

I looked up, and my stomach dropped. That soldier Hans had directed to our blanket, only now he was standing in front of me, and we were alone.

My instant reaction was to lie, play dumb. "Me?" I touched

my chest with one hand. "You must have the wrong person." I went back to my handbag, but he walked closer. So close, the tips of his shoes were nearly touching mine. I smelled his cologne. Musky, with the scent of whisky from drinking.

"From the Lech, no?" He dug into his pocket and pulled out a paper heart, smiling like a child with a shiny penny but with bloodshot eyes. I heard Engle's voice again, now much closer to the wall. I found myself competing to hear his voice over my own as I argued with the soldier.

"Today? No—"

He reached up and swept a lock of hair from my eyes.

I gulped. I could either run up the stairs, down the hall, and back to the bar where I'd come from, or give him what he wanted and buy myself a few more seconds listening to Engle on the dancefloor.

The woman giggled at something Engle said, and something inside of me clicked. I smiled, taking control of the situation in a way I hadn't when I was on the blanket with Hans.

He handed me his flyer, as if that was what he was told to do.

"Yes. It was me." I smiled slyly, stuffing the flyer away. "Good to see you again." I reached up, grabbing him by a tuft of hair and pulling him close to me for a kiss no other woman could match.

He was probably eighteen, though he looked and felt like a man much older, making groaning noises you'd usually make in private. His hands felt their way up my hips to my waist, then to my chest. I saw where this was going, so I turned him around and had him put his back to the wall.

He pulled his lips away. "What's your name?" He looked dreamily into my eyes, slightly out of breath.

"Be quiet," I rasped before kissing him again, but this time with my eyes open, listening to Engle give the woman a twirl as she laughed and laughed, just like he'd made Junie laugh. I thought I heard something about a parachute, but I couldn't be sure. Parachute and umbrella sounded the same in German with the wall muffling his speech.

"Does this have something to do with the dogs barking in the hills?" the woman asked, then the rest was inaudible other than something about a meeting.

Dogs? Who is he meeting? Ava?

The music ended, and so did the dancefloor chatter.

I pulled away from the soldier while still in deep reflection.

"Where are you going?" He puckered his wet lips, and when that didn't work, his hands tightened around my waist, one reaching to lift up my skirt. "We're not done."

"I'm tired." I wiped my mouth. "And my boyfriend is coming back any second." I pushed him away with both hands to his chest.

"So, that's all?" He looked shocked, and when I nodded, he straightened his jacket in a huff. "Hans was right. You are different, not like the lonely women near the line."

"What line?" I asked.

"The Gustav Line, of course."

It took me a second to realize what he was talking about—the last mission. "How different?"

"If you see Francesca, tell her I said hello." He lifted his chin. "She had a very soft bed."

Francesca from the villa?

"If you're not going to follow your own flyer, why be here?"

I blinked, digging my hand into my pocket for his flyer, then hastily unfolding it for a read once he was gone, immediately noticing it was different from the flyer Cora had showed us in Rome.

Dear frontline soldier!

When will you have leave again?

When will you be able to forget your arduous soldier's duties for a while? We at home know of your heroic struggle. We understand that even the bravest get tired sometimes and need a soft pillow, tenderness, and healthy enjoyment.

WE ARE WAITING FOR YOU:

For you who must spend your leave in a foreign town; for you whom the war has deprived of a home; for you who is alone in the world without a wife, fiancée, or a flirt.

WE ARE WAITING FOR YOU:

Cut our symbol from this letter. In every coffee shop, in every bar and railway station, pin it to your lapel so that it can be clearly seen. A member of our association will soon contact you. The dreams you had at the front, and the longings of your lonely nights, will be fulfilled. We want you, not your money. There are members everywhere because we women understand our duties to the

HOMELAND AND TO ITS DEFENDERS. THE LEAGUE OF LONELY WAR WOMEN IS HERE FOR YOU.

WE, OF COURSE, ARE SELFISH, TOO. WE HAVE BEEN SEPARATED FROM OUR MEN FOR MANY YEARS. NO INHIBITIONS NOW: YOUR WIFE, SISTER, OR LOVER IS ONE OF US AS WELL. WE THINK OF YOU AND GERMANY'S FUTURE. THAT WHICH RESTS, RUSTS.

THE ASSOCIATION OF THE LEAGUE OF LONELY WAR WOMEN

My God, Babs was right. We were expected to sleep with them.

The piano player announced he was taking a break since the dancefloor had cleared out. I shoved the flyer away. *Damn it.* They left. I raced upstairs to see if I could catch them leaving from the privacy of my room and find out if they were indeed going to Ava's. Junie answered the door dressed in the frilly nightgown she had bought from Frau Schneider.

"I was starting to worry—"

I walked briskly to the window where I pressed my face to the glass, looking for signs of Engle walking across the street, but I saw his parked car instead. A valet stood watch, tossing up his keys every few minutes and looking at his watch.

Junie turned on the radio for noise. "What's going on?"

I flicked off the lamp, reducing the reflection in the window. The evening hour brought in a misting of rain, darkening the pavement below and spattering on the glass. "I'm looking for Engle," I said because it was true.

"Why?"

"There. See his car?" I pointed to the street, and she backed away when she saw the sleek lines of Engle's black Mercedes 770. "He was downstairs again." I looked up and down the street with my nose pressed to the glass. "I swear I heard him talking about Ava as if he knew her."

"Oh, no. We're not back to Ava and coincidences, are we?"

I braced the window ledge, rethinking today, in his car, and even in the biergarten the night before, for anything I'd missed between him and Ava. I whipped around. Junie had talked to him at length.

"Junie. When you talked, was he…" I wasn't sure what I was searching for, but if anyone could answer some questions, it was her. "Cordial?"

"He was charming." Junie turned for her bed.

"Did he mention Ava?"

"I don't like it when you talk like this."

"Talk like what?"

She pulled back the covers. "You know," Junie said, climbing into bed. "Crazy. It's because of Babs and Kitty, isn't it? You think they are gathering separate intelligence because of who they were with. Trust me, they aren't. It's too dangerous. They are good analysts, and as much as we don't like them, they are smart enough to know it."

"I'm just being cautious," I said to put her mind at ease. "I know you think Ava is sincere, but I want to make sure she and that SS officer don't have some kind of an agreement between them."

"Cautious or digging up bones?" She sat bolt upright in bed. "This better not be an effort to get ahead of Babs and Kitty. It could get us killed. It's not just you on this mission."

"I know, Junie. I know—"

She pulled the radio's electrical cord from the wall, and all turned quiet. "Get some sleep."

I turned around, waiting to see if Engle would come walking out of the hotel for Ava's apartment, like I suspected. Or maybe he was already inside? His car was still parked, and the valet was still playing with the keys. Back and forth my eyes traveled, second by second, when something caught my eye in the dark recesses of the balcony below Ava's apartment. The burning cigarette of someone else who was also silently watching Engle's car.

Ava said that the apartment was vacant. I whispered for Junie, but she was dead to the world with the covers thrown over her head. "Hey ... there's someone in the apartment below Ava's," I said anyway, but now the light had flicked on in Ava's apartment.

Her curtains were closed like she'd always had them, but I could see two shadows walking the room through the narrow curtain gap, growing larger the closer they moved toward the lamp near the window, then smaller once they returned to the door. I could barely make out Ava's blonde hair at times. Looked like one handed the other something, maybe a paper, maybe notes on us, or perhaps a payment, a tip?

I clamped my hands over my mouth before turning and rasping for Junie, but she'd thrown her pillow over her head. "I'm serious." I tried tugging her hand to get her to move. "You have to look!"

By the time I turned back around, Ava's apartment was dark and Engle's car had disappeared.

Chapter Eleven

I woke from a nightmare the next morning, panting, sweaty, and holding my chest. Junie was already up and buttoning her dress. "What's wrong with you?" she asked, giving me a suspicious side-eye.

"I … ahh…" I pulled back the covers for some air, closing my eyes.

Engle was leading a death march, and my grandfather was on his knees after having fallen in the snow, hungry and weak, begging to be set free. Engle, dressed in a pressed SS uniform, flicked a lit cigarette at him, and while he laughed at my grandfather from the back of his throat, he suddenly turned and looked directly at me as if I were a voyeur and asked, "How was the soldier you tasted?"

My eyes popped open.

"Viv?"

I was still breathing heavily and took a second to collect myself. "I had a nightmare."

"About what?"

"Doesn't matter." I scrambled for the window to see if anything had changed since last night, but Ava's curtains were dark, and the apartment below looked still and empty.

"What did you want to tell me last night?"

"It's not what, Junie, but who." I turned around, bracing the window ledge behind me. "I have proof Ava lied to us."

She stopped buttoning her dress mid-button. "What do you mean 'lied'?"

I plugged in the radio for some noise. "Ava told us that the second-floor apartment was vacant. Remember? Even told you to go downstairs and open it up. It's not vacant. She has a secret renter."

Junie hadn't blinked, which made it hard for me to gauge her thoughts.

"Well, aren't you going to say something?"

Junie started buttoning again. "That doesn't make sense."

"That's what I've been trying to tell you. She had a visitor late last night, too. They were talking closely, possibly whispering, and it looked like they passed each other notes. What if it was Engle? Remember, his car was outside, and I saw him downstairs. I think I heard him talking about her as well."

"It could have been anyone in her apartment. She used to live here. It wouldn't be odd for her to receive a visitor."

"Yeah, but late at night? And it just so happens Engle was downstairs and possibly talking about her?"

"It wasn't that late. And he's always downstairs. He must be staying at the hotel. We saw him in the hallway that first day."

"Well, someone was in her apartment. And someone was below it."

Junie sighed, and I tossed my hands up and went into the bathroom to get ready, brushing my teeth vigorously, wondering what plausible explanations Ava could give that would make sense, only nothing was plausible. I let the water pour out of the tap into the drain and looked in the mirror.

Junie applied lipstick over my shoulder. "Look, Viv, I know you don't like her. I don't like her either. But it doesn't make sense for her to turn on us. You're the best analyst I know. Surely, you must see that."

I turned off the tap to fold my arms. "I'm supposed to forget about what I saw?"

"No," she said. "I know you're going to ask her about it, but do me a favor and don't do it in front of Pudge and Dot."

She meant, don't upset Ava first thing in the morning or create a scene in front of the others. I agreed, but it was only because I didn't want the locals to see—or raise suspicions about us.

We were making our way down the hallway to the elevator when I saw that soldier from last night. He motioned to his buddy, and they walked faster. I ushered Junie into the elevator and closed the door with a rapid push of the button.

"What is going on now?" she asked.

The doors closed, narrowly missing them. I only had a few seconds to spill the beans before we got to the lobby. "I should have said something on the tram, but I wasn't sure if I could trust Babs or not. Then, last night, I found something out."

She gave me a stressed look. The elevator passed the first floor and was now headed toward the lobby. She motioned for me to spit it out.

"Cora told them they'd be expected to sleep with the Germans as part of the mission."

"Babs told you this? I don't believe it." She shook her head. "She's lying."

"That's what I originally thought, but now there's something else." I pulled the flyer from my pocket. "I had an encounter with one of those soldiers who passed by us just now, and he seemed to know a lot more about the League than I did." I shoved the flyer at her.

Junie's eyes grew to the size of walnuts as she read. "'The longings of your lonely nights will be fulfilled…'" She looked up. "No inhibitions!"

"The text that was missing from the flyer she gave us is bolded on this one. Cora gave us a draft in the chapel. This is the real one."

The elevator dinged.

"Come on." I stuffed the flyer away, walking out to a lobby full of guests checking out with their luggage. The soldiers that were on our floor had come down the stairs and were clearly looking for us. We ducked outside.

"You'll show the others?"

I nodded.

"Dot, especially, will have a tough time with this."

"I know."

Pudge and Dot joined us moments later, suggesting we go to breakfast and wait for Ava there. I pulled Pudge back a step to let Junie and Dot into the restaurant first.

"I heard something last night. I think Engle went to see Ava."

Pudge's eyes widened. "Does Junie know?"

I nodded, moving out of the way for customers who were leaving.

"What did she say?" Pudge asked, but I had to wait to

answer because the waiter appeared and showed us to the back table.

"Not much," I managed to whisper.

"Not much?"

We sat down together. The waiter handed us each a menu while also announcing that they were out of most things except for eggs. We promptly handed back the menus. "Eggs it shall be," Junie said.

I felt for the flyer.

Both Pudge and Dot looked at me oddly, and rightfully so. I felt like I had a grenade in my pocket about to explode. "There's something you both need to see." I slipped the flyer across the table to Dot.

She guardedly opened it with Pudge looking on.

I folded my hands on the table, only to unfold them, waiting for a reaction.

"I knew it!" Dot shook her head, tracking every sentence with her finger as she read. "I just knew, but nobody was interested in listening to me." She glared at Pudge after pursing her mouth. "Were they?" She handed back the flyer.

Pudge was quiet as a mouse, as were we all. The eggs came and went, and after paying, we still hadn't said a word about where Ava was or what our plans with the soldiers would be like that day.

"Where is Ava?" I finally asked, breaking the silence. "What if she left us. What if—"

"She didn't," Junie said.

"Cora sent her. Need I remind you? We can't trust her," Dot said, but before any of us could respond, Ava breezed through the restaurant doors, looking like a million bucks with a clean white dress on, bright pink lipstick, and set hair.

She threw her hands up in surprise as if she'd been looking all over for us.

"We have to trust her," Junie said.

"There you are!" Ava grinned. "Ready to shop?"

Junie motioned for us to follow Ava outside. We'd talk more about the flyer later, I supposed, and about Ava. We hooked arms and walked down the street like old friends from the Faith and Beauty Society. Passersby were coming out of the woodwork with the nice weather and started to crowd the pavement, especially near the fountain in the square where chairs and a podium draped in Nazi Party flags had been set up. Some sort of concert was about to start.

Two German bombers flew over the square. "Messerschmitts," I said, then shivered from the noise. Dot discreetly covered her ears while nobody else had.

The buzz of the propellers faded over the mountains.

"We should split up. Talk to as many soldiers as we can in the square, in shops, and throughout Füssen." Ava pointed to a hat shop. "Let's start there."

Junie agreed to go with Dot this time, while Ava, Pudge, and I went into the hat shop.

Ava turned to me, grinning, when I wanted to rip into her and barrage her with questions, but I'd promised Junie I wouldn't make a scene, so I'd have to wait. I pulled open the door to a clattering song of doorbells. Ava walked in first, one hand poised in the air like a teapot spout with me and Pudge walking closely behind.

There was a slight gasp from the shop owner at the same time I elbowed Pudge.

"What is it?" she asked.

"That woman was with Engle last night."

"Are you sure?" Pudge asked.

The woman looked like she'd seen a ghost instead of Ava, her mouth hanging open and hats effortlessly slipping from her grasp to the floor, with Ava looking equally caught off guard.

"Ingrid?" Ava asked.

"Ava?" The hats were still at Ingrid's feet. "You're back." She cleared her throat after a long pause. "What a surprise."

I tried on a hat, asking Pudge how I looked, but my ears were firmly on Ava and Ingrid. Back from where? From seeing her in the apartment or back from France? Either way, she was lying because I heard her talking to Engle about Ava's return last night, so why the act?

Ava shifted one shoulder before looking distracted by a hat on a stand that wasn't her type at all. "Is this your shop?"

Pudge and I looked at each other. The tension was palpable, to the point where I decided neither had seen each other in a long time. Engle must have gone to her apartment alone last night.

They had a conversation about the weather, the hats, and how Ingrid was a shop owner—which sounded incredibly phony—before things took a different tone. Ingrid straightened. "Why are you here in Füssen?"

"I have some unsettled business."

"Oh?" Ingrid looked confused.

"My accountant has been stealing from me. I came to collect."

"All the way from France?" she asked. "I would imagine you'd be quite busy there with the invasion."

Ava scoffed. "I left France last May. I've been in Berlin mostly, where my other properties are," she said, which sounded believable, especially when Ava said it out loud and with her exaggerated hand movements. "You are looking well, Ingrid," Ava added. "Not easy to do with the rations."

Ingrid softened from the compliment and even offered to pick a hat out for Ava, free of charge, which Ava refused.

"I really shouldn't," Ava said. "Given—" She cleared her throat.

"I've moved on," Ingrid said.

"As have I."

"Good!" Ingrid said.

"Are you staying for the concert in the square? Should be a lovely—"

"I have to go." Ava was about to turn around, but Ingrid stopped her with a reach of her hand.

"I hope to see you again. We have much to catch up on. Would you like to meet later? I know a great little place we could go."

By now, Pudge and I had walked close enough to join their conversation if we wanted.

"No … no…" Ava shook her head. "I'm afraid I can't. Some other time." She looked at her watch. "Oh, I'm late for an appointment. I must be off." She rushed out under the sharp clang of bells as if we were strangers, brushing past both of us.

I stepped forward, hat in hand, while Ingrid watched Ava walk away. "I'll take this lovely hat."

"Ahh…" Ingrid pulled her attention back, scrambling to pick the hats up at her feet and trying to look in control and calm as her hands trembled. "That's wonderful. I love this shade. It's one of a kind."

In the right light, the hat took on another look. It wasn't maroon, but a strange pink color I couldn't name. "How extraordinary," I said. "I chose the right one, then. One of a kind."

"Just like you," Pudge said.

I smiled. "Just like me."

Ingrid reached for a hat box, and while her back was turned, Pudge motioned for me to say something a little more meaningful. I inched closer to the counter. "I just couldn't help but overhear. We're on holiday." I hiked my thumb to Pudge. "Did you say you know of a great little place to have a drink?"

"Yes. I do…" She glanced at the tag, suddenly looking embarrassed by the price she had to charge.

"Not a problem." I dug around in my handbag. "A treat for all the hard work I've been doing back home. Now, where is that place?"

She wrote the tally in her ledger. "The biergarten at Hotel Hirsch. Do you know it? It's not much of a biergarten, actually, more of a place to have a drink while waiting for dinner, but it's become quite the sociable spot lately."

I looked at Pudge. I had to say something.

"I'm a guest at the hotel." I snapped my fingers as if I had just recognized her. "In fact, I think I saw you there last night."

"You did?" She gently set my hat in the box and added some tissue paper.

"I can't forget those gorgeous earrings of yours."

"These?" Her hand immediately went to her ear to play with one of her rhinestone earrings. "They were a gift from a dear friend. In fact, she just left."

Ava had given her a gift, and she was still wearing them despite their apparent falling out. They'd been close once. Maybe they still were, and the entire display they put on was an act.

She handed me the box. "Have a lovely visit in Füssen. And who knows, maybe we'll bump into each other again. Perhaps at Hotel Hirsch."

I handed her more than enough reichsmarks to cover the hat and possibly even a second one, which pleased her greatly. "This is too much."

I pushed it away. "A hat as lovely as this would be worth twice as much in Munich. Keep it."

She promptly pocketed the extra. "Thank you."

I turned to Pudge once we were outside and the bells were muffled. "Ava gave her the earrings."

"Ava is full of secrets."

"We need to confront her about this," I said. "We simply can't go on this way."

We found Ava having what looked like a tense conversation with Junie and Dot by the fountain in the middle of the square. "Not here," Ava rasped, pointing to the violinists gathering in the square and those who arrived early to get a good spot. "Meet me in the park." All four of us started to follow, when she put her hand out. "Junie and Viv only, to avoid suspicion."

"What are we supposed to do?" Pudge asked. "Wait?"

Ava left like the wind, the back of her white dress bouncing off her calves and her heels clipping across the cobblestones.

"She's worried about a crowd." Junie hooked my arm. "Wait here." We left them standing by the fountain and headed to the park. Once we were clear of listeners, Junie leaned in.

"What happened in the shop?" she asked.

"Ava knew the shop owner. A woman named Ingrid, and it wasn't a pleasant reunion."

"What do you mean?"

"You should have seen it, Junes. They had daggers for each other. I've never seen anything like it."

"That would explain her aloofness. She was breathless at the fountain before you joined us, flustered in a way she's never been before and wouldn't talk."

"There's something else." I looked at her. "Remember when I said I thought I heard Engle talking about Ava in the biergarten. It was with Ingrid."

Junie looked shocked.

"I'm going to confront her. There might be a scene, Junie."

"Do your best to be discreet."

We reached the park and caught up to Ava. She led us behind one of the bushier trees for privacy. "Did you say anything to Ingrid after I left the hat shop?" she asked me.

"First, there are some things you need to answer for." I crossed my arms. "You have a tenant in the apartment below yours when you told us it was vacant."

Ava's eyes widened. "How do you—" Her lips pursed.

"We had a very private, very incriminating conversation in your third-floor apartment the other night, and all the while someone was in the apartment below?"

"Have you been spying on me?"

"Call it what you like," I said, then paused while she considered if I had spied on her. "I saw him through my window last night on the balcony. I also saw two shadows very close to each other, but that was coming from the gap between your window curtains."

She held her chin up. "That was my accountant."

"I don't know many accountants who visit their clients at night."

"You don't know my accountant," Ava said. "Besides, he

owed me money. I'd meet him at midnight if that meant I'd get the money he owed me. I told you about him already, and you heard me telling Ingrid about him."

A wind whistled through the birch trees, just brisk enough to knock a few yellowing leaves to the ground. What she said made sense if one was to look at it her way, but there were two sides to every story. "And the apartment below yours? Explain that one." I tapped my foot.

"You should be relieved it's occupied. You were worried people would wonder why I hadn't asked you to stay with me, being old friends from the Faith and Beauty Society—sisters practically, the closest three women can be in Nazi Germany. Now, the problem is solved."

"But you sent Junie to look at that apartment. Told her where to find your hidden key and have a look inside. What if she was caught?"

"I didn't know it was occupied at the time. Frau Schneider managed the building while I was away, and she allowed him to rent the room. I found out yesterday morning, on my way to breakfast. She felt sorry for him. He came here on leave to nurse a wound only to find his wife had left him for another man."

"Gunther?" I asked.

She looked surprised. "That's his name. You know him?"

"He frequents the biergarten at the hotel."

"I've never met him," Ava said. "I only know what Frau Schneider told me."

Junie turned to me. "Viv…"

Ava looked appalled all of a sudden. "And how dare you question me after that stunt yesterday."

"What stunt?" My eyes narrowed.

"Making contact with other agents right out in the open when we all told you not to."

"Viv," Junie said again.

She didn't say it out loud, but I knew Junie was questioning if I was satisfied with Ava's answers because she was.

"I've answered your questions," Ava said. "Now, answer mine. What did you say to Ingrid? You didn't tell her we were friends, did you?" She grabbed my arm and gave it a yank, which surprised me. "Did you?"

"Let go." I tried wiggling free, but her grip was fierce and left a red mark. "I didn't say much of anything. I bought a hat. And no, she doesn't know we were together."

"Good." Ava snatched the hat box from my hands.

"What are you doing?" She pulled away when I reached for the box.

"People will talk. They should think I bought something from her." A couple walked by. Ava smiled and laughed, swinging the hat box until they passed as if we were having a girly chat.

"You're worried about her—this Ingrid?" Junie asked. "Who is she?"

"We can't talk about this here," she rasped. "Too many people can see us now—hear us." She tried to walk away, but Junie pulled her back.

"No, tell us now."

Ava closed her eyes briefly, her hands curling tightly around the box's braided cord. "We were the closest of friends. She knows almost everything about me. She even visited me in France, but I had an affair with her husband."

I threw my hands up. "You had another affair?"

"Shh! Keep it down!" She looked down both ends of the

path. "That's why I wanted to carry the hat. People will think we are still friends, or at least reconciled, if she said something."

"Can't you keep your knickers on for one second?" I asked.

Ava shot me a glare.

"Does she know you were in a POW camp?" Junie asked, and with that, Ava looked unsure.

"We haven't spoken for so long. She couldn't know."

"Are you sure?" Junie asked.

Ava reluctantly shook her head.

"We should break up," Junie said. "Not see each other for a few days."

"I agree," Ava said. "If Ingrid does know about the camp, there will be signs. I'll see it in the faces at the biergarten, whispers on the street and in the shops. I'll know."

"Are you nuts?" I asked. "That biergarten is the last place you should go. We've already been seen there together. Don't come to our hotel."

She closed her eyes again. "Fine."

"Yes, conveniently keep your distance," I said flippantly. "Safe in your apartment while we mingle with the enemy."

Ava's eyes popped open. "You act as if I did this on purpose," she said. "Someday, you'll realize you had a friend in me—an ally—and when that day comes, I won't be saying I told you so."

I scoffed. "Yeah? What will you say?"

"You're welcome."

"Come on, Junie." We walked back the way we came while Ava walked toward her apartment.

I hooked Junie's arm.

"I know I said I'd drop it, but damn, Junie. Now this with Ingrid?"

We'd made it back to the square where the village was almost ready to start the outdoor concert of strings, with all the violinists in Füssen coming out for the occasion and taking their seats. A Nazi Party banner unfurled from a marquee above our heads with great fanfare.

"I believe her," Junie said. "Even after the way she acted, I can tell. Can't you?"

Pudge and Dot were waiting by the fountain. I had to come to a conclusion about Ava one way or the other, and whatever that conclusion was, I'd have to bring Pudge and Dot on board, too.

"What did she say?" Pudge asked.

"There's a story there. A long and sordid story between her and Ingrid."

"Should we be concerned?" Pudge asked.

We moved to a bench in the far corner of the square for a modicum of privacy, near a wooden pole with Hitler Youth flyers pasted to all sides. Dot crossed her arms with her back to the pole and kept a lookout for prying ears, while we huddled around and talked about Ava.

"Affairs, double-crosses, and a bad friendship describe it all," I said before going into detail and spilling all that Ava had told us. What followed was a moment of quiet, almost as if they'd expected as much, but they were also disappointed.

"I knew she was up to something," Pudge said.

"Now, wait a minute," Junie said. "It doesn't mean—"

Ingrid burst from her hat shop with a loud clang of bells, only to clip past us on cobblestones in the direction of Ava's place, head down, the "Closed" sign dangling in her front window.

"I'll bet you a fat dollar she's going to you-know-who's apartment," Dot said.

"She could be closing her shop because of the concert," Junie said.

The thought of Ava being back in town was probably grating on Ingrid's nerves since their encounter, and there'd be only one place to really have it out, really say her piece, and that would be in the privacy of Ava's apartment.

Violins were warming up, each playing a different piece from the selection. More planes flew overhead. This time, they were not in formation.

Pudge pulled me to the side. "Remember last night when we talked about opportunity? We need to know what they're talking about. What if Ingrid drops something about Engle? It's believable to think she might. Something about his past or his work?"

I gasped. "What if she mentions where Engle lives?"

"What are you whispering about?" Junie asked.

I closed my eyes briefly, then turned. "I think I should go listen. Eavesdrop on them at her apartment. I've done it a million times back at Grosvenor Square. I can do it here. It's the only way to be sure Ava is really on our side."

"How? Listen through her door in the hallway?"

There was a better way. Gunther's apartment. I didn't think I could get invited back to his place, but I did think I could sneak in. I knew where the key was.

"That soldier, Gunther…" I looked at my watch. "He's at the hotel biergarten right now. I know it. The bartender told me how often he visits, and I'd bet everything in my pocket he's on a stool drinking a half-liter of beer."

Junie folded her arms. "What if you get caught? You may have befriended Gunther to a degree, but he's still a German soldier. And if Ava catches you, she'll never trust us."

"It's a calculated risk," Pudge said to Junie. "I think she should go. We have to know."

Junie looked to Dot for her opinion. "What do you say?"

"Pudge is right. We have to know whose side she's on."

More planes, only this time the entire squadron, flying so low, there wasn't a bare ear to be had in the square, everyone trying to protect themselves from the noise as they looked toward the sky with their mouths open.

I grabbed Junie by the shoulders. "I'll be careful. I promise. If I haven't heard anything useful in the first few minutes, I'll get the hell out of there," I said, but there was no way I was going to leave if they were talking about Engle. "All right?"

She nodded once.

We walked back to Hotel Hirsch without a word passing between us. The street traffic had thickened, most on their way to the square for the concert, while the others, mostly soldiers, were headed to the beer halls for day drinking.

I unhooked my arm from Junie's, turning toward Ava's apartment building while she walked straight ahead to the hotel with Pudge and Dot.

Now was my chance.

Chapter Twelve

I snuck up the stairwell of Ava's building, first taking my shoes off to muffle my steps and being careful not to touch the broken handrail. Didn't take long before I heard the mumblings of a conversation coming from above. My heart thumped wildly. I'd never broken into someone's apartment before, and what if Gunther decided to leave the biergarten early? I shut my eyes, chastising myself for worrying about that—I didn't have time, and it was too late.

I snatched the key above Gunther's door and let myself inside. The apartment didn't have much furniture other than a simple bed, a Wehrmacht rucksack on the floor, a desk, and gobs of paintings on the wall, all reproductions similar to the ones Ava had upstairs, including a duplicate of *The Reckoning* by Duval that she had hanging next to her bathroom.

I listened carefully, but they were still dancing around what had got them so upset, talking about the weather and the soldiers. I inched closer, following their voices with my eyes to the ceiling, when I bumped into a desk. Papers cascaded off, falling to the floor. Handwritten letters, from what I could tell.

"What are you really doing here, Ingrid?" I heard, which redirected my attention.

I moved the desk chair to stand on, carefully lifting it away to place next to the wall, and put my ear to the plaster where the echo of their voices was amplified.

"I want to know why you're back," Ingrid said. "In Füssen."

"I already told you. People owe me money, and I've come to collect. Surely, you can understand—"

"I don't believe you," Ingrid said. "You have plenty of money. Why here, why now when you have the whole of Germany?"

There was a pause, and for a moment, I wondered if Ava was going to tell her the truth. The chair wobbled, making me unsteady when I pressed my ear to the plaster just a little harder.

"Why do you think I'm here?" Ava asked.

I knew Ingrid had walked to the window because I heard Ava ask her not to open the curtains. Ingrid mumbled something.

"I can't hear you," Ava said.

"There's buzz within circles," she said clearly. "I heard it myself last night from an officer of the Reich."

"What kind of buzz?" Ava asked.

"Whispers of a spy among us. In the village. In Füssen."

"You think I'm a spy?" Ava laughed heartily. "I gave up being a spy when you did, deary."

My mouth hung open. Ava wasn't just worried about

Ingrid. Ingrid was worried about Ava keeping her secret! That explained the urgency. *That's why she's here.*

"When did you leave France?" Ingrid asked.

"After you," Ava shot back, and just as quickly. "I realized my future was in Germany after my husband was killed. This is where my properties are, my wealth. Plus, it was too dangerous. Sorry about your husband, but he was only a husband on paper, wasn't he?"

"I cared for him," Ingrid said.

"As I cared for mine, to an extent." Ava offered Ingrid a cigarette, but she declined, which meant Ingrid wasn't planning on staying much longer.

The chair squeaked from being unbalanced.

"Now, what do we do?" Ingrid asked. "I heard you are in town with some friends. Is that true?"

"I'm here alone. Doesn't mean I haven't bumped into a few friends since I've been here. Why does that matter?"

"I told you there's talk about a spy, but the newest information is that there might be more than one."

"Who told you this?" Ava laughed again. "I honestly thought you were joking. Of all places! Füssen is hardly Berlin, Ingrid."

"Joseph Engle told me," she said, and I closed my eyes. "He's become a close friend. Do you know him?"

Ava paused. "I've heard of him. He is from Füssen?"

"No," she said.

I waited breathlessly for her to say where he came from and, more importantly, where he was living now, but she switched back to talking about spies. "The Abwehr's dogs found something in the forest. Parachutes, from what I understand."

My hands clamped over my mouth with that, and now the chair was rocking back and forth. I caught myself on the desk, making a slight noise, but not enough to bother them.

"I thought those parachutes might have something to do with you, Ava. Do they?"

"You think I parachuted into Füssen?" Ava laughed again, only this time deep from her throat. "Oh, Ingrid, you really do have an imagination."

Ava was handling her questions well, but I just wanted them to get back to talking about Engle.

"Ava, I'm going to be blunt… Is my secret safe with you?"

"As safe as my secret is with you, I suppose. I have to trust that you're not going to tell your friend Joseph Engle about my past."

"He's gone. I don't know when I'll see him next."

Engle is gone?

"Well, once my affairs are settled in a few days, I will leave as well," Ava said. "Then we most likely won't see each other again."

Ingrid walked to the door. "We were friends once, Ava. I'd like to think—"

"We are still friends, Ingrid. You are wearing the rhinestone earrings I gave you, are you not?"

"I suppose I am."

"We were caught up in a war where we did what we had to do at the time, didn't we?"

"So that is all, then?" Ingrid asked.

"Yes. I'm satisfied. Are you?"

"Yes."

Ava's door opened and closed, followed by the rapid click of Ingrid's heels down the stairwell.

I knew I'd find out something, but that was a lot to unpack. They were both spies, and both had motives to get the other arrested or, at the very least, to disappear. And Engle. Damn, I was so close to finding out more about him, too.

I put the chair back and quickly gathered Gunther's letters off the floor before leaving. They were from his wife. Her name was Marlene, and she'd been waiting for him, just like the bartender had told me.

She'd heard about the League of Lonely War Women and accused him of finding one of his own for comfort. She'd met Engle in the hotel restaurant. He was attentive, charming, and understanding. After a passionate three-day love affair, she went back home with a promise from Engle that he'd call for her after the war. Gunther had no illusions about Engle; he'd watched him in the restaurant long enough to know he'd used his wife and wouldn't be calling. But no amount of letter writing would convince her that Engle was a womanizer. In the end, she asked for a divorce.

I abandoned the letters for a notebook, something with worn edges and ink-blotted pages. A twist of the locked doorknob startled me, and I dropped it, making a loud clack on the floor.

"Hallo?" It was Ava. "Someone in there?"

I set the notebook back on the desk. My heart was pounding. *Boom, boom, boom*. She tried the doorknob again, and my hand went to my pocket. Oh, the relief I felt from having the spare key. I was safe, but then I heard Frau Schneider call out to her in the hallway, where they had a chat that ended with Ava asking for the other set of spare keys.

My stomach dropped.

"The one that's usually above the door seems to be

missing," Ava added. "And I heard a noise. A squeaking noise, it sounded like, followed by something hitting the floor. I'm sure it's nothing, but I want to make sure it's just the one tenant inside."

"I understand, and I do have that key right here..." I heard, followed by a jingle of keys.

I panicked, tiptoeing to a storage closet just as I heard a key slide into the lock. I tucked myself in between Ava's mothy spare coats.

The front door cracked open, and then silence, a crackling quietness where the slightest movement felt like an explosion of noise. I squeezed my eyes closed, clutching my handbag.

"What is it?" Frau Schneider had followed her inside.

"I clearly heard a noise." It sounded like Ava had walked to the middle of the apartment only to stand in place. "And you are sure he doesn't have a guest staying with him?"

"I told him no visitors."

There was a pause, as if Ava was listening to see if she could hear movement, or maybe she was looking at the mess of letters.

"My imagination must be getting the better of me. Now, was there something you wanted, Frau Schneider?"

"I wanted to thank you for Klara's documents," she said, which Ava shushed her for speaking about.

"No need to talk about this out loud."

"I thought we'd be safe up here. That's why I'm mentioning it. I owe you, for what it is worth. Nobody has questioned her legality. But if they do, at least I have documents that don't say she's Jewish. You really are a magician."

Documents? How did she have time to get documents? The accountant. Of course, that's why he visited her so late. Frau Schneider was right. Ava was a magician.

"And her parents are dead, you said?" Ava asked.

"One can only assume."

"Her father was my estate agent years ago. It's the least I can do."

They walked back into the hallway, where their voices turned muffled after softly closing the door. "And about the rental. I wanted you to make money from the apartment. Again, sorry about your friends. They bought several items from me the other day, so I feel awful about the situation, but I'd already rented it to that poor soldier by the time I talked to you. I hope they understand—"

"Yes, they understand," Ava said. "Thank you, Frau Schneider. But please, don't rent the apartment after he leaves. I am entrusting you. I want my things exactly as they are when I return. From my paintings to my other furnishings, they are a comfort to me in this changing world."

I stepped out of the closet, hearing them a little clearer.

"Are you leaving again?" Frau Schneider asked. "You just got here."

"I need you to make sure the doors to the back of the building are locked at all times. I had an unexpected visitor just now, and I don't like surprises. At least when people enter from the street out front, I can hear them."

A knock from somewhere got both of their attention. "That's the repairman for the handrail," Frau Schneider said.

"Now?"

"You asked me to find someone as soon as possible."

Ava sighed. "Yes, yes. I did ask you. My friend had a near fall, or she thought she had a near fall. Anyway, make sure he works quickly." What followed was the repairman talking in the hallway and Ava's footsteps running upstairs and closing her door.

I made fists. I was the friend. I thought maybe I'd slip out anyway. The repairman wouldn't know who I was. Or that I wasn't supposed to be there. I got ready to escape, hand on the doorknob.

"You don't mind if I watch, do you?" Frau Schneider asked. "In case it comes loose again, I'll know how to fix it."

I hung my head. I wasn't going anywhere anytime soon.

I peeked out the window curtains and kept an eye out for Gunther while I waited, then decided to flip through that notebook. I thought it was going to be more of the same, notes to his wife. Love letters and passages, but I quickly realized the notebook wasn't just any old notebook, but in fact, a dossier on Engle that contained the most comprehensive, detailed notes on any subject I'd ever seen outside the records room in London.

My heart beat a little faster.

I knew it was him because of how Gunther described his car, where he drank, and the women he was keeping company with. Ingrid was at the top. There were notes on where he thought he was living, but the notes were in some kind of code, probably to keep it a mystery in case the notebook was found. In the back, Gunther had a list of sources as if he were a correspondent and preparing a big story. But this kind of story would get him hung from the nearest lamp post once he attached it to a name.

"Gunther," I breathed. He surprised me.

The repairman had finished, and after Frau Schneider paid him, the stairwell grew increasingly quiet. I decided to take the notebook with me, bring it back to the OSS, and made haste for the door.

My heart was racing from having such information in my handbag, then nearly flew out of my chest when I heard the tramp of jackboots coming toward me upstairs. Frau Schneider shrieked, asking why the Abwehr was there. "What do you want?" she cried.

I crouched next to the door, swiftly curling into a ball in the corner.

"Where's Ava?" one shouted shortly before bypassing Gunther's door for the next floor up. A series of kicks to her door followed, then trampled steps from her kitchen to the window, calling for Ava to come out of her hiding spot.

"You are being charged with treason…" I heard echoing through the walls.

I slipped out, running down the stairs so fast that I nearly twisted my ankle. People had gathered to watch, see who they were going to drag outside by the hair, so I slipped through the interior door that led into Frau Schneider's shop, spying her frantically pacing with a distraught and tearful Klara at her side.

I calmly walked between the dress racks. "Good day, Frau Schneider," I said as if it were any other day.

I don't remember crossing the road, but I do remember entering the hotel lobby. Chatter from arriving guests about bags, trains, and timetables had given way to conversations about the commotion across the street.

I pulled the lacy collar away from my neck, feeling dizzy and flush, looking for Junie, then Pudge, or even Dot, but they were nowhere to be found. *But I made it back,* I thought, eyes closed and taking a breath. I fingered the notebook in my handbag. Nobody had caught me.

Through the biergarten doors, I saw Gunther's beer on the bar, his stool pushed back, and the bartender calmly cleaning a glass. The only thing that would pry Gunther from his stool was Engle or the sudden appearance of the Abwehr, I imagined, especially if he thought they were searching his apartment and not Ava's.

If my heart was pounding before, it was nearly jumping out of my chest now.

I turned, walking up to the bartender. Beer suds slipped down the inside of Gunther's glass from taking a sip not long ago.

Soldiers crowded around the windows to look across the street. "Who is it this time?" I heard, followed by, "Hang her in the square!"

"Where's Gunther?" I asked the bartender quietly.

He paused, looking at the soldiers, then glancing to the back behind the bar. "Follow the hallway all the way down. Better hurry."

I ducked behind the bar and down the hallway, where a cool alley breeze whistled through a half-open door. I burst outside just in time to see Gunther lumbering away on his injured leg, head down, hands in his pockets. "Wait!"

He was a little horrified to see me running after him. "What are you doing?" He took a guarded look behind me as I caught my breath.

There was no time to act coy. I didn't have time to spare, and neither did he.

"I know you have information on Engle. I want to expose

him." His eyes bulged. "I want him dead," I added because only someone who would risk their life would say such a thing about an SS officer. "Tell me... He's elusive, why? Where does he go at night? Where does he live?"

I could tell he was struggling by the way his eyes strained.

"Please," I said, but that wasn't enough because he shook his head. I had to tell him more, something earth-shattering. "I found your notebook. But that's not why the Abwehr are in the apartment you rented. You heard something you weren't supposed to?" He shook his head. "You stole something—"

The light changed in his eyes. That was it. He'd stolen something—something he'd want back, something the Abwehr was willing to conduct a raid for.

"Who are you?" He dropped his hands, but it wasn't out of curiosity. He looked scared.

"I'm your friend. Trust me. You have proof of something?"

"It's too dangerous," he said, trying to turn away, but I pulled him back.

"I'll scream if you don't tell me," I said, hands clenching his jacket. It was an empty threat, but he didn't know that, and I had to pretend I was serious. I took an inhaling breath. "I said I'll—"

"It doesn't matter now because I can't go back. It's too dangerous."

I gulped. "I can."

His eyes skirted over my shoulder to the door I'd just come out of. "Someone can hear us."

"No, nobody can hear," I tried not to sound desperate, but it was nearly impossible. "We're alone."

He closed his eyes briefly. "It's behind the big painting. After the war, it'll be all you need for an international court trial, which is sure to come." I released my hands from his jacket, but instead of walking away, he wrapped his strong arms around me and squeezed. "Be careful." Then he was gone, walking the length of the alley and disappearing into the foot traffic.

I stumbled backward a few steps before turning around and doing my best to act normal, slipping through the biergarten's back door and passing through the lobby. I didn't know where Pudge, Dot, and Junie came from, but they appeared and followed me into the elevator.

I closed my eyes, head thrown back. *He hid something behind Ava's painting. My God. My God...*

Junie pushed the button to go up. "You've been gone for over an hour," she rasped as the elevator squealed its way up through the floors. "And the Abwehr... What happened?"

I clutched my chest. "Not here."

Inside the room, Junie snapped at everyone to get under the bed covers to conceal our voices even more after turning on the radio. "Well?" Our breath was warm, and our faces were close. "So help me, Viv. If you don't spill—"

"Ingrid accused Ava of being a spy," I blurted. "But that's not the worst part. The Reich found our parachutes, and they're searching for us. I heard them arresting Ava moments ago."

Junie gasped. Pudge and Dot covered their mouths.

"Do they know who we are?" Junie whispered.

I bit my thumbnail. "They will soon, that's my guess." I was waiting for Junie to say we had to flee, take the first train out of Füssen, but there were two problems: we needed Ava's help to escape—she was our way out—and I wasn't leaving until I found what Gunther had hidden behind her painting.

"When does the next train leave?" Junie asked.

"How can we get back to Rome, or France for that matter, without knowing a safe route?" Pudge asked.

"We'll have to find a way through Switzerland," Junie said. "There are hidden routes, and ones that cross the Rhine to France. You've read the reports, they do exist. We just have to be smarter than the Germans."

"A train to nowhere feels like a better option than staying," Dot said.

I had moved on from my thumbnail to my fingernail after biting it to a nub. How was I going to get across the street without anyone noticing, much less Junie?

"Viv?" Junie asked.

I looked up, nail between my teeth.

"What's in your handbag?" she asked, and my hand immediately went to the bulky part where I had the notebook stashed. "Did you take something from Ava's apartment?"

"No." I turned into the blanket, digging into my handbag. "But I think I have a timetable in here somewhere…" After searching for a few seconds, I shrugged. "I don't have one."

Junie tossed the bed covers off and stared at me for a moment before calling Dot to the window. They whispered over the road noise. I heard something about leaving on the midnight train, or maybe it was the morning train. Pudge thought there wasn't a train at all except to the front lines, through Austria.

Junie turned off the radio. "We're going to get a drink," she said, leaving with Dot, which we understood to mean they were going downstairs to hear what the news was from across the street and to find a train schedule.

Pudge confronted me after the door closed, whispering in my ear. "What are you hiding?"

"You better sit for this," I said.

She sat down next to me on the bed with her hands bracing her knees. I pulled the notebook from my handbag.

"A journal?" She thumbed through the pages.

I whispered into her ear. "His wife left him for Engle, and he wanted revenge. All of Engle's comings and goings, theories of where he lives … and code. He'd only write in code if it was something that could get him hung."

"This is golden," she whispered back, then mouthed the rest. "The OSS will love it."

"Yeah," I breathed. "But there's something else. Something … big." I turned the radio back on.

Pudge threw the covers back over us.

"He hid something behind one of Ava's paintings."

She didn't blink for several seconds. "How do you know?"

"I chased him down in the alley and asked the right questions. The opportunity presented itself, and I didn't have anything to lose. He thought the Abwehr were looking for him on account of it, and he was fleeing."

She was at a loss for words. "Well, what did he hide?" she finally asked.

"I don't know. Something he stole. Something valuable enough to get arrested by the Abwehr. He said it would be all the proof an international court would need to prove his identity and guilt. But I was there, Pudge. They went up to Ava's apartment to arrest her, not him. So, it's still there, whatever it is, waiting to be uncovered, hidden behind one of Ava's god-awful paintings. It must go hand in hand with what's in this notebook."

She gasped. "What are we going to do? We're going to leave soon. Maybe as soon as the girls come back."

"We have to find a way into that apartment."

"And how are we going to do that? Even if we did manage an excuse, the Abwehr are swarming the whole building."

We tossed the blanket off to look out the window. There were two Abwehr cars still parked below, and the crowds had dispersed. Frau Schneider was talking to an officer on her front step, shaking her head. Klara was sweeping and looking unassuming.

We both heard footsteps in the hallway, and it wasn't Junie or Dot by the sound of them. We huddled under the bed covers again, whispering.

I cupped my hand to keep my voice extra low. "We'll have to wait until the Abwehr leave."

"And delay our escape?" Pudge whispered back. "The girls will never agree to that."

I snapped my fingers. "My hat. It's a liability being over there, if they didn't find it already. I can make a case to get it back. God, that's it. That's how!"

"Does it really matter now about the hat?"

"It will have to, and Junie will smell a rat if I push the subject. She just will. You'll have to insist it's what needs to be done."

She sighed, but my heart was speeding up, because I didn't know how much time we had left to discuss it with Junie and Dot away. I pulled the blanket away to take a few fresh breaths, then slid back under. "Will you do it?" I asked. "This is our last chance to dig up some bones on Engle. Whatever Gunther has, it's big. You know this—"

"Aren't you worried about getting caught?"

"We'll never get this chance back." I squeezed her arm. "Pudge, this is—"

"I know!" Pudge rasped. "We need in, if it's the last thing we do in Füssen."

She threw off the covers, and we stared out the window toward Gunther's apartment.

Chapter Thirteen

We waited for Junie and Dot to come back. Pudge paced the small hotel room, arms folded, while I clutched my handbag on the bed, checking my watch every few seconds. They'd been gone for more than thirty minutes. One Abwehr lorry remained, parked along the curb.

I stood, hearing a noise. "Was that the elevator?"

Pudge stopped pacing. "They're back," she said, just as Junie and Dot came walking in while the radio was off, which made the noise of an opening door more jarring. "You've been gone for—"

"Shh…" Junie put a finger to her lips, first checking the street down below, then coming back to the bed and having a seat with Dot. Pudge turned the radio on, and I threw the bed covers over us.

"There's a train that leaves in an hour," Junie whispered.

Pudge and I looked at each other.

"But it's to the front lines, soldiers only."

I huffed as if it was the last thing I wanted to hear, but inside, I was relieved.

Junie checked her watch. "There are two trains that leave close to midnight, each a minute apart. One to Munich. The other will get us about ten miles from the French border."

"Munich is a death sentence. We'd never get out of Nazi Germany if we went there," I whispered.

"We can find a clandestine route across the border to France—free of document checks and soldiers—and if we can't, there's always the river," Junie whispered back.

I chewed my fingernails again, my mind drifting back toward Gunther's apartment when I should be thinking about the trains. Junie's stare lingered a little too long.

I dropped my hand, wiping my wet fingertips on my dress.

"What do you think, Dot?" Junie asked.

"It feels dangerous waiting here at the hotel. Let's leave. Doesn't matter where to."

Now was the time to bring up the hat.

I reached for my chest to act surprised. "I just remembered something." Both Dot and Junie's heads turned to face me. "The hat I bought at Ingrid's is in Ava's apartment. I must go get it just as soon as it's clear to do so. I know it's dangerous, but I'm willing to—"

Junie scoffed. "Why take the risk? We're leaving."

Pudge inched forward when I looked at her. "Because..." Pudge whispered. "Because the Germans can track us down. Don't you see? They won't think much of the hat initially until someone recognizes it as one of Ingrid's. She said it was one of a kind. That directly ties Ava and Viv together. They'll know exactly who to look for then, and will come after us, and not just in Füssen. They'll check all the train stations and roads from Bavaria to Berlin."

"Pudge is right," I said.

"Who cares about the hat?" Dot said. "We told anyone who would listen that we were old friends of hers. Faith and Beauty, remember?"

"Füssen is full of Ava's old friends, who she's been gladly talking to, and we've not made a big enough impression either way to stand out," Pudge said. "But if they find the hat, it means Ava and Viv were in contact after we left the shop, and before Ingrid made it to the apartment. And, some could say, in secret."

"Maybe she talked her way out of an arrest and is still in there," Junie said. "She's savvy and strong. Doesn't change the fact we need to leave, given they found our parachutes, but we can hope."

I threw off the bed covers for a look out the window. For a moment, I allowed myself to think that Ava had talked her way out of an arrest, until I saw that her window was open, then worse, that her curtains were fluttering against the outside of the window as if nobody was inside that apartment, despite the empty Abwehr car still parked out front. "I don't think so."

"Did anyone see her being hauled away?" Junie whispered. Now, we were all at the window, trying to catch a glimpse. A delivery lorry arrived to unload in front of the hotel, providing enough rumbling engine noise to hide our voices without using the blanket. "We'll have to stay in this room until right before we leave. So that nobody sees us and asks questions."

"I agree," Dot said.

Junie started to turn for the bed, but I pulled her back when

I saw the last of the Abwehr leave. "I can sneak over there now and get the hat," I whispered. "Nobody will know."

The lorry drove away, and we had to huddle again. "We settled this, Viv," she said, once under the bed covers.

"I didn't settle it." My eyes flicked to Pudge. "You agree with me, don't you, Pudge?"

Dot gave Pudge a look, which gave her pause.

"I do agree it is best," she finally said. "Slip up there now while the Abwehr are gone. Just be quick."

"I don't like it, Viv. Not one bit. It stinks." Junie folded her arms. "Remember the last time you wanted to do something I knew wasn't a good idea?" She stuck her arm out of the blanket to turn the dial on the radio up just a hair more. "We almost died from a flying bomb, and if that wasn't bad enough, we almost lost our jobs. And what about what happened at the river with Babs and Kitty. If that comes back to bite us, I don't think I'll be able to forgive you. You promised me you wouldn't risk our lives for something dumb."

"This isn't dumb, and you don't have to bring all that other stuff up, either."

"Don't I?" she asked. "I feel like I have to remind you about everything."

"Think about it, Junie," Pudge said. "Once they make the connection between Ava and Viv as being more than acquaintances, they'll alert all the checkpoints and every train station in Germany. We might get away tonight, but we could get caught tomorrow."

I reached for both of her arms. "Trust me, Junie—"

"Don't!" She closed her eyes tightly. "We're not in London. This isn't a trip to the pub. This could get us all caught, when you said yourself that Ava had protected us. It's possible the hat isn't even there. But if you go looking in her apartment and the Abwehr come back, or worse, they are still there, we're done. Finished."

I folded my arms. "I feel it in my bones, Junes. I have to go."

"No, you don't have to go," she said. "Not this time."

"You talk too much, Viv," Dot said. "Just listen to your partner." Dot moved out from under the blanket to lie down on the opposite bed. "Don't go."

"Leave without me if I take too long," I whispered. "Head to the station and make a getaway." I took the bed covers off to have another look out the window, and then Pudge and Junie crawled out. A moment passed. I expected Junie to have the last word, or even Dot, but they were not engaging.

I turned off the radio, and the room turned abnormally quiet.

"Later," Pudge mouthed, but I had no intention of letting this go.

We waited hours until the sun had set behind the buildings and the air outside had turned cool. Every now and then, we would hear footsteps pass in the hallway or the elevator, which caused us to become very still.

I thought about how many seconds it would take for me to make it up the steps to Gunther's apartment door; fewer than Ava's, as it was one floor down. Maybe twenty seconds, if I took my heels off, and I'd have to take my heels off to avoid the noise. I squeezed my handbag, feeling the edge of the notebook.

"We should leave," Junie announced. "I'll tell the concierge we need a taxi to meet soldiers at a beer hall across Füssen. Once safely inside, we'll tell the driver to take us to the train station."

"That's a good idea," Dot said.

I decided that the only way to get into Gunther's apartment was to do it behind Junie's and Dot's back.

Junie whispered into my ear, "We probably shouldn't leave at the same time—wait a minute or two, all right? The noise of four people in the hallway would cause alarm at this hour. See you downstairs."

Pudge's eyes shifted to mine after the door was closed.

I bit my fingernails, then waved her over so I could whisper into her ear. "They'll leave without us if we take too long, won't they?"

"Once they figure out what we've done. Yes."

"Good. That will keep them safe in case anything happens."

We snuck out the back entrance and down the stairs to the alley where nobody could see us. On the curb, we saw Junie and Dot negotiating the cost for a ride. A few couples dribbled out of the lobby into the street, drunk from the biergarten or full from the restaurant, all looking for private time, walking down the lamplit streets of Füssen with their arms slung over each other, some singing songs.

"Let's get across," Pudge said.

I pointed to a shadowy part of the street where we could cross without anybody seeing us, especially Junie and Dot. "Take off your shoes." I hooked her arm as we stepped into the street and immediately felt the cool and damp cobblestones under my feet. "Three minutes tops in the apartment,"

I whispered. "You take one wall and look behind all the paintings. I'll take the other."

My heart pounded with every step. I looked over my shoulder just before walking into the apartment building. Junie and Dot were getting into the car. "We'd better hurry."

Inside, the building was deathly quiet. The interior door to Frau Schneider's shop was closed and dark through the glass, but most importantly, there was no sign of the Abwehr. I held my handbag close, and we ran our way up.

"Here," I whispered in the dark outside Gunther's door. The pounding in my chest was now drumming in my ears. "Remember," I said, shoving the key into the lock, "you start on one side—"

"I know!" she rasped. "We're taking too much time."

We burst into the dark apartment about as loud as two bulldogs. I was a little shocked by the lack of light—nothing from the streetlamps outside was filtering in through the loosely closed curtains, and we couldn't tell one painting from the other.

"Open the curtains," I whispered. The lamp turned on.

"Hallo, Fräulein," a voice said.

Pudge and I froze, one foot in front of the other.

Abwehr.

"Two Fräuleins, what a surprise."

My stomach sank. I had waited for the Abwehr to leave, but I did not count the officers. I looked at Pudge, but she still hadn't moved.

"Who are you?" He casually lit a cigarette.

Gunther's rucksack was still on the floor where he'd left it, and the paintings appeared undisturbed. I cleared my throat. This officer had stayed behind, but apparently had no idea what to look for, if anything. He might not even know who Gunther was.

Pudge finally moved, but only her eyes. Through the curtain split, headlamps shone on the wall from a car driving away. Junie and Dot. It was then I started thinking on my feet.

"No, who are you?" I crossed my arms. "This isn't your apartment." I took a different posture, one of defiance, cocking my head in a "how dare you" sort of look. "And what did you do with Gunther?"

His nose wrinkled. Not what he expected to hear, was my guess, because he took an incredibly long time to answer.

"Who is Gunther?" He clipped across the wood floor, hands behind his back.

I gripped my handbag a little tighter, which drew his eyes downward.

"What are you hiding?" he asked, at the same time reaching for the shoulder strap and snatching my handbag away. "What do we have here?" He pulled Gunther's book out.

"Give that back," I said, but he stepped away as I tried grabbing for it, flipping through the pages.

"What is all this writing?" His cigarette bobbed between his lips.

I huffed. "I demand to see Frau Schneider."

"You are spying on someone?" he asked, now turning the pages slowly, but my lips were sealed, at least until I'd come up with a story.

Pudge elbowed me to answer.

Footsteps pounded up the staircase. Another Abwehr officer. "Ah!" He waved the officer in. "Perhaps Officer Schmitz can get you to talk."

I turned, and my jaw dropped. He was the one I saw Babs

and Kitty with at the river. Schmitz took the notebook from the other officer. "Is this book yours?" he asked, glancing at the pages.

"It's not," I said. "It belongs to the soldier who is staying in this apartment. I was returning it."

They discussed the notebook and the apartment. From what I gathered, they only became interested in it when they found out Ava owned the building. He told Schmitz we'd snuck into the apartment and surprised him while he was having a cigarette.

"If you were returning it, then why did you sneak in?" Schmitz asked.

"Because I didn't want the soldier to know I took it." I scoffed, which might have been too much, but I had to show some confidence. "We dated for a night."

"For a night?" He smirked.

I fluffed my hair. "Yes. Does that bother you? He was obsessed with his wife's lover, and I'd had enough. I thought I'd take his notebook. It meant a lot to him for some reason, but then I decided I was being petty. I had the spare key, so I thought if I could sneak back in and return it, he wouldn't know. I also didn't want him to say I stole it. I only possessed it while I was mad at him."

He studied me.

"Frau Schneider, she rented him the room. She'll tell you all about Gunther, and that's she's seen me here."

Pudge gave me a confused look after I demanded they bring Frau Schneider upstairs but there was one thing I knew about Frau Schneider after hearing her and Ava: she loved Klara. She wouldn't have risked her life to get her phony documents if she didn't. I'd have to subtly threaten her with exposure if she didn't cover for us, all the while not alerting the officers.

Schmitz snapped for us to sit on the bed while he and the other officer talked privately in the corner. He opened the window, pointing to our hotel, then to the street.

My eyes skirted over the paintings, large ones, small ones, some with gold frames, and some with brown, and that godawful Duval painting above the desk, before coming back to Pudge. It was under one of the bigger ones, somewhere. "Trust me," I mouthed.

The officers broke apart, one leaving, hopefully to get Frau Schneider, with Officer Schmitz bending down to meet my gaze, getting so close I could smell the ale on his breath. "I recognize you from somewhere." His eyes turned beady as if trying to place me, but I knew the Abwehr enough to know that he knew exactly where he'd last seen me.

"I don't know where we could have met before."

"Where are your friends?" He looked exaggeratedly around the apartment.

"Friends?" I asked.

I heard the main door open and close down below, followed by footsteps. Sounded like three people instead of two. *He made Klara come, too.* I closed my eyes. I didn't want that.

"Oh, there they are. Your friends." He clapped once. "Come in."

I turned to look and nearly slipped off the bed. It wasn't Frau Schneider and Klara, but Junie and Dot. They didn't leave after all.

"Little whores from the river," he said. "Didn't think I'd

remember you?" He snapped for the other officer to bring Frau Schneider up.

I could see it in Junie's eyes: she wasn't just disappointed, she was livid, and also scared, albeit she held her composure very well. Dot looked more disgusted at Pudge, who looked down and away.

If only they had driven away.

I could hear Frau Schneider's voice from down below. She would be just as surprised to see us in Gunther's apartment as the Abwehr were. I decided the only way to make sure she didn't make a fuss, was to repeat something from her private conversation with Ava; it was my only leverage.

"I'm sorry," I mouthed to Junie, but she remained stoic.

Frau Schneider walked in, resisting. "It's late. After today, what is the meaning of this—" She was dragged in by the elbow, wearing her nightgown and cap.

I straightened. "Hallo, Frau Schneider."

She was so startled all she could do was blink and blink.

"There appears to be a mix-up," I said.

She pulled her elbow away from the officer to walk closer, still not saying anything, looking at Pudge, Junie, Dot, and then back to me. "What mix-up?" She played with her collar. "What's the meaning of this?"

"This notebook is Gunther's." I pointed. "They think it's mine and refuse to let me go. You've seen him with it, haven't you? I had a jealous moment and took it, but I was bringing it back..."

Junie folded her arms. Now, she knew I'd lied to her when I said I didn't take anything, and also, she knew I lied about the hat.

I kept talking. I had to keep talking.

"Now, who has egg on their face?" I pointed to myself. "Gunther must have found himself someone else to spend the night with because he's not here, yet his things are, and you know what? I'm not a magician," I said because she'd used that word when talking to Ava. "I can't make him love me. Right, Frau Schneider?" I smiled. "Not a magician."

"Is this true?" Officer Schmitz asked of her.

"I brought the spare key back." I set the key that she and Ava had been discussing on the desk. "I had it all day. You understand, right, Frau Schneider? How's Klara? I hope all this commotion didn't disturb her."

She looked stiff like a statue, cold, frozen, and stunned.

"So, again. Would you please inform these fine officers that the notebook belongs to Gunther, and if they have any questions, they should direct them to him. I was returning it."

"The notebook is Gunther's," she finally said, turning to the officers. "And if you have questions, you should talk to him."

"You've seen him with it?" he asked.

"Yes," Frau Schneider said. "He keeps it on his desk with those letters."

"If that's everything, officer. Are we free to leave?" Junie asked. "We have an evening planned at a biergarten across the square."

He folded his arms around the notebook, and it was then I realized that I'd never see that notebook again, much less know what was behind Ava's painting. "Yes, you are free."

"I'll show them out," Frau Schneider said.

My eyes danced over the paintings—which one, which one was it—when my eyes settled on the Duval painting. *The Reckoning*. That was it. *That's the one.*

Pudge pulled on my sleeve. "Come on. It's done."

We walked into the hallway. "I'm sorry," I said to Junie. She walked a little faster down the stairs to avoid me, while Dot steered clear of Pudge. At the bottom of the stairs, I turned to Frau Schneider.

"I'm sorry, Frau Schneider," I whispered. "I meant no harm."

I saw the relief on her face once she realized I had no intention of acting on my threats. She nodded once, and we broke for the road and the car that had been waiting for us.

Junie and Dot didn't say a word the entire drive to the station. I was waiting for it, though. Like a pressure cooker, the weight of the unspoken words felt like boulders on my chest and shoulders. Eventually, Dot would let Pudge have a piece of her mind, but Junie was going to let me have all of hers. I'd have to weasel my way out of this one with more than an apology and a promise.

The station was unusually crowded for so late at night, with soldiers on leave coming in from the front and dispersing aimlessly into the streets looking for women, if they didn't already have one waiting for them. With so much commotion and uniforms, documents weren't being checked thoroughly. Pudge and I walked up to the ticket window to buy tickets, while Junie and Dot stayed behind, whispering to each other.

"A sleeper car, please," I said, thinking that would give us some privacy to talk. "Four."

"Munich?"

"No," I said. "The other train." I paid for the compartment, which took every last reichsmark I had left. We started toward the platform. "They are not going to be kind," I said quietly to Pudge. "Are you ready?"

Junie and Dot walked two steps behind us.

"I don't know. Dot might never speak to me again after this stunt, much less when she finds out the breadth of our secret. She never wanted to come here to begin with." Pudge glanced once over her shoulder. "What about you?"

"Junie needed this job, and it's clear I messed things up for her." It was my turn to look over my shoulder. "She's mad. The angriest I've ever seen her."

Pudge put her arm around me. "We did what we had to do, Viv. We had orders to keep our side mission from them. We still have orders."

"We had orders not to go digging up bones, too, but that didn't stop us. We should tell them. What does it matter now?"

She tugged on my arm. "Because we don't know what Ingrid told Engle or if the Abwehr figured out who we are yet," Pudge said. "You heard about the interrogations when you were in the Corps, didn't you? They'll do whatever it takes if they think you're hiding something. The less they know, the better, just like Cora said. We're protecting them both by keeping quiet."

"As soon as we're in Rome, we're telling them everything."

"Agreed."

We found our train, one of two steaming on the tracks. I pointed to our carriage. One with big windows and hanging curtains, which Pudge immediately closed. We all sat down, Dot and Junie close and stiff.

"Sorry," I said.

Dot crossed her arms and legs tightly. "I didn't want to accept this mission. I was persuaded to come, and you put my life at unnecessary risk."

Junie inched forward in her seat. "How could you? I asked

you point blank. Did you take something? And clearly you had, though from Gunther's apartment. Why? What are you really up to, Viv?"

"I'm not up to anything."

"Oh, yeah?"

"Yeah," I said.

A few seconds passed, but now we were both crossing our legs at the knee with one foot swinging back and forth.

She scoffed. "I knew it. It's all a competition to you. Isn't it? I felt it when we saw Babs and Kitty at the river. We almost got caught back there. Killed maybe, like Ava."

"We don't know what happened to Ava," I said. "We certainly don't know whether she was killed."

Junie rolled her eyes. "It's Nazi Germany, Viv. There can be only one outcome."

"What you two did was unforgivable," Dot said. "Disregarding orders, and a competition?"

"It's not like that, Dot," I said, shaking my head.

"You mean to tell me that taking Gunther's notebook had nothing to do with Babs and Kitty? You didn't think about them the moment you slipped it into your handbag?"

I shook my head, lips pressed.

"There's still something else you're keeping from us," Junie said.

Dot looked up, and so did Pudge.

"Why did you go into that building? The hat was a cover to meddle in Gunther's apartment. What's in there? What's so important?"

I paused, collecting my words, but there was little I could say. "I'll tell you in Rome," I said through my teeth. "Not here, all right?" I gave Pudge a glance.

"You have to trust us," Pudge said, which got a scowl from Dot. "Trust Viv, at least."

"Trust Viv?" Junie turned to me. "You know what? You've changed, Viv. Since the moment we landed in that forest, you've been different. Scared, though you've never used that word, but I've seen it. Nervous. God, how you've been nervous. And for what? You know how to be German, so that's not it. It's because of the competition. You were consumed with getting ahead. Being undercover inside Nazi Germany, and gathering intelligence the way an analyst does, wasn't enough for you. Certainly not worthy enough, or special enough, to include in a letter home to your parents. Am I right?"

The conductor announced that we would be leaving soon.

I closed my eyes. "Tell me everything is going to be all right between us, Junie. Tell me it's okay. Like you always do." I reached for her hand, but I felt the fabric of the seat instead because she'd moved. "Junie?" I opened my eyes to find her standing.

"I need some air," Junie said. "Dot?"

Dot got up, following her out, presumably to have a chat about their rotten partners.

I pressed my palms to my eyes. "If only they knew," I said. "Ah, this isn't fair."

"When is anything fair?" Pudge said. "If the brass find out we told them, and they will, we'll never find work in the U.S. Army again. And if we tell them, and we're caught, it puts them in actual danger—more than we might already be in."

"I hate this." My throat began to ball up. I loved Junie more than anything in this world. All I kept thinking was that once we were in Rome, she'd know the truth about Engle and why we'd done what we'd done.

"I hate it, too," Pudge mumbled before slumping forward and holding her head.

Time passed, and the conductor announced that everyone should be in their seats, but Junie and Dot hadn't come back. I started to get worried, lifting my head from my hands and looking at the closed door. Something wasn't right. I felt it in my bones, but it also twisted my stomach, making me sick.

"They should be back by now." I stood, but Pudge had already got up to have a look in the train car. Nobody was there. She even had a peek into the next car along.

The conductor walked briskly by, yelling at Pudge to take her seat. There was a small argument, propelling me to step into the corridor.

"Our friends are gone," Pudge said to the conductor. "We can't leave."

"All passengers are on the train," he said, pointing to our carriage. "Now, if you please."

My stomach took another sour turn.

I threw open the curtains. Pudge gasped first because I had covered my mouth. Junie and Dot had walked off our train to board the one to Munich. Steam puffed into the air only to settle on the platform in a hazy mist. I banged on the glass.

"Where are they going?" Pudge cried.

"They're going to Munich."

"But that's a death sentence," she said. "Why would they do that?"

My hands slipped from the glass, plummeting into my seat. "Because they think it's safer than being with us."

Chapter Fourteen

A few days later, Pudge and I walked up to the villa in Rome, dressed in button-fly men's fatigues given to us from the Seventh Army. After taking the train as far west as we could, we'd crossed the Rhine into France, then had to wait for a transport plane to Italy after Cora wouldn't dispatch one for us. I couldn't remember the last meal I'd had that wasn't from a tin can or a soldier's helmet.

The sun set between the buildings, leaving an orangey-pink glow above the ramparts. Prostitutes lingered in the narrow street or waved scented scarves from their upstairs bedroom window. One of them whistled at us, followed by some laughs.

All we had thought about was our partners and prayed they had beaten us to the villa or at least sent word that they were safe.

"Ready?" Pudge asked.

"As ready as I'll ever be."

We didn't bother knocking; we busted in, flinging the door open to see greasy little Hector, who we had met on our first day. "You're back too soon." He scrambled to close the door behind us, which felt more like a coffin lid sliding shut. "Cora won't like this—"

"She knows," I said. "Are we the first ones?"

"There's more of you coming?"

Pudge and I looked at each other. We beat Junie and Dot.

"Where's Cora?" I asked, but he was fumbling his words, still stuck on the idea that there were more of us arriving earlier than expected. "We'll find her ourselves."

We left him and walked down the long hallway to the terracotta courtyard, where the Morale Operations Branch had grown and now looked more like OSS headquarters than Cora's departmental team.

One by one, service men looked up at us from their makeshift desks, some with fake documents, others with parachutes—they were sending more agents.

"Where's Cora?" I asked.

One of them pointed down the hallway, and we turned. Shoes click-clacked against the tiles, growing louder and louder, followed by Cora's voice talking to her assistant about the newest flyer to be dropped over the Gustav Line.

Moments before she emerged from the hallway, I spotted Hal. Looked like he was delivering something and was on his way out. We both perked, making eye contact, but the sharp cut of Cora's voice entering the courtyard got me to look away.

I straightened.

She stopped by the dry fountain, but appeared to have no idea we were there. The courtyard turned quiet after Pudge cleared her throat. It was the silence that got her attention, looking around to see what she was missing.

"Hello, Cora," I said.

She smiled slyly. "I knew you'd find a way here." She slapped the papers she'd been carrying against her leg. "In my office." She pointed to a door.

We followed her into a small room that looked like it had been a cleaning closet because it wasn't quite the size of a bedroom or a formal sitting parlor, and it had a working, closing door.

"I was surprised to hear you were back in France so soon." We shook our heads at the cigarettes she offered us from her case. "Glad you're home safe."

"This is hardly home," I said back.

"Have a seat." She sat down in her chair behind the desk and had a smoke. We remained standing.

"Why didn't you dispatch a plane for us in France?" I asked.

"A good agent will find their own way back, and look at you two. You're here." She smiled. "But before you tell me how that happened, why don't you tell me why you left Füssen early." She pretended to look over our shoulders. "Where's Ava and your partners?"

"There were a few hiccups," Pudge said.

She leaned back in her chair, hands folded. "Hiccups?"

"Well, one hiccup," I said. "Joseph Engle."

"What?" She sat up. "You saw him? In Füssen?" She held her forehead with the cigarette smoking between her fingers. "Please tell me you didn't talk to him—"

"We rode in his car," Pudge said.

Her eyes popped. "You didn't."

"Junie talked to him at length," I added, "but of course, she had no idea who he was, because I was under orders not to say anything."

She shook her head, hands now bracing her desk. "I explicitly told you how delicate the operation was. You could have ruined things. Not only did you put all of my agents working undercover at risk, you jeopardized the entire Morale Operations Branch of the OSS. What if you still have?"

"Pipe down, Cora," I said, which made her scowl. "Give us a break, all right? We were just in Nazi Germany. Besides, it's not like we meant to."

She thoughtfully collected herself. "Start at the beginning."

"First, tell us about Engle. We deserve to know. Why does the OSS want him? And don't tell us it's because he was the commandant at Flossenbürg. There's something more to it."

She took a few puffs of her cigarette. Then she stood, moving to her bookcase, where she pulled out a bound notebook. "Look here." She flipped it open to a photograph—trees, maybe a forest, and an open mass grave of American soldiers. "I can't tell you how we obtained this photograph, but I can tell you that sometime after D-Day, they moved American POWs to Flossenbürg. This is Engle's doing."

Pudge looked away, shaking her head.

"My God."

"The OSS wants him for war crimes." She stubbed out her cigarette after sucking it down to a nub. "But he's managed to keep his face and signature off every official record. As if he knew there was no path to victory and he'd have to be held accountable one day. That's why the situation is so delicate, and you were ordered to observe. But it sounds like you disobeyed your orders. Riding in his car. How could you?"

"We didn't know his identity until later."

She promptly lit another cigarette. "Now, where's Ava? Where's Junie and that other one?"

"Dot," Pudge said. "Her name is Dot."

"Yes, Dot. Where are they?"

We told Cora everything, right down to the reason Junie and Dot left us on the train. "When we went back into Ava's apartment building, they thought it was part of a competition we had with the replacements you sent—Barbara Bennington and Kitty Meyer—and we'd put their lives at risk." She appeared to be listening, especially when I mentioned the painting, but kept telling me to write it all down in my report, which would come later. "They knew about clandestine routes over the Rhine because we discussed it. But Hector said we are the first ones."

"Why would you think they made it before you if their train went east and yours went west?"

"Wishful thinking."

"Well, when I hear from my contacts in France and talk to them, I'll let you know."

"You must tell them there was a misunderstanding. I know you won't divulge the mission over the wire, but at least tell Junie and Dot there's more to the story. Please."

She nodded, stubbing out her second cigarette. "Of course." A smile flashed on her face.

A housekeeper burst into her office, scaring us, but not Cora. She squeezed in between me and Pudge to reach the trash can, leaving little to the imagination when she bent down.

"*Mi scusi*," she said, emptying the trash and looking incredibly sexy while doing it.

I gave Pudge a look, and she appeared to be thinking the same thing: she was one of the lonely women from the previous mission, and a local prostitute from across the street.

I pulled the flyer from my pocket, the one I got in Füssen. "There's one more thing, Cora—"

Pudge reached for my arm, stopping me from saying another word while the housekeeper made her way out. "Not now," she said to me, then turned to Cora. "Can we be excused?"

"Good, yes. I have work to do." Cora smoked her cigarette. "I want your reports sooner rather than later, understand?"

Pudge pulled me out of that office and into the hallway.

"What was that about? I want to confront her about the prostitutes, tell her we know, and also that it wasn't right to lie to us, giving us a draft flyer and not the real one."

"We can't." She shook her head. "Not until after she follows through with Junie and Dot. She holds our lives in her hands regarding them. We can't risk upsetting her now. After. We'll have to wait until after."

I closed my eyes, taking a hard breath. Pudge was right. She had thought things through while my mind was in a vengeful state. "All right."

We walked into the courtyard where it was business as usual, Cora's team was putting together the next drop of lonely war women. I looked anxiously for Hal over all the bobbing heads.

"He'll be back. He knows where you are."

"Yeah."

In the kitchen, we found Francesca standing at the counter folding the napkins for breakfast the following morning. Her slick dark hair had been brushed out to hang long in the back, showing off her girly waves.

Manzo was at the stove. "You're back?"

"Not you too, Manzo. No more questions, all right?" Pudge said.

He stared at us, his mouth ajar. I wasn't sure of his expression, which denoted a bit of sadness. "And Ava? Did she…"

"I don't know where she is. We're the only ones back."

He paused, looking at his cauldron of ravioli, then to the opened cans of Chef Boyardee on the floor. "I see." A second later, he blew out the flame, untied his apron, and left without a word about dinner.

"What was that about?" I asked Pudge.

"I'm sure losing a turned agent to Nazi Germany has to be disappointing. Even if they didn't like each other."

Francesca threw her hands up after Manzo left and relit the flame, cursing in Italian and giving us glares.

"Francesca?"

She turned her head only, taking Manzo's spoon, but I saw the fire in her eyes.

"Thank you," I said.

Francesca's legs had bruises that had turned green and yellow from blows that had been inflicted weeks ago. She *was* the Francesca that German soldier talked about, and we were the lucky ones.

I got up and took the spoon from her hand; she didn't have to do Manzo's job as well. She didn't have to wait on us or cook for us. She gazed into my eyes for a second, as if she understood my gesture, before going back to her napkins. I dished up bowls for me and Pudge, but she decided she was more tired than hungry and left to find a bedroom.

I ate by myself, thinking of Junie, but not so much about

what happened, but what was going to happen. "Viv?" I heard from behind.

I turned. "Hal?" I smiled. "I thought I'd never see you again, not after the airport that night. Sorry for ignoring you earlier. I had something—"

"It's okay," he said. "I understand."

He was dressed in his uniform and looked a little tired, I imagined, from poring over maps and analyzing data for OSS missions. "Are you working with Cora here at the villa?" I asked.

"No. I deliver reports sometimes. My office is near the airport."

"Oh?"

He pulled out a chair. "Is this seat taken?"

Francesca had snuck out, leaving a lit candle on the counter, a thank you for being nice to her, maybe. I didn't know. But what timing.

"I didn't plan that," I said, pointing to the candle.

"Well, perhaps I did."

I smiled.

We had quite a conversation, but not about the OSS, about home. Where he grew up and where I grew up. I was surprised by the things we had in common. However, considering we weren't born that far from each other—Ohio and Maryland—it made sense.

"How long are you going to be here?" he asked.

I shrugged. I really had no idea, and what was I going to do? I wasn't about to go behind enemy lines as a lonely woman again. "I'm waiting for my partner, who's gone missing. After that, not sure. Maybe back to London, maybe back to the U.S." I looked at my hands, rubbing them under the table before folding them on top. "Right now, it's all uncertain. What about you?"

"I heard I might be sent back to the U.S. to train some new recruits."

Train? He was high up the chain in the OSS, someone important.

"Do you know what we did?" I asked.

He examined my face, possibly taking note of every smudge of dirt. "I know you did something for Cora, and by the looks of you…"

I immediately ran my hands through my hair, trying to clean myself up the best I could, but it was too late for that.

"You were somewhere undercover. Somewhere dangerous and had to claw your way back. I can only guess you speak German fluently since you're here."

"I do. And yes, to all the rest of it." I paused. "Hal, I—"

"I know you can't tell me everything. I'm not asking."

"You don't understand. I don't care if you know, but I'm bound to keep quiet for other reasons. Cora's orders." I certainly wasn't about to blather all my secrets now. Cora said the side mission with Engle was delicate, and now I had to be delicate with what I said outside of the circle. Like Pudge had said, she held our lives in her hands when it came to Junie and Dot. "I can tell you one thing. Wherever I end up after here, I'm not going to work with Cora. Not ever."

My hands turned to fists just remembering her voice, leaving me frustrated.

What if Pudge and I were chosen for the side mission, not because we were the best, like she said, but because of our past as girls who pushed orders and had a personal stake in catching Engle, in hopes we would dig up bones? She did make a point of telling us he was the commandant of Flossenbürg Prison when she approached us with the details.

I tipped my head back, groaning. "I think I've been had by her, and now Junie is missing."

"I'm sure your partner will show up. If not tomorrow, maybe a week from now. But she'll show up."

He placed his hand on mine, which was a shock because the last touch I'd had from a man was in Germany, and it was not kind. "Hal?" Next, we were holding hands.

"Yeah?"

My stomach fluttered when he looked at me.

"I'm glad we met."

Days passed, yet there was still no sign of Junie and Dot. Pudge and I had completed our reports, listing every single detail we could remember about Füssen, Engle, and the soldiers. We waited for Cora to finish chewing someone out in her office.

"I can't stay here any longer, Viv," Pudge whispered.

"You're leaving?" I was surprised.

"There's a war going on. I don't feel useful in Rome. I'm going to make my name in this organization, one way or the other. Then I'm going to retire to that beach I've always talked about. I can't get there in the League of Lonely War Women."

I didn't want to think about what it would be like with Pudge gone, too.

"What about you?" she asked.

I wasn't like Pudge. The fire that burned inside of me in the days leading up to the promotion was long gone. "I don't know."

Cora's door opened, and Francesca walked out, napkin to her eyes from crying. "Francesca," I said, but she kept walking. "Francesca!"

She turned. "Watch out," she said in perfect English. "She breaks promises."

Pudge and I blinked and blinked. I think I was more surprised she spoke English so well. Cora called us in, then got up with her smoking cigarette and closed the door behind us.

"I see you have your reports. I have already relayed the information you informally provided regarding the soldiers and their morale. The brass are very pleased." The cigarette bobbed on her lips, her eyes roving over my report before moving on to Pudge's. "Now..." She looked up, setting her cigarette in the ashtray. "I have some bad news for you."

I squeezed Pudge's hand.

"Ava is dead," she announced.

I gasped. Even though I didn't like Ava in the beginning, in the end, I knew she was genuine and didn't deserve to die. "That's awful—"

"How do you know?" Pudge asked.

Cora didn't look like she wanted to be questioned, picking her cigarette back up with a slow flick of the ash. "An agent in the field said a woman matching her description was hanging in the square. We assume, given what you told us about how things were left in Füssen, it was her."

"An agent in the field told you?" I asked, wondering if it was Junie or Dot, or one of the other women who were due back any day.

"Someone who was on Engle's trail but lost him. Engle has

retreated into the fabric of society, protected by his friends and colleagues. We are back to square one."

"And Junie and Dot... Have you heard from them?" I asked.

"That's what I wanted to tell you two. Sit down." Pudge and I sat because we knew this was going to be bad news, and the fact that it was coming from Cora was just the icing on the cake. "They made it to France."

I gasped, but this time in relief. "Oh, thank God." I turned to Pudge, smiling.

"I knew they would make it. I knew it!" Pudge patted my hand. "Are they on a plane back to Rome right now?"

"You told them about the misunderstanding?" I added.

Cora smoked her cigarette, staring at me.

"You told them?" I asked, sternly. "Right, Cora? You promised you would."

"They decided to go to London. Work out of the offices there. Perhaps they've had enough of me. But I think they're still mad about how things ended in Füssen."

"Why didn't you tell them the truth?"

She scoffed. "If I said something about a misunderstanding, then the next thing that would follow would be an explanation, and what would I say?" She shook her head. "Spies are listening in on the wires. The OSS can't risk a word of this getting out."

"You promised."

"Preserving the integrity of the mission is more important than a misunderstanding between friends. Surely, you can see how self-centered you are to insist that I am wrong."

"Now, what?" Pudge asked. "Where do we go from here?"

"I'm glad you asked." She sat up, smiling. "Ladies, I'm

reposting you. You're heading to France. There's word of Vichy collaborators near Nancy, which might put Patton's advance in danger, and we need two women to go undercover and sniff them out."

I shook my head.

"You are declining?" Cora asked.

Pudge looked shocked as well.

"I'll only accept London. I'm not going to France."

She stubbed out her cigarette after a little threatening laugh. "Let me be clear. You can stay here and work for me or go to France. If you don't like either of those, then your only option is to talk to someone at the airport and see if you can be their secretary or serve donuts to the boys."

My lips pursed. "Donuts?" There had to be something else, and I quickly thought about all those planes on the tarmac and which ones I could hitch a ride with.

"And here's a warning for you, Viv, the last one you'll get from me. If, for some reason, you end up in London or anywhere near Junie and Dot to tell them about Engle before this mission is completed, I'll have you court-martialed."

"Viv?" Pudge said.

"And here I thought you were smart," Cora said. "At least Pudge has enough sense to go to France, don't you, Pudge?"

"I'll go."

"Good. Now, I have other work to do. Pudge, your transport leaves in an hour. Be ready."

We both walked out to stand near the fountain. Girls recruited from all over had just arrived and were finding their way to the chapel with their duffel bags to hear Cora's speech. They examined us, probably trying to figure out what their mission was all about, just like Junie and I had done when we'd arrived.

"Take the post, Viv. Soon, our boys will break into Germany, and who knows what will happen then. I'm not going to stop trying to find Engle, even if it means going behind Cora's back."

"I can't." I shook my head.

She grabbed me by both shoulders. "Come to France."

My eyes welled with tears. Not because I was sad that she was leaving me too, but because I didn't have the strength to join her. "Pudge, I'm exhausted. I feel like Cora just stole a piece of my soul. Without Junie, I'm nothing, definitely not someone who can work with a different partner, given what has happened. Not in the OSS, anyway. And we can't even set the record straight for fear of being court-martialed? And how long did she say the Engle mission might last? A year? Five years?"

"I don't know."

I pulled the flyer from my pocket, flapping it in the air. "And what about this, huh? I guess it doesn't matter now that she lied to us." I tossed it into the bin.

Pudge let go of my shoulders. I think she understood. I hoped she did.

"I don't blame you for leaving, but I can't retire knowing he's alive and out there enjoying life, even during a war. I don't know if I ever will."

"You're going to keep looking?" I asked.

"When the opportunity arises, I will."

I gave Pudge a hug. "I'm going to miss you."

"I'm going to miss you, too."

Cora left her office for the chapel, giving us a brief glance before click-clacking away. "Now," I heard her say to the new girls, "I know what you're wondering. You're wondering who is the best…"

"Once Engle's found, there's no reason to keep secrets," Pudge said. "Cora can't control that. It's only a matter of time."

"I hope you're right."

We kissed each other's cheeks, then she was gone. Headed up to our bedroom to pack her duffel bag and fly out. I didn't know what to do with myself—other than to go and pack, too—because I wasn't about to stay at the villa.

A soldier came in to take Junie's things away.

"Wait." I tried reaching for her duffel bag, but he shoved her belongings into it—fatigues, her helmet, her shoes. He reached for her jacks on the nightstand, and I beat him to it. "Not these," I said, clutching them in my fist.

His superior came into the room, standing in the doorway. "You've got everything? Let's go. Flight leaves in thirty." I saw another person carrying Dot's bag away.

The soldier looked at me, hesitated, then walked out of the room with Junie's things, all but the jacks. Hal caught me on the stairs, slowly walking out because I still wasn't sure where I was going.

"Hey." His smile was like a breath of fresh air in that villa. He smoothed his hair back, and when my eyes met his, my stomach fluttered.

"You're back," I said. "I'm so glad you came back."

We held hands.

"I wanted to see how you were."

"I'm leaving," I said.

"Where?"

"I... I don't know. Cora told me to go to the airport and see if anyone needed a secretary. I'm not about to serve donuts."

"Your partner, Junie," he said. "She never came back?"

I looked down momentarily. "She's in London."

There wasn't anything else to explain. Whatever I'd been mixed up in had imploded, and it explained why I was looking for independent work. He lifted my head by my chin.

"You can work with me, in my department. It's nothing glamorous, just analyzing field reports, if you're up to it. I know it probably doesn't stack up to what you were assigned to do with Cora, and I know you can't tell me, but—"

"Really?"

Hal was nice, even great. I'd be a fool to say no, and something in the way he spoke to me, something in the way he held my hands, felt safe.

"Yeah."

I smiled, and I hadn't smiled in days.

"You know, we never got to finish that dance," he said.

I hooked my arm in his and headed outside where his jeep was waiting. "Are you asking me on a date?"

"Is it out of the question? We're owed at least another two minutes of dancing to 'In the Mood', and a chance to finish our ales afterward, where we can talk about how close we live to each other back home."

"You remembered the song?"

"Remembered? I haven't stopped thinking about you, Viv."

I smiled again.

Chapter Fifteen

April 6, 1955
Washington D.C.

When the phone rang at precisely ten in the morning on Wednesday, April 6, I thought it was Hal, saying he had forgotten his lunch again. Not that I would deliver it because I'd never set foot in his office, nor did I plan to. What wife doesn't visit her husband at work?

Viv Cunningham, that's who.

Oh, I'm sure my name has come up many times around the water cooler with the typing pool. "Hal's wife doesn't call or come to visit him. Poor thing, and he never has a lunch."

I love Hal, and I wish I could visit him at work, but of course, I cannot, because he works in the same building as Cora at the CIA. I still haven't forgiven her for the way things ended in Rome, and most importantly, how she said she'd have Pudge and I arrested if we told Junie and Dot the truth before they found Engle.

Brring!

I cleared my throat before picking up the receiver. "Hello, darling! Forget your lunch again?" I asked, but then I saw his lunchbox wasn't on the kitchen counter, so he must have taken it.

"Mrs. Cunningham?" It was a voice I recognized, but not one I immediately placed.

I straightened. "Yes, this is Mrs. Cunningham," I said, somewhat hesitantly.

"This is Pam at Dr. Hopp's office."

"Oh, yes." I relaxed, holding my forehead. Pam was Doctor Hopp's nurse. "Sorry, Pam. I don't know where my head was just now. Did I forget my sweater on the coat rack again? I can come later—"

"No," she said. "We have the results back from your blood test."

Pam paused with what sounded like a hand over the receiver to talk to someone else, her voice slightly muffled, asking for my medical record. Years ago, I would have wanted to crawl through the receiver and strangle Pam for keeping me on the hook, but I'd become used to hearing the results of a negative pregnancy test. So much so that I'd asked Dr. Hopp's office not to call me unless the news was favorable, and I had stopped telling Hal that I was taking tests.

"You there?" she asked.

My hands started to shake, then my knees, realizing why she was calling. "You have positive results?"

"Yes," she said, then in a total breach of etiquette, addressed me casually, woman to woman. "Congratulations, Viv."

I gasped quietly. "What?"

"It's true. I'm holding the results right here in my hand," she said. "Dr. Hopp would like to see you next week. Is there a time that suits you?"

I nodded incessantly even though she couldn't see me. "Yes." I gulped. "Yes! Next week." But I hung up the phone without making the appointment. I sat heavily on one of my kitchen chairs.

I'd given up hope that I'd ever have a baby, and I think Hal had too, though he never showed it, always very patient and loving whenever the subject was brought up.

I picked up the phone to call Hal, but suddenly couldn't remember his phone number. Even if I could have remembered it, my shaking fingers wouldn't have cooperated, but then it occurred to me Hal was probably in a meeting. I'd have to wait another hour.

I tapped my fingers on the table. *Who else? Who else, who else, who else?*

The truth was, I didn't have anyone to call. I sat alone at the kitchen table, listening to the clock tick.

I was pregnant. I smiled.

I raced into the spare bedroom to pull boxes from the top closet shelf, trying to find the things I'd bought over the years for the baby but had stuffed away months ago. New rattles and blankets with tags still attached. Photo albums without any photos. Giant poncho dresses for me, ones I never believed I would wear. I dug all the way to the bottom, laying the things out on the carpet with the cat coming in for a peek, delicately pawing at the blankets, when I found something else in the box, buried underneath all the baby things. Something I did not intend to find.

A photograph of Junie and I in London, dressed in our

uniforms, arms draped over each other's shoulders, smiling, her pretending to choke me with my tie. "You were right, Junie," I breathed. "That army doctor didn't know anything." The smile on my face slowly faded when I saw her jacks at the bottom of the box, hidden in the corner. I briefly held them before returning them to the box.

She was so close, yet so far away on the other side of the city. Professor of American Studies is what I read last in *The Evening Star*, with a specialization in America's mafia and gangs, which I would have never imagined, but I supposed it made sense: the Nazis were thugs, and her skills as an analyst would have been relevant to that field and probably suited her well. I wondered if she knew where I lived, that Hal and I were married, and also that I didn't stay in the OSS after Rome, or continue on with the CIA after the war, like Pudge. Instead, I was a private investigator, catching rich senators cheating on their wives with their secretaries in cars and bars.

I hoped she would never find out about that last part.

"Viv?" I heard from outside, followed by a knock on my door. It was Mrs. Bunn from across the street. I put the baby things back in the box before setting off downstairs.

She delivered our mail a few times a week, insisting that the postman had mixed up the deliveries, but we knew she was just being nosy and took the mail from our box. Hal thought about installing a mail slot in the front door, but she was harmless and I enjoyed her company.

I smoothed my hair into place and wiped my eyes in the hallway where she couldn't see me through the screen door, before emerging like I had been doing a bit of laundry, and not thinking about all I'd gained and lost.

"Good morning, Mrs. Bunn." I wanted to tell her my news,

but I couldn't, not without telling Hal first. I couldn't risk the neighborhood finding out before him—an image of Hal getting an outside call dispatched to his office from the grocer to say congratulations flashed in my mind, and all this would happen before lunchtime.

"Hello, Viv." She held up the mail. "Again, I got your mail. Dadgummit."

"Please, come in, Mrs. Bunn." She wore a blue dress with a white collar and smelled as sweet as lilacs and vanilla. It wasn't her perfume; it was just how she smelled. We walked into the kitchen, where we usually had our chats, and I poured her a cup of coffee from the percolator.

"How's life?" she asked.

I laughed. "Now, that's a heck of a question, isn't it?"

She giggled. "I suppose. What I mean is, I thought I heard a little squeal of enjoyment coming from across the street. Thought now was as good of a time as any to check up on you. And I have your mail, of course." She batted her hand.

She knew. Of course, she knew. We shared a party line, and she must have picked up her receiver at just the right time when I couldn't hear the click.

I pressed my lips together, head shaking. "Nope. Nothing new. How's life with you, Mrs. Bunn?" A good distraction usually did the trick. "Did Jessica start her new job?"

"Jessica!" She tossed her hands up, one hand still clutching my mail. "That daughter of mine. Yes, she's working at an auction house, and I can't believe how much some of those paintings are selling for. Picasso, for example. Thousands of dollars. As much as a new house." She rolled her eyes. "It's just a bunch of lines to me…"

I was pouring her that cup of coffee, nodding, but I was not paying attention, and instead was thinking about how I was going to tell Hal my news. I didn't want to blurt it out over the phone, I'd decided, but how?

The phone rang as Mrs. Bunn was rambling. I set the percolator down.

"Hello?" It was Pam calling me back to make that appointment. I shot Mrs. Bunn a look. Aside from Hal calling, this was the other conversation I didn't want to have in front of Mrs. Bunn.

She gave me a strange look, taking a delicate sip from her coffee cup.

"Yes, sorry about that," I said, making sure not to mention Pam's name. "The line must have disconnected." I gave Mrs. Bunn a smile. "Next week is fine. Any time. I'll make it work." We settled on next Wednesday morning.

After hanging up the phone, an odd and awkward moment of silence followed. We both knew what that phone call was about, but neither of us was going to say anything. If I admitted what we both knew, even if I asked her to keep it a secret, she'd inadvertently tell everyone on her prayer chain within minutes. If I acted dumb, that might hold her off until Hal got home. Plus, I had no idea if she heard the entire conversation, half of it, or just the last part.

"Well, I should go!" She stepped away from the counter. "The Maytag repairman will be by soon." She twisted her watch. "Was supposed to be here at the top of the hour, now that I recall."

I pulled a coffee cup from my cupboard. "Repairmen are never on time, are they?"

She played with her dress collar. "You know, Viv, you can

tell me. Anyone on our street having an affair? I won't tell anyone." She crossed her heart. "Hope to die."

"Mrs. Bunn, you know I can't—"

She shook her head. "I know. Can't blame a girl for trying, though, can you? I think your work is very intriguing. I always wanted to be an investigator. Did I tell you that? I had a knack for it, once."

I wanted to laugh because she still had a knack for it, even if she didn't realize it.

"In fact, I tried to join the OSS, but for some reason, I wasn't selected."

"What did you do in the war? Your husband, Ron, was in the Navy, right?"

"Yes. Pacific Theater. I volunteered in the SOE. Served donuts mostly." She shrugged. "I bet you'd be a fantastic fraud investigator with Hal. Did you ever think about joining him in that line of work?"

That's what we told everyone Hal did for a living—insurance fraud. I shook my head. "I'm happy where I am."

"Now, come to think of it, that's a horrible idea."

"Why is that?" I asked.

"Well, I love Ron, and we've been married twenty-five years, but if I had to go to work with him, see him every second of the day … well, that would be murder!" She laughed from her belly, which got me to laugh. "Enjoy your coffee."

She turned for the door but then spun around as I reached for the percolator. "Oh! The mail." She laughed again. "I almost forgot." She flipped through the letters in her hands. "That one's mine … yours … mine…" She pulled the last piece of mail from the pile. "A postcard."

I perked. "Postcard? I don't know anyone on vacation."

"It's from Manhattan."

"Manhattan? What's the address?" I motioned with my chin for her to flip it over as I poured my cup of coffee.

"No address. Just a message." She put her glasses on, squinting. "And it's the most peculiar message…"

"What does it say?"

"Just…" She looked up. "It's only three words. 'I found him,' and that's all it says."

I froze, pouring my coffee without so much as a blink, even as it spilled over the rim and splashed onto the floor.

"Viv?" She lunged for the percolator. "Viv!"

I screeched to a stop outside the CIA building, the front tires hitting the curb and saving my car from breaking through the fence. Mrs. Bunn must have thought I'd gone crazy, rushing her out of the house only for me to race out seconds later, not even taking a moment to clean the coffee off my kitchen floor. I would have to come up with an explanation for her later, maybe something to do with cheating husbands and how I'd caught one. She'd enjoy that story.

Walking up to the CIA building was a bit surreal. It was the first time I'd seen it in person, though I knew exactly what streets to take to get there, and how long it would take me in traffic. A man held the door open for me; another tipped his hat. Typists whispered to secretaries on breaks.

I pulled my shoulders back at the reception desk where a beautiful brunette sat smiling, not a hair out of place, and her lips wet with butter-colored lip gloss. "Mrs. Cunningham."

"You know me?"

"Yes, of course." She picked up her phone. "I'll tell Mr. Cunningham—"

"No." I put my hand out. I didn't want her calling Hal. "I'm here to see Cora Hughes," I said, then remembered her married name. "Cora Jones. Tell her Viv is here."

Her face was unnaturally frozen, with the receiver slowly moving away from her face, Hal's secretary in a state of confusion on the other end of the line with her voice blaring.

"Cora?" the receptionist asked. "There is nobody by that name here."

I shifted. "Yes, there is."

She hung up the phone and called someone else. "Code X," she said, then whispered, "Yes, right now." She pointed to the empty chairs after hanging up. "Please, have a seat."

I smiled. Cora was on her way. "I'll stand and wait."

She swiveled around in her chair to answer another call, in her perfect black dress, with perfect make-up and that perfect smile. She was an asset to the CIA; I could see that. She could hold in her emotions like a robot and maintain that plastic smile as she lied to my face.

The lobby was congested but bright, thanks to sunlight shining through a skylight. Everyone seemed to be whispering to avoid their voice traveling. I would have never thought, after all these years, I'd come to see Cora at the CIA. I wasn't sure I'd be able to whisper like the others when I saw her. I slipped my hand into my purse, feeling the postcard's sharp edges.

A man wearing a black suit approached me as I waited. "Mrs. Cunningham." He reached for my elbow.

"Don't touch me." I stepped back when he went for another reach.

"I think the air is fresher outside," he said, pointing toward the door. "If you please."

Everyone in the lobby turned to look.

"No, I don't please." I folded my arms. I was not budging from this place without seeing Cora first.

He waved to another man for help, but before he could reach me, I saw Hal down the hall behind the reception desk, oblivious to what was going on in the lobby, or that I was in his building. I clipped away with the men swiftly on my heels. "Hal!" I waved, and they stood down.

"Viv?" He nearly dropped the papers he was holding. "What's wrong?" The concern he had for me was evident in his firm grip as he took my hand, his searching eyes, and his strained face.

"Nothing is wrong." I took a deep breath, waiting until the receptionist's goons had completely left the lobby, but they only stood in the corners, watching and presumably waiting. "What does Code X mean?"

His eyes skirted over the lobby and to the receptionist. "It means intruder."

"That's fitting."

"Viv, darling, what are you doing here?"

There was so much to tell him, the least of which was that I was pregnant, but I certainly wasn't going to tell him in the hallway and then dash away right after to see Cora.

"I know this is going to come out of the blue, but you'll have to trust me and not ask any questions. At least not right now."

He nodded.

"I came to see Cora," I blurted.

His eyes bulged.

"Remember, no questions." I looked over both my shoulders. The goons appeared to be gone for now. "The receptionist said she doesn't exist. Tell me which office is hers."

He paused, but it wasn't because he didn't trust me; it was because he worried about me. "Wait here." He told the receptionist I was going to be in his office for an hour so I could get a visitor's badge.

That done, we walked down the carpeted hallway. Secretaries came out of their offices, only to retreat at the sight of Hal's wife, whispering, "Why is she here?" I imagined them all whispering over the water cooler later and making up ridiculous stories.

Hal closed the door to his office. My picture was on his desk; more than one actually. He had a window, too. "I've always wanted you to come here."

"I know you have. I'm sorry I can't stay." I reached for his hand. He knew I blamed Cora for what had happened between Junie and me, but even after all these years, he still didn't know the details. He definitely didn't know about Engle. "Now, which office is hers?"

"Second floor. Last office on the left. Take the stairs."

I kissed his cheek, but he pulled me back when I turned toward the door.

"Viv, I—"

"No questions."

"It's not that. Be careful. Cora doesn't get visitors, if you know what I mean."

I had a feeling. When the receptionist said she didn't exist, I realized Cora didn't exist on paper, and that made her important—possibly more important than Hal at the CIA.

"I understand. Also..." This one hurt. "Don't take any outside calls until I see you."

"Outside calls—"

I kissed him again and left for the stairs, walking the short two flights up to Cora's floor.

My heart started pounding as soon as I was an office door away from her. I heard voices, but I couldn't tell if they were coming from another office. My palms turned sweaty. This, I did not expect. I pulled the visitor's badge from my collar to slip it into my dress pocket.

A man walked out of Cora's office, surprising the both of us. I smiled, and he gave me a glance, then walked on after a brief pause. I could tell Cora knew he'd run into someone in the hallway because it was quiet. Too quiet for her.

I stepped foot in her office as she was lifting from her chair to see for herself.

"Hello, Cora." I closed the door behind me.

She hovered over her chair for a moment before sitting back down. Her phone rang, and I didn't have to guess who that was. "Yes. She's here now."

"The receptionist is too late," I said.

She hung up. "As I see."

I pulled the postcard from my purse and silently slid it toward her, text side up. She examined both sides, gazing at the Manhattan illustration on the back a few seconds longer than what was necessary before setting it back down.

"You're looking well, Viv."

I scoffed. "That's all you have to say?"

"You know, I never wanted you to leave the OSS. You were one of the best."

"What's the plan, Cora?"

She set her pencil down to fold her arms and kick back in her swivel chair. A graying curl fell onto her forehead, reminding me just how much time had passed since I'd last seen her. "Plan for what?"

"You know what I'm talking about." I pointed to the postcard. "I know Pudge's handwriting. She found him. Evidently in Manhattan, otherwise, she wouldn't have chosen that particular postcard. Now, how do we go and get him?"

"Viv…" She frowned. "The world has moved on since the war. Nobody cares about Nazis. We have a new enemy—communists—in case you've been living under a rock." Her chair squeaked as she tipped further back, testing its tension. "Anyway, to answer your question … there is no plan." She shot straight up in her chair and grabbed her pencil. "Thanks for visiting, though. Good to see you." She gave the postcard back, pushing it across her desk with two fingers.

My mouth hung open. "Nobody cares about hunting Nazis? Cora, what are you saying?"

"People care, Viv. Governments don't. Not like they used to." She pointed to Pudge's postcard. "And Pudge is on thin ice already for going off assignment. Heads will roll when the brass find out she went rogue. Again."

"I don't believe nobody cares. There's always a way. What are the prerequisites needed for a plan? Witnesses to come forward about his crimes? Positive identification from me that he's Joseph Engle? Because I'm willing to testify, even if it means coming clean about what we did in Füssen for the OSS and the Morale Operations Branch. Tell me. What do I need?"

"Why do you care?"

"Why do I care?" I repeated.

"Yeah. I hear you're doing pretty well for yourself. Married a respected agent and live in a big house in Cathedral Heights. Why are you so concerned with Engle, especially after all these years?"

"He's a war criminal—murdered my grandfather at Flossenbürg. Pudge's grandfather too, in case you forgot. And, on top of all the other evil deeds he's done, he got away. It's not fair."

"Is that really the only reason, Viv?"

I twisted my hands while I decided if I was going to answer.

"It's been ten years since the end of the war. Have you reached out to Junie?" she asked.

"I sent a letter once. Not to talk about Engle, of course." I looked down for a pick at my nails.

"And?"

"Return to sender."

"Yes, well. The CIA isn't in the business of mending friendships. In fact, we couldn't care less."

"But what about catching a notorious SS officer living in America as a free man?"

Cora looked like she was thinking about it, especially when she swiveled around in her chair to look out the window.

"Tell me what the CIA needs to approve this mission. Who do I talk to—"

A secretary walked into the room with a clipboard and a pencil. "I need you to sign—" She grimaced. "Sorry. I didn't know you had a visitor." She tried to step back out, but Cora waved her forward.

I waited patiently for them to finish, listening to their barely audible chit-chat about missions and signatures, the details making me think Cora was the lead on many projects.

Cora was back at her desk once they were finished, picking up her pencil again as if I weren't there.

I cleared my throat.

Cora groaned. "Listen, Viv—"

"Who do I have to talk to?"

"Me. I make the initial decision, then I move the request up the chain. But even if it is approved and we arrest him, we'd need evidence to convict, even for a Nazi. Something that directly ties Engle to his duties in the SS."

I scoffed. "And how am I supposed to get that?"

"You mean you don't happen to have a piece of Reich stationary with his signature on it?"

"Oh, wait. What's this?" I said, pretending to pull an imaginary piece of paper from my pocket. "Of course, I don't. Damn it, Cora." I pressed my palms into my eyes.

Think, think, think.

"Like I said, the U.S. government has other priorities. Without a smoking gun, there is little I can—"

I pulled my hands away. "What about the painting in Füssen?"

She looked confused. "Viv, I don't have time for this—"

"It was in my report." I paused because she still looked confused. "The one I gave you in Rome, didn't you read it?"

"Of course, I read it, but it's been ten years, and I've moved on—the entire organization has, as I explained."

"If you read it, then you would know that there is something very incriminating about Engle hidden behind a painting in Füssen. My source at the time told me point blank that it would directly implicate Engle and his role in the Reich."

"Well, what is it?"

"I don't know. We had to flee before I could find it, barely escaping the Abwehr. If Ava was still alive, I'd pay her a visit. It was her painting. Maybe it's still in Füssen?" For a moment, I thought about traveling to Germany—it felt a little like grasping at straws, but it was all I had.

"Ava?" Cora's face had changed—she was no longer confused. She had information. I could tell by the way she blinked her eyes.

She got up, hand to her mouth, and headed to the window.

"What is it?" I raised my voice. "Cora!"

She whipped around, hands twisting behind her back, just as Pudge walked in, surprised at first to see me in Cora's office, then appearing as if she'd expected it.

"I see you got my postcard." She set a file folder thick with papers on Cora's desk. "We need to talk."

Chapter Sixteen

I hadn't seen Pudge in years, since before Hal and I moved into Cathedral Heights. Her wavy hair lay exactly the way it did after we landed in the forest all those years ago, slightly tussled, sandy-blonde, and cut just above her shoulders. It was as if she'd never aged—Eva Braun back from the dead, except Pudge wasn't a Nazi. If the CIA had their heads on straight, and clearly, they didn't after listening to Cora, they would have dispatched her into the field, perhaps to east Berlin where the CIA could keep an eye on all those communists they were so worried about.

"You look good, Pudge," I said, sitting back down.

Pudge flipped her file folder open, giving me a side-eye. "You too, Viv."

Cora tapped her desk with her fingernail. "Now that we've had our little reunion, you have a lot of explaining to do, Pudge."

"Before you start in on me," Pudge said, flipping through what seemed to be fifty pieces of paper, before pulling out one, "take a gander at this, will you?" She placed the paper in front of Cora, who didn't even glance at it. "I figured sending Viv that postcard was going to get me in hot water. But it was a risk I was willing to take. I found him, and we're going to get him, whether you like it or not."

Cora laughed. "Mmm. Hmm." She lit a cigarette and had a smoke.

"He's a war criminal," Pudge said.

"I have to admit, Viv almost had me believing it was a good idea, while you're now starting to make me regret ever allowing her to stay. Answer this. Why the postcard when you could have talked to me first?"

"Would you give me the time of day if Viv wasn't in your office right now?"

Cora thoughtfully smoked her cigarette. "Probably not."

Pudge reached for the paper, physically wrapping Cora's fingers around it. "This is my report."

Cora finally had a look.

"Engle came over here on a visa for scientists," Pudge said. "Only he never was a scientist or will be. He's a photographer in Manhattan. Goes by Stephen Jansson. My guess is he changed his name to a Swedish one so that people wouldn't question his accent. He lied to the U.S. government, Cora. And one thing I know about Uncle Sam is that he'll forgive a mass-murdering Nazi if it fits into a political agenda, but he will never forgive someone who lied and continuously takes advantage of the laws."

"Displaced Persons Act, it says." Cora set down Pudge's report. "Looks like he arrived just a year after the war. He has been here a while."

"Manhattan. Enjoying life as an American," I added. "That's a hard pill to swallow."

"Looking for him has become an obsession for you, Pudge. And for Viv, from what I can tell. Will it ever end? Even if I get the okay to go after him, will it be enough?"

"I'm about to retire, do something meaningless and mindless for a change," Pudge said. "But I can't, not without finding Engle. It's my last open assignment." Pudge crossed her arms. "Well, are you going to approve it? We can have him arrested by tomorrow afternoon with your say-so."

"If only it was that easy," Cora said. "I need a few things first. You won't like them."

"Why do you have to make this so hard, Cora?" Pudge sat down, palms to her eyes like I'd done earlier. "All right," she said, all breathy. "What do you need?"

"I was telling Viv that even if a request to pursue is approved, there will be no court in America, or Germany for that matter, that will convict him without something tangible linking him to his crimes. An official signature. Something!"

Pudge laughed. "Well, for that, we'd need to bring Ava back from the dead."

My eyes darted to Cora, who stubbed out her cigarette. "I was about to tell Viv when you walked in. Ava is alive. She didn't die in the war."

"What?" I wasn't sure what I was expecting, but it wasn't that. It seemed so improbable that she'd escaped.

"Alive?" Pudge ripped her hands away. "How?"

"I don't know, exactly. About a week after you two left, she walked into the villa looking for her paycheck," Cora said. "She refused to talk about what happened, and she wouldn't write a report worth anything. She married Manzo."

"Manzo?" I questioned. "The sergeant turned cook, turned..." Cora nodded as I talked. "He would never—"

"He did." Cora shrugged. "There was a war going on, and I didn't ask questions."

"Finding Manzo shouldn't be too hard. Records must have information on him," Pudge said. "And from what I know about Ava, she wouldn't have left the continent without her precious things, which means there's a paper trail."

I was starting to feel a sense of hope. "Pudge," I breathed, standing. "You're right. There would be records, wouldn't there?"

"Whoa, whoa, whoa," Cora said. "I need authorization, and for that, I'll need the team back together first, then positive identification. It's policy. Then we can worry about finding Ava."

"We are the team, and I already told you I can identify him along with Pudge," I said. "Start the authorization paperwork now."

"You don't understand." She cocked her head. "With today's CIA and all the paperwork required, I would need all four of you, including Junie and Dot, since they were there."

"What?" I looked at Pudge, mouth hanging open. "Pudge..."

"And when I say identify, that means you'll have to make contact with him. Viewing him at a distance will not qualify."

"They weren't part of this specific mission," Pudge said. "This doesn't make sense."

"Four sets of eyes to confirm," she said. "What is the matter with you two? This is what you wanted all along—to tell them about the mission and Engle, and now I'm giving you the go-ahead to do so."

"They don't need to be involved. After all this time, they'll believe us when he's caught," I said. "When the story is splashed across the evening news, when they read how long we've been looking for him and what lengths we went in order to catch him. I already told you Junie returned my letter and won't speak to me. There's no way she'd agree to do this."

Pudge had no expression. It was as if she'd been waiting the entire time for that final ax to drop on us and was not surprised. Her eyes shifted to mine, and then, in a surprise move, she winked.

I relaxed, taking my hands off Cora's desk.

"Now listen, Pudge." Cora pointed her cigarette. "Don't even think about going after him yourself. Viv is a civilian, and anything less than a coordinated mission from the CIA is breaking the law. Understand? Get the team together, and then we can proceed." She set down her cigarette to point her finger. "I mean business, Pudge. You need to walk the line between now and then and your retirement, or so help me."

Pudge nodded, grabbing my hand and shutting Cora's door between us. "We need to talk," she whispered, "but not here. I'll come by your place tonight. Late. Eleven o'clock. I'll be discreet."

"The house next to mine is for sale, and nobody's home."

"I'll park in front of that one. Be ready."

She nodded, then turned around and left while I walked back downstairs to Hal's office, hoping to catch him, but it was empty. I wrote him a note, leaving a lipstick print. *See you for dinner*. I placed it on Hal's chair, mostly because I didn't want anyone to think it was from his secretary, when I heard the most annoying, nerve-wracking voice in the hallway.

Barbara Bennington.

I knew she worked here. I'd just forgotten, or didn't care. I closed my eyes, hoping she'd pass by without looking inside, but she stopped just inside Hal's doorway. "Vivien Cunningham," she said, and I opened my eyes. "When I heard you were in the building, I didn't believe it."

I turned around, smiling. "Babs!" I gave her a pitiful hug. "How are you?"

Her hair was in a tight bun, which made her look smart. "I prefer Barbara. All grown up!"

"Aren't we all?" We stared at each other with silly smiles on our faces.

"Well..." She peeked into Hal's office. "Looks like Agent Cunningham stepped out. I'll just leave this report on his desk. It's for his trip at the end of the week." She reached around to place a yellow file folder on his desk.

"Good seeing you," I said.

Her gaze lingered for a bit before she left. "Yeah, you too, hon."

I adjusted my purse strap. Still, after all these years, Babs's voice sent shivers up my arms. And she worked *with* Hal? I didn't blame him for not telling me. He knew I wanted nothing to do with his organization or with the people I'd worked with.

I glanced at the folder. I'm not sure what came over me, but I had the urge to see what Babs had compiled. Were her reports still just as good? And maybe, I wondered, could I do better? I closed the door to all but just a crack and had a look at her report.

I read something about an agent he was working with in Israel.

Hal was working with the Mossad?

Hal's voice and footsteps came down the hall, and I swiftly

placed the papers in the folder. I turned around just before he opened the door, hands behind my back. Big smile.

"Viv! You came back."

The folder had closed on its own. "Hello, darling." I kissed his cheek, but he closed the door so we could have a private, passionate kiss, which gave my heart a flutter.

"Now, that's what I call a hello," he said, holding me.

"I was just leaving you a note." I gazed into big blue eyes. "Thank you for earlier and for not asking questions." I wasn't about to tell him what was going on, and I knew he wouldn't press either because he trusted me.

He smiled oddly, and that gave me a panic.

"Did you take an outside call?" My heart pounded.

"No." He looked confused. "You told me not to. Viv, what's going on?"

I took a relieving breath, patting my chest instead of clutching it. "It's a surprise." I nodded. "That's all." I shook my finger at him. "Now, don't spoil it. You had me worried just now." I kissed his cheek goodbye. "See you at home. And be hungry. I'm making your favorite—Steak Diane."

I accidentally passed by Babs's office as I left. "Bye-bye, Viv," she said, and I closed my eyes. She sounded like a bird or a cartoon. I almost laughed because Junie would have appreciated my imitation of her.

"Ah, Junie," I said to myself. "I miss you."

Mrs. Bunn knocked on my door precisely at five in the afternoon, arriving with the bottle of brandy I phoned her about, but didn't actually need.

"It smells wonderful in here, Viv. Steak Diane?"

"It is." She followed me into the kitchen. "Thank you for coming over so quickly," I said. "I was halfway through the sauce when I realized I didn't have any brandy." I closed my liquor cabinet so she couldn't see I had my own bottle, before opening hers and pouring a splash of liquid into my saucepan.

"Smells heavenly." She took a deep breath. "Looks like a good cut of beef, too. Special occasion?"

"That's the other reason I asked you over, Mrs. Bunn. I know you heard my call this morning."

I let that statement hang in the air.

"What call?" She looked so convincing, her mouth forming an "O". She even managed a dip in her eyebrow for added concern, which almost resembled a frown.

Mrs. Bunn was one of those people I'd want on my team if I was in the field—it really was a shame she wasn't chosen to join the OSS. They missed out on a good investigator.

I sighed. "Mrs. Bunn..." I opened my arms to her. "I know you know."

She beamed. "Congratulations, Viv." She walked around the counter, and we hugged.

"Thank you. I also want to thank you for not telling anyone my big news before Hal got home." Of course, I didn't actually know if she'd told anyone or not.

She giggled with a swat of her hand. "Absolutely."

I tried handing her the brandy back after I was done using it, but she refused. "Go ahead and keep it. Put it next to the other bottle you have in your cabinet." She smiled.

"You caught me."

"Yes. But I understand."

I continued to cook my steak, the sauce bubbling and filling the kitchen with an incredible savory smell. Mrs. Bunn watched.

"Hal will be home soon. I'm going to tell him over dinner."

She put her finger in the air. "Gotcha. I'll let myself out," she said, but I walked her to the door anyway.

She chatted about the weather and the house that was put up for sale next door, wondering how much it was going for, before adding, "Do you know anything about Mr. Cohen down the road? He's been gone for quite a while. Some say to Israel. And why would he leave a wife at home for so long to go over there? Sounds unbelievable to me."

We stood in my open doorway with the screen held open. "I don't know Mr. Cohen."

"Oh, you don't?" She looked surprised I didn't know him. "I just assumed."

"You assumed his wife hired me, is that right?"

She giggled. "Now you're the one who caught me. Yes. I was fishing."

"Mrs. Bunn, if I didn't know better, I'd say you were the neighborhood gossip."

"I'd like to think I'm the protector. Neighbor watch. He walks his dog first thing in the morning and last thing at night. I've seen him late … about eleven o'clock at night when he's not on one of his overseas trips. Who walks their dog that late?"

"That does seem rather late," I said, but what surprised me the most was that *she* was up that late. Pudge said she was coming by at eleven to talk to me. I hoped she'd be discreet like she promised.

"Yes, it sure does." She stared off into the distance, lost in her thoughts, but as luck would have it, Hal pulled into the driveway just then.

"Don't say anything, Mrs. Bunn," I reminded her as she headed down the walk. She turned, motioning to her lips like a zipper.

"Good evening, Mrs. Bunn," Hal said, but she walked by, motioning to her sealed lips.

Hal watched her walk into her house from our front door. "That was strange," Hal said.

I gave him a kiss. "You know Mrs. Bunn—such an odd one."

I picked up the evening paper from the step and followed Hal inside. I had the table all set with candles, even though it wasn't dark enough to use them yet. The entire bottom floor of our home smelled like brown gravy and brandy.

"Smells good in here." He took off his coat and set down his briefcase, which popped open just slightly. I saw the yellow folder Babs had given him. "I heard you saw Barbara Bennington today."

"Do you work with her often?"

"Not often." He gave me a smooch near the stove where the gravy bubbled around steak and mushrooms.

"Good. I was worried about your health for a second. Her voice will drive you mad."

He laughed.

"She said you had a trip at the end of the week."

"Unfortunately. I'll be gone for two days. Come with me."

"Where are you going?" I stirred the sauce.

"New York."

"I wish I could, but cheating husbands in the greater D.C. area are keeping me incredibly busy."

I dished up the plates while he scanned the newspaper.

"Quit and join me at the CIA, then." He set down the newspaper to wrap his arms around me, but I was taking my apron off. He nibbled on my neck where it tickled.

"You'd never get any work done."

"Neither would you," he said.

"I'm quite happy catching cheating husbands with my private firm."

He glanced at the den where I had my office. Files were stacked, and my tickler file was as fat as a stuffed pig, and not from being overloaded with business, but because the work had lost its zeal, if I was honest with myself.

I placed the steak dinner down in front of him.

"If you say so."

I had a seat opposite him, placing my napkin on my lap. It was time. "Hal…" He looked at me over the steaming steak. "Darling…" I said, but now my hands had a nervous shake to them. "I have something to tell you."

I held my breath when he smiled.

"You're expecting?" he blurted.

I clutched my chest. "Hal Cunningham! Did you know?" I wadded up my napkin and tossed it on the table as if I was upset, but I wasn't upset in the slightest. We both got up from the table, and he took me in his arms.

"I'm a CIA agent, trained to catch spies," he said.

"You mean, you called the doctor's office?" I asked.

"No, I just had a hunch after you asked me not to take any outside calls."

"It's because of Mrs. Bunn. She picked up the line when the doctor's office called and heard everything." I squeezed him extra tight. "I didn't want to chance her telling someone and then that someone calling to congratulate you."

"I figured," he said. "But does your news have anything to do with seeing Cora today?" He loosened his grip on me.

"No, and you know I wouldn't have gone to see her if it wasn't serious."

"I just don't want you getting mixed up with anything to do with Pudge. I know her work, and she's not always on the up and up."

"Let's eat." My perfectly cooked steak dinner was getting cold, and I wasn't about to let Engle, Cora, or Babs ruin my big evening.

I sat down, napkin in my lap and fork in my hand when I caught a whiff of the steak, which wasn't as pleasant as it was seconds ago. I covered my mouth in horror from a sudden rush of salty water coating my throat and tongue.

"What is it?" he asked.

I dropped my knife. "Oh, no," I managed to say seconds before I took off running for the bathroom.

That night, I lay fully clothed in bed with the covers pulled up to my chin, waiting for Pudge and her headlamps outside. A car drove by and I perked up, only for the light beaming through the windowpane to sweep across the wall instead of stopping. Hal turned over beside me, tucked away for the night and softly breathing.

In the span of twelve hours, my life had taken a drastic turn, with two of my dreams colliding in grand fashion. Most women would be lying in bed awake, wondering which color to paint the nursery. I was thinking of all the ways I'd confront Engle.

I closed my eyes briefly. *God, where are you, Pudge?*

Just after eleven o'clock, I finally saw a pair of headlamps pull up next door to the vacant house that was for sale. I crept downstairs after carefully getting out of bed, stopping only to slip on my shoes, but turned sharply when I heard Hal snore, knocking his briefcase off the side table in the dark.

I froze, waiting to see if he'd heard, then hastily placed it back on the table.

Outside, I traipsed across the dewy lawn to the curb. A small dog barked somewhere, which immediately got me to look at Mrs. Bunn's big front window to see if she was still awake, thinking it was her dog, but the reflection was black as night from having the curtains drawn.

When I hopped into Pudge's passenger seat, I was breathing heavily and waiting for her to say something urgent, but instead, she smoked her cigarette and stared blankly out the windshield. The leather was chilled against my skin. A new Buick. Probably Pudge's pride and joy.

I folded my hands. "Pudge?"

"Viv." She flicked ash from her cigarette. "You sure nobody is home at this house I'm parked in front of?"

"Yeah. It's for sale, been empty for weeks."

She took a long drag from her cigarette. "We're going to have to talk to Dot and Junie."

"What? They won't believe us, not unless we have Engle first."

"I know Cora. Been working for her the last eight of my ten years with the CIA. She's killed more assignments of mine than I can count because I didn't follow her specifications, even when my intelligence was plumb. She'll kill this one as well, if we don't bring the girls on board like she asked. It's her need to control and manipulate. We have to do what she says if we want Engle."

I crossed my arms, staring out the window with my mouth ajar. I thought for sure Pudge was going to swoop in with some incredible plan. Why else would she insist on talking to me so late at night and in the dark? She'd certainly been in the CIA long enough to come up with one, especially when her back was up against a wall, but then I thought, maybe that's the problem. She'd been in the CIA and under Cora's thumb for too long.

"Having two more witnesses isn't a plan," I said.

"If you come up with one—a legal one—let me know." She sucked on her cigarette until it was a little nub, smashing it into her car's ashtray. "I worked so hard to find him, too. Bastard almost caught me." She shook her head from remembering.

"Tell me the story."

She sighed, tipping her head back. "I wasn't supposed to be staying over in Manhattan, which is probably the first thing that irritated Cora. I was on my way back from Berlin. I was undercover there for three weeks."

I was glad to hear they weren't wasting Pudge's talents and had sent her to Berlin like I thought they should do. "Three weeks undercover? Well, you were one of the best, as I recall."

"That's debatable." She reached for another cigarette. "I was at the end of my mission and doing pretty well, that is, until I came across information about Engle. He has a sister. To begin with, it was by happenstance that I met her. She owns a café and was hanging a photograph of a woman…"

I sank down in the seat and listened to her story. Pudge questioned the photographer's Swedish name after the café owner said he was her brother and lived in Manhattan. "That's what got you on his trail? A name and a city?"

"Hardly." She rolled down her window to let a little fresh air in. "It was the photograph she was hanging. I recognized the landscape as the Füssen countryside, particularly the beach along the Lech, and the woman…" She turned to me. "Ava's old friend, Ingrid."

I covered my mouth. "Ingrid? The hat shop owner."

She lit her cigarette. "I never forget a face."

"Is Ingrid in Manhattan also?"

"I didn't see her."

"All this time, he's been right under our noses." I tasted something sour and just hoped I wasn't going to vomit in Pudge's car. "Makes me sick." I held my stomach.

"He's paranoid. I followed him into an alley but felt like I was the one being followed. The tiny apartment I rented was broken into, and I was left pretty shaken up by a man with bushy eyebrows in the alley, asking who I was and what I wanted with the photographer."

"What did you say?"

"I said I was lost in the city after a night out. That seemed to appease him, but it was clear to me Engle hired himself a goon to keep himself safe." She turned away, a little disbelieving shake to her head while looking out the windshield. "How's it going to be, Viv? When we realize that we don't know them anymore?"

Now I was shaking my head. "I don't know."

"On my way over here, I was thinking, what if we were wrong all those years ago? We chose to follow one set of rules and disobeyed the others. We should have told them then. The moment we touched down in Füssen."

"Easy to say now, but at the time, we were worried we'd be putting them at risk by telling them. Remember? We did the best with what information we had at the time."

"Yeah," she said. "I suppose you're right."

I realized that the window curtains at Mrs. Bunn's house were now open. I inched forward, straining to see with a few blinks of my eyes.

"What is it?" Pudge took a look.

"Nothing," I said. "Well, maybe something. My neighbor. I think she's up and watching us. Her curtains were closed when I walked out here." I sat back. "She's harmless. A gossip, but harmless. I'll have to come up with a story to explain why I'm in a car late at night with a stranger. She loves my stories." I looked at Pudge. "Life as a private investigator isn't without its excitements."

"When I retire, the most excitement I want is fresh ice in my beach drink."

I reached for her hand. "I missed you, Pudge."

"I missed you, Viv. Now, what's the plan to get our partners back? Catching Engle depends on it."

"I suppose it starts with a visit," I said.

"You should go first," she said.

I twisted in my seat, hand to my chest. "Why me?"

"Because Dot will be easier to convince if Junie is on board. What time should I pick you up?"

I took a deep breath. She was right. I just didn't want to be the one to go first. "Ten. Hal will be gone by then and won't ask questions. The last thing I need is for him to think we're working on something. Especially now that I'm having a baby."

She gasped. "You're pregnant? Viv—"

"Yeah. Found out this morning, right before everything hit the fan with Cora. Can you believe it?"

"I'm happy for you." She squeezed my hand. "And Junie will be too. You'll tell her?"

"I don't know." I swallowed hard because, on top of everything I had to say to her about Engle and the mission, I wasn't sure if it would have an impact, and that hurt most of all.

"Where should we start looking for her? The last known address I have is—"

"I know where she is. Just be here tomorrow."

I got out of the car, traipsing back up to my front door, and saw Mrs. Bunn's curtains fluttering to a close.

Chapter Seventeen

I sat at my kitchen table the next morning, waiting for Hal to leave. I had already called ahead, reconfirmed Junie's office hours at the university, and made an appointment with the department secretary, posing as a student with a question. I slipped my hand into my skirt pocket and felt for Junie's jacks from the box upstairs. She had no idea it was going to be me.

"All right. I'm off!" Hal reached for his briefcase, then bent down and kissed me goodbye, and right on time. Everything was moving along smoothly, which I hoped was a good sign of what was to come.

After he left, I finished a few last-minute housekeeping duties, dumping out my coffee cup, wiping the sink basin, fixing my hair one more time, and smoothing on some red lipstick. I slung my purse over my shoulder, at the same time having a look out the window, expecting to see Pudge, but to my shock, it was Hal.

He'd never left, and worse, he was talking to a man with a dog on the sidewalk.

I looked at my watch and then at the clock, my pulse quickening. The man adjusted his thick glasses as if he had all the time in the world to talk. The hall clock chimed. Pudge would be pulling up any minute, and then I'd have to explain. That was the last thing I wanted to do.

"Good morning!" I shouted, walking outside. They both waved. I pretended to check on my roses. "Hal! Don't you have work?" I tapped my watch, and that seemed to do the trick. Hal ended the conversation and got into his car. The man walked off.

I pretended to go back inside but turned around in the doorway because Pudge had pulled up in her Buick just after Hal drove away. I made my way over.

"Yoo-hoo!" Mrs. Bunn called from across the street. "Viv…"

She rushed over with her hand in the air, but it wasn't a wave; it was more of a signal not to move. I froze with Pudge's car door just out of my grasp.

"Good morning, Viv. Sorry, I won't be long. I can see you have somewhere to go." She leaned in closer. "Did you hear some strange noises last night? We might have had a prowler in the neighborhood. A car, a dark car, parked just there." She pointed to Pudge's Buick. "And it stayed for a good half hour."

"I didn't hear anything," I said, but I didn't have time to play games since I knew she saw me. "All right. It was me." I shrugged.

Her eyes gleamed.

"I was meeting with a colleague." I motioned with my eyes to Pudge sitting in her car. "It's a case we're working on, a high-profile case. A senator."

She covered her mouth in surprise, but then looked rather serious. "I see."

I looked down both directions of the street for added intrigue. "You know, you should come to work with me. You're very good at noticing small details."

She turned a shade of pink, then blushed a deep red. "Oh, Viv, I couldn't go to work."

"Why not?"

She stopped laughing to ponder that question.

"I have to go now, Mrs. Bunn." I reached for the door again. "Have a good morning."

"Oh, but one more thing," she said. "Why did you say you didn't know Mr. Cohen?"

"Mister who?" The exhaust glugged from the Buick's tailpipe.

"Mr. Cohen. I mentioned him yesterday, remember? He's the one that took the long overseas trip. You said you didn't know him, but you just waved to each other."

"I was waving to Hal."

She laughed, hands in the air. "Oh, yes, of course."

I got into the car, sitting heavily on the leather seats, watching Mrs. Bunn walk back toward her house. It was almost scary how much she knew about the neighborhood and how effortless she made it seem.

"Everything all right?" Pudge asked.

"Yeah," I said. "That's the nosy neighbor I told you about."

Mrs. Bunn threw open her window curtains, but instead of watching us from her couch, she popped up near the kitchen window, her curly head of hair barely visible over the ledge.

"I guess everyone has one." Pudge put her car in gear. "Now, where do we find Junie?"

"Georgetown University."

She stepped on the accelerator, driving the opposite way

Hal had gone. Both of us were quiet. I had been too focused on whether or not Junie would be in her office, that I hadn't thought about what I'd actually say when I got there. I imagined the secretary would be a student herself, maybe with a ponytail or brushed-out curls. And Junie...

My palms sweated.

"Are you nervous?" Pudge asked.

"Does a bear do its business in the woods?"

A laugh bumped in her throat. "Same old Viv, just a little more grown up. Don't worry. You still know each other. No matter how much time has passed." She tapped her heart. "It's in here. All those hours spent together in the war, each other's right hand—that dependency. It never leaves you."

Pudge was right about dependency. I wouldn't have made it to London without Junie, and she wouldn't have made it to Rome without me. All those recommendations, all those targets, and sleepless nights. I pointed to the exit Pudge needed to take.

My heart beat a little faster the closer we got. "Why does climbing Mount Everest seem more manageable than talking to her?"

"Because you love her," she said. "You always have, just like I love Dot, and we hurt them in the end. All you can do now is tell her the truth. It's all you have to offer."

We entered the downtown area and were getting closer to her building. The cherry blossoms were in full bloom, which brought out the bees, many meeting their demise on Pudge's windshield. "This is why I don't come down here in the day. It's colorful, gorgeous, love the spring! Hate bees. Ah, I should quit my griping. It's better than Manhattan where I found

Engle. Now, that place could use a cherry tree or two to brighten it up."

"Where exactly did you find him?"

"A shabby basement bar near Broadway."

"Broadway?"

"Off, off Broadway. The area where only the strong survive. Cheesy lounge singers and comedians who get locked up for swearing. Policeman who patrol for a price."

"That sounds appealing," I said. "I wonder if he'll recognize me."

"One hurdle at a time, Viv." She pulled into a parking lot and into a spot just outside the main faculty building. We both looked up at the office windows through the pink-blossoming cherry trees. "First, you need to go in there." She pointed.

My heart wasn't racing; it was pounding. "I…" I looked at my hands when they started shaking, then felt sick and held my stomach. "I don't know if I can do this."

"What do you mean you can't do this?" She reached over and opened my door, only for me to close it.

"I need a second. Or two, or three…" I took a few deep breaths with Pudge watching me. She must have realized I wasn't feigning a sickness and let me be. It had been a long time, and now the day was here. We'd meet. Face to face. And I had a lot to answer for.

"Hey, let's talk about something else," Pudge said. "Until you feel better." She looked at her watch. "So, what if you're a little late? You get the whole half hour. Right?"

I nodded. "Yeah. Talk about something else." I turned to her. "Go."

"I can tell you about work. Babs. She's a pill, but she is a good agent. She'll get promoted soon."

I groaned. "I don't want to talk about Barbara Bennington. Something else, please." I closed my eyes.

"Kitty, well, she left a few years back. Yeah, married someone in accounting. Thought she couldn't have it all—a career and a child—so she quit."

My eyes sprang open. "She quit? But she'd made it so far! Most likely riding Babs's coattails, but she made it nonetheless, a real modern woman on paper, at least. I bet people listened to her, too."

"Oh, she quit all right. I remember because there was cake, and I never forget a cheap cake."

I laughed.

"You can have it all, Viv. If you wanted."

It was quiet. I looked at my hands, which had stopped shaking. It was time. Now or never. And if I couldn't get in there and defend myself after all these years, then I'd never be able to.

I opened the car door.

"Good luck," Pudge said, leaning over the seat. "And don't forget, if you can't get Junie on board, then I won't be able to get Dot. No pressure. Just telling you how it is."

"Thanks, Pudge."

I shut the car door and started walking.

I opened the front doors to the building, only to find that instead of a lobby and a receptionist, as I had thought, it was a narrow hallway with classes in session. The door slammed shut behind me, and a student told me to shush, closing their classroom door amid glares and gawks. The smell of old books and stagnant air was suffocating, sending me right back to the WAC training facility in Daytona.

Junie tapped her pencil on my notebook until I looked up. I'd looked over all my exam answers and checked them twice. "Trust me. You got a perfect score. Turn it in."

We'd been partners for weeks, eating our meals together, living together, studying together, telling each other our hopes and fears, but how well do you really know someone until you trust them with your secrets, and boy, did I have one. I just didn't know what she'd say when I told her. Would she take pity on me? That's exactly what I didn't want.

I looked over my paper again while she crossed her arms. I knew the moment I stopped focusing on the exam, my thoughts would turn down a dusty, bumpy path, and back to this morning when we'd had our medical evaluations.

"Look, Viv." She offered to take my paper to the front to be graded. "If you aren't sure now, you'll never be."

"Shh!" someone hissed. There were a handful of WACs still taking their exams, and Junie wasn't one for being quiet.

"Is there something else bothering you?" she whispered.

I closed my eyes. I wasn't about to tell her there, in that stuffy training room that smelled of old books and dust. "Here, take it."

We bought some Scotch at the PX to celebrate the end of testing even though I wasn't fond of whisky. "You know we're the best, right, Viv? Nobody can match our record. We deserve to celebrate. That promotion in London is as good as ours."

She ran ahead of me and did a little twirl, her brassy blonde hair twisting in the sunlight and that smile of hers... The last thing I wanted to do was spoil things, and I tried like hell to stuff my thoughts down and not ruin the moment; I'd done such a good job of it while taking the exam.

"Aren't you excited?" she asked. "I can't wait for you to write that letter to your parents." She squinted for effect. "Take that, hotshot brother. Vivien Allen is moving up the ranks!"

She poured me a glass of the Scotch once we'd reached our barracks.

"To us," she said, clinking her glass to mine. I mustered a smile. "There's nothing we can't do."

I took a sip, but it did little to no good, and sat on my bed with my head in my hands, overwhelmed with what I'd learned that morning and unable to hide it any longer.

"All right, will you tell me what's going on?" She looked at her drink as if that was the problem. "If it's the Scotch, I'll get something else."

"Oh, Junie…" A look of horror washed over her face when I burst into tears like a silly cartoon. No matter how much she tried to calm me down, I couldn't, for the life of me, dry up. The hiccups came next.

"You're scaring me, Viv," she said. "Does this have something to do with the exam?"

I shook my head.

"The doctor?"

I looked up.

She immediately sat next to me for comfort, and my entire life history flashed before my eyes. How I'd had my appendix out when I was a child, and although I came out of it fine, there had been some damage.

"What did the doctor say?"

I'd been holding my breath. "I can't have children," I blurted, and that isn't something someone should blurt, but I felt better for saying it out loud once I decided to tell. "The doctor said my insides are mostly scar tissue."

"Ah, Viv. I don't know what to say."

She let me cry into her shoulder, and I felt bad for ruining the day and our celebration. "I'm sorry." I wiped my cheeks of tears. "Forget I said anything." I filled my glass to the rim with Scotch, spilling some on the table. "Right now, we should be celebrating." I took a gulping drink with my eyes closed, the liquor scorching the back of my throat and pooling hot in my stomach. "That drink might have made things worse." I sat heavily back down on the bed after trying to stand.

"Viv." She put her hand on mine. "You don't have to pretend. Everything will be all right. You are so much more than—"

"I'll be alone." I wanted to tell her I was scared. "Nobody wants to be alone."

She shook her head feverishly. "Vivien Allen, you won't be alone, you hear me?"

"My mother says a woman who doesn't marry is a lonely woman."

"Your mother is wrong. If a man doesn't marry you because you can't have his babies, then he isn't worth marrying at all."

I wiped my eyes until I could see a little clearer.

"Listen to me, Viv. You're never going to be alone. We have each other. Partners till death, and maybe even after. And Annie too—my little girl. I'll write to her, and she'll know all about you before she even meets you in person."

"You mean it, Junes?"

"Yeah. We'll be neighbors. Only you'll have a husband, and I'm perfectly fine not having one. You already know my secret, that I'm not a widow and never had a husband. Now, I know your secret. We're stronger for it. Our boys over the pond have to trust each other, and we should be trusting each other, too, even if it hurts sometimes."

She slung her arm over my shoulders, giving me a side hug. "It's going to be okay. Wanna hook fingers on it?"

I smiled, and we hooked our pinkies and gave them a little shake.

A woman's cold touch on my arm shocked me into the present. I yelped, hand to my chest, but she acted like I was the problem, giving me a glare.

"Shh! There are classes in session," she rasped. "Are you a student?"

I saw a sign directing students to the second floor for office visits and started my way up.

She called out to me from below. "Hey!" she rasped. "Are you a student? Come back here!"

I walked up to the department secretary, who was sitting at her desk. The bronze nameplate said, Brenda. "Hello, Brenda." From the bottom of the stairs, I heard the woman asking someone for a security guard. "I have an appointment with Junie Knight," I said, then corrected myself. "Professor Knight."

She gave me a look, probably thinking I looked too old to be a student.

"Is there a problem?" I asked.

She tapped my appointment slot in her ledger, which I'd made under a fake name. "Ruth Evens?"

I nodded.

"You're late."

"Car trouble." I looked down the stairs again. "Can I see Professor Knight?"

She nodded once. "Office seven. On your right."

I fully intended to breeze right into her office for momentum, only I stopped an arm's reach away in a place where she couldn't see me, but I could see her. She was reaching for a book on the bookcases behind her desk.

"Brenda," Junie said, thinking I was the secretary. "Cancel my eleven o'clock. If they can't make it on time, then I don't have time for them."

I wondered what her reaction would be when she turned around and saw me with no warning.

"Did you hear me?" Junie asked, her back still to me. "Brenda..."

I stepped inside. "Hey, Junes," I said, and she froze with her arm in the air and the book she was reaching for in her hand. "It's me."

She took a second before finally lowering her arm and whipping around. I thought I saw a smile lift her cheeks before the shock took over her face. "Viv."

Her hair was more refined than when we were partners, no longer brassy and tucked into a well-managed bun. The eyeglasses were new, but not surprising considering our age.

"I missed you," I said, which I hadn't planned but couldn't resist once I saw her.

She sat down stiffly. "You're my appointment?" She read from a piece of paper. "Ruth Evens."

"I know it must come as a surprise to see me..."

She squeezed her eyes closed, and I took a seat before she could order me out, arms clutched around my purse in my lap. "The night we left Rome for Füssen, Cora pulled Pudge and me aside. We were selected for a special side mission and ordered not to tell our partners."

Her eyes sprang open. This wasn't what she'd expected, which I hoped meant that she'd hear me out. I glanced once out the door, thinking I heard that woman from below.

"The German..." I got up briefly to close her door. "The German officer that drove us to the river—Joseph Engle—he was wanted by the OSS for reasons I only came to fully understand once Pudge and I made it back to Rome. He's a war criminal, commandant from Flossenbürg, leader of the death marches there, and responsible for the mass murder of hundreds of American POWs. You remember that Flossenbürg is where my grandfather was murdered."

Junie hadn't blinked.

"I didn't go into Gunther's apartment because of a competition with Babs and Kitty. I went in to get evidence on Engle before we left, because it was my only shot. You always said I talked too much, but the truth is, I couldn't talk about this. I was willing to risk my safety for it, but I wasn't going to risk yours. It's the only reason I didn't tell you the truth in Füssen. Why I lied."

She finally blinked. I waited for her to say something as she began to blindly pick at the corner of a piece of paper on her desk. But after a few seconds, the silence was starting to get to me, and I wasn't sure if what I'd said was working.

"Aren't you going to say something?"

"You were ordered to do surveillance?"

"Not exactly."

"But you just said—"

"There was one stipulation. We weren't supposed to go digging up bones, as Cora liked to say. We were there to observe, but after I learned that there was something in that apartment that would sink Engle, Pudge and I agreed we had to dig a little and thought the risk to our lives was worth it. We hoped you'd drive off without us."

"Why are you telling me this now?"

"I wanted you to know. I've always wanted you to know. I sent you a letter."

She was studying me—from the way I sat in her chair to the way I held my hands and how they were folded. I thought about asking her how they escaped Nazi Germany, but I still had to tell her about Engle living in Manhattan, and that was more important.

"That's not the only reason you're here. I can tell."

I smiled hesitantly because maybe she still knew me, at least a little bit. "He's living a secret life in Manhattan. Pudge found him—she works with Cora at the CIA—only the brass at the CIA won't touch him unless we can identify him. All four of us—a mission."

She ripped off her glasses and dug her palms into her eyes.

"Do you believe me?"

A commotion erupted in the hallway—someone was coming. The woman from downstairs had found me, and by the sound of it, she'd brought a security guard with her.

He opened Junie's door without knocking first. Blue uniform and a baton at his side.

Junie bolted to her feet. "What is the meaning of this?"

"Escort her out," the woman said, pointing at me, "she's not a student." Her lips pursed.

"What does it matter to you?" Junie asked.

The woman looked astonished that Junie would talk to her in such a way, then a little disgraced. "She was loitering downstairs, Professor."

Junie addressed the security guard. "She's my eleven o'clock."

At that point, the woman realized she'd messed up and

Junie's secretary shooed them all out. The office turned quiet again.

"I guess I lost my touch." I blew on my nails to see if she would laugh. I thought I saw a smile.

"Yeah."

I wanted to tell her that I was pregnant but didn't have the guts just yet. "Annie, is she…"

"She's in middle school and plays the clarinet. Both of us are doing well."

"You're a professor. No surprise, of course. I always knew you'd be a success, a real modern woman, someone who has it all." I looked at my hands. "Does Annie… Does Annie know about me?"

She hesitated. "I see a wedding ring on your finger. Hal?"

I nodded. The way she dismissed my question was telling. I wasn't about to tell her about the baby now because I wasn't sure if she would care, and that would crush me. I just needed her to believe me first. The rest would come later.

A lump formed in my throat. "Junie, do you—"

"Listen, Viv. I'll think about it, but I can't promise anything."

I stood. "I understand. But I'm afraid we only have a couple days before the CIA scraps all discussions on this matter, giving Engle a free pass. If you decide to go forward, meet me at the south bench at Waterfront Park tomorrow at noon. You know where it is?"

She nodded. "Why would they scrap all discussions?"

"The United States government doesn't care about Nazis anymore." I reached into my purse for her jacks. "Only communists."

"I see."

I held my chin up, feeling the jacks in my closed palm.

"I have a lot to think about. This is very shocking and hard-to-digest news." She rubbed her forehead. "You understand, don't you?"

I placed the jacks on her desk. "It was good to see you again, Junes. For what it's worth." I turned and walked away because I couldn't bear looking at her face any longer where she wasn't my friend and hadn't forgiven me, especially after I spilled all my secrets.

"Viv?" she said, followed by a clearing of her throat. "Vivien."

I stopped in the doorway, my back to her.

"It was good to see you, too."

I nodded once, my eyes welling.

Chapter Eighteen

I jumped in the front seat of Pudge's car and shut the door, clutching my purse like a life preserver. Pudge smoked the last of her cigarette while staring out the window. Students walked by with their books, plaid skirts, and ballet flats, probably whispering about who the older women were.

"Well?" I said after several seconds of silence. "Aren't you going to ask me about it?"

"What's there to ask?" Her eyes shifted. "I can see for myself. She doesn't believe you, does she?"

I let go of my purse to fold my arms. "I don't know."

She scoffed. "You don't know?"

"Yeah, that's what I said."

Pudge crushed her cigarette into a mountain of butts, an entire pack's worth, it looked like, with ash spilling over the sides of the tray, sprinkling her console and floorboards.

A minute or so passed, and we just sat there. I realized she was nervous about seeing Dot, and about how if things hadn't worked out between me and Junie, then they probably wouldn't work out for her and Dot.

"I asked Junie to meet me at Waterfront Park tomorrow at noon if she was in. That's how we left things."

"Why noon?"

"Why not?"

"Did she listen to everything you said?" she asked, and I nodded. "About Engle, Manhattan, and how we had orders?"

"Yes..." I was still nodding. "I said it all. I asked if she believed me, and she didn't answer." I sat up slightly. "She did say that it was good to see me."

Pudge perked. "She said that?"

"Well..." I hoped she was being sincere, but after thinking about it once again, I couldn't be sure. "I said it to her first."

"Oh."

"Can we go? It's your turn."

Driving away from Georgetown felt like a huge weight had been lifted, but in the same breath, another weight had replaced it. We headed out of the city.

"Was it hard getting Dot's address?" I asked.

"I know where she lives." She gripped the steering wheel tightly. "I've known for a long time."

"You've seen her?" I asked. "But I thought—"

"I haven't seen her since Füssen. And before you ask, yes, she's married, and Mary is eight, Jackie is seven, and Pip is five. There's a baby, but I don't know her name. I haven't seen her house. Just know where it is." She pointed up ahead. "Not far now."

I stared at Pudge while she drove. She'd been watching Dot's successes from afar, like I had done with Junie.

"I guess you could say we're hopeless dreamers," I said. "Or hopeful dreamers."

"Or just plain fools."

We'd headed out of the city and into Burnt Mills, a residential area with corner grocery stores and butcher shops. Housewives called their children in from outside or let them out to play. A mailman walked by, delivering that day's parcels.

"I'm nervous," Pudge said.

"I'm nervous for you."

I tried to think of something else to talk about—the streets, the homes, my breakfast that morning—but somehow, the conversation veered back to the CIA.

"You want my job?" she asked. "Soon to be vacant. Cora is a nightmare, but otherwise, it's fulfilling work."

"I like what I'm doing," I said.

"Hal doesn't mind you working?"

I looked at her. "Hal wants me to be happy."

"Are you, though? Happy catching cheating husbands?"

She turned onto Alder Avenue, a picturesque little neighborhood with uneven sidewalks, grassy green lawns, and clay flowerpots. Ivy grew heartily up brick chimneys, and neighbors waved to other neighbors. "Looks like something from *Life Magazine*, doesn't it?"

"It really does," Pudge said. "It's exactly where I always thought Dot would end up."

Dot had found herself a little slice of American bliss. Good for her, I thought. Then I felt bad because Pudge was most likely going to upend her perfect world in a matter of minutes.

Pudge came to a stop under a shady tree, its leaves quivering from birds making nests in its branches. She turned off the car, and the glug of the engine was replaced by a distant dog bark, a woodpecker pecking, and a child laughing from somewhere.

There were two powder-blue homes across from each other, nearly identical with white dormers. "Which one is hers?"

A woman with a baby on her hip walked out of one, following her husband to his car where they kissed. Another woman across the street helped her small daughter with a watering can for her roses.

"There she is." Pudge shakily pulled a cigarette from her pack and stuck it in her mouth.

Both looked similar—petite brunettes with children. "Which one?"

"Lady with the baby." She pointed at the woman who was now waving goodbye to her husband as he drove back to work, presumably having finished his lunch hour. Afterward, she took the baby to the fence line and chatted with the mailman while he dug into his satchel for her mail.

Her hair was shorter than it had been during the war, set with curls that brushed against her white dress collar and a strand of pearls. She was just far enough away not to recognize us through the windshield, but close enough for us to notice the details.

Pudge took a heavy breath. "I can't do it."

I shifted in my seat. "What do you mean 'you can't do it'?"

She struck her lighter over and over again until her thumb had turned raw. "Damn thing." She tried shaking it.

"Relax!" I took the lighter away and was able to get a flame on the first try. "Take a moment."

She inhaled that cigarette, then collapsed in her seat,

exhausted, and she hadn't even gotten out of the car yet. Dot was still talking to the mailman, but for how long?

"Pudge, it's been a few minutes. You have to talk to her before she goes inside."

Her eyes were closed. "One more second."

I gave her a second, and then some more. "Pudge—"

"We met on the first day." Her eyes popped open. "We trained together and finished each other's sentences. Hell, it wasn't a matter of if you want ice cream, it was what flavor you wanted."

"I know all this."

"Did you know she never wanted to go into Nazi Germany? I didn't just talk her into it. I begged her to do it, for me. That's what I said to her. I know everyone thought I said something inspirational. She even covered for me once in the villa kitchen when you asked, but that wasn't the case. I ruined everything then, and I might ruin this, too."

My stomach twisted into knots. We'd come all this way, and I'd already talked to Junie. "What are you saying?" I gulped. "Pudge?"

"If I don't talk to her, then there's still a chance. It's an open wound that will never heal, but at least it's still open."

"No!" I held my temples where my head was pounding. "And what about Engle, and what will I tell Junie tomorrow at the park? That you didn't have enough courage to tell Dot the truth, or that she didn't believe you? Both are detrimental."

"You don't know if Junie will be there."

"We've waited more than ten years for this," I said sternly. "What happened with our partners was a misunderstanding. They need to know the truth. It's time, Pudge. They need—"

The mailman had walked away, leaving Dot at the fence with her baby, looking right at us. She'd seen us.

"Oh my God." I tapped Pudge's arm. "She sees us. You have to go now. What will she think?" I tapped her arm again, but this time gave her a little push.

"Don't you think I see that?" she seethed.

After taking a second to look at her face in the rearview mirror, Pudge got out of the car. "Here goes nothing." She flicked her cigarette in the road as she walked off.

Dot never moved, and I think it was because she was flabbergasted to see Pudge walking toward her. I dug into my purse for my own cigarette and waited nervously, trying to ascertain how it was going by judging Dot's body language, but Pudge was blocking most of the view. A mere three minutes later, Pudge was on her way back, and Dot had gone back inside.

She got in the car, slightly out of breath. "My heart is still racing."

"What did she say?"

"Her baby was darling." Her voice wavered. "A little Dot if I ever saw one. Big brown eyes—"

"What did she say?" I flicked my cigarette out the window.

"She listened. That's it. She just listened, and I told her everything—from our secret mission to all of Engle's crimes. Afterward, she just blinked. I asked her to say something, but I think she was too stunned because she kept blinking. That's when I walked back." She took a deep breath, hand to her chest. "You were right, Viv. She had to know the truth, and I got it all out. It's in her hands now."

"And she didn't say a thing?"

"Not a word."

I rubbed my face. Deep down, I thought Pudge would have better luck than me, and now it appeared we were in the same boat. Pudge started the car, eager to get out of there, but in her haste, she flooded the engine, and it wouldn't start.

I tossed up my hands.

"I didn't mean to."

We waited for what seemed like an eternity. A housewife walked by with her dog, looking into my open window, but it was more of a stare, trying to figure out what two women were doing parked on her street. I waved. She waved back.

I turned to Pudge. "Try it again," I rasped.

Dot had snuck up behind us on Pudge's side of the car and tapped on the glass. "Why are you still here?"

Both of us shot up in our seats. Dot leaned in after Pudge rolled down the window, resting her arms on the door. "Viv, you're looking well."

"Dot."

"You two have a lot of nerve showing up here."

She took pointed looks at both of us. We never said a word as she examined us. I thought maybe Pudge was too petrified, because her eyes were locked on something far away through the windshield. I was just waiting to see what Dot was going to say.

"I've spent ten years putting my OSS days behind me."

"How is that going, Dot?" I asked, which earned me a glare from Pudge.

"Viv—"

"It's all right," Dot said to Pudge. "Because it hasn't been going well. I need to think, and whatever my decision is, I'll be doing it for me and my family." She ended with a prolonged look at Pudge, which I took as a direct reference to how Pudge talked her into the Füssen mission to begin with. She walked away, cutting right through the road toward her house.

Hal walked through the door just after I put the pasta on to boil. He set his briefcase on the kitchen table and pulled his tie away from his neck. I chopped herbs for the spaghetti sauce. "How was work?" he asked.

I was still chopping, trying not to think about tomorrow and what would happen if Junie didn't show up. I closed my eyes. God, I had to stop thinking about it, or Hal would know I was up to something.

"Viv?"

My eyes popped open. "Sorry, darling. I was…" I shook my head, thinking. "Daydreaming. What did you say?"

He kissed both my cheeks. "How was your day?"

If he had looked into the den, he would have seen that I still had a stack of paperwork to do and my tickler file was still fat as a pig. Normally, I would have gone into a big explanation of what I'd done, but this time I kept it simple.

"Quiet." I stirred the sauce after sprinkling in some fresh oregano. "I've been working on this sauce for a while. I hope you love it."

I gave him a taste from the spoon after blowing on it.

"Did you tell everyone at work our news?" I asked.

"Just a few colleagues I can trust. I didn't want to tell any of the women because it would spread like wildfire, and since I still plan to recruit you…"

I laughed. "You're not recruiting me."

He shuffled through the mail. "That's what you say, but

you never know. You made it into my office, and I never thought that would happen either." His eyes lifted from the mail just as mine lifted from the herbs.

I set the knife down. "I'm serious, Hal. I'm not working for the CIA. It's OSS redesigned, and I know how they work. You know most men want their wives at home, especially when they find out they're pregnant."

"I'm not most men. Besides, how many men can say they have a wife who was in the OSS, operated secret missions in Nazi Germany, and lived to tell about it?"

"I don't know…" I pretended to count on my fingers.

"Not many, if any at all."

"Did you ever work with Kitty Meyer? I heard she quit after becoming pregnant."

"Not directly, but Viv, Kitty Meyer doesn't hold a candle to you. I believe you can do it all."

I kept stirring the sauce. I wasn't going to disagree with him about not holding a candle to me. I'm sure Babs typed out all her reports.

Hal opened his briefcase on the table and shuffled through his papers. I saw that yellow file folder Babs had given him and a photo—a man, looked like a passport photo—but I could barely make out the features because of the angle his case was situated.

I picked my knife back up. "What were you talking to the neighbor about this morning?" I chopped that basil until there was hardly anything left of it.

He looked up from his papers, hands deep in his briefcase. "This morning?"

"Yeah." I reached for the parsley next.

He gave me a confused look.

"Out on the sidewalk before you left for work," I clarified. "Has a beard, walks his dog…" I turned down the gas and set the sauce to simmer.

"Oh!" He threw his head back as if he just remembered. "Mr. Cohen? He lives down the street." He went back to his paperwork, but I was still looking at him. "He walks his dog at the same time I leave every morning. Nice fellow. A little talkative. He asked me about the house that's for sale next door."

"I see." I untied my apron. "Mrs. Bunn said he's suspicious."

"Suspicious? Suspicious how?"

"Well, maybe she didn't use that exact word. She thinks he might be cheating on his wife."

He laughed. "Why would Mrs. Bunn think that?"

"She said he was gone on some overseas trip for quite a while. Not that traveling overseas is suspicious, but she did wonder how plausible his story was."

Hal snapped his briefcase shut. "He was overseas?"

"He didn't mention it?" I asked. "I'd think that would be something to mention."

He shrugged after giving it a think. "No. Mostly, we talked about the paperboy and how he always seems to miss our front step. Were you hoping for a new client with his wife?"

I laughed. "Maybe."

"Watch out for Mrs. Bunn," he said.

"Why?"

"A gossip is like a flying bomb. Sneaky and unpredictable. I wouldn't be surprised if Mrs. Bunn thinks I'm cheating on you by the end of the week because I have that business trip and will be away."

"She's harmless, Hal, really. She's a protector of the neighborhood. In fact, she'd make a great agent. That's who you should be recruiting."

He rolled his eyes. "Sure. Neighborhood gossip catches communists. I can see the headline now."

"Well, why can't you see it? Mrs. Bunn is an analyst at heart. I think she has skills. Stranger things have happened. Besides, with what the CIA is up to these days, it seems like the world is upside down."

"What do you mean?"

"Ahh…" I hesitated because when discussing the CIA, I was also indirectly referring to him. "All right, fine. I'll say it. Why aren't you interested in catching Nazis anymore?"

He looked a little uncomfortable, squirming a bit under his loosened tie. "Where did you hear that?"

"Cora," I said, then followed up with, "I heard her talking with her assistant, and it's been on my mind ever since. She said the United States government doesn't care."

"Communism is the current threat, but that doesn't mean I don't care. You know how nations are, on to the next war."

"Yeah, but Nazis, Hal. We were there and saw what they did."

"What can I do about it? I'm an agent out of hundreds with files on my desk a mile high. Also, every mission is covered in so much red tape that it takes box cutters to get through."

I scoffed, reaching for the parsley to chop again even though I'd taken my apron off. "I'm sure you can think of something." He opened his briefcase. "Don't you have any ideas in that briefcase?"

He gave me an eye, his meaning clear—be careful what you ask—because as a civilian, I wasn't supposed to know. But after peeping through his files at the office, I already knew he was working with the Mossad or at least had some connections.

"Well, if you are working on something, I hope you arrest them. In Europe and here in America. Make them pay…" As I talked, I realized I was doing exactly what I shouldn't be doing —going into detail. I set the knife down. "I know!" I smiled. "Let's make them listen to Liberace for hours on end," I said, which got him to laugh. "That should do the trick. They'll give up whole families just to make the music stop!"

He kissed me on the mouth, leaving a smear of lipstick on his lips. "I love you."

A knock on the door got us both to look. "Hello! It's me. Mrs. Bunn…" She knocked again. "Yoo-hoo!"

I washed off my hands. "Speak of the devil."

"She's been listening to us," Hal said.

I moved to answer the door.

"Wait," Hal said. "Don't answer it." He snapped his briefcase closed. "She'll never leave."

"Shh!" I opened the door. "Hello, Mrs. Bunn. Come in."

She walked in hesitantly, as if she'd heard Hal and I talking. "Is now a bad time?"

Hal spoke up from the kitchen. "Well, actually—"

"It's fine, Mrs. Bunn."

"Are you finished with the brandy?" she asked. "I know I told you to keep it, but now I haven't time to run to the store, and I need some myself."

"Sure," I said, motioning for her to follow me into the kitchen where she and Hal said hello to each other. "Here you go."

She held on to the bottle with both hands. "Thanks," she said, but instead of walking away, she paused, almost as if she was searching for something else to talk about. "How was your day?"

"Oh, ahh... It was good. Yours?"

The phone rang, which was the perfect excuse for Hal to leave and take the call in the front room. She waited until he was out of earshot. "So, how is your friend?" she whispered.

"My friend?"

She looked once toward Hal in the other room after hearing him talking. "The one in the nice car this morning."

Hal was on his way back in.

"She's fine," I said, then swiftly changed the subject. "How's your daughter, Jessica? She's working for an art auction house, you said?"

Hal stepped one foot in the kitchen to grab his briefcase, then stepped right back out.

"Yes, she is. I'm so proud of her. She's become quite the detective working on provenance for art that made its way over from Europe." She waited for me to say something as I stood over my boiling pot. "You know, stolen art. Never can be too careful. She's been keeping a list of art owners along the eastern seaboard. There's this one painting she's been trying to negotiate the sale of, but the owner is German and stubborn as anything. She refuses to talk to anyone if it isn't in her own language because she doesn't trust American contracts—"

She looked into my pot after I stared too long and saw my noodles had overcooked.

I turned off the burner with a huff.

"I hope that's not my fault," she said, but it kind of was. "I better let myself out. Dang it for me to go on talking about my daughter and that Duval painting."

"What did you say?" She was halfway to the door. "Mrs. Bunn, wait!" I dashed to the front room and blocked the door. My heart was pounding. "A Duval painting?"

I smiled.

"Yes. Are you familiar with art? It's got a funny name." She snapped her fingers repeatedly. "The Wrecking Ball, the Wrecker…"

My heart stopped. *"The Reckoning?"*

"Yes, that's it!" she said, but Hal sounded like he was going to come downstairs. I shooed her outside, offering to walk her back to her house.

"Tell me more about the seller," I said once we were near the sidewalk. "A German woman, you said? Mrs. Bunn, I might know who it is. What a coincidence if I'm right."

Her eyes lit up. "Does this have something to do with a case you're working? A mistress or cheating husband? You've got me very curious."

I nodded. "Yes. That's right. It's an incredible story, actually." I gulped, giving me a chance to come up with something. "My client wanted to double-cross her husband with his own money and buy the very painting he gifted to his German mistress, but for triple the cost."

Mrs. Bunn gasped. "You don't say…"

"Only she couldn't bring herself to talk to the woman who stole her husband. Understandably. If it's the same person, I might be able to help Jessica and my client all in one transaction. Did you know I speak German fluently?"

She shook her head. "I didn't know that, no."

I looked back once through my screen door to see if Hal was there. All seemed clear. "Mrs. Bunn. I think I should talk to your daughter. If it's the same person, we can both make a few bucks."

"I'll go write down her number." She ran inside her house and came out with Jessica's telephone number written on a piece of paper. "What's her name?"

"Who?" I asked.

"The German mistress."

"Oh! Ava Manzo. Accent, gorgeous. Blonde. Will drive a hard bargain." I laughed nervously, which got Mrs. Bunn to laugh.

I stuffed the number in my pocket. "Thank you."

"I know this probably isn't protocol, but would you mind telling me more? You know, if your client gets the painting back? I love a good double-cross."

"Absolutely." I winked. "You've been a great help."

"I have to tell you, this is much more intriguing than Mr. Cohen."

We both turned, walking back into our respective homes. Only once I was inside mine, I put my back to the door, processing what I'd just learned from Mrs. Bunn. Could it be? God, what luck if it was Ava. My heart was still pounding. My story was almost too good. I wanted to laugh.

German mistress.

Hal yelled down from the second floor. "Honey, what's for dinner?"

"Ahh…" My pasta dish was ruined, and I was too scattered to cook anything else. "Reservations, darling!"

Hal laughed. "All right. I'll be right down. Angelino's tonight?"

I chewed on my fingernail, thinking of Jessica and when to call her. Hal's briefcase was slightly open, back on the kitchen table and barely visible from the front room, but I saw what appeared to be Babs's report sticking out.

"Yeah, that sounds fine." I moved closer, unable to resist, pulling the yellow file out before Hal made it downstairs, and rifling through the papers to find that photo. I gasped. It was Mr. Cohen.

That's why Hal was talking to him. He's with the Mossad.

"Damn, Mrs. Bunn," I mumbled to myself. "You really should be an agent."

"Ready?" Hal asked, coming down the stairs. I quickly tucked the file back inside his briefcase because the last thing I wanted, among other things, was for him to think I was interested in Babs's report. "Viv?"

"Yeah?"

He walked into the kitchen to see me smiling with my hands gently clasped.

"Can we make it an early night?" I asked. "I have a big day tomorrow." I reached for my sweater.

"Oh? What do you have planned?"

We walked to the front room.

"Well, I could tell you, but then I'd be breaking client trust." I shrugged.

He put on his jacket. "You're going to a museum with Mrs. Bunn, aren't you?"

I grabbed my purse. "A museum?"

He opened the door for me. "I heard you talking about art."

I smiled. "You caught me."

Chapter Nineteen

The following morning, we arrived at Waterfront Park ten minutes early. I slid into the empty space beside Pudge, tightening my trench coat amid the graying skies. A light breeze whistled through the trees, giving me a shiver. I'd been a wreck for hours and searching for things to do around my home, but no matter how hard I cleaned, the floors didn't shine enough, and the windows weren't clear enough. The laundry wasn't dry enough. I had made a conscious decision not to think about Junie while at dinner last night because I didn't want Hal to think anything was off, but saving all my nerves for the morning was starting to make me ill, and proving to be more than I could handle.

I rubbed my trembling hands for warmth. "It's cold."

Pudge's gaze shifted from the river to my hands. "That's not because of the cold. That's nerves." She pulled her hands from her pockets. "Mine are shaking, too. Did you get some sleep last night?"

"Not a wink. You?"

She shook her head. "Not. A. Wink."

A dog, loose off his leash, ran up to us for a sniff of the grass. I yelped, throwing my legs onto the bench, but he ran off before his owner could catch him. I was still holding my chest.

"You're not making it any better."

"I'm afraid of dogs, all right?" I checked my watch. It was almost time. I looked down the path, near the lapping river, and over my shoulder to the parking lot where I thought I heard a car door close. Still no sign of Junie or Dot.

"Is Hal still in the dark about all this?"

"He thinks I'm going to a museum today with our neighbor."

She turned to me on the bench. "Viv, what do you want out of this?"

I scoffed. "Isn't it clear?"

"No, it's not. Let's say Junie and Dot help us identify Engle. Is that enough? I remember their faces on the platform in Füssen, the disappointment, the disdain, and the disbelief that we'd crossed them. Even if they believe us about the second mission and why we did what we did—"

"I want forgiveness," I blurted. "Then maybe we could start over, maybe I'd be able to meet Junie's daughter, and she could meet my…"

My hands went to my stomach, scrunching my jacket in my palms. It pained me to think that I'd never get to tell Junie my news. But what good would it be to tell her I was expecting if she had the unforgiving coldness of a stranger? That's why I didn't tell her yesterday.

"Forgiveness." Pudge nodded. "That's it. It's been forgiveness this whole time, hasn't it?"

"I suppose so. But, Pudge, believing our story, forgiving us for keeping it from them, and catching Engle feel like three distinct and unsurmountable mountains to climb." I looked at my watch again. "In a few minutes, this may all be for nothing anyway. What if they don't come?"

Pudge turned back around with a fold of her arms, and together, we watched the geese fly up the river, and the ducks float down. She held a swatch of her blonde hair back when the breeze flitted over us. I pulled my coat tighter by the lapels.

"I guess we'll have to give up and move on if they don't come. But Viv, I've spent every day of my career at the CIA trying to make sure that day never comes." She grabbed my wrist to look at my watch. "One more minute. They should be here by now." She looked over her shoulder toward the parking lot and once more down the path.

Another five minutes passed, and now it was past noon and our deadline. I felt sick. Sicker than I'd felt with my head hanging over my plate of Steak Diane the other night, a gut-wrenching feeling when you realize that all hope is lost.

I put my face in my hands, ready to tell Pudge how sorry I was for not succeeding with Junie, when a voice behind us said, "Hey, you two see our partners around here?"

Both of us spun around. I think Pudge was the first to clutch her chest. Dot and Junie had arrived together.

My heart pounded. "You…" We both stood, staring at them like idiots because we were stunned. "You're here! You believed us?"

"Well, yeah," Junie said.

"It was the forgiving part we needed help with," Dot added.

I gulped. "Do you forgive us? We were worried for your safety, and Cora's orders were in our heads—"

Junie opened her hand, showing me the jacks. "I can't believe you saved these all this time."

A little cry peeped from my mouth. "Does that mean…?"

"I forgive you, Viv," she said, just as Dot forgave Pudge.

I threw my arms around her for a hug.

"Is that a tear, I see?" she asked, after pulling away, but she also had tears.

"Nah, it's dust." I wiped my eyes. "Sorry. I don't usually cry."

"Me neither." She dabbed her cheeks dry. "Don't tell anyone at the university, or I'll lose my reputation."

We shared a laugh. "It's been so long. It's strange. I'm so happy you're here, but it is strange, right?"

"Yeah." We hugged again.

That dog was back, sniffing around our feet. Dot tried to shoo him away when she saw I had ducked behind Junie. The owner came running up soon after, attaching his leash.

"Is there somewhere we can go?" Junie asked. "Somewhere private?"

We agreed to go back to Pudge's apartment a few miles away because we couldn't go to Junie's office, and I certainly couldn't bring them back to my house. Hal would find out, somehow, and Mrs. Bunn might be the one to tell him. We walked back to our cars.

"When did you believe me?" I asked Junie. "Was it before the woman from downstairs busted through your door?"

"I believed you immediately. I knew it took a lot for you to come see me. It was the forgiving part that took me a moment, like Dot mentioned, which happened after a long phone call with her last night. There was a lot to talk about, more than you know. Something we've been carrying with us."

"Carrying with you?" I asked. "I don't understand."

"We disobeyed orders, too, Viv."

Pudge and I stopped in the grass, but Junie and Dot kept walking.

Pudge lived in a dinky apartment in a seedy part of Georgetown along the canal. We pulled up to see Dot and Junie waiting for us on the curb, clutching their purses and looking up at the windows, most of which were covered in aluminum foil or cardboard to keep the rain and wind out, and possibly peeping eyes.

We sat in her car with the engine running. "Have you been thinking about what Junie said?" she asked. "Because I sure have."

"You think Cora put them on a secret mission also? It would be just like her to do that and make them promise not to tell us."

Pudge turned off her engine. "I don't know, but we're about to find out."

We both reached for our door handles. "Wait! Are you going to tell Junie about your condition?" she asked.

"I plan to." Junie waved. We waved back. "I'm waiting for the right time."

Pudge gave my hand a pat, and we got out of the car. I was a little taken aback by the state of her neighborhood. It's not the place I would have thought a CIA agent would be living, but then again, it was the perfect cover. She assured me it was safe.

Pudge walked up the cracked concrete steps. "These old

Queen Anne buildings…" Pudge said over her shoulder as she jammed the key in. "They look decrepit, but I promise, my apartment is fine. And my neighbors are at work, so nobody will hear us." She got the door to open only after giving it a shove with her shoulder. "This way."

We walked up the dark staircase to her apartment on the third floor, sounding like a herd of elephants on the creaking steps. I wasn't going to say it, but it strangely reminded me of Ava's building back in Füssen. Only instead of a huge penthouse apartment filled with art and luxuries, Pudge's apartment was nearly empty, except for a rug, a few chairs, and a brand-new beige couch with perfectly fluffed pillows and cushions. So perfect, I wondered if anyone had ever sat on it.

"Spend much time here, Pudge?" I asked.

We stood in the living room, looking up and down the bare walls, arms folded to stay warm.

She turned the baseboard heaters on. "I'm on assignment most weeks. But it's clean. Have a seat."

A blast of stale and dusty warm air radiated from the baseboards. Junie and Dot sat on the couch, and Pudge and I pulled up the chairs. I wasn't in the mood to waste time. "Were you working a side mission like us?"

"Something to do with Ava?" Pudge asked.

"Or Cora—"

"No, nothing like that." Junie folded her hands on her lap. "It's about the rule we broke to get out of Germany. Cora didn't tell you?"

Pudge and I shook our heads.

Junie exhaled. "I don't know where to start?"

"How about the beginning," I said.

"Yeah," Pudge said. "Right where you left us on the train and boarded the other one to Munich."

"We didn't board the train to Munich," Junie said.

Pudge and I looked at each other. "Then where did you go?"

"We were angry," Dot said. "As you can imagine. It took us a while to unpack all that had happened."

"We weren't sure what other things you might have been hiding."

"Understandable," I said. "But where did you go?"

"We left on foot and walked to the next village along, and that's where we caught a train," Junie said.

"To where?"

She hesitated. "It was a split-second decision, and it wasn't easy. We weren't sure what kind of reception we'd get."

I started to wonder why she was evading such a simple question. "Where did you go?"

"To Starnberg," Junie blurted. "To see your cousin, Ina."

"What?" I breathed. "How did you even know where to find her?"

"You talked a lot, Viv," she said. "I paid attention."

It took me a moment to realize what Junie meant. Over the months we'd known each other, I'd told her countless detailed stories about my grandparents and their big house in Starnberg and Ina, my dear cousin, who still lived there.

"It wasn't hard to find."

I stood, hand to my mouth, peering thoughtfully outside through a gap where the aluminum foil had separated from the glass. "But you put my cousin's life in danger."

"She welcomed us," Junie said, "as soon as I told her I knew you from when we were children. We stayed the night …

just long enough to make a plan in an area where we weren't suspected of being outsiders. She had no idea you'd become a spy. How could she?"

"The first order Cora gave us was to not contact family," Dot said. "So, you see, Junie and I had a lot to talk about last night—a lot to come to terms with—after hearing your story. How could we continue being angry after hearing what you had to say, when we also broke the rules and put someone's life in danger for the sake of something bigger?"

My eyes started to dry and itch from being blasted open for more than a minute, listening in shock.

"Are you angry?" Junie asked.

"Am I angry?" I wasn't sure what I was. They had risked my cousin's life to save their own, and disobeyed an order that was meant to keep innocent people safe. But in the same breath, Pudge and I had done the same thing, so it wasn't right of me to be mad, especially after all this time.

I finally blinked and sat back down.

"Did Cora find out?" I asked.

"Oh, yes." Dot and Junie flashed each other a look. "Cora knew everything after reading our report and demoted us. Sent us to London straight from the field hospital in France after crossing the Rhine."

"She demoted you?" Pudge appeared just as floored by this news as I was, because Cora had told us quite a different story. "We weren't told that part."

"What did she tell you?" Junie asked.

"We knew you went to London, but she made it sound as if you'd chosen that assignment as a way to not see us again. We demanded she tell you the truth about Engle and our secret mission, since it was clear she wouldn't let us do it, but she said that would have to wait because of the sensitivity of finding him and the OSS's larger objectives."

I folded my arms. There was so much to digest. So much misunderstanding. Cora had the chance to make things easier, but instead, she'd thrown gasoline on a fire by not telling us the truth about Junie and Dot.

"Why didn't you go around Cora?" Dot asked, looking at Pudge. "There must have been a dozen planes to get you back to London. I'm not saying we would have given you the time of day, but still, I always wondered why, considering how things were left between us all."

"She threatened to court-martial us if we got within arm's reach of you two," Pudge said.

"Yeah. If we wanted a chance to talk freely, our only option was to find Engle. We've been waiting all this time for a break. Thank God Pudge found him."

"I sent Viv a postcard that she couldn't ignore," Pudge said. "She ended up sneaking onto Cora's floor and walked right into her office unannounced to confront her. You should have seen her face when I walked in, too." Pudge laughed, which drew a laugh from Dot and Junie.

I was still thinking about their escape. We had made it across relatively easy. Their journey must have been treacherous, not knowing who to trust. It was risky to reach out to my cousin. She could have turned them in, and they had no way of knowing until they knocked on her door. "But, how did you know my cousin would let you in?"

"I just had a feeling," Junie said.

"In your bones?" I asked.

She smiled. "No, just a feeling."

We each reached for the other's hands. "So much time has

passed. We were all friends. The best of friends. And look what happened to us."

"We're still friends," Junie said.

"Nothing says friendship like catching a Nazi," Pudge said. "Now does it?"

We all had a laugh, and after having another hug between us, we started to make plans.

"I must tell you, Pudge," Dot said, giving the bare walls another glance over. "I never expected you to end up in a place like this."

"What's wrong with my place? Besides, I don't spend my money on frivolous things like furniture. I save it, you know, for that beach I plan on retiring to." She pointed to her wall calendar, which had all the days marked off until her retirement at the end of the month. "Pineapples, sand, and maybe my toe in the water."

Dot looked impressed by the calendar. "You're really going to do it, Pudge. After all these years. Retire to that tropical beach you wanted."

Pudge flipped the edge of the rug back, exposing a secret compartment in the floor. "Well, I haven't done it yet." She pulled a file out. "Here's everything you need to know about Engle." She plopped the file on the coffee table. "Now, before you say anything, I realize I shouldn't have this file in my apartment, but I don't trust Cora with it, and I don't trust the CIA, given what I know about them."

"What do you know?" Junie asked.

"I know that things disappear. Things that don't suit their interests, and I wasn't about to let ten years of information disappear just because I kept my notes on Engle in a file cabinet at work."

"Sounds like nobody at the CIA trusts anyone," I said.

"We don't," Pudge said.

Dot laughed. "So, nothing has changed since the OSS days, huh?"

"Sounds like it," Junie said.

Pudge told them how she'd found out about Engle in Berlin through his dimwitted sister. She went on to talk about his little studio in Manhattan in a sketchy downtown neighborhood, and how he frequented an underground bar that played jazz music in the evenings. "He likes his gin and tonics. Always a different woman on his arm."

"Sounds like one of the husbands I have a contract to follow," I said. "Shouldn't be hard to find him. Bar. Drinker. Womanizer. Manhattan."

"One of us will have to talk to him, confirm his accent, tattoo, and facial features."

"I'll do it!" Dot raised her hand like we were in school.

"Dot, no," Pudge said. "He'll think you're a woman to prey upon. And you're a married woman, and he's a Nazi."

Dot slowly lowered her hand. "This is part of the reason I agreed to come. I spent these last ten years being ashamed of what I did in the OSS. Hitting on German soldiers and riding in cars with the SS. Letting some touch my bare knees…" Her fingers went to her mouth, feeling her lips. "Let some of them…" She straightened with a clear of her throat. "I told my husband last night what happened in Füssen. He was surprised, but forgiving and inspiring. He was in the OSS like me and now works for the State Department. He knows what kind of woman I am. It just took me ten years to figure it out."

"What kind of woman are you?" I asked.

"A strong one. A woman who will do what is right for the right cause."

I nodded while Pudge patted her hand. "And that's what got you here today?"

"That, and the fact that someday my daughters will find out, and I'll have the pleasure of telling them that I helped catch a notorious SS officer living in the States. I don't think many mothers can tell their daughters that."

"No," I said. "Well, except for Junie."

"That's exactly how I feel, Dot. It's one of the reasons why I agreed. I wanted to help finish what Viv and Pudge started. Any more children on the way?" Junie asked, looking at Dot's stomach.

"Why? Do I look it?" She sucked her stomach in, then let it out. "No. We're done, and I'm getting old." She laughed at herself, but Dot hardly looked old. Her hair was still dark and shiny, and her skin was bright and fresh. Dot was beautiful. She'd always been and probably always would be.

"Good," Junie said. "I wouldn't feel right going after Engle with you in a delicate condition. I wasn't prying. I just had to ask."

"I understand."

Pudge perked. "Well, Viv has some—" She pointed to me.

"Information about Engle," I blurted. "Something that isn't in that file," I gave Pudge a look when the others couldn't see —a subtle shake of my head, followed by a serious expression. I couldn't follow that with my news. Junie wouldn't come, or wouldn't let me come, and I wasn't about to miss this for the world.

"What is it?" Junie asked.

"Ahh..." I coughed into my fist as an excuse for the delay

in answering. "Actually, it involves Ava," I said, thinking on my feet. "All this time, Pudge and I thought what was hidden behind her painting must have been lost in the war because she died. But she didn't die. She escaped."

Dot sat up, and so did Junie.

"If you can believe it, she married Sergeant Manzo."

Junie's mouth hung open, but it was Dot who gasped. "I can't believe it."

Pudge nodded. "Cora confirmed. Speaking of, I'd better call Cora and tell her the news that you're both in. She said that after we get the team together, she'll start the paperwork to make this a proper mission."

"Put a kettle on for tea, too," I said. We chatted while Pudge was gone, avoiding the subject of Engle until Pudge was back. After a few minutes, we started wondering if there was a problem, but we heard whispers coming from the kitchen, so she must have made contact with Cora.

I got up to see what the problem was, finding Pudge standing over the stove, heating the kettle with the phone pressed to her ear.

"We are, Cora," Pudge rasped into the receiver. "We're planning it right now. We'll be in New York tomorrow, and we'll call you when we're finished. But you better have an answer for me as well."

I heard Cora talking, even though Pudge had the receiver to her ear.

"Watch it, Pudge. If you weren't retiring in ten days, I might try to have you formally written up."

Pudge huffed.

"All I'm saying is that the team is back together, following your orders, and we expect you to come through, honor your word and get us an approved mission."

I pulled the phone away from Pudge when Cora laughed.

"Cora, it's Viv. Is there a problem?"

"I don't have any news for you. As of right now, there are no promises on my end. Stand by, and I'll let you know in a few days if you can proceed."

"Wait. No promises? But you said—"

"That's right. No promises."

Cora hung up, and I was left staring at Pudge, who had heard Cora's last words. She'd promised us that all we had to do was get the team back together, but clearly she'd lied. I slowly handed the receiver back to Pudge.

"Everything all right in there?" Junie shouted from the couch.

"Yeah," I said. "Everything is fine."

Chapter Twenty

Pudge and I were still staring at each other when Dot and Junie walked into the kitchen. "What do we do?" I mouthed, a second before the kettle peeped like a train whistle, cutting the silence of the apartment in two. "Pudge—"

"I don't know." She took the kettle off the heat and held her forehead.

"What did she say?" Junie asked, setting Engle's file on the kitchen table. "You did reach her, didn't you?"

Pudge turned around, backside to the oven with a fold of her arms. "Oh, I got a hold of her. Though I wish I could get a hold of her neck!"

Their faces were a mix of concern and confusion, and rightfully so. We had the looks of two people who didn't want to tell them the truth.

"Is she backing out?" Junie asked.

"Tell us exactly what she said." Dot put her hands on Pudge's shoulders until she lifted her eyes and couldn't look away. "Exactly."

Pudge took a deep breath. "I told her we were together again, a cohesive team, ready to go to Manhattan to identify Engle, when she turned squirrely, jabbering about clearances and communists. She ended the call, saying something about not making any promises." She rubbed her face with a moan. "Basically, we don't have the backing from the CIA to go forward, even though we've done exactly what she asked."

Junie's mouth hung open. "You're joking."

"I wish we were," I said. "You'd think we had learned our lesson with her. The prize was just too great, I suppose. We were blinded by thoughts of catching Engle."

Junie tossed her hands up.

I gasped when the truth suddenly dawned on me. "Cora didn't think we could get Junie and Dot on board," I said. "That's why she had us jump through this hoop to begin with. Damn it, that's what happened. Isn't it? I thought it was strange she insisted on all four of us when it was just Pudge and me on the mission to begin with."

"With Cora, that sounds about right," Pudge said. "It was her way of killing the assignment before it even got started, but we surprised her, which means she'll just be more difficult now because we called her bluff."

I closed my eyes. I should have known not to trust Cora.

Dot had been chewing on her red fingernails. "Guys. What happens if we continue with our plan? Go to New York preemptively."

"What happens?" Pudge asked. "You mean, besides breaking about a hundred laws?"

"Well, we'd be breaking some laws," I said. "Not a hundred, but probably pretty close. Impersonating a CIA agent would most likely be at the top of the list for us."

"She's itching for a reason to fire me before my retirement date," Pudge said. "It may be the final straw if I go."

"What happens then?" Dot asked.

"She'll have you all arrested."

We stood quietly in the kitchen as the wall clock ticked. Condensation from the kettle beaded on the window above Pudge's sink. Nobody wanted to back down now. I could feel it in the air, but most importantly, I could feel it in my bones.

"Let's go to New York anyway," I said.

Junie nodded, followed by Dot.

"You're sure?" Pudge asked all three of us. "I can't protect you if we're caught."

"The thing I worry about the most is Engle," I said.

"Me too," Junie said.

"Me three," Dot said. "He doesn't deserve to live in America. Or live at all."

A door opened and closed one floor down. Pudge's neighbor had come home early. "Come closer." Pudge motioned for us to huddle around the kitchen table, where we dug into Engle's file, analyzing every act and circumstance. We decided to approach him at the dingy alley bar the following evening. "We can take the train into the city. There are two that leave just after ten in the morning. We'll be there by the afternoon. I have an apartment near his photography studio with a great view of the bar and his window. Paid for a month's stay last time I was there. The landlady is eccentric, but she'll stay out of our hair."

"Tomorrow," I said. "Then it's settled."

Hal was leaving in the morning for New York, but I wasn't sure what time, though I knew he'd be gone for two days and that was plenty of time to identify Engle. He'd never know I'd left. And Mrs. Bunn, I'd tell her I was on a stake-out or something. She'd eat it up.

"In the meantime, we can still hope Cora comes through. She didn't say no. She said no promises. I would hope, at the very least, she's moving the request up the chain of command. No telling how fast she's moving it, but if she does get clearance, then we will be one step ahead."

"But what if she doesn't come through, and we've identified him? I don't think I can sit back and watch Engle live his life after that," Dot said. "Can we hand him over to the British or the mafia? Nobody likes a Nazi, and don't you have connections, Pudge?"

"To kill him? Oh, yeah," Pudge said. "I'll just ring up the mafia. Let me get my address book."

"We need to talk to someone from the Mossad," Junie said.

"Mossad?" I stood, having a think while chewing my fingernail.

"You know someone?" she asked.

"Would you believe I might?"

I'd have to go behind Hal's back, but what if I'd misunderstood and Mr. Cohen wasn't with the Mossad after all? What if Hal was investigating him rather than working with him? I could really mess things up for Hal. Mrs. Bunn said he walked his dog in the morning and at night.

I put my hands on my head, still thinking.

"Viv?"

"I have this neighbor," I blurted. "I've heard rumors, but nothing is certain." I couldn't tell them I'd been snooping in Hal's briefcase because then they might ask me for my husband's help, and I couldn't—I wouldn't—do that and risk getting him in trouble. "He's been gone overseas, leaving his wife at home for long stretches."

"Israel?" Pudge asked. "Or is going overseas his alibi for an affair?"

"I don't know, but it's worth a shot. I don't want to sound like Cora, but no promises." I thought about how I could manage a secret conversation with him without Hal knowing, much less Mrs. Bunn across the street when all she does is watch the neighborhood. "I'll see what I can do to make contact. Let's focus on Engle first and identifying him."

We talked a little more about the final details before agreeing to meet at the station in the morning. We said goodbye by the door, but I was yawning. They all three stared at me, especially after I had to cover my mouth and turn away.

"Sorry. I'm suddenly exhausted." I smiled. "Long day, I suppose, for all of us." I yawned again.

"Not that long." Dot laughed. "Careful. The last time I yawned like that in the middle of the day, I was pregnant." She laughed again, and Pudge shot me a look.

Junie thoughtfully placed her hand on my shoulder. "Tomorrow?"

I nodded. "Tomorrow."

I was still yawning when I got home. Deep, powerful yawns that closed my eyes. Pudge dropped me off about ten minutes before Hal was due home. Mrs. Bunn was already looking out her window, and Pudge hadn't even put the car in park yet. "Are you ready for this?" she asked.

"Aren't you?"

"You were tired back there because you're pregnant. Junie will see through it."

"Maybe. But by then, we'll be in New York, and what can she do about it? I'm going to tell her, but I wasn't about to bring it up after she said she had concerns about Dot."

"I understand now, but you're on borrowed time, Viv. Junie is smart. Now, what about this neighbor? You really think he's a Mossad agent?"

"Possibly. He's elusive, but my nosy neighbor gave me some good information about him. I'm going to research that a little further, but there's something else... I have a phone number—someone who might be able to help us find Ava."

Pudge raised her eyebrows with that one. "You sure you don't want my job when I retire?"

"And work with Cora every day? No thanks." I got out of the car. The paperboy threw Mrs. Bunn's newspaper into her bushes, which got her to come out of her house. With her preoccupied, now was the perfect time to try her daughter. "See you tomorrow."

I raced into my kitchen and pulled her daughter's phone number from my purse. "Operator? Yes, can you connect me to 2L-N9, please?"

I waited for the connection, then panicked when it rang because I hadn't thought about what I would say. I couldn't tell Jessica the truth. The phone kept ringing. I heard a click and spun around to look out the window, and to my horror, Mrs. Bunn had gone back inside. *Damn.* Of course, she was listening. I told her I needed her daughter's help with one of my cases, and she had probably been waiting for me to call, too intrigued about the mysterious German mistress not to.

"Bastard cheating husband, he's about to get his…" I mumbled between rings just so she'd hear.

"Honey?" Hal called from the front room, and I slammed the phone down into the cradle.

"Yes?" My heart was thumping, wondering if he'd seen me getting out of Pudge's car because he must have pulled up just as she drove off.

"Where are you?" I heard him set his briefcase on the table in the front room.

"In the kitchen." I stuffed my coat into the cupboard just before he walked around the corner. My whole body had heated up to a million degrees. I tied on an apron.

"How was your day?" He kissed my warm cheeks.

"Good. Yours?" I gave myself a fan when he wasn't looking. My heart was still thumping.

"Everything all right?"

"Of course." I smiled.

His eyes wandered over the clean kitchen. Usually, I'd be halfway through cooking dinner by now. I pulled a pound of hamburger from the refrigerator and the tater tots from the freezer.

"Dinner will be ready soon." I smiled again.

Hal went up to change while I made dinner. I checked the clock while browning the beef. I'd have to wait to call Jessica again because it was just too risky with Hal so close.

I set my mind on Mr. Cohen and turned down the heat.

Mrs. Bunn said she'd seen him walking his dog around eleven o'clock at night. Maybe I could wait until he passed by our house. Then, I could confront him on the corner between Maple and First. That way Mrs. Bunn wouldn't see us, if she was up and looking, and neither would Hal, as long as he was dead-to-the-world asleep and snoring.

I yawned forcefully, closing my eyes.

And I'd have to stay awake.

I put the casserole in the oven to bake, and after cleaning the kitchen, setting the table, and pouring a vodka martini for Hal, I slipped on my oven mitts and unveiled that night's dinner.

"Tater tot casserole," I announced.

We both sat down to eat like a regular couple, as if he really did work for an insurance company and I was a housewife with only the home to look after, when the truth was, he was a spy—and now, so was I.

I watched him eat from across the table. "Oh, no…" I covered my mouth from the overwhelming odor of onion and creamy gray mushroom soup. "I chose the wrong dish to make tonight," I said, which got him to laugh.

I pushed my plate to the side, but I could still smell the onion and ended up laying my napkin over the golden-baked tater tots, which helped. "What time do you leave tomorrow?"

He perked. "Have you decided to go to New York with me?"

"Oh, yeah, sure. Official CIA mission. Count me in." I rolled my eyes, taking a drink of water so he couldn't read my face, which I was sure was on the verge of betraying me.

"I'll leave the name of the hotel and phone number on the counter before I leave. Just in case of an emergency."

"There better not be an emergency." I set my glass down and tried to think of a delicate way to bring up what sort of business he'd be doing in Manhattan so that I'd know where he'd be. "Will you be busy in Manhattan during the day?"

He smiled slyly. "You want to know what I'm going to New York for. What mission I'm on."

"I didn't say that."

"No, but you asked for my schedule. If I say I'll be busy in the day, then you know I'll be at meetings, and there's no real mission there. If I say I'll be busy in the evening and early morning, you know I'll be undercover and most likely meeting someone in secret. You want to know if I'll be in danger."

"Will you be?"

"I'm a professional." He got up to wash off his plate, kissing my forehead on his way to the sink.

I turned in my chair. "Russians or Nazis? Oh, that's right, no more Nazis. Russians? Sniffing out the communists on this trip, are you?" I batted my eyelashes.

"You know I can't tell you."

"Yeah, well, you kind of just did."

He pulled back the curtain to see Mrs. Bunn watering her roses. "How so?"

"You didn't deny it." I twisted my hair, thinking about how ridiculous the CIA's priorities had become. "I'm sick of communists, just like the next housewife, but eradicating our old enemy is good business. And if you believe that, then tracking down war criminals living in America isn't what I'd consider in addition to the workload. It is the workload. If I were in the CIA, I'd remind them of that."

He'd turned away from the window and folded his arms while I was talking. "Where did that come from?" He smirked. "That speech was for someone else. That's for—"

"All right, it was for Cora. What is wrong with her? She's a lead in her department, and she cares more about communists than Nazis. There has to be something that can be done, Hal. Can't you do something?"

"What makes you think I'm not?"

"Because I live with you, and if you were hunting Nazis, I'd know about it."

"I agree." He scooped me up in his arms. "Just like I'd know if you were *hunting* Nazis."

"Yeah, hunting Nazis in my apron sounds about right." I laughed a little too nervously. "Sometimes I think following cheating husbands is like hunting Nazis. How long is your trip this time? I absolutely hate it when you're gone. Do you need help packing?"

I eyed the phone over his shoulder where I'd left Jessica's number scrunched up in a ball of paper, then Mrs. Bunn through the curtain gap where she was still watering her roses. I needed him to go upstairs.

"I'll be back Sunday after dinner. And for the record, I'm going to New York for some boring meetings. No danger, so don't worry." He kissed the nape of my neck where it tickled.

"You promise?"

"I only have to worry about cab drivers who don't have enough change, and too much traffic. Not like worrying about night raids back in London."

He paused, looking into my eyes, smiling, and I was reminded of when we first met.

"Hal... How did you know I was the one that night in London? Out of all the girls, you knew you'd marry me. You said it. I remember it quite well."

"It was just a feeling I had."

I perked. "In your bones?"

"No, nothing like that. Just a feeling."

His eyes wandered to the counter where I had a pad of paper. "I better leave that note about my details right now before I forget." As he wrote the hotel information down for me, I nonchalantly rested my hand over the ball of paper with Jessica's number on it. "Nine o'clock."

He hadn't noticed.

"What?" I pulled my hand away with the note in my palm.

"I'm leaving at nine o'clock tomorrow."

"Oh?" I was pleasantly relieved he wasn't on one of the ten o'clock trains. "We have time to eat breakfast together before you leave. That'll be nice."

I drank an entire glass of water I poured from the tap.

"Everything all right?"

I nodded, wiping my mouth with the back of my hand.

He kissed my forehead again before going upstairs to pack. I set my glass down, waiting until I thought he was in the bedroom, listening to his carpeted footsteps crack on the ceiling, walking from one end of the house to the other, before unraveling the ball of paper.

I peeped through the curtains to make sure Mrs. Bunn was still outside as I picked up the receiver. The operator answered. I cupped my mouth to keep my voice low. "Jessica Bunn, please. 2L-N9."

Hal was whistling upstairs, getting his suitcase out of the closet, and starting his packing. A few seconds passed of dead silence.

"Hello?"

"Hold please."

I waited for the connection with a tap of my foot. Mrs. Bunn looked like she was finished outside, setting down her watering can and brushing off her skirt. The phone rang, and my heart jumped, but it rang again and again, and I feared she was taking her time getting to the receiver. "Pick up," I rasped, now giving the counter a click of my fingernails, looking out the window for Mrs. Bunn, but she was gone. "Pick up!"

"What was that, darling?" Hal shouted down from the top of the stairs, then rushed down to get something from his briefcase in the front room.

I hung up.

"Nothing," I said when suddenly my phone rang, startling me clear into the ceiling with a yelp. "Hello?" I said, carefully into the receiver.

It was Mrs. Bunn. She waved to me from between her window curtains when I looked. "Hi, Viv. You know, I was thinking about what you said the other day."

I exhaled, eyes closed. "Hello, Mrs. Bunn." My heart was still beating out of my chest. "The other day?" I repeated because, in that second, I could barely remember that morning.

Hal walked into the kitchen for a drink of water, silently questioning who I was on the phone with. I gestured across the street.

"You said if you didn't know me better, you'd think I was the neighborhood gossip."

"Oh, that. Ahh… Mrs. Bunn, I—"

"It's all right. I just want you to know how much I value your opinion, and I've been thinking about what you said. I have an insatiable appetite to know things, but I want you to know that you're the only one I talk to. I listen, but rarely talk. If you understand me, dear."

Hal set his glass in the sink.

"I understand, Mrs. Bunn. Have a good evening." I set the receiver in the cradle.

"What was that about?" Hal asked.

I was starting to wonder myself. I told her I understood, but I had no idea what she was getting at, and then it hit me. She'd seen me with Pudge a few times, and it appeared I was racing back home before Hal caught me, so it couldn't be work related. She either thought I was doing something illegal or I was having an affair, and Pudge was my transportation.

God love her; she really would make a good agent.

Which made her slightly more dangerous.

Later that night, I lay in bed close to eleven o'clock, yawning and trying mercilessly to stay awake. Hal rolled over with a snore, and I stuck one leg out, feeling for the floor with my toes. Another snore, and I slipped out of the covers as quietly and as motionless as I could. I waited, peeping over the side of the bed to see if he'd heard.

Another snore, this one a little louder and longer.

I tiptoed out of the bedroom and down the stairs, where I put my trench coat on over my nightgown and the hood over my head, drawing the strings to conceal my face.

I peeped out the front window, making sure the coast was clear—Mrs. Bunn's front window was dark from her pulled blinds. I ran my hands over my face to rub some life into me and had another look, this time down the street, along the sidewalk.

A dark shadow was coming with a dog by his feet. I looked for my shoes, but I was running out of time. I heard him clip-clopping past my front lawn on the sidewalk.

"Ah, forget about the shoes," I said aloud, then chased after him, quietly closing my door and traipsing through the dewy evening grass in my bare feet.

Once I reached the sidewalk, and passed the empty house next door, I gathered I was about twenty feet behind him. A dog barked from behind a fence, which got his little dog to bark. He pulled on the leash, stopping on the sidewalk, which allowed me enough time to narrow the gap between us before he continued on.

He turned around at the curb under a birch tree, allowing the light from the streetlamp to eclipse his face and shine onto mine. "Mrs. Cunningham, is that you? It is late."

I moved out of the light. "Look," I said, tightening my waist tie, "I don't have time to dilly-dally, so I'm going to cut to the chase."

The metal tag on his dog's collar jingled slightly in the dark at his feet. It was all I could do to keep my heart in my chest with being so close to a dog. At least it was a small dog, but those always seemed the most aggressive. I lifted my chin.

"I know you are with the Mossad, and I know someone I think you would be interested in. A high-ranking SS officer. The former commandant from Flossenbürg Prison, Joseph Engle."

He started walking again.

"Wait!" I grabbed his arm. "Aren't you going to say something?"

"How did you know to contact me?" He looked over my shoulder.

"How did I know?" He wasn't aware that Hal was with the CIA. I had to tread delicately and divert all attention away from my household. "Do you know where you live? You can't break wind on this street without Mrs. Bunn finding out. You should be more careful. Now, listen, in about twelve hours, I'm going to be on a train to Manhattan, and in about ten hours after that, I'll have him ready for the Mossad to take—wherever you want to take him. He's been living as an American this whole time."

He tried to walk away again, and I panicked. "Ludwig Klein," I said.

He turned around. "Who?"

"My grandfather, Ludwig Klein, and countless others, American POWs to be exact, died at Engle's hands. Who did you lose at the hands of the Nazis, Mr. Cohen?"

He pulled me into the darkest space under the tree until we were standing in someone's yard. Cold and damp leaves stuck to the soles of my feet. "Why isn't this request coming through proper channels?"

Typical. A question he knew the answer to.

I scoffed. "Because of the Soviet Union. The CIA prioritizes catching communists over Nazis. It's a new war, as you know. Why am I contacting you specifically? Because my department doesn't follow official codes of conduct. We're outliers."

A few seconds passed with him staring at me in the dark. I felt like I had him on the hook, but for some reason, he seemed unsure whether or not to take the bait.

"You have proof of his role in the Reich?"

"Would I be standing out here if I didn't?" I hoped he couldn't tell I fibbed on that one.

"I need to talk to my superiors first." He reached into his pocket and pulled out a card. "Call this number tomorrow from a payphone." He gave the leash a tug and left with his dog trotting behind him into the night.

I reached for my chest to claw my pounding heart back

down my throat. Either I was getting too old for this kind of excitement, or I was out of practice. I wanted to think I was just out of practice.

I snuck back home and quietly closed the door. Hal called for me from the bedroom, groggy and still half-asleep.

"Where were you?" he asked.

I slipped into bed. "Nowhere. Just downstairs." His feet slid toward mine for a bit of footsy but my toes were still cold and damp from being outside, so I pulled them away. I kissed his cheek.

"Go back to sleep," I whispered.

Chapter Twenty-One

It was two minutes past eight in the morning, and I wasn't sure why Hal hadn't left for the train station. I cleaned our breakfast dishes in the sink, keeping one eye on the clock and the other on the phone for the call I needed to make to Jessica.

"Hal?" I took off my yellow rubber gloves and drained the sink basin of water.

"Yes?" He was in the living room, casually reading yesterday's newspaper. His suitcase was all packed and ready by the door.

"Aren't you going to be late?"

He looked at his watch. "I have plenty of time."

"But you're taking the nine o'clock train," I said with a little laugh. "You'll have to leave now if—"

"You must have misunderstood, darling. I'm leaving the house at nine. Taking the ten o'clock to Manhattan."

My stomach sank. "The ten o'clock?"

"Yes, why? My cab will be here in an hour."

I held on to the doorframe.

"Is something the matter?" he asked.

"Whew!" I smiled, pretending to wipe perspiration from my forehead. "I thought you were going to be late, is all." I had my own cab coming at nine and wasn't sure how I'd explain that if they both showed up at the same time. "Coffee?" I asked, but before he answered, I headed to the kitchen to pour him a cup.

I'd also packed, but my small travel case was hidden under our bed. Mrs. Bunn was outside eyeing Mr. Cohen closely as he passed by with his dog, which he probably took as a threat after what I'd confessed to him last night. I waved like a good neighbor, but he did not wave back.

I stood at the counter, staring out the window over Hal's cup of coffee until it turned cold.

"Darling?" Hal called.

I dumped it in the sink, then felt my belly where my baby was living through all my nerves. "It won't always be like this," I whispered. "I live a calm life, I promise." I shook my head. "That's not true. It's mostly like this. Forgive me, will you?"

Hal poked his head into the kitchen. "I thought you were bringing me coffee?"

"Oh, ahh…" I frowned. "It made me sick," I said. "I'm sorry. I had to dump it out."

"It's all right." He gave me a hug—one of those embraces you give your lover just before they leave for a year or forever, but this was always the way Hal hugged me. "I'm going to miss you. Put your feet up while I'm gone, and don't cook anything that will make you sick."

I nodded.

He went back to reading the newspaper. I chewed my

fingernail nervously in the kitchen until the first cab pulled up outside. "Ride's here!"

I'd never been so happy to see Hal leave. I rushed him out of the house.

"Don't let the meter run!" It didn't matter if it was my cab or his, because they were both going to the train station. I just couldn't let them both show up at the same time.

Hal climbed into the back seat. "Watch out for flying bombs," he said.

"What?" I closed the door, and we talked through the rolled-down window.

"Flying bombs." He motioned with his head to Mrs. Bunn who was still outside with her watering can. "Our neighbor."

"Ah!" I laughed. "I will."

"Honey, call me tonight about nine o'clock, will you? It's not every day I leave my pregnant wife at home alone."

"Sure, sure, sure…" I kissed him goodbye again through the window. "I'd love to."

I wiped my brow where I was sweating, watching him drive away when the other cab drove around the corner from the opposite direction.

I dashed back inside, frantically locking up the house and closing all the curtains. I wouldn't have had to hurry if things had gone like they were supposed to go that morning. By the time I'd made it outside, it wasn't just my brow that was sweating, but my armpits, too.

I forgot my travel case upstairs, but at least I had my handbag.

"Please hurry, driver. My train leaves at ten." I had one foot inside the car when I noticed Mrs. Bunn. She wasn't even trying to pretend to mind her own business across the street—

she was standing still and staring at us with the water can by her feet, having taken in the entire scene: Hal leaving and me appearing to rush away behind his back.

"Actually, hold on," I said to the driver. I walked across the street to talk to her. "I have to explain something."

She batted her hand. "No need to explain to me, Viv. I'm just out watering my roses and minding my business." She whistled with a glance to the clouds, which only made her look guilty, a deliberate act to let me know she was definitely making up stories in her head and I needed to put an end to it.

"I know you're wondering what the heck is going on across the street, and the truth is…" I leaned in to whisper. "Hal's got a business trip and I'm going to surprise him. Would you mind looking after the house for the next couple of days?"

"Oh!" She tapped her chest. "I'm enthralled. I can't wait to hear about it. Anything I can do here to help? Have you talked to Jessica yet?"

"I haven't," I said. "But I hope to soon—"

"I went ahead and told her the name you gave me—"

"I gave you a name?"

"You did! Ava. You must have forgotten. But I didn't. Well, turns out that is the seller's name." She snapped her fingers. "And what was that last name…? Manzo! That's it. Jessica said her name was Ava Manzo. Lives in Brooklyn." She nodded several times.

My legs felt a little wobbly. I was right. My God, I found her.

"Are you well? Come, sit down." She urged me to take a seat on her porch chair.

"I'm fine!" I said. "I really must go. Thank you, Mrs. Bunn. You've been a great help."

She beamed. "No problem, Viv."

I climbed into my cab, my heart thrashing. "Train station."

He looked at me through his rearview mirror as I held my chest.

"Floor it."

Junie arrived at the station the same time I did. I headed straight to the payphone. "It's her. I found Ava."

"Where?" Junie asked.

"Brooklyn."

"You talked to her?"

"Not yet."

We'd made it to the phone. "Keep a lookout for Hal. He's also going to Manhattan." I dug in my pocket for the card Mr. Cohen gave me. "Might be on the same train."

I dialed the number.

"Who are you calling?" she asked.

"The Mossad." I turned my back to her in case it was bad news. The phone only rang once before a man picked up on the other end. It didn't sound like Mr. Cohen, but it must have been because he knew too much about our visit last night for it not to be.

Dot and Pudge found us by the phone and were talking to Junie, who was filling them in. They gave us our train tickets.

I turned even more toward the payphone for privacy. "Do you want him or what?" I rasped into the receiver.

Cohen asked me particulars about Engle, specifically where I'd seen him and what I planned to do to catch him. Engle wasn't going to take lightly to being restrained was his next contention. I didn't bother to tell him it was Pudge who'd seen him and not me, and I had no idea how we were going to restrain him. Then he asked me if I was sure that he was *the* Joseph Engle.

"As serious as a heart attack," I said. "I'm at the station now. Give me twelve hours. Do we have a deal?"

"Call me back once you have him."

"Call you back? But—"

He'd hung up, and I hit the phone with the receiver. "Damn you!" I said, then tried to find another coin to call Jessica before we had to leave.

"What did he say?" Junie asked, but I was too busy dialing because I needed that proof, and I needed it now.

Both trains headed to Manhattan whistled.

"Never mind that," Pudge said, pulling me away and leaving the receiver dangling. "We better start walking, or we'll miss our train."

We started toward our platform, following Pudge and Dot. "What did he say?" Junie asked. I wasn't sure how to put it all into words, especially in the limited time we had before reaching the train. "It's been more than ten years since we've seen each other, but I know when you've spent cash you don't have."

Junie did still know me. Maybe she always had.

"I told the Mossad I had proof." I glanced over my shoulder, looking for Hal. "Proof of his role in the Reich."

"But we don't have proof yet."

"I know," I said through my teeth.

I needed to get a hold of Jessica now more than ever. If only things hadn't gotten screwy with Hal this morning, I might have had a chance to call her from the house.

Passengers rushed past us, only to clear up ahead because they were hopping on their train. The two trains side by side on our platform were both headed to New York. Then I saw Hal, looking handsome in his gray suit and carrying his briefcase.

"Wait!" I froze in place, tugging on Junie's arm. Dot and Pudge stopped in response. I held my breath, looking this way and that for a place to duck into, but then, by the grace of God, we watched Hal hop onto the other train going to Manhattan that morning, without a care and without seeing us.

I held my chest. "Oh, thank God." I exhaled, so glad we were on separate trains. We boarded our train and made our way into the private compartment Pudge must have spent an arm and a leg to book. I pulled back the window curtain, watching Hal take his seat on the other train.

Pudge snapped the curtain closed. "You talked to the Mossad?"

My head pounded. "Yes."

"Tell us everything," Junie said.

"They'll take him, but only if we can connect Engle to his crimes. They want proof, and I told them I already had it."

"But we don't even know what that proof is," Pudge said.

"Yes, but I had some good news this morning. I found Ava. She's in Brooklyn."

"That *is* good news!" Dot said.

"We can't celebrate yet, though. I still need to make contact with her, and it's not that easy because I have to go through someone else." I pressed my palms into my eyes. "I have a headache."

The girls talked about ways to get Ava's painting. "We could have her come to us," Dot said, but Pudge liked the idea of having a messenger bring the painting to her rental in Manhattan.

I moved my hands away from my eyes. "There's one more thing. The Mossad agent asked me how we planned on restraining him long enough to be picked up."

We were quiet, each of us watching the other.

"How many laws have we broken so far?" Dot asked.

"More, once we restrain him," Pudge said. "We could possibly be charged with kidnapping. Cora warned Viv and me about this very situation."

"Fingers crossed Cora will come through. Make us official," Dot said, and there was a pause, followed by a laugh from us all, even me, through the pounding of my headache.

"You know, it's not too late to turn back," Pudge said.

"We've already discussed this," Junie said.

"Yeah," Dot said.

"We discussed moving forward with identifying him. This is different." Pudge looked at me.

The last thing Dot needed was to be sent to prison when she had a husband and kids. Junie would lose her job and her daughter. And me... Well, I needed to keep Hal from finding out. It was the only way to protect him, his job, and the life we'd built for ourselves.

I felt the bulge in my stomach, slightly below my waist.

"Viv, are you still in?" Pudge asked.

I nodded. "Yeah. Now, what's the plan?"

Pudge motioned for us to move in closer. "This is what I propose..."

She recapped in detail what we knew about Engle's habits. What his workday was like, what he ate, and at what time he walked down his fire escape at night and entered the basement dive bar. Pudge's rental was a small apartment in the building across the alley, which didn't just have a great view like she'd said, it had a direct view into Engle's photography studio where he also slept.

"I didn't want to say anything before, but I did bring something." Pudge pulled a cellophane bag with white powder from her purse. "Since Dot is going to talk to him at the bar, you'll have to give him this," she said, handing Dot the bag. "Sprinkle it in his gin and tonic and give it a swirl. Then we'll have about thirty minutes before he passes out. So, we'll have to work fast to get him out of there and up to my rental."

"What is it?" Dot asked.

"Best if you don't know. Just don't drink it yourself. CIA approved. I've seen it knock out at least a half dozen Russians in my time. It should take care of a Nazi just the same. Also, the last time I was there, he had a goon looking out for his safety. He was paranoid before, and probably even more paranoid now."

Dot shoved the cellophane bag into her purse.

In New York, I found the nearest payphone, heels clicking and looking every which way for Hal with the girls following closely behind. They crowded around me as I made the call to Jessica. She answered on the second ring. I straightened.

"*Yeah, who is it?*" she said, smacking her chewing gum like a teenager, even though she was an adult.

"Hello?" I cleared my throat. "Jessica? This is Viv Cunningham, I'm your mother's neighbor—"

"*Oh, yeah, I know who you are,*" she said, still smacking her gum. "*Ma called me, said you might give me a buzz. You're looking for some broad named Ava who owns a Duval?* The Reckoning, *to be exact. She told me all about it.*"

"Yes, yes…" I closed my eyes briefly, just wanting her to cut to the chase. "I heard you know her? Ava Manzo?"

"*Yep! Talked to her yesterday for ya. Told her you were in the market to buy her painting. I have to say, Mrs. Cunningham, I really appreciate this, helping negotiate the sale—*"

"Wait! What did you say?" My heart raced. "You talked to her personally? Mentioned my name?"

"*Yeah, that's what I just said. Is this connection all right? And to confirm, you'll bring the buyer and seller to an agreement, and I'll receive the commission? Ma said you had another investment in this.*"

I gulped. There was no other way than to lie to her. "Yes. Absolutely. Did you tell her my exact name?" I asked. "Viv."

She smacked her gum. "*Yeah. Viv Cunningham. That's your name. Right? She was surprised you were looking for it, but she's willing to meet.*"

"What's her phone number?"

"*Yeah. I can't give you that. She said she didn't want you calling her home and upsetting her husband. I can relay a message to her. What do you want me to say?*"

I snapped at Pudge for the address of where we were staying. "Jessica. This is very important. Relay exactly what I say. Word for word."

"*Yeah, go ahead,*" she said, but I could tell she wasn't writing anything down.

"Write this down!" I yelped, closing my eyes. "Jessica. Write this down. Tell me when you have a pencil."

"Okay, okay..." There was a commotion that sounded like spilled pens and a desk drawer opening. *"Go ahead, I'm ready."*

Junie and Dot left to hail a cab to save time.

Pudge handed me the address. "Tell her to meet me at the Mowry building on the corner of Bowery and Grand Street tomorrow at..." I looked at Pudge because we hadn't talked about a time when she mouthed eight o'clock. "Eight."

"Eight o'clock?"

"Yes. That's right. Eight o'clock in the morning," I said. "Tell her to bring *The Reckoning* by Duval from the second-floor apartment in Füssen."

"Second floor?" she asked.

"Be very specific about the painting from the second floor," I said again. "That's the only one I'm interested in," I said, then added, "because she has some fakes, and obviously, I want the real one."

"Ah, I see now," she said, then talked as she wrote. *"Has some fakes..."* She blew a bubble with her gum that popped through the phone.

"Don't write that part!"

"Which part?"

"The part about the fakes." I took a deep breath. Mrs. Bunn's daughter was proving to be difficult, and I desperately needed her to get the message right.

"I won't say that part. I graduated from high school, Mrs. Cunningham. I'm not a dummy. Bring the Duval from the second-floor apartment to the Mowry address. Eight o'clock. I have it all written down."

"Second-floor apartment in Füssen," I said again. "*The Reckoning*, Jessica. *The Reckoning*—"

"In Füssen. Yes. Got it." She hung up. I wanted to scream.

"Let's go."

Pudge and I met Junie and Dot in the cab line, where our car was waiting.

"She's bringing the painting. Eight in the morning. Ava." I said her name as if I didn't believe it. "After all these years."

They both looked a little stunned. Then we prayed because we still didn't know what it was, or if the evidence concealed behind that painting had been removed between the war and now. I didn't even want to think about that.

Pudge sat in the front, telling the driver where to go, but instead of driving into the heart of the city, they drove into the sweaty armpit of the Lower East Side with rundown tenements and shoeless children running rampant in the streets.

"You didn't say he lived here!" Junie said, which got us all to look at her because she didn't just sound surprised. She sounded concerned.

The driver had driven half a block too far. "Stop here..." Pudge said, patting the back of his seat, but when the driver didn't stop, she yelled, "Here!"

He slammed on the brakes.

"Out..." Pudge pushed us to open the doors and get out of there. "It's a scam," she said once we were on the street. "They drive an extra two blocks away, to a place a woman shouldn't have to navigate back from, and then demand more money to drive to the original address."

"Pudge?" Junie said. "You didn't say he lived here. Lower East Side in the triangle."

"I did tell you."

"No. I heard you say Manhattan. A sketchy downtown neighborhood. I most certainly would have remembered if you'd said something about Bowery Street or mentioned gangs."

"What gangs?" I asked.

Men with greasy hair and blue jeans shouted to us from across the street. "Hey, cheeks! Yo, broads!" Followed by laughter and hand gestures.

"We have to keep moving. Standing on the street only means one thing." We followed Pudge to a building where the main door faced the dank and dark alley. I wasn't going to say it, but the building Pudge took us to looked remarkably like her apartment building near the canal—brick with dirt on dirt and grime. "Compliments of the government," she said. "Second floor. Mrs. Cecchetti lives on the first floor."

"The landlady?"

"Mmm." Pudge pushed open the door after jamming in the key, and we made our way up to the second floor. The apartment was unapologetically bare, with minimal seating and a kettle in the kitchen. "That's his studio," she said, motioning out the window. "Late tonight, he'll throw open the curtains that are blackening out his windows to let the moonlight in, and make his way to the basement bar." She pointed to a set of stairs that went down and down and down. "Dive Five. That's the name it goes by on the street, but in truth, it doesn't have a name because it doesn't exist on any map."

"Why Dive Five?" I asked.

"Because—"

"Because after five drinks, you're passed out, broke, or suffering from a broken nose," Junie interrupted, turning away from the window. "I helped teach a class on the rise of post-war gangs in Manhattan. Dive Five is well-known. That's what

I wanted to tell you outside ... about the neighborhood and the gangs."

"What does that have to do with us?" I asked. "We're just talking to Engle and slipping him that drug Dot has."

"If we're going in there," Junie said, motioning toward the Dive Five, "then it has everything to do with us."

A knock on the door interrupted us before we could hear more. It was a delivery Pudge had called ahead for before we left Washington, a dress shop that owed her a favor. The delivery boy didn't look at all pleased to have a delivery in this neighborhood. He waited for the tip as Pudge pulled garments from the bag, her cigarette hanging from her bottom lip.

"This is too classy," Pudge said, referring to the fabric.

"That's all we had. Now, look, lady. I don't want my bicycle stolen, so if you'd kindly…"

She paid him what they'd agreed on, then pulled a jar of pickles from her cupboards. "Plus, here's an extra quarter. I need you to deliver these to Mrs. Cecchetti on the first floor." She talked through a smoking cigarette.

"Lady, I—"

"Fine, two extra quarters." She pushed the coins into his palm, and a short time later, after he walked away, we heard Mrs. Cecchetti shout up the stairs.

"*Grazie, tesoro!*" she said, followed by a smooch noise.

"Special pickles from Poland. Can't get them here." Pudge shrugged. "It's why she stays out of my hair."

The dresses were undoubtedly thin and cheap, and the trousers were shorter than I'd seen back home. Black jackets went with the trousers, and there were scarves for all of us. Junie was pacing. Pudge threw a dress at Junie and trousers at me.

"What's so bad about the Dive Five?" I asked.

We changed into our clothes as she talked. "Well, for one, there was a murder there just a few weeks ago. It's rough. There are rules to follow, and knowing a slick Nazi like Engle, he knows every one of them. If we don't follow them, we'll stick out like sore thumbs."

"What rules?" Dot asked.

"It depends. I'll have to wait until we get inside to see what the crowd is like. Just … follow my advice, all right? This isn't like Germany, where we can blend in. This isn't even America. This is the fringe, where the locals decide what the laws are."

"Pudge, you didn't know?" I asked.

She shrugged. "I said it was sketchy."

"I understand why he lives here," Junie said. "The locals are not concerned with Nazis, and if they were, it would be second fiddle to the threat of turf wars. He's probably very comfortable."

We waited and watched Engle's window for hours. Pudge ordered takeout, and even during dinner, there wasn't any movement across the alley. We talked about how we were going to restrain him.

"The Mossad agent made it sound like they'd take a while after we gave word."

Pudge pulled a long rope from her kitchen cabinet drawer and counted out the yards. None of us said a thing. She looked like she'd handled rope before and had tied someone to a chair.

At half past seven in the evening, we saw light in Engle's photography studio.

"Guys?" Dot said, waving us to the window. He'd opened

his curtains. Seconds later, a man emerged, opening the window and climbing down the fire escape.

"It's him," I said. Even in the darkening hour, I could see his slick hair, which he'd let turn white. His profile, chiseled jaw, and muscular build were not surprising. He was still strong and agile ten years later. "My God, it's really him…"

"I told you," Pudge said.

"It's extraordinary, isn't it? Seeing him again," Junie said.

"Yes." He took my breath away and for all the wrong reasons. I watched him disappear into the basement bar.

"So, it's official," Dot said. "We've identified the bastard."

Pudge wanted to leave right then for the Dive without going over the plan, but I stopped her.

"We'll hang back. Dot will do the talking, but only after we know it is safe. She'll slip him the drug and invite him up for a nightcap." I pointed to the rope. "Pudge will tie him up. And then I'll place a call to the Mossad."

"You make it sound so easy," Dot said.

"Just like the old days. Just like Füssen, only this time, we'll get what we came for because we're ready for it, and we're making up our own orders. What could go wrong?"

I pulled my scarf away from my neck, and then all four of us made our way into the alley and down the dark stairs into Dive Five.

Chapter Twenty-Two

We entered the bar just in time to see Engle take a seat at a table in the far corner, as if it were his regular table. A bartender dried a glass with a rag behind the bar, serving a few men on stools with shots of what looked like Scotch. A lounge singer sang sultry songs from her two-man band to a couple who were lip-locked, hands all over each other.

The place was relatively peaceful. We took a booth near the door. "Tell us about the gangs, Junie."

The waitress brought us a round of Scotch without asking, as if that was what every woman asked for. I asked for a glass of water.

"The crowd that's in here now, I can tell some are locals—Engle and that couple in the back necking—but the others…" She subtly pointed to the man sitting on a stool at the bar, his two goons beside him, and the women who slunk by, purposely trying to catch their eyes. "That's a loan shark. Also,

Dot, about those rules you must follow when talking to Engle…"

Junie observed the women a little longer before finishing.

"This is the crowd I was afraid of."

"Why are you afraid?" Dot asked.

"Because this is where the women take a backseat. They're submissive. When you approach him, you'll need to ask permission to sit and then take the seat beside him, not across. Also, ask him for a cigarette, don't smoke one of yours. Look around…"

We took guarded glances around the bar. Women were sitting side by side with men, not directly across from them.

"It's considered aggressive among these types to sit across from someone unless you're their equal," Junie said. "Also, don't order your own drink. Let Engle do it for you."

"I'll go sit across from him," Pudge said, joking.

"Me too," I said.

"I'm serious," Junie hissed. "We'll be tossed out of here if you don't follow the rules." She looked at her watch. "And there's something else."

"God, what else?" I asked.

"Turf wars happen frequently, and we don't want to be caught in one. We'll know when we've overstayed by watching the loan shark at the bar. When he and his goons leave, we should leave as well. In fact, it's best if we're out of here in two hours, before ten o'clock." She twisted her watch around her wrist. "Or earlier."

"I've worked under pressure before. Try cooking dinner with four kids hanging off you." Dot stood from the booth and smoothed her skirt, showcasing her hourglass figure. You would have never known she had children hanging off her at home, like she said. "It's been a long time since I tried to act sexy. Like riding a bike, right, ladies?"

"You have the drug?" Pudge asked.

Dot patted her skirt pocket. "Yeah." She pulled her shoulders back. "Here goes nothing."

"Wait!" Pudge grabbed her elbow. "Good luck."

Dot slunk away.

I drank my entire glass of water in four or five gulps.

Would he recognize her? No, he wouldn't. He barely saw her, except for those few minutes in the back of his car. "What if he recognizes her?" I asked anyway.

Pudge looked at me. "Then get ready to run because he'll be pounding up those stairs, and by the time he's in the alley, we'll have to be on the ground with him."

"Jesus, Pudge, have you done this before?"

"Twice. Once in Vienna and once in Paris. This will be my first time in New York. I think I'd rather be in Vienna, honestly."

"She's talking," Junie said under her breath.

There was a moment of breathlessness among the three of us as we waited to see if Engle would offer Dot a seat. When he placed his hand on the chair next to him, my heart stopped.

"Ask her to sit, you bastard," I breathed.

"Shh," Junie said. Then, to our relief, he kicked the chair out with his foot, and Dot sat down. He offered her a cigarette. Dot barely smoked, but she lit that sucker like she smoked packs a day.

I nearly collapsed on the table. Now we had to wait.

"Have you ever been caught?" I asked Pudge. Junie gave me a look. That wasn't something you should ask at this stage. I shrugged my shoulders at her.

"I've been chased a few times. A chase that made me think my life was about to end. Most recently, the night I wrote you the postcard."

"You were chased? By who?"

"Engle has a goon, remember?" She glanced around the bar. "He isn't here. I'd tell you if he were. He has a heavy brow and a square jaw."

"I remember. But you didn't say anything about fearing for your life. Maybe you really were the best this whole time, Pudge."

"Do you ever wonder what would have happened if we'd all stayed together?" She downed the last of her Scotch.

I wondered all the time. But there was also something else, and I thought now was as good a time as any to bring it up as we waited and watched.

"Junie..." I pulled the scarf completely from my neck when it felt too much like a tie. "Does Annie..." I cleared my throat because this was hard. By the time Junie had made it back home, she would have still been wrestling with what had happened, and Annie would have been still so young. If she were to mention me, it would be later in her life, and because she still cared.

"Junie, does Annie know about me?"

She put her drink down, and that's when I reached for my chest, thinking she'd told Annie only the worst parts.

"What did you say?" I asked.

She laughed at my expression. "Oh, I told her about how the boys called you sweet cheeks."

My mouth dropped.

"Shh!" Pudge rasped, looking over her shoulder and to each side, over the booth. "You'll blow our cover."

"No, we won't." Junie pointed. The prostitutes of the Lower East Side had descended into the Dive Five, laughing and making a clang as they searched for an empty table. A glass crashed on the floor, a shot glass one of them had thrown instead of dropped, making a ruckus as the jazz singer kept on singing.

Dot laughed with Engle, even playfully touching his hand. Everything was progressing and moving along as we had hoped.

"I told her about my best friend," Junie said. "About the girl I went through training with, roomed with, and went to Rome with. How we were the best, once, and how I wouldn't be who I am today if I hadn't met you."

My eyes filled with tears, but I didn't dare blink. She reached across the table for my hands. "You did?"

She nodded.

Pudge watched us, then narrowed her eyes at me. She wanted me to tell Junie my secret.

"Junie, there's something—"

"They're getting up," Pudge exclaimed.

Engle had asked Dot for a dance. Of course, he wanted to dance with her. His drink was left on the table, and from what I could see, it looked like he'd drank at least half of it.

"Another round?" The waitress was back, giving us glares for reasons unknown. Pudge gave her a five-dollar bill and told her to leave, which she was happy to pocket.

"Sorry," Pudge said. "Go ahead."

I looked at Junie, the words on the tip of my tongue, but now wasn't the time either, not at the Dive Five and not with Dot dancing with Engle. "I'm glad you're here," I said. "Working with me again."

"I'm glad, too." She looked at her watch. "When this is all over, I'll need to make a call. I told Annie I was on a business trip, and it's not like me not to call."

"Call?" I gasped, remembering that, for some reason, I told Hal I'd call him that night. "What time is it?" I twisted, looking at the clock on the wall, then looking at my own watch. "I told Hal I'd call him at his hotel."

"He'll understand if you don't," Pudge said.

"No, you don't understand. If he calls, Mrs. Bunn might answer because we share a line, and I told her I was surprising Hal in New York."

Pounding came down the stairwell, and we all looked. Three greasers in blue jeans looked around the room, knuckles in their palms. "You better make that call, Viv, because it's going to get ugly in here." Junie urgently tapped my hand to scoot out.

I asked the waitress to use the phone, and she directed me to ask the bartender. The loan shark left after tossing a few bills on the bar. "Can I use your phone?"

The bartender poured a glass of Scotch, spilling half of it on his fingers when he picked the glass up and transferred it to a tray. "It's not free."

"How much?" I looked at my watch again.

"Two bucks." He folded his arms when I complained, winking at the waitress who'd obviously told him we had the cash.

"Fine." I pulled two dollars from my pocket, and he pulled a broken rotary phone out from under the bar, covered in tape and ink from a pen used for writing numbers. "Do me a favor. Buy a new phone with that, will ya?"

"Yeah, yeah." He left to talk to another customer.

I dialed the hotel. Shouts came from the front of the room, and it didn't take long to figure out that they came from those greasers who had their knuckles in their palms. Pudge and Junie waved for me to hurry up.

The phone rang. "Come on, pick up," I said out loud before the front desk answered.

"Hal Cunningham's room, please."

"Who's calling?"

"Who's calling? His wife. Connect me, please."

My heart beat a little faster when the jazz singer stopped singing, and angry voices were amplified. Dot and Engle were on the move. Pudge waved for me to follow them.

Hal answered. "Hello, darling."

"Hi, Hal," I said, then stuck my finger in my ear to hear better. "How are you? How was your journey?"

One of the greasers flipped the waitress's tray over, glass crashing all over the floor. Junie was waving frantically now. Dot and Engle were making their way over. He was a little wobbly.

"Sorry for my loud radio program," I said, thinking quickly. "It's quiet over here, otherwise. Just relaxing, looking out the window, and waiting to talk to you. Mrs. Bunn is asleep because her curtains are closed."

He laughed. "Who is the nosy neighbor now?"

I yawned. "I'm so tired. Can I call you tomorrow?"

"Yes, darling—"

I hung up just before one of the greasers threw a pitcher of beer at the wall and started a brawl. Dot and Engle ducked out and up the stairs. Pudge followed behind.

"Run!" Junie shouted, grabbing my hand, and we ran through the splash of beer dripping from the ceiling, reaching the alley in time to see Dot lead Engle toward Pudge's apartment.

He stumbled over his own feet, waiting for Dot to open the door. Pudge came up from behind and supported him, handing her the key, but it was on a ring with other keys, and she had to search.

"Easy now, big fella," Dot said.

"Hurry up," I said. "Open it!"

She found the key and jammed it into the lock. Junie and I pushed them into the hallway.

"Hey!" A man ran up behind Pudge in the dark before she could close the door. "What do you think you're doing—"

She socked him in the nose, and he fell backward like a cut tree in the forest, landing among the spilled garbage. All I saw were eyebrows.

"Who is that?" I asked.

"The goon!" Pudge kicked his foot to make sure he was out. "Let's go!"

We somehow managed to get Engle up the stairs and reached Pudge's rental, Mrs. Cecchetti yelling at us to be quiet the whole time. We scuttled him in through the door before he collapsed on the apartment floor, unable to stand.

He looked up at us four, blinking and blinking, before settling his eyes on Pudge.

"You… I've seen you before," he said, his speech slurred.

Pudge got some rope to tie him up. "Shut up and give me your hands." She lunged at his hands while he lay on the floor, but he managed to finagle a pistol from his back waistband. He appeared unsure who to shoot, waving it first at Pudge, then at me.

Junie flung herself in between me and the bullet, but when

he pulled the trigger, nothing happened. Pudge grabbed him by the shirt collar. "This is for Füssen," she said, pulling back her right hook, but I beat her to it and clocked him with the kettle from the kitchen.

Dot put her hands to her face, screaming. Junie grabbed the gun from the floor.

Pudge tied Engle up like a hog, then, in a quick-thinking maneuver, stuffed a rag in his mouth. She was sweating, I was sweating, but Junie was stone-cold quiet, opening the barrel of the gun.

"The bullet got jammed."

I held my chest, feeling my life pass before my eyes, and not sure how I felt about that. It had been a while since I'd been that scared.

Mrs. Cecchetti pounded up the stairs, telling us to be quiet when she walked in on us standing around Engle, Junie with the gun in her hand, and Pudge on her knees from having just hog-tied him.

Mrs. Cecchetti froze, her hands clamped over her mouth. "What on earth—"

"He's a Nazi, Mrs. Cecchetti." Pudge stood from the floor, wiping her brow. "A real Nazi from the war, living a secret life right across the alley."

Mrs. Cecchetti dropped her hands.

"I'm sure you lost someone in the war." Pudge motioned to Engle. "Well, whoever it was, you can take it out on him."

Her face turned sour. "I lost my brother." She walked right up to him and kicked him in the stomach. "Dirty Nazi!" she shouted.

We scrambled to hold her back before she got another kick in. We didn't want Engle dead, not yet, anyway.

He moaned on the floor but was mostly out.

"Who…" Mrs. Cecchetti looked a little scared of us all of a sudden. "Who are you?"

"Angels. Promise," Pudge said.

"CIA," I said because we needed her silence, and Pudge was going to retire soon, so what did it matter? "How else do you think Pudge was able to get you those pickles? All the way from Poland is what I heard."

"There are two more jars in the cupboard," Pudge said. "Take them. Just give us a day or two, and we'll be gone."

She scooped the jars in her arms. "Dirty Nazi," she mumbled again, but refused to leave and stared at him as a warning if he moved.

I turned to Junie. "You almost took a bullet for me," I said.

She reached for my hand. "You're pregnant. What did you think I was going to do?"

"What? Who told you? Pudge—" I said, but Pudge shook her head.

"Nobody told me," she said.

"Then how'd you—"

"The tiredness, bloated belly, oh, and that glow around you." She smiled.

I hugged her. "You can tell I'm bloated?"

She laughed. "See, Viv. That army doctor didn't know anything after all. Just like I told you." She pulled away. "Congratulations. You deserve it."

Engle moaned a little louder on the floor, but this time, he opened his eyes. Now, I was the one who kicked him, which got him to clam up.

"Well, now that you've got that secret out of the bag. Can we get on with it?" Pudge asked.

I turned to Mrs. Cecchetti, who still had the pickle jars in her arms. "Can I use your phone?"

Mr. Cohen said his team would take the train up from D.C. in the morning, but only after I assured him that Engle was tied up and that we had irrefutable proof of his role with the Reich.

"So, what is behind that painting?" Dot asked.

"That's the million-dollar question," I said. "I don't know." I looked at my watch. It was nearly six in the morning, and the sun was rising over Manhattan and spilling into the alleyways.

Engle had roused enough to become coherent. His eyes were closed, but I could tell he was listening by looking at his eyes moving behind his eyelids.

"Whatever it is, it's sure to send SS Officer Joseph Engle to the gallows," I said.

He opened his eyes. "You have the wrong man," he said firmly. "I'm a photographer."

Pudge got up from her seat to light a cigarette. "You gonna tell him, Junie? Or am I?" She pointed to her inner arm.

Junie pulled his shirt sleeve up. "If only you didn't have the tattoo of your blood type on your arm. I'm sure you regret that decision now. Did you know most SS officers got the same tattoo? And there's only one that we know of who got it in the wrong spot, lower on their arm. That identifies you. Shame."

"Whoever you think I am, I'm not him."

We all laughed at that one.

"I..." He tried sitting up the best he could with the ropes and his hands behind his back tethered to his ankles. "I've seen you before."

"You've seen us all," I said. "Füssen, about ten years ago."

His face dropped, which got us all to howl. Pudge a little more than the rest of us.

"You," he said, looking at Junie. "You're that whore from—"

I kicked him in the stomach for that remark. "Watch it, pal."

He groaned and moaned. Dot couldn't bear it any longer and covered her ears. "Don't do that, please. We are not him. We're too good."

Engle's head swung toward Dot when she spoke. "And you…" He smiled. "I know you."

"You don't." She pulled her shoulders back.

"Yeah. That voice, pleading for help. All Jews look like you—"

Dot kicked him in the face without even taking a breath, leaving an instant black eye on him, and a lock of hair flopped in front of her eyes, which she quickly fixed. "Look what you made me do. And I'm a lady."

Pudge handed her a cigarette, which she gladly took and smoked quietly by the window.

A knock on the door got us all to look. Junie checked at her watch. "That can't be them already."

Pudge looked through the peephole before opening the door. It was Ava. She was early and she was dressed to the nines with a fitted white dress and a fox stole. She lingered in the doorway like Marilyn Monroe, waiting for our reactions, but Junie could only muster a dropped jaw.

"Hello, friends," she finally said, sauntering in.

I stuttered. "Av—Ava." I swallowed. "Thank you for coming."

She made her way over to Engle in her stilettos. "Well, well.

Look who we have here. Joseph Engle, SS Commandant of Flossenbürg Prison, among other things."

He shook his head. "No."

"Oh, cut the crap, Joe. We know who you are."

"Ava," Junie said. "Good to see you so well."

She spun on her heel. "Good to see you four." She took pointed looks at each of us, ending on me. "And you, Viv. I must say, I was surprised to hear you were looking for me. I didn't know why, of course, until you requested I bring the painting from my downstairs apartment in Füssen."

My heart sped up. "Did you bring it?" I asked, because she only had her purse with her.

"I did better than that." She pulled an envelope from her purse. "Do you remember what I said to you in the park, just after we visited Ingrid's hat shop?"

She handed me the envelope, which I quickly opened.

"I said that one day you'll realize you had a friend in me—an ally—and when that day comes, I won't be saying I told you so."

I pulled out a photograph, a very revealing photograph of Engle dressed in his Reich-issued commandant uniform. I closed my eyes briefly. It was better than I had imagined. Not only was Engle in his uniform, but he was at the camp with notable other officers that had already been charged with war crimes. This was what Engle had tried so hard to keep out of Gunther's hands. And now it was in mine.

"But I decided, what the hell." She winked. "I told you so."

"Thank you, Ava. I'll never be able to repay you for this."

"I know." She smiled. "And you're welcome."

Engle lifted his head from the floor, trying to see what I had, but I left him to guess. I showed it to Junie, who clicked her tongue, and to Pudge, who shook her head. Dot laughed, flicking her cigarette on him.

Ava told us that she'd escaped down the back stairwell of her apartment. She knew I was in Gunther's apartment and had enough sense to leave before the Abwehr showed up. She made it back to Rome using contacts and connections.

"I'm sorry," I said. "You were our partner the whole time. I knew it then, that night that you left. I never got a chance to tell you. What made you come? You must have hated us these past years."

"Well, anytime I can help put a Nazi behind bars, I will. That idiot at the auction house drives me crazy with her chewing gum. I'd rather not go through her in the future if you need anything else from me." She handed me her phone number, then turned on her heel for the door.

"Wait!" I wondered what she did to earn Manzo's trust, but considering Ava's many talents, it didn't take much to guess. "You married Manzo?"

She laughed. "Guessing by your face, you are surprised. Yes, well, turns out we have the same personality. Fiery and passionate."

"But he hated you," I said, then recoiled a bit because she was married to him now, after all, and it sounded a little harsh. "You threatened him in the plane while he tried to throw you out of it."

"Like I said, we are both passionate people. I was driving a hard bargain and changed our terms. I was never pregnant, nor did I need an abortion, and he saw right through my lies. I just wanted to see how far the United States Army would go for me—a test before I gave my life for that mission. Turns out, quite the distance. In the end, he thought I was charming." She fluffed her hair. "And I can be charming."

Reclaiming her possessions back in Füssen after the war was her only request before coming to America. And thank God for that.

She waved goodbye and left as elegantly as she had arrived, leaving us all a little stunned.

A team from the Mossad showed up a few hours later. They couldn't dispute the photograph. Mr. Cohen was especially impressed, and grateful.

Two members of his team took Engle by the armpits, and one other grabbed his feet. Mr. Cohen walked behind him with the photograph.

"Are you going to kill me?" Engle cried on his way out.

"Who do you think we are, Nazis?" Mr. Cohen said before closing the door.

At the train station, we made one more call.

"Yeah, Cora." Pudge held the phone far enough away from her ear for us all to hear the conversation. "This is Pudge. Junie is here, Viv, and Dot. We have a message for you."

"Well, I have a message for you, Pudge. I'm delighted to say I have clearance for you four to proceed. If you make your way to New York and identify our subject, I can move things along. I'll need a report and a—"

"Hold it right there, Cora."

"Pudge, I'm not playing games here—"

"Neither are we. Consider Engle not a problem anymore. Oh, and also ... I'm retiring early." She looked at her watch. "In fact, I retired the moment I placed this call. And if you check with HR, you'll see I already turned in my paperwork."

"You did?" I mouthed.

Pudge covered the receiver. "I have a friend in HR who owes me."

"Oh, you're retiring today?" Cora laughed. "After I just approved the mission?"

Now, it was Pudge laughing, which got us all to laugh.

"That's what she said, Cora," I said.

"Yeah, clean out your ears," Dot shouted into the receiver.

"Hi, Cora. Junie here. Have a great day!"

Pudge hung up, and we all laughed again. Passengers walking to their platforms gave us looks, but nothing could keep us quiet after that call.

Chapter Twenty-Three

We made it back to Washington just before dinner. Dot asked Pudge to accompany her home so she could introduce her to her husband and children, then promised to have us all over for dinner real soon. Junie said goodbye next to our cabs.

"You'll be by next week?" I asked.

She nodded. "With Annie."

We hugged. "Ah, Junie. It's so good to have you back."

"It's good to be back. But what are you going to do now? You can't go back to catching cheating husbands and wives after all this, can you? You really are one of the best, Viv. You have something special. Have you talked to Hal? He's with the CIA, maybe he—"

I gasped. "Hal!" I grabbed Junie by the shoulders. "Junie. I have to go."

Hal's train was twenty minutes behind mine. I didn't have time to dawdle and talk at the station. I needed to get home! I hopped in the cab.

"Hurry driver." I tossed money over the seat. "Speed if you have to."

"I'm not getting a traffic ticket, lady."

"Just drive!"

He stepped on it, but we were caught in rush-hour traffic on the turnpike. From the back seat, I felt like I was practically sitting on the dashboard, tapping my fingers on the driver's headrest. "Can't you go around?"

He just looked at me, and we moved about two feet more when he let his foot off the brake. I checked my watch. My twenty-minute buffer had dwindled to three, and trains were always a few minutes early or late, and I had no way of knowing which side of the coin Hal's train would land on.

We'd made it to the off-ramp, which led into the residential area about five blocks from my home. I saw my reflection in the side mirror and let out a horrified gasp.

I quickly fixed my hair, licking my palms and smoothing it back the best I could. Staying up all night and sleeping on the train had really done a number on my complexion. Maybe Hal wouldn't notice.

We inched forward another two feet, and to my shock, I saw another cab in the next lane also creeping along, and in the back seat, Hal. He nonchalantly read a newspaper, having no idea I was next to him.

I dropped to the floorboard behind the driver.

"What are you doing?" he asked.

I closed my eyes. "Just keep driving."

"We're at a standstill."

Cars honked from another traffic jam, but this one was from an accident that blocked the road. I peeked out the window. I was only a few blocks away. If I ran, I might be able to beat him. I opened the car door and made a decision. I had to run.

I don't know if it was once I was on the road, or when I passed the stop sign at the bottom of the off-ramp that I realized I had to ditch my shoes.

I ran through yards, hopping a fence into my neighbor's yard where her dog chased me as I screamed my head off. I made it to Mrs. Bunn's yard, but she was in the front watering her roses. I snuck around the side, behind her back, and made a break for my house.

I was almost to my yard, almost to my door, when she called out to me.

"Viv!" She looked down the road. "What are you doing out here? Where's your cab?"

"Oh!" I was out of breath and tried to hide it. "He let me out on the wrong street, so I decided to walk." I looked at my watch. A few minutes had passed since I jumped out of my cab. A few minutes closer to when Hal would be arriving.

"Was he surprised?"

"Who?

"Hal, of course. The big surprise." By the twinkle in her eye, I wasn't sure if she was sincere or if she knew I hadn't met him in New York.

"Yes. He was, thank you for watching the house." I turned and walked toward my door.

"Viv, your shoes…"

I whipped around. I had to tell her something, or she might come over later and bring it up.

"Are you in some kind of trouble?" She lowered her voice. "Did something happen in New York between you two? I really hope not. You are my favorite couple, and I—"

"Truth is, Mrs. Bunn, I was working." My shoulders dropped. "I try to keep my work life secret, but you really are a natural. Now, this is top secret, but I know I can trust you. I was working with the CIA to apprehend a known Nazi commandant living incognito in New York. He's caught now. We hog-tied him and now he's off to Israel to answer for his crimes."

Her face was frozen, eyes wide and unblinking.

"Now, if you'll excuse me, I must start dinner before Hal comes home. You understand, right?"

She burst out laughing. "Oh, Viv, you sure tell some whoppers!"

I looked over my shoulder, laughing along. "Don't I? I'll catch up with you tomorrow, Mrs. Bunn. I have lots to tell you about the German mistress and the double-cross."

Her eyes glowed. "All right, Viv. See you tomorrow!" She went back to her roses, and I opened my front door.

The house smelled stale and vacant, having been locked up for so long without anyone home. I paused in the entryway with the door closed, my heart pounding while standing in place. "Honey?" I said, just to be sure. No answer.

I raced to open all the window curtains, and when I opened the kitchen window, I saw his cab had just pulled up. I turned on the radio and flung a handful of flour on the counters as if I'd been baking for hours.

"Darling?" he called from the door.

I hastily tied on my apron. "In here!" I checked my breath. He'd know. I didn't have time to race up to the bathroom. I reached for the brandy and took a guzzle, swirling it around before spitting it into the sink.

He walked in, and instead of giving me a kiss on the cheek,

he went for a full-mouth kiss. "Tough day?" he asked, tasting the brandy on his lips.

"Just a celebratory drink because you're home!" I poured him a glass on the rocks. "Drink?"

"I'm glad to be home. What are you making?" he asked, looking around the kitchen where I clearly had made a mess, but had nothing to show for it. "I'm not hungry. Don't go to any trouble tonight. I'm going to knock off early. Will you join me soon?"

After giving me another kiss, he took off his hat, hung his jacket, and walked upstairs.

I found the nearest chair and had a seat. *God, that was close.*

Later that evening, after he'd gone to bed and I'd cleaned up, I slipped under the sheets in my satiny nightgown.

He roused just enough to hold on to me for a snuggle.

"I missed you," I said into the dark. I felt bad for keeping my secret from him now, and I was trying to think of a good way to bring it up, but how could I, with him nearly dozing off again. I closed my eyes, settling into his arms.

"I'm proud of you," he said.

"Thanks, but keeping the household going isn't hard at all. Really, Hal." I got just a little more comfortable with the covers over us, and my bare feet toasty and warm.

"I'm talking about with Engle," he said, and my eyes popped open.

It was quiet between us. I wasn't sure what to say or what not to say.

I sat up slightly, looking at his face in the dark. "How did you—"

"It was Barbara Bennington's idea to bring you that folder."

I turned on the side lamp, and he sat up, closing one eye and shielding the other with his hand.

"Babs?"

"She knew you couldn't resist a peek at one of her reports. Our hands are tied at the department, and if I brought it up to you, I could be subpoenaed later, so I kept quiet. You really are one of the best, Viv. Please reconsider working for the CIA."

I sat still for a moment, holding my breath and letting his revelations wash over me like a cool wave.

"You can breathe now."

I smiled. "Hal Cunningham." I playfully hit him with my pillow. "All this time, you knew what I was up to?"

He laughed. "Are you mad at me? It was almost worth it to see you go to such lengths with the flour."

"Well, if you think that's impressive, you should have seen Engle's face when he woke up on Pudge's floor tied up like a hog…" I turned off the light, and after telling him what had really happened while he was gone, I went to bed one happy woman.

A week had passed since I'd left Junie at the train station, and I was waiting like a nervous schoolgirl for her and Annie to visit. She said they'd arrive at nine that morning, but it was already five minutes past. I paced the carpets.

"Relax, Viv," Hal said. "It's Junie and her daughter. Not the Queen."

"Feels like the Queen." I paced some more.

The tea had been made, and I had baked fresh cookies that

morning. All was perfect, or as perfect as I could make it. "And the cookies don't make you sick?" Hal asked.

"Wouldn't that be a shame if they did?" I laughed. "No, they do not."

He kissed my forehead. "Don't worry so much. She's going to like you."

I gave the napkins an extra fold and was rearranging the cookies on the platter when I heard a car drive up. Junie got out first, followed by Annie who looked just like her mother, only younger. Brassy blonde hair that had been smoothed straight. A pink dress and white collar.

I passed by the corkboard near the phone where I'd pinned Pudge's postcard, straightening it just a hair. I'd received it the day before, postmarked from Miami. She'd retired to that tropical beach after all, promising to come back at the end of the month for dinner at Dot's house.

Knock! Knock!

I had already smoothed my hair back a dozen times before they'd even made it to the door, and when I answered, instead of saying hello, I was breathless.

"Come… Come in!" I finally said.

Hal reintroduced himself to Junie and said hello to Annie, while I grinned. I was sure Annie thought I was crazy, when in fact, I was just elated to finally get to meet her. After inviting them in, I sent Annie ahead to the kitchen. Junie and I followed.

"She looks just like you, Junes," I said. "She's beautiful."

We talked and drank our tea. I think Annie was surprised to hear I knew so much about her from when she was little, especially about the jacks she played with her mom.

"Trust me, your mother got in trouble more times than what was allowed for having her jacks out while in London."

Junie laughed, agreeing, when she noticed something out my kitchen window. It was Mr. Cohen. He was walking his dog. When he stopped at the edge of my lawn to tie his shoe, I knew he wanted to talk to me.

"Wait right here." I left them with Hal in the kitchen.

Mrs. Bunn was out watering her roses, as usual, trying to learn as much from us as she could without looking guilty.

I took my watering can with me to avoid making it look too obvious. "Hello," I said once I reached the flowerbed at the edge of my yard. Mrs. Bunn looked over, oh so nonchalantly, but I saw her twinkling eyes and the way she adjusted her glasses to see better.

"He's secure," Mr. Cohen said.

I nodded. Engle was answering for his crimes. The plan had worked, whether or not the CIA liked it. Hal had heard indirectly that Pudge was blamed for it, but that she'd already retired by the time Engle was handed over, so there was nobody to actually charge with insubordination, especially since the Mossad publicly was taking full credit for finding him, kidnapping him, and shoving him on a chartered flight out of the country. Allegedly, there was no mention of him being hogtied in the report, or so I was told, but that image would live in my mind for eternity, and it made me smile, nonetheless.

The CIA was too bothered with a rogue communist uprising in the Bronx to care about a missing Nazi, and with Pudge retired and out of the way, Cora had no incentive to make a stink about what had happened, at risk of overwhelming embarrassment for her.

Cohen stood stoically, subtly adjusting his tie instead of walking away.

"Something else?" I asked.

"I have a message for you from my superior, if you are willing."

Hal had come outside to get something out of the back of his car. He looked over, gave a wave, and then walked back inside. Turns out Hal had never spoken to Mr. Cohen in an official capacity and had just been covertly investigating him. His cover as an insurance-fraud agent was intact.

I poured water over my daffodils. "What message?"

I thought he'd relay some tidbit about Engle. His last words before he left America? An apology? No, Engle wouldn't do that, not sincerely, anyway, but I wouldn't put it past him to say and do whatever he thought was necessary to try and save himself.

"Will you consider working for the Mossad, Mrs. Cunningham?"

I scoffed. "I don't think working for government agencies fits me, after all. I'm busy with a side gig catching cheating husbands."

"I thought you'd decline." He pulled a card from his coat pocket. "Still, there are secret organizations that have asked me about you. One in Europe wanted me to pass this on…"

I took the card, which had only two names and a country on it. "Mr. and Mrs. Westerfeld?" I read.

"Not their real names, of course. But one of many private teams that, let's say … hunt Nazis. There's a bounty, usually paid to you directly. This is something you might consider?"

I didn't know such teams existed. In fact, I thought the CIA was my only choice, but now that I considered it, in those brief seconds while I emptied my watering can over my flowers, with Mr. Cohen's dog licking my shoes and Mrs. Bunn still looking at us from across the street, I thought ... maybe?

"In what capacity?"

"They need an analyst in the United States. Judging by your conduct with the Engle affair, I trust you have a long career in undercover work and in this area?"

I felt my stomach over my dress. Although the opportunity sounded enticing, I was expecting a baby. I was going to be a mother, and I most certainly wasn't going to take long-haul flights to Europe to read a report or deliver one.

"Card says they're in France."

"You will work from home. As I understand it, you will analyze information sent by courier. Undercover, of course. Probably a milkman or a postman. I am just passing on the information, you see? I don't know the particulars, but I was asked to get in touch. Would you like me to respond to them with interest?"

I thought about it. For a moment, I even saw myself poring over reports, and I couldn't help but think how this would get under Cora's skin, which was just the icing on the cake. But I didn't want to work alone. Not anymore.

"I imagine you'd have to quit your current work or get someone else to take your place. Mr. and Mrs. Westerfeld require devotion. Do you know someone who could take it over?"

Mrs. Bunn waved from across the street as if she'd just walked outside. She wore her favorite floral dress, which she must have thrown on in haste because she still had a pink curler in her hair. I waved back after she mouthed, "All right?"

"I think I know just who to ask," I said to him. "What about a partner agent to analyze the information with? Can I have one?"

"I'm sure they would be most appreciative." He watched Junie come out of my house, walking toward us.

"Everything all right?" Junie asked.

"I'll get in touch," I said to him, and together, Junie and I watched him walk away with his dog. I folded my arms. "He just offered me a job. Some outlier husband and wife team that hunt Nazis for a bounty. Can you believe it?"

Junie's eyes popped. "What did you say?"

"I said I needed a partner. The best come in pairs, isn't that right, Junes? So, what do you say? Do you want to take a sabbatical from your position at the university and hunt Nazis for a spell? Like old times, only different. Real modern women who have it all."

We walked back toward the house, her arm over my shoulders. "I'm listening."

I pointed to the house for sale next door. "Well, while I'm at it… What about buying that house? I'm having a baby, and I'm going to need your immediate advice, and I'd rather not fight Mrs. Bunn over time on our party line. Oh, it'll be wonderful. I'll borrow cups of sugar, and you can borrow milk and…"

"Viv?"

I was decorating her house in my head, what her office would look like, green with pink stripes and wall-to-wall carpeting. Of course, maybe we'd share an office on occasion because we'd have to go over all those files together anyway, analyzing every single mustache, café conversation, and suspicious visa this side of the Mississippi.

"Viv!"

"What?" We paused in my doorway.
"I knew this would happen."
"You did? How?"
She winked. "I felt it in my bones."

Author's Note

The story of Viv, Junie, Pudge, and Dot is entirely fictional and meant to entertain, but the League of Lonely War Women campaign actually existed. Furthermore, their situational spaces and experiences in the Women's Army Corps, in Rome, and while attempting to catch Engle during the Cold War were inspired by real events and people. Again, this is fiction and meant to entertain, but as with all my books, my intention was to make the story plausible, and it wasn't hard to do within this framework.

The League of Lonely War Women was created by OSS officer Barbara Lauwers, in the summer of 1944. As part of the Morale Operations Branch of the Office of Strategic Services, this campaign was considered black propaganda, intended to lower morale among German soldiers by using a simple yet cunning strategy: convince the weary German soldier that a paper heart pinned to his lapel would attract a patriotic lover while on leave. The true brilliance of this campaign lay in its insidious suggestion that their wives or sweethearts might be indulging in infidelity back home. Essentially, the League of Lonely War Women aimed not just to provide comfort but to erode the very morale of the enemy from within.

The heart was prominently featured on leaflets scattered among Axis troops, and Barbara and her team produced nearly 300,000 leaflets from their covert operations in Rome between July 1944 and the end of the war. The operation was so expertly executed that even *The Washington Post* had been deceived, publishing an article in the fall of '44 titled, "German soldiers on leave from the Italian Front have only to pin an entwined heart on their lapel during furloughs home to find a girlfriend." This news story was drawn from a flyer found on a captured German soldier, penned by Barbara Lauwers herself (the flyer I used in this story is a slightly edited version of one of her originals). The prologue is a fictional account of how that happened (the newspaper story ran in October of '44, but in my book, the story was published earlier, and the flyer was found by the Third Army).

The picnic scene at the Lech River was inspired by a photograph I saw many years ago of German soldiers on leave, resting on a beach with women draped all over them. The image has stayed with me for more than ten years (I guess I knew one day I'd write about it). Engle was also inspired by a real person, an SS officer who managed to keep his name and face off all incriminating documents, then quietly slipped into the fabric of society after the war, as if nothing had happened.

The characters of Viv, Junie, Dot, and Pudge are figments of my imagination, but Cora was inspired by Barbara insofar as being the head of the campaign. Ava was also inspired by a real person: a woman who was turned and worked for the OSS, dropping by parachute into Nazi Germany, where it was rumored she threatened her handler with the need for an abortion. I thought that story was a good Easter egg to include, but there are many Easter eggs in this book, including Viv and Junie's recommendation to bomb the tire factory, which was discovered by a WAC analyst in London who noticed the serial numbers.

The Westerfelds and Viv's job offer at the end of the novel was inspired by the real-life Nazi-hunting couple, Beate and Serge Klarsfeld, who had an incredible and extensive career finding Nazis and bringing them to justice, starting in the early 1960s. There were quite a few independent teams hunting Nazis during the Cold War, and honestly, I think that is a whole different book worth exploring (which I would love to write).

I don't remember exactly when I discovered the League of Lonely War Women, but I do have a file dated June 2020, while writing *A Child for the Reich*, that contains the initial premise of this story and a note to "research later." At this point, I already had the outline for *The Secret Pianist* drafted and another book on my mind, so I guess good things take time to percolate.

If you were entertained by this story, please consider leaving a review on the retailer site where you bought the book. I also invite you to check out my other wartime novels.

Thank you for reading!

Acknowledgments

Huge thanks to my editor at HarperCollins UK, Charlotte Ledger, and the amazing team at One More Chapter. You make the magic happen with your sharp editorial eye, gorgeous covers, brilliant audiobook narrators, and all-around expert packaging. I'm also so grateful to my agent, Kate Nash, along with Saskia Leach and the wonderful staff at the Kate Nash Literary Agency, for their support and for always cheering me on. And to my readers (and especially to my fellow history nerds), thank you for coming along on this journey. I hope this story swept you up, kept you turning the pages, and left you thoroughly entertained.

A TALE OF COURAGE, SACRIFICE, AND THE HAUNTING ECHOES OF A LIFE ONCE LIVED IN THE SHADOWS

In the underbelly of Cold War Moscow, Mae Pierce, once a formidable OSS agent, has found herself once again thrust into a perilous mission that could spell redemption or ruin.

Posing as a model at the American Exhibition, Mae is haunted by the ghosts of her past and the weight of a life she thought she had left behind. As she navigates the treacherous waters of deceit, betrayal, and the ruthless Russian Mafia, Mae realizes that the stakes are higher than she ever imagined.

In a game where trust is a luxury and survival is paramount, can one broken agent rise from the ashes to confront the Cold War's most hidden secrets?

COMING MAY 2026
PRE-ORDER IN PAPERBACK, EBOOK AND AUDIO!

SISTERS. TRAITORS. SPIES.

When a British RAF Whitley plane comes under fire over the French coast and is forced to drop their cargo, a spy messenger pigeon finds its way into unlikely hands…

The occupation has taken much from the Cotillard sisters, and as the Germans increase their forces in the seaside town of Boulogne-sur-Mer, Gabriella, Martine and Simone can't escape the feeling that the walls are closing in.

Yet, just as they should be trying to stay under the radar, the discovery of a British messenger pigeon leads them down a new and dangerous path. Now, as the sisters' secrets wing their way to an unknown contact in London, they have to wonder – have they opened a lifeline, or sealed their fate?

AVAILABLE IN PAPERBACK, EBOOK AND AUDIO!

AN EMOTIONAL WW2 HISTORICAL NOVEL INSPIRED BY A TRUE STORY

Since her husband, Josef, joined the Czech resistance three years ago, Anna Dankova has done everything possible to keep her daughter, Ema, safe. But when blonde haired, blue-eyed Ema is ripped from her mother's arms in the local marketplace by the dreaded Brown Sisters, nurses who were dedicated to Hitler's cause, Anna is forced to go to new extremes to take back what the Nazis have stolen from her.

Going undercover as a devoted German subject eager to prove her worth to the Reich, the former actress takes on a role of a lifetime to find and save her daughter. But getting close to Ema is one thing. Convincing her that the Germans are lying when they claim Anna stole her from her true parents is another…

AVAILABLE IN PAPERBACK, EBOOK AND AUDIO!

A GRIPPING WORLD WAR 2 NOVEL WITH A GHOSTLY TWIST YOU WON'T BE ABLE TO PUT DOWN

In the shadow of the ravaged battlefields of Verdun, where the scars of the First World War never healed, Vianne, struggling to hold onto her crumbling family chateau, takes in her traumatized nephew Blaise after the arrest of her sister by the Nazis.

But when Blaise says he can see eerie figures in the fog and whispers from the forbidden forest beyond the fence, it seems something ancient and sorrowful stirs in the soil where soldiers of the Great War once bled. As strange guests arrive at the old house and secrets surface, Vianne must face the terrifying possibility that the brutal SS aren't the only horrors she must face…

AVAILABLE IN PAPERBACK, EBOOK AND AUDIO!

ONE MORE CHAPTER
YOUR NUMBER ONE STOP
FOR PAGETURNING BOOKS

The author and One More Chapter would like to thank everyone who contributed to the publication of this story…

Analytics
Imogen Wolstencroft

Audio
Fionnuala Barrett
Ciara Briggs

Design
Lucy Bennett
Fiona Greenway
Liane Payne
Dean Russell

Digital Sales
Laura Daley
Lydia Grainge
Hannah Lismore

eCommerce
Laura Carpenter
Madeline ODonovan
Charlotte Stevens
Christina Storey
Rachel Ward

Editorial
Janet Marie Adkins
Rosie Best
Kara Daniel
Charlotte Ledger
Federica Leonardis
Laura McCallen
Jennie Rothwell
Sofia Salazar Studer
Emily Thomas
Helen Williams

Harper360
Emily Gerbner
Ariana Juarez
Jean Marie Kelly
emma sullivan
Sophia Wilhelm

International Sales
Ruth Burrow
Bethan Moore
Colleen Simpson

Inventory
Sarah Callaghan
Kirsty Norman

Marketing & Publicity
Chloe Cummings
Grace Edwards
Katie Sadler

Operations
Melissa Okusanya

Production
Denis Manson
Simon Moore
Francesca Tuzzeo

Rights
Ashton Mucha
Alisah Saghir
Zoe Shine
Aisling Smyth

Trade Marketing
Ben Hurd
Eleanor Slater

The HarperCollins Contracts Team

The HarperCollins Distribution Team

The HarperCollins Finance & Royalties Team

The HarperCollins Legal Team

The HarperCollins Technology Team

UK Sales
Isabel Coburn
Jay Cochrane
Leah Woods

And every other essential link in the chain from delivery drivers to booksellers to librarians and beyond!

One More Chapter is an award-winning global division of HarperCollins.

Subscribe to our newsletter to get our latest eBook deals and stay up to date with all our new releases!

signup.harpercollins.co.uk/
join/signup-omc

Meet the team at
www.onemorechapter.com

Follow us!

@onemorechapterhc

Do you write unputdownable fiction?
We love to hear from new voices.
Find out how to submit your novel at
www.onemorechapter.com/submissions